I0657965

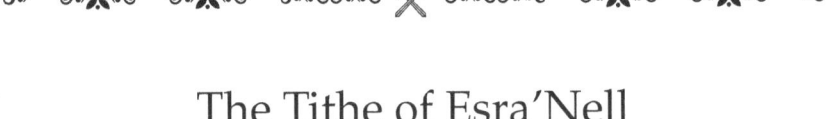

The Tithe of Esra'Nell

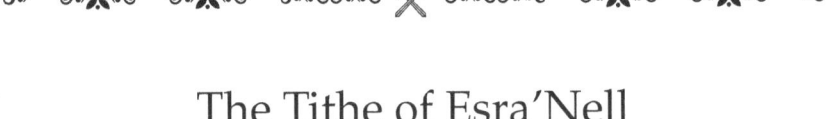

"It brings me great pleasure to mark the release of this special edition of The Tithe of Esra'Nell.

"This date, five hundred years after the founding of the Alliance, seems a fitting one to commemorate the legendary heroes who laid the foundation for a long and lasting peace between the two great peoples of Lorem, and all of their kingdoms therein.

"I hereby gift this copy, bound in precious gold, to the Archives of the Alliance, and I commend it to any and every citizen of Elandria—it is really quite good."
Excerpt from the speech of Queen Amaryllis III,
Ruler of Elandria and Keeper of the Alliance

Praise for the Original Tale

"A magnificent and scintillating telling of the adventure underlying d'Barouse' unsurpassed performance of the ultimate tale."
Ariadne Spinoza,
Most Pulchritudinous Critic of the Elandrian Critics Guild

"Utterly false: unmentionably crass and untrue: a vicious attack on my person: an unentertaining addition to the campaign of falsehoods distributed about my character and deeds. Bad."
Hupert Ainsworth,
from his prison cell

"... but in truth it is really quite entertaining, and could be said to be mostly accurate, despite its comparative brevity..."
From the introduction to 'A Focus on Folk Tales, vol. X'
by J. D. Wright

"Vastly downplays how handsome I truly am."
Artyom Tilin

The Tithe of Esra'Nell

James S. Bennett

Based on a story by
Louise Horsley

An adventure with
Dominic Caltabiano,
James Roberts,
&
Blake Thomas

Illustrated by
Tania Crossingham,
Kyle de Silva,
&
James Roberts

refrontal
Press

Copyright © 2017 by James S. Bennett
All rights reserved. This book or any portion thereof may not be reproduced or used in any manner whatsoever without the express written permission of the publisher, except for the use of brief quotations.
Story and characters used with permission.
ISBN 978-0-6480447-2-7
Prefrontal Press
prefrontalpress.com
Distributed by www.lulu.com
First printing 2017

Lettrine (dropcaps/initials) illumination © 2017 by Tania Crossingham
All rights reserved. Not to be reproduced or used in any manner whatsoever without the express written permission of the artist.
www.tania-crossingham.com

Cover illustration © 2017 by Kyle de Silva
All rights reserved. Not to be reproduced or used in any manner whatsoever without the express written permission of the artist.
www.artstation.com/artist/kursid

Map of Arcana © 2017 by James Roberts
All rights reserved. Not to be reproduced or used in any manner whatsoever without the express written permission of the publisher.
Map prepared using stock material provided by DeviantArt users popzel127 ('Compass Rose'), Ramaraunt ('Parchment'), and StarRaven ('Sketchy Cartography Brushes').
Used with permission.

This book was created using the memoir class in the typesetting package pdfLATEX. Additional packages utilised include palatino, ulem, fourier-orns, graphicx, microtype, pdfpages, lettrine, ragged2e, and endnotes.

Also available in .epub and hardcover formats.

Contents

Map of Arcana

Adeline

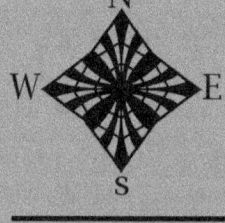

N
W E
S

10mi

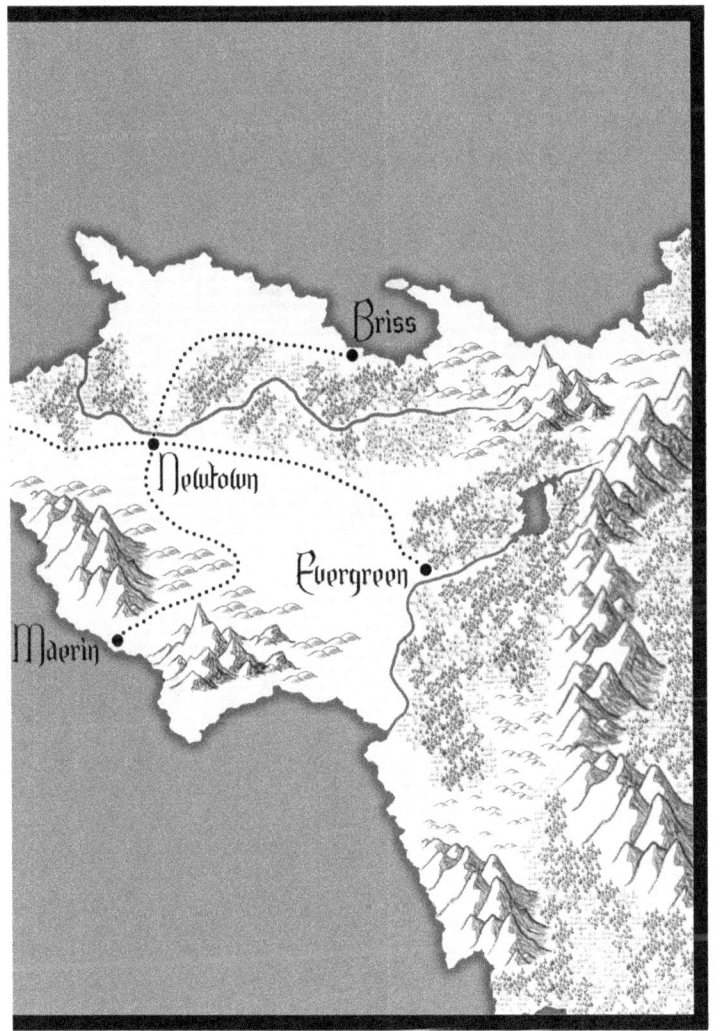

Acknowledgements

Y first role-playing game experience was highly enjoyable. Between sessions I took to writing as a means of remaining immersed in the world so ably crafted by Louise Horsley, herself a first-time Game Master. Thus did this book begin life.

Several people have contributed greatly to bringing the story to this point. Foremost is Louise, who created the world of Lorem and brought its locations and peoples to life. A *very* close second are my fellow players—Dominic Caltabiano, James Roberts, and Blake Thomas—who are responsible for the quirks and perks of Ed, Artyom Tilin, and Alfazar d'Barouse respectively. It has been a joy to tell these characters' stories, and I thank Dom, James, and Blake for their enthusiastic assistance and detailed feedback.

Special mentions must also be made of Joshua Harbort, who has vigorously debated various plot points with me, and helped to ensure that Lorem's theology is self-consistent; Courtney A. Landers[1], who provided the sassy back-cover 'blurb'; Chris Slee[2], who was extremely helpful in navigating the turbulent waters of self-publishing; and Henry Goeldner[3] and Nicholas Wyatt, for strong yet sensitive editing and style advice.

Lorem has been brought to life in picture form by four artists. The amazing cover art is the work of Kyle de Silva[4]. Tania Crossingham[5] is responsible for the great initial characters featured in the print book. Both of these professional artists were punctual,

v

professional, and gratifyingly enthusiastic; I highly recommend them. Readers of the e-book will miss out on Tania's work because of technical limitations. Do not worry; you will get to enjoy some character art by Louise Horsley! I asked Louise to do some simple sketches as reference for the cover art, but she turned out such beautiful illustrations that I had to share them. Credit for the excellent map goes to James Roberts, who obligingly went through about six (extensive) revisions before we settled on the version included here. I must profusely thank these two amateur artists for turning out great work in the midst of their university degrees.

I also wish to give credit to those who prepared the stock materials used in the map (as listed on the copyright page) for their gracious permission to make use of their work.

Thank you to my ePub test readers: Itia Favre-Bulle, Daniel Green, and Nicolas Mauranyapin.

Thanks must also go to Tihan Bekker, Elizabeth Bennett, Simon Bennett, Rebecca Bennett, Ann Bui, Nick Evans, Conrad Lauf, Tim Mew, Mitch Mitchell, Sophia C. Morgan, Lucy, Mark Simmonds, and Mitchell Webster for support and encouragement along the way.

Finally, thanks to my parents for looking after me in so many ways. Surprise, I wrote a book!

---

[1]Mental health researcher,
www.courtneyalanders.wordpress.com
[2]Historical fencer and French buff,
www.longedgepress.com
[3]Comic book author and novelist,
henrygoeldnersblog.tumblr.com
[4]www.artstation.com/artist/kursid
[5]www.tania-crossingham.com

Prologue

UGEN was roused by an ear-piercing scream. He came instantly alert, wide-eyed and frightened, clutching his blanket. Something thrashed in the bed next to him where Elanor should have been, but darkness obscured its form.

Though he was young, Bugen quickly figured out what was going on; attacks like these were an all too common occurrence in Elandria.

A clammy hand pawed over his legs and he kicked out at it, trying to disentangle himself from the twisted bedsheets. He rolled onto the floor and crawled away, as far away as he could get in the tiny hovel he shared with his sister. Bugen was desperate to hold back his tears, though he knew not why.

The scream sounded again.

Cold air gusted through the window which Elanor had carefully bolted shut before tucking her little brother in. The moonlight streaming through behind it revealed two humanoid silhouettes looming over the bed, struggling with his sister. Each figure was roughly as big as Bugen, but they had glowing eyes and gossamer wings which glinted faintly.

Elanor threw off one of the creatures, then twisted in the other's grasp, scrabbling for the tiny knife she kept under her pillow. Bugen saw metal flash as her hand darted forth once, then again, and half a wing fluttered to the floor. The injured Fae screeched and lashed out with wicked nails, scoring deep furrows across her face.

1

"Elanor!" Bugen cried involuntarily, hoping that his sister yet lived. She was the only family left to him.

"Bugen! Get out, get out n–"

Elanor's frantic instructions were cut off as the beast bit into her arm, making her yell in pain and drop the knife. Seizing the opportunity, the other Fae bounded across the bed and grabbed fistfuls of her hair, dragging her towards the window.

Feeling helpless, Bugen obeyed. His tears dripped onto the packed-earth floor as he scurried towards the door on all fours. Elanor's screams rang in his ears, and Bugen frantically thought that someone must have heard; someone must be coming. *Please.*

The door burst open easily and Bugen ran out into the crisp night air. Pausing, he looked around for any assistance, or more threats, but all was still. The boy rubbed at his red eyes. "Help, help!" he sobbed, but the thin sound seemed to evaporate into the night with nary a trace.

Deciding that he must take matters into his own hands he ran around to the back of the hovel, where he and his sister stacked firewood. Elanor's warnings about how dangerous the axe could be only spurred him on. There it lay, well-used but kept sharp and bright by her careful ministrations. He lifted the heavy, unfamiliar weight and made ready.

"Somebody help!" he screamed again as he turned and made an ungainly dash towards the door. Rounding the corner, he nearly ran straight into one of their Fae assailants: the one which Elanor had maimed. It was carrying her by her legs, lifting her out of the window with the help of the other creature, which was still inside. She had stopped struggling.

Terrified by what that could mean, Bugen aimed an awkward blow at the Fae without stopping to brace himself properly. It struck home, but the weapon twisted in his grasp and did not bite correctly. Hissing, the creature tripped Bugen; his axe went flying and his face hammered into the unyielding ground.

Not willing to give in, Bugen sprang to his feet and charged the Fae again, bare-handed and screaming incoherently. It nonchalantly back-handed him away, using strength seemingly beyond its stature. Now sprawled on the ground, Bugen turned to face his adversary once more. His body ached terribly; his front teeth were loose in his gums; his eyes were puffy and reddened; but the boy was not about to let go of his sister without a fight.

The creature let loose a horrible call, and in response another Fae descended from the sky on sparkling wings. It slammed Bugen into the dirt and pinned him there while the other two made off with Elanor. He caught a glimpse of her face as they took her; it was disfigured by claw marks, and she bore an enormous bleeding lump on her temple. No amount of squirming, writhing, kicking, or screaming could free Bugen from his captor's unnatural strength. Weeping and nearly spent, Bugen launched one final assault.

It failed.

With its prey now subdued, the third Fae spread its glistening wings and grabbed the boy's ankles, ready to drag him into the sky. It crouched and launched itself towards the moon, then its headless corpse crashed to the ground beside Bugen.

Aghast, Bugen peered upwards and beheld his saviour. The woman's robe of red and yellow shone almost golden in the moon-light, and her sword seemed sharp enough to slice through the very darkness of night. She looked very old to him.

She carefully wiped the Fae's blood from her weapon, then sheathed it and knelt beside the boy. He sat and inspected the stranger wordlessly. Emotions warred within Bugen; he hated her for arriving too late to save Elanor, but he was also grateful for his own deliverance and the simple company of another human. After a few moments the latter won out, and Bugen dissolved into tears. "Forgive me, child," she said gently. He rushed into the glowing woman's embrace, and she tenderly lifted him and carried him back to the town's only inn.

Bugen was soon bundled into a warm rug and cradled beside the inn's warm hearth. "Sleep now," the priestess told him. As con-sciousness faded, he heard only snatches of her conversation with the innkeeper. "Is there nobody here that can care for him?" she as-ked. There was a brief but significant pause, then an unconvincing reply in the negative.

He slept, and in the morning they left.

Chapter 1

Land Ho!

What needs to be said of the Fae? Everyone knows of them—pixies, nymphs, kelpies, hobgoblins, fauns and sidhes, amongst others—to one degree or another, for there is almost no escaping them. Not even on the ocean can one be sure that any number of the bombastic array of Fae are not close at hand.

Fae blood runs thick with untamed magickal power, of a more elemental variety than that wielded by our arcanists. Some are capable of feats which violate our understanding of magick. Others have the ability to project powerful illusions, warping our perception of reality and twisting our minds. Many are shapeshifters who perversely play on our emotions by taking the form of innocent children or alluring women. As a rule, Fae of all shapes and sizes are potentially lethal.

There are few who study these creatures—and fewer who do not employ the sword as their chief means of enquiry—as most people simply desire a means to evade or eradicate the threat that they represent. And who can blame them? I for one cannot. Neither can I shake the feeling that there is a rich ecosystem—nay, even a society, no matter how brutal—lying uncovered in the lives of the Fae.

Journal of A. Higgens

F ANYONE had cared to look, they would have seen the cleric standing by the port rail of the trade vessel *Steadfast*. It was curious that nobody was looking, as the man's garb was quite striking; a quartered yellow and red tabard worn over bronzed scale maille betrayed his alignment to the Sun goddess, Sol, and his ever-present buckler and cruciform sword marked him as a warrior priest.

It had been some twenty years since Bugen-Kynes was adopted into the priesthood by Priestess Sabine. Twenty years of emulating her example, studying, training, praying, and worshipping the Goddess of Light. Though it was a life of constant toil, the bond that he had made with Sol made it well worth the effort. To be entrusted with even a little of Her divine power was a charge both great and terrible.

And yet, for all this, his understanding of the Fae remained essentially nil.

Bugen's green eyes carefully surveyed the expanse of ocean which had surrounded them for the last month, idly wondering at how remarkably dynamic the wind and waves were. The ship rolled underfoot as a stiff breeze propelled the *Steadfast* towards their destination—Arcana. It was a long way from anywhere in the Kingdom of Elandria to the New World, affording Bugen much time for introspection.

It was at times like these—times of waiting, with nothing immediately demanding his attention—that he thought of Elanor. He brought out his memories of her for conscious inspection less frequently nowadays. Though cherished, they were not particularly clear anymore: like a favourite book read so often that the binding was failing and the spine coming loose. The one exception, of course, was the night that she was taken. Bugen remembered that with sharp-edged clarity.

It surprised Bugen to realise that he did not hate the Fae for what they did to Elanor. Unlike the majority of humanity, who quickly came to loathe the Fae, the priest suspected that there was some profound explanation for their actions. He wanted to know the truth of things before passing judgement, one way or another.

Loud words flitted across the deck on a gust of wind, and Bugen turned to investigate.

Ah, yes: that would be why no-one cared to notice the young priest. The sailors not at the helm or in the crow's nest were gathered around a fellow who was sitting with his back against the wall of the ship's cabin. Bugen had heard he was named Ed, though they had not been formally introduced. A tightly curled yet messy red beard and bald pate gave Bugen the impression that at some point the man's head had been removed, only to be replaced upside-down. Ed scratched his chest languidly, then did the same to his dog as he continued his tale.

"The creature had me pinned up against the wall, it did," he said, slamming himself back against the cabin wall, "and it grabbed me round the middle while it tried to do me for. But it bit off more than it could chew, ya see, 'coz I had my cold iron knife tucked into me shirt, and I thrust up," he demonstrated drawing a knife and thrusting upwards repeatedly, "and stabbed it right in its damn Fae heart!"

The sailors looked on, some with a measure of guarded scepticism, and many with equally well-hidden awe. "What happened then?" one called out from amongst the crowd.

"Well, its bloody Fae insides burst out and drenched me in blood, if you can call it that. Damn well got in all of the cuts it had laid on me, including this one 'ere." At that, Ed reached across and opened his filthy shirt to reveal an ugly wound stretching right the way diagonally across his chest. Matted hair was plastered into the gash. Even from the other side of the vessel Bugen could tell that the cut had been suppurating for a time now.

Apparently unperturbed, Ed merely poked the raw flesh again before closing his shirt and looking up at his audience; he appeared to be rather enjoying himself.

"Wow, you actually killed one!" said a younger sailor, who was slightly wide-eyed.

"Course I did, didn't I?" replied Ed. "I hate the damn Fae," he growled before hawking a great glob of phlegm over the railing. "Ever since those bauchans tried to–"

"No more questions!" an angry voice proclaimed from near the stern, pausing after every word so as to ensure that the listener fully comprehended its meaning before moving to the next.

Ed was suddenly bereft of attention, as all eyes moved towards the helm.

"Go and bother someone else with your cursed inquisitiveness. And take your notebooks and your pet *squirrel* with you!"

A leather bag came flying down from the raised rear deck, hitting the timbers with a resounding thud, and a skinny boy, scarcely nineteen years of age, arrived shortly after it, skidding down the stairway at a fearsome rate. He was trailed by a bright-eyed creature, grey to red, looking like a fox one moment and a raccoon the next.

At first glance the lad seemed a regular rich-boy. He had the green-about-the-gills look of one who was unaccustomed to travel by ship, resulting in the loss of a few pounds during the trip. This had caused his finely tailored clothes to hang just a little loose on his frame. The image of privilege was reinforced by the finger's length of wavy brown hair sprouting from above his clean-shaven face, and the pair of spectacles perched upon his slightly upturned nose. The more observant would have noticed that even in his flustered state the boy carried about him an air of curiosity and brilliance that was found in few true adults. They may also have realised that the leather-bound notebooks which spilled from the sack did not contain sketches or drawings, but rather notes and diagrams of more precise nature.

The young man looked back towards the helmsman, collected himself, and jovially called back, "I enjoyed our little chat!" before tucking yet another book into his fine shirt and strolling across the boat to retrieve his bag, smiling at the chuntering of the angry steersman which could be heard above the waves. The sailors, knowing full well what the angry muttering meant, quickly scattered across the ship and made themselves look busy.

"Did you jus' interrupt..." Ed grouched at the newcomer, indicating the dispersing crowd. He let out a great sigh. "I was jus' getting into it!"

"Ah, stow it Ed," the lad responded, waving one hand dismissively as he began re-packing his bag. "You already told them last week. Besides, you're a Fae hunter, not a storyteller."

"Yeah, and you're an arcanist, not a blasted theatre critic." That explained the creature; it was likely the lad's familiar.

"You are too intellectually infantile to appreciate the fine arts," sniffed the mage in a manner which left Bugen wondering why he was trying to pick a fight.

"Oh, that's how it is? You're too waif-like to lift a weapon like a real man, Artyom," Ed shot back.

"Is that what you call yourself? That's cute." The lad—Artyom—still had not made eye contact with Ed. "Remember that paralysis I saved you from back in Ludland? Who lifted whom?"

"Fine. You win that one," Ed conceded. "But don't forget that I bailed you out of that kelpie business back in Frederheim."

"Okay. You tell the story too often for me to forget anyway."

Ed's face broke into a rough smile. "You're a blasted pain in the rear, but useful enough to keep around," He crouched to help the mage gather his books.

"I'm a utility mage, baby," Artyom agreed absently. "Got spells for everything. Sort of."

Bugen listened in with half an ear and decided that Ed and Artyom must have known one another for a reasonable period prior to being signed on for this voyage. Like most Fae hunters, they probably travelled from town to town and hired out their services as necessary.

And Fae hunters were *always* necessary.

"Did I hear someone say 'theatre critic'?" came a smoother and deeper voice from below-decks. Bugen looked toward the nearest hatch and caught sight of a cloth-swathed head as it hove into view. "Please don't use such filthy language onboard," the head instructed Artyom and Ed. "The sailors know enough curses already."

"Alfazar!" Artyom replied as a full body emerged from the hatch. He seized Alfazar's hand and enthusiastically pumped it.

Alfazar cut a striking and somewhat intimidating figure. The man was tall and proud, with a strong jawline, bright brown eyes and olive skin complemented by a flowing blue shirt over baggy navy pantaloons. Despite the elaborate clothing, superb control and grace could be seen in his movements. The man did almost literally *cut* a fine figure, for he was festooned with knives; a great array of them was strapped across his belt and across two bandoleers gracing his shoulders. Although deadly, their primary purpose was in fact performance, as Alfazar was a travelling Graean bard-cum-acrobat of, rumour had it, quite some repute.

"I was merely expressing my opinion," Artyom explained, "That somebody as unlearned in the Arts as Ed should not try to perform them: especially when one as esteemed as yourself is on the same vessel."

Ed glowered at the mage, but said nothing.

"Well, thank you," Alfazar graciously accepted the praise. "Still, I would not malign those who wish to share their talents," he continued, probably in an attempt to appease the hunter.

"Well, of course," agreed the young arcanist. "Except that Ed has no—"

"Land ho!" came a rough voice from the crow's nest.

"Oh! Finally!" Artyom changed tack mid-sentence. He did not even bother to hide the tone of relief in his voice.

Bugen privately agreed; although he did not feel unwell aboard ship, he missed the feeling of solid rock underfoot. Furthermore, it seemed that Ed and his partner were now less likely to get into another argument.

The crew were also happy with the news, though perhaps they were drawn more by the promise of a warm bed, cold ale and salty wenches. "Alright you dogs," shouted the helmsman, "you know how it is. Make sure she's prettier than the other girls, or you'll be sleeping in the bilge!" The sailors were busily stowing loose items and clearing detritus from the deck when it finally dawned on Bugen that the tiller had been referring to the *Steadfast* itself... or, rather, 'herself'. Evidently appearances were important in Adeline. None of the other harbours they had berthed in had inspired a cleaning spree.

Bugen just moved closer to the rail and tried to stay out of the way of the crew as they went about their beautification; his inexperience would make him worse than useless to them.

Ever the insular type, he lapsed back into introspection.

So little was known about the Fae. Legend and hearsay had it that they were unknown before their sudden appearance some centuries ago, whereupon the creatures began stealing into human homes and snatching children. Then, as now, the Fae chiefly preyed upon families living far from large settlements, particularly those near to forests and water sources. Some people believed that the Fae were a plague on those of mean living—the poor, the reclusive, and the outcast—but the young priest lent this idea little weight. Despite the many wild theories which he had heard, if Bugen were a betting man he would happily wager a large sum that nobody knew the truth.

Of course, the young cleric did not have a large sum with which to bet. There were those who did, however; those who had lined their pockets with the wealth of Arcana. Bugen had been summoned to Arcana—albeit indirectly—by one such man: Sir Hupert Ainsworth, the leader of the expedition which had discovered the isle in the first place. Ainsworth was directly responsible for the presence of three others aboard the *Steadfast*. As Bugen had been informed, the band were intended to be colleagues of a sort, with an as-yet unknown directive.

He suspected he might be seeing more of the trio behind him.

Some hours later, Bugen watched an over-zealous sailor supervise as Ed cleared his woodsman's gear from the deck. The grumbling man's equipment consisted of a smattering of leather armour, skinning knives, a small bow, an axe, and a sidearm which could not decide whether it was a large knife or a small curved sword. The priest dredged his memory to find the correct term: a kukri. Once these items were all secreted somewhere about Ed's person he moved off to stand at the bow, trailed by his dog. There he again joined Artyom in conversation.

The wind drowned out all voices except those nearby ("Put those cards away, slackers! Can't you see there's a priest right there?"), but Bugen could see Ed's body language becoming more frustrated as time went on. He parted his shirt again briefly, then after an animated exchange Artyom turned and strode across the deck. Bugen, not wanting to be judged an eavesdropper, turned away.

As a result, he did not realise that the mage was heading towards him. "Hey, priest. I need your help for a minute," Artyom announced, not even bothering to introduce himself.

Bugen stood at the railing and gathered himself for a moment—he had been a little startled, to be honest, but he was not about to let that on—then turned to face the arcanist. "Okay," he said evenly. Questions rose to his lips, but Artyom had already set off again. Bugen hurried to catch up, making his maille jingle a little.

Once he got to the bow Ed extended a hand and shook the priest's. Wondering what sort of mess he was going to be caught up in, Bugen began to introduce himself. "Ho there, priest," Ed cut in, looking reluctant about the situation. "The arcanist here,"—he indicated Artyom with a jerk of his thumb—"tells me this here wound is going to end up pretty nasty... 'spose you'd best take a look." Bugen mentally sighed with relief, glad that he had not been called over to settle some sort of fight.

The priest inspected Ed's trophy wound with a practised eye. He quickly confirmed what he already suspected from his earlier glimpse. Angry red skin and the weeping of the cut indicated a deep infection had set in. In this case things were already too far gone to rely on mundane healing; Bugen could not in good conscience allow this sickness the possibility to develop further, or—Sol forbid—spread.

"Aye, the cut is filled with some pestilence," said the priest. With no further ado he closed his eyes, placed his left hand lightly on Ed's chest and murmured a short phrase. Upon its completion Bugen's palm briefly shone a brilliant yellow, and, Artyom noted, a glowing circle quartered by two spokes flared into being on the man's buckler, held in his right hand.

Ed gritted his teeth for a moment, then relaxed. All trace of the wound was gone. To indicate his thanks, Ed poked the region again, as though to confirm that he was not being duped, and proceeded to poke his thigh. "At least you let me keep this one, eh?" he said with an unconvincing grin, before sidling off. Bugen was left wondering whether the man was toying with him or not. Maybe Ed felt a little emasculated by the healing?

Artyom also departed, only pausing long enough to say a brief, "Thanks," and pronounce his intent to gather his belongings from his cabin. Bugen was alone once more. He moved back to his accustomed position at the port rail, then stood, mesmerised by the approaching isle.

Those aboard the *Steadfast* could begin to make out the broad strokes of Port Adeline. In the foreground they could see the gentle swell rolling in toward the port, protected by a natural harbour formed by a rocky portion of the otherwise sandy coastline. Numerous ships' masts were silhouetted against the city itself, delineating the extent of the docks. Though a great many buildings were gleaming invitingly in the midday sunlight, Bugen's attention was held by the abundant greenery; the backdrop to the scene was formed by forest-clad mountains atop leagues and leagues of verdant farmland dotted here and there with barely-visible settlements. Any child of Faust could not help but be impressed by Arcana, even at this distance.

"Reminds me of Graea," Alfazar opined from alongside the priest. Bugen had not even noticed the bard approaching.

"I have never been to Graea," the cleric answered. "It looks nothing like Faust, though," he continued.

Alfazar chuckled in agreement. "Not foreboding enough to be Faust. And far too hot."

"Aye, it is that," agreed Bugen.

"I imagine you're the fourth member of our little band, then," Alfazar half-stated, half-asked.

"It is likely."

"Priests must accompany all expeditions of the State, after all," the bard nodded. "Are there many of your Order in Arcana?"

"I do not believe so," Bugen answered. There were relatively few of his Order anywhere anymore. After all, the human world was now for the humans, not the gods.

"Must rankle a little, no?"

Bugen was surprised by the piercing question. Were his thoughts that transparent? He turned to face the bard directly. "It does," he responded without inflection. "But there is little to do about that, besides continuing to serve."

From this new angle the priest could see that Alfazar was already packed and ready to leave the *Steadfast*; his small bag sat propped against the gunwale. Bugen surmised from this—and their discussion—that the bard was a well-seasoned traveller. Not eager to dwell on the current topic of conversation, Bugen asked "Why are you here?"

With a glance over at the priest, Alfazar reached up and hoisted himself into the ship's rigging. "I felt stale," he replied, now looking directly at Bugen. "The stories of a New World are what I'm here for." With that, Alfazar climbed halfway to the crow's nest, peering ahead to the rapidly-approaching port. The man looked for all the world like a pirate, with his black hair streaming from beneath its veil in the wind. "This is some view, priest," he called down to Bugen, voice carrying smoothly above the brisk wind in the rigging. "Perhaps you should come and take a look." The suggestion was part rapscallion and part serious, but the cleric could tell that Alfazar meant no harm. Bugen just returned the man's smile.

Their ship finally drew level with the entrance to the harbour and a call came from above to reef all of the sails. As this was done a number of smaller vessels, powered by the long oars protruding from their sides, came alongside the *Steadfast* and tethered themselves to it without waiting for the larger ship to slow. They then proceeded to deftly draw their charge through the coral reefs which fringed the entrance to the port. Bugen could see that sections of the mysterious, colourful rock had been blasted away, probably by arcane means, to provide passage for larger ships. Once clear of this, the tug vessels then guided the *Steadfast* through busy wharfs and docks.

Whilst most people would have been entranced by the variety of ships in harbour, or perhaps the menagerie of people and goods that they were transporting, Bugen was occupied by the strength and skill which allowed a few dozen men to manoeuvre a three hundred ton ship through the tight quarters.

The pilot vessels finally brought the *Steadfast* to the end of her long journey at an unoccupied berth lying alongside a pier, and a gangplank was thrown down with a loud crash. Alfazar climbed down from the rigging in his sure-footed way, threw the priest another grin and a nod, then made off along the gangway. "Be seeing you soon."

Ed and his dog mooched off after the bard, keeping their distance from Artyom for now.

"Alright, let's get off this tub!" came the mage's voice from behind a teetering pile of books and sacks; Bugen had not noticed the heap's approach during the commotion of docking. A passing member of the *Steadfast*'s crew caught the mage's comment and threw Artyom a filthy look, which was promptly ignored.

"Aye," came Bugen's reply, short but not terse, as he stooped to collect a bag which had already escaped the arcanist's grasp. Maybe this was why Ed was keeping his distance.

Together they moved down the gangway, one showing almost gay levity at having arrived, the other carefully assessing the new setting and his place in it.

Chapter 2

Ainsworth

Humans played out a kind of perverse internecine warfare for time immemorial before their unification under a single kingdom; the inhabitants of Faust, the large and inhospitable northern continent, looked on Graea, a smaller and rather more clement landmass to the southwest, with jealous eyes, whilst Graeans often pillaged the Faustian coastal towns and made off with hoards of the coal and iron that were hard to come by in their homeland. All that changed nine hundred and forty-nine years ago, when the unified Kingdom of Elandria was formed. The Unification set the stage for an unprecedented level of cooperativity, economic growth and technological innovation. Since then humans have largely been at peace with one another, despite minor insurgencies flaring up from time to time. In this new era many have found the time and inclination to venture further afield, searching for new lands. A few have even succeeded. Thus it was that some thirty years ago the island of Arcana, to the southeast of both Faust and Graea, was discovered by the now-wealthy philanthropist and self-avowed magick enthusiast Sir Hupert Ainsworth.

Excerpt from *Exploration in the Modern Age* by E. A. Tilin

HE wharf was teeming with sailors, coming and going; there one was counting his money out, ready for a night on the town, and over there another was performing the same action, but wondering when it was that his companions had cut his purse. A long line of carts and barrows carried exotic products ranging from clothing to foodstuffs. The whole scene of bustling energy impressed upon the arrivals the shear burgeoning wealth of Adeline.

Even the dockside pubs and brothels looked tasteful in Port Adeline.

At the end of the wharf stood a man dressed in a fine suit and wearing a monocle, trying to maintain an air of superiority and sophistication as he conversed with Alfazar. Bugen had the impression that his accustomed aura of confident aloofness was not so easy to project in the face of the bard's easy self-assuredness. Ed and his dog were already lounging against a nearby pole, looking far less out of place than the finely-dressed man.

"Ahhhh," said the fop, glad for an excuse to regain control of the conversation. "Here they are. You must be the arcanist," he said as he proffered a hand toward Artyom. The hand was quickly withdrawn once it became apparent that the lad could not even see it past his pile of belongings, let alone spare a limb to shake. "And that makes you our... esteemed priest of Sol." He briefly grasped Bugen's hand, but it was clear that the man's attitude towards the priest was rather lukewarm, almost derisive. "The other two members of the party. I am Ignatius Davenport," stated the man, addressing the whole group now, "*majordomo* to Sir Hupert Ainsworth."

Ed grumbled something under his breath: Bugen thought he caught the words 'butler' and 'inflated', and he suspected that

Davenport had also, for the man's countenance darkened momentarily.

"I will guide you through our prosperous city to Sir Ainsworth's residences," said Davenport as he polished his monocle with a handkerchief. "Do keep up, I haven't time to chase *every* lot of adventurers that come through these parts."

With that, the pompous little man reinserted his eyeglass and strode off through the crowd, which seemed to part before him. Evidently those with a position under Ainsworth commanded much respect in Port Adeline. The four 'adventurers' fell in behind him. Alfazar smoothly strode alongside Davenport, calmly surveying the surroundings. Next came Artyom, excitedly peering out every which-way from behind his mound of belongings, with the priest walking beside him, still carrying the leather bag which the mage had dropped back onboard the ship. Ed slouched along behind the rest, with Buhbuh at his heels.

They made their way up a broad boulevard, paved with exceptionally wide and flat flagstones, that swept towards the city proper.

The city was entirely enclosed by walls, as were all major towns, but central Port Adeline seemed unique in that Bugen could not describe it as possessing 'battlements'. Though undoubtedly sturdy, the walls seemed to be primarily designed for decoration rather than defence. They were furnished from some local rock shot through with veins of purple and silver which glinted in the sunlight. This, the perfectly paved road, and the bustling traffic combined to give quite a striking first impression.

Davenport kept up a brisk pace, and Bugen began to swelter in the oppressive heat and humidity. As beads of sweat started rolling under his arming jacket he mentally noted that he would need to oil his maille more often than in the cold, dry climes of Faust. How their guide managed to keep his suit so clean and dry was a mystery to the priest.

Gradually even Davenport's position was not enough to ensure them a clear path, and the companions were swept up in the general crowd heading towards the wide gates of the city.

As they neared the portal they were accosted by a short man

brandishing handfuls of pamphlets. "New to Adeline, eh?" asked the man, keeping pace with them in the throng. "You'll be wanting some maps then, eh?"

Bugen demurred, slightly worried that the man would demand a fee for the map, and a little more worried about losing track of Ignatius in the close press. The others, however, gladly took maps from the short fellow, who then melted back off the side of the road. The man had taken no money; evidently he was employed to ensure people knew their way about the city.

Bugen stole a quick glance at Alfazar's map. It was immediately evident that the city walls did not just encircle the town; they divided it into eight sectors. From the different colourings on the map Bugen presumed that each sector was devoted to a different activity.

The flagged road continued straight through town to the point antipodal to the travellers, lined on both sides by tall, graceful buildings of beautiful stone. Those which were completed were decorated with intricate sculptures, soaring columns and brilliant murals, but a large proportion were swathed in scaffolding, as though they were caterpillars waiting to emerge triumphantly from their cocoons. Off to the right could be seen the entrance to the market sector, bedecked in the bright colours of cloth, crops, and other produce.

At the far end of the city, opposite the coastal gates, rested a stately construction, which, despite the splendour all around, drew the eye like a lodestone draws iron. Ainsworth's residences.

Bugen was following Alfazar, who stood out by dint of his clothing and bandoleers, past the entrance to the market plaza when he heard it. First the crowd went quiet, then a great collective sigh seemed to go up. This was immediately followed by the sight of two men dressed all in black, obviously town guards, chasing a third man through the arch joining the bazaar to the central boulevard. The third fellow was clad in black also, but only a loincloth thereof. He bore marks about his wrists and ankles, and the pallid complexion visible beneath the unkempt stubble and close-cropped hair closed the deal; the man was clearly a prisoner. "It's never just one!" he cried, though his thin chest heaved with the effort of running. Spittle flew through the air. "Never just one, no! She always needs more. It's never just one!" He came to a halt as the guards drew level with him.

The crowd had drawn back from the three men, leaving the four newcomers nearest to the prisoner and his pursuers. Davenport stood near the edge of the street, attempting to look dignified. Despite these reactions, nobody seemed particularly worried: there was almost an air of routine about proceedings.

"That's far enough Higgens," said one guard, as the other positioned himself between the prisoner and the city's main gate. Both were wielding truncheons.

"Again?" someone could be heard muttering from near the archway. "That's the third time this month."

"It's never just one," said the prisoner again, quieter this time, his wide eyes flitting between the troupe and the guards. "Never just one."

Artyom just blinked, peering around his mound of belongings. Alfazar looked at the man, inscrutable, and Ed gave off an air of mingled curiosity and wariness. The priest stood ill at ease; it was clear that this Higgens character was of no immediate danger, and Bugen was inclined to sooth the man's evident anxiety. "Who is this man?" asked the cleric.

"Alfonz Higgens," came the reply. "Formerly a priest of Knowledge. Nowadays, the man's deranged. You shan't get anything else out of him, bar what you've already heard. Now come along Higgens: back to your cell with you." With that the two guards grasped an arm each, not ungently, and led the former priest back through the marketplace.

"She always needs more. It's never just one!" Higgens implored Bugen over his shoulder. The latter could do nothing but watch as the former was escorted back to, no doubt, a dark and solitary cell.

"Alright, nothing more to see here people," proclaimed Davenport, stepping forth from the rest of the crowd. The onlookers rapidly began diffusing, until after a moment or two there was no indication that anything untoward had ever occurred. "Onwards then," Davenport instructed the four travellers, indicating that they should continue along the main avenue.

Still a little shaken, Bugen tried to distract himself by examining each building along the road. Two facts were clear to him. Firstly, money abounded in Port Adeline. Secondly, so too did magick. The latter was clear from the manner in which the structures were being constructed. Very little seemed to be carved by hand or lifted into place by the work of a man's back. It was this fact that made the first evident; the services of mages did not come cheaply.

Within a few minutes, and with no further mishaps, the group of five had reached the far end of the road. They quickly mounted the stone steps and ascended towards great white and gold doors, shut firmly and attended by two guards. These were attired like the two encountered on the other side of town, but with a fine gold filigree stitched about their shoulders. Probably some mark of rank, Bugen surmised.

At a nod from Davenport the men drew the doors apart and cold air washed out of the opening. "That is sooo awesome," said Artyom with delight, quickly recognising that some magick was responsible for the beautifully cooled air. Even Alfazar, who was well-travelled, had not seen a luxury like this before. All four men hesitated at the threshold.

Davenport, already inside by this stage, wrinkled his nose at the thought of the hunter's dog and the arcanist's familiar entering the building, but contained himself. He had his orders. "This way, if you please." He guided them up a marble staircase with gilded bannisters, alighting on a relatively small landing with a patterned wooden floor. Two doors, the miniature twins of those stationed at the entrance, were set into the facing wall.

Large brass handles were grasped by two gloved men dressed in black tailcoats, revealing a richly-appointed oak-panelled room beyond. The air carried a faint smell of whiskey and expensive cigars; evidently Ainsworth was a man who enjoyed the 'finer things' in life. After performing a quick circuit of the room, Bugen's eyes came to rest on the figure seated at the leather-topped desk at its centre.

The man, clearly Sir Hupert, was almost grotesquely obese, confirming Bugen's supposition. Above the besuited body—one almost felt sorry for the buttons straining to hold the man's waistcoat closed—sat a head bearing a generally jovial demeanour, partially obscured by a neatly-trimmed white beard and bushy eyebrows.

"Arty Tilin, m'boy," boomed Ainsworth. "Come in, come in. How's my favourite nephew?"

The lad promptly dumped his belongings on the landing and dashed into the room. "Excellent, Uncle," replied Artyom vigorously, pumping Hupert's hand as the whole group filed into the room. Davenport took up his station behind the desk, standing at attention almost like a soldier, whilst Ed plumped himself down on the nearest couch. Alfazar, who was on the whole more accustomed to dealing with those of high station, politely inclined his head toward Ainsworth before taking a seat opposite him. Bugen remained standing stiffly to the left of the great doors, which had been closed from outside, noting that Ainsworth still had not deigned to acknowledge the presence of anyone in the room bar the arcanist.

"Oh, it's fantastic to see you Arty," continued Ainsworth, waving a hand around airily. "It's been, what, almost ten years? Why, you were but a little boy last I saw you! How do you like my little town, eh?"

"It's simply fantastic Uncle," agreed Artyom, somehow managing to be more enthusiastic than sycophantic. "There's just so much happening here. And the magick... it's everywhere!"

"You've not seen the half of it, m'boy," Ainsworth commented with a knowing grin. "You simply *must* see the mages' sector. I shall let the Archmage know that you'll be taking a peek soon."

"Excellent." replied the boy. "When can I have a look?"

"Ahhh, but we have business to attend to first," said Ainsworth, his face falling a little. "Business always comes first, you know," he continued matter-of-factly, gazing down at his desk.

"I've called you all together," the man announced, lifting his eyes and looking at Alfazar, Ed and Bugen for the first time, "to deal with a little public relations problem that I'm having." Ainsworth settled himself deeper into his chair, looking somewhat irritated. "You see, I've made my fortune in Arcana. When I found this place no-one could even believe the quantity of gold hidden in the land. The riches of the soil didn't stop there; we soon discovered a whole new set of farm crops. Sugar cane, tobacco, many previously unknown fruits... all thrive in Arcana. We became the envy of all the Kingdom. Yet, despite this natural wealth, the *real* reason that Arcana has taken off with the common folk is that *there are no Fae in my country.*"

Bugen found this pronouncement a little unnerving, seeing as the population of Port Adeline was under the rule of the King, not Ainsworth.

"The problem is that some rumour-mongers have been frightening the townsfolk with stories of Fae sightings over the past few weeks. One or two children go missing and a few people see some strange lights at sea, and all of a sudden there must be *Fae* in Arcana." The latter comment was laden with sarcasm. "Well, I won't have a bit of it!" he said, punctuating his declaration by loudly slapping his desk. The man's ample jowls wobbled on for a goodly time after the sudden motion. "These childish tales are cutting the immigration rates like there's no tomorrow, and a lack of common people means a lack of gold and crops to export. If things get too much worse, I'll have them wanting to *leave* Arcana soon!" It was clear that he found the very thought borderline heretical.

The four men remained silent for a moment, each digesting what Sir Hupert had just laid before them. It was true that a great deal of Arcana's appeal lay in the fact that the Fae were apparently not present in the new land.

Alfazar was the first to speak. "Well, Sir Ainsworth... although there are those in our party who are inclined to hunt and destroy the Fae," he motioned towards Ed, "I gather that you have brought us together to fulfil a rather different purpose."

"Well, of course," began Ainsworth, clearly irritated. "There *are* no Fae, so there's no need for –"

"What are we to do then, Uncle?" cut in Artyom, before the man could build up a head of steam.

Ainsworth regarded the boy with narrowed eyes, then sighed. Bugen had the impression that he would have brooked interruption from no-one else. "You and your companions are to be my messengers—or maybe my 'ambassadors'—to the outlying towns of Arcana. I want you to *dispel* these rumours; soothe the townsfolk where you can, bribe and coerce them if you must, but I need these rumours *crushed.*"

General silence met this pronouncement, broken only by the arcanist whipping out a notebook and charcoal. "Crush... rumours," Artyom said, writing the heading on a blank page, before brightly looking up and staring around at his fellow ambassadors. "So, what do we have to go on?"

At a nod from Ainsworth, Davenport deposited onto the desk a sheaf of papers. Artyom immediately began sorting through them; apparently the lad was to be their unofficial leader.

Bugen moved closer, seeing two maps spill forth.

"Here," indicated Davenport, leaning over the desk, "is Newtown, the first settlement that Sir Ainsworth formed beyond Port Adeline itself. There have been two murders in the township over the past month, which is unusual, but both victims were adults, not children, so we do not believe that Fae are involved... despite what the gossips might say." He moved his manicured nail across the page. "There are three outlying settlements surrounding Newtown, each about a day's travel by horse. To the south lies Maerin, a diminutive fishing community; the small cane farming and gold mining settlement of Briss lies to the north; and between the two, about half a day's march from either, sits Evergreen, nestled up against Darkwood, the forest which carpets the foot of the ranges."

"That'd be Fae territory, if they're 'ere," mused Ed, earning a filthy look from Davenport. Ainsworth restrained himself.

"What news from the outer settlements?" enquired Bugen.

"Four children have been taken recently from Darkwood—we do not believe these disappearances are linked with the murders in Newtown—and fisher-folk at Maerin report seeing strange lights abroad at sea."

"The peasants have probably just had a bad batch of homebrew," growled Ainsworth. "At any rate, there's absolutely no reason to believe that Fae of any description have made their way to Arcana." Davenport nodded sycophantically in response to this comment.

Artyom finished scribing down these pieces of information and moved onto the second map. It was evident that the parchment showed a larger region of Arcana. The inhabited area, sitting to the north-west of the continent, occupied a rather measly portion of the page. "Here," said Davenport, "is shown the extent of our continent which has been explored, largely by Sir Ainsworth. The settled regions are bordered to the east by the Staufen Mountains, which were the source of much of our alluvial gold. Nobody yet lives in that range, nor past it."

"Pray tell, what sits beyond the Staufens?" queried Alfazar, indicating the rest of the map.

"As it says, performer, that is the Bone Desert," supplied Ainsworth. "A most perilous region, ringed around by the Great Arcan Forest: none who penetrate the secrets of far Arcana ever return from their adventures there. Animals, foul weather, shortages of provisions, difficulty of navigation: all of these may be responsible for their deaths. I was never so foolish, despite my yearning to discover more of my country."

Another unnerving comment, thought Bugen. The man was full of them.

Artyom regarded the map intently for a moment. "Uncle, these markings are usually reserved for portions of maps which are uncharted..." He continued to frown in concentration, whilst the others looked at the lad in mild astonishment. "Yes, I am a cartographer, like my father before me," he said dryly, with nary an upward glance. After a moment all of them transferred their attention to the cross-hatched region of the page, circular, nestled in the centre of the Staufen mountains.

"Yes, well," began Ainsworth uncomfortably, "you've not yet appreciated the scale of the mountains ringing that particular region. These surrounding hills are really only measly undulations by comparison. And when I say 'ringing', I mean *completely* encircling. They extend some leagues upwards, though their true height is unknown, and our most gifted arcanists have failed to find any means of scaling or otherwise bypassing them." The man folded his hands over his ample stomach. "It... plagues me, I admit."

Ignatius spoke up in an attempt to salvage Hupert's mood. "You must understand," he declared in warning tones, "that this second map is provided for reference only, as your commission concerns only the inhabited regions of Arcana." It was Ainsworth's turn to nod now, his jowls following half a cycle out of phase with his head.

"What be our... commission?" asked Ed; if he was *not* being paid to kill Fae, he at least wanted to know what he *was* being paid.

"That will depend on your success," Ainsworth replied whilst eyeing the hunter. "Quell these rumours and you will be well rewarded,"—his eyes drifted over Alfazar and Artyom, coming to rest on Bugen—"or in your case, your Order will be well rewarded."

Bugen's superiors had warned him that Ainsworth would rather have nothing to do with the divine and their servants, and that Bugen's presence in this group was only in grudging acquiescence to Elandrian law.

"If the rumours persist I will be... displeased," Ainsworth finished pointedly.

"In the meantime, your needs will be covered by our treasury," supplied Davenport, speaking into the silence. He took the remaining papers from Artyom and showed them to the rest of the group. "Whilst you are within Port Adeline you may acquire whatever you need by means of these letters of credit," explained the man as he distributed the notes. "You should outfit yourselves as you see fit, within reason, whilst in our city. We will also supply coin to be spent in the outlying settlements, if necessary: one hundred pieces each should cover any sundries, accommodation or... coercion that need be purchased." This amount of wealth staggered Bugen, who would live comfortably for many years on such a sum. "Finally, we have arranged for horses and a cart for you to travel with. They will be delivered to your lodgings this night; simply inform any of the city guard where you wish to stay and show them your letter of credit."

"Now, be gone. Return before the Festival and you may claim your reward," said Ainsworth in dismissal. Bugen knew that the Festival of the White Lady would be held in two weeks: that should give ample time to visit all of the Arcanan townships.

"Wait, Uncle," said Artyom, as the others stood and made to leave. "Are we the only group you have commissioned?"

Sir Hupert regarded his adopted nephew for a moment before answering. "No: I have hired two other bands also. They were briefed this morning. Most likely they have already left town, though I know not where they head beyond Newtown. Now go, and be sure to visit the mages' sector, Arty."

The doors were opened and the companions filed out; they could hear Ainsworth calling on Davenport to deliver him a brandy. On the landing Bugen stooped and took up one of Artyom's bags, the same one which he bore off the *Steadfast*. Artyom, meanwhile, was so preoccupied by the maps that he walked straight past his pile of belongings.

Tamtem looked brightly from the bags to his master, then seemed to shrug as he followed the group down the marble staircase.

The whole group stopped, as though by unspoken consent, just inside the large doors; Bugen suspected that they were all reluctant to re-enter the humid atmosphere which awaited beyond. "Well, I'm off to the mages' sector," stated Artyom needlessly. He looked at the remaining three. "What will you be up to?"

Surprisingly, Ed was the first to pipe up. "I want to learn more 'bout this Higgens character," he said, stroking his beard and looking thoughtful. "After that, I'll probably head off to the markets, pick up some supplies."

"Well then," grinned Alfazar, "I shall perform. My heart yearns for a decent crowd."

Bugen finished. "I too wish to speak with Alfonz Higgens. Thereafter I shall seek out my brethren in the House of the Sun. It seems that my path goes with Ed for the time being. Where shall we all meet at the conclusion of our errands?"

"Let's go to Findlay's Inn," suggested Ed, scrutinising his map. "It's near enough to the centre of town, close to the markets." The others readily agreed, each not being fussed with pursuing more upmarket accommodation, though it lay well within their collective grasp.

With that decided the group pushed the great doors open. Ed brandished his paper under the nose of the nearest guard. "We'll be staying at Findlay's," he told the man with no preamble, before striding off with Buhbuh and Bugen close behind. Alfazar breathed deeply and rolled his shoulders, anticipating a performance with pleasure, and Artyom briefly consulted his own map before moving off in the opposite direction, anxious to sample more of Adeline's magick.

Chapter 3

Misstep & Mishap

"There's never any break for us, we Fae hunters. They're always out there, always waiting, always ready to take our children and kill us if we get in the way, and if we don't stop 'em, nobody will. No wall is worth as much as a Fae hunter, and we're worth a lot to all the Faustian and Graean peasants out there.

"There's only one guaranteed break for us, and it's a lucky few who live to see it. The Festival of the White Lady! Once every hundred years the blood moon hangs over Elandria and great swarms of banshees appear—got no idea where from, mind you—and give the Fae what–for. 'Course I've never seen it. I'm thirty, and though that's old for one of us, it's nowhere near a century.

"Ahhhh, I'm looking forward to it though! Two weeks with naught to do but sit back, eat, drink, and be merry. Might have to find myself a handsome chap in a little seaside village somewhere...

"They'll be back, of course, the Fae: they don't stay away for long, no matter how bloody the banshees make 'em. Fortunately, rumour has it that children born during the Festival of the White Lady are destined to make pretty damn fantastic Fae hunters... s'long as they don't put me out of business, I'll be happy. Mind, I wouldn't mind being put out of business, if you take my meaning.

"Well, first things first: I've got a job offer in Arcana coming up. Just a little jaunt, nothing major. Then the Festival! I'm fairly sure there's a flagon and hammock with my name on it in that little town they've got there... what's it called, Bevin? Nah, was it Nerrin? Ach, who cares, so long as my man's there!"

Yasmin Eyre, acclaimed Fae hunter

ﹰ   ﹰ﹅ﹰ   ﹰ﹅ﹰ   ﹰﹰﹰﹰﹰ ✕ ﹰﹰﹰﹰﹰ   ﹰ﹅ﹰ   ﹰ﹅ﹰ   ﹰ

 HE gaolhouse was nestled under the section of the city wall which encircled the markets. Entering through a forbidding doorway, Ed and Bugen found themselves in a small waiting room. Against the right wall was a bench on which sat two hunched, old women swathed in shawls. A dark hallway speared off along the length of the wall, from which there was little to be heard except the distant mutterings of imprisoned wretches.

Bugen turned to the man seated in the guardroom to the left of the entrance. "Excuse me," said the priest through the small window. The guardsman didn't look up from the scroll that he was frowning at, but did grunt an acknowledgement that he had heard something. "We wish to speak with Alfonz Higgens," Bugen continued. At this the guard did look up, now frowning at the pair before him.

"Hmmm. You'll need to wait here for a moment while I check with the higher–ups," spoke the man, stroking his chin. "What be your business anyways?"

Ed simply poked his paper through the bars. The black-clad man unfurled it, took a long look, deepened his frown, and handed the sheet back, then left the guardroom through a tight passageway.

"Oho!" screeched a new voice. "*Another* priest. Sun by the look of ya. Are they gonna replace the Sun priestess too? Oho, but she is a fiery one, eh? I like listening to her sermons: they're funny."

"Aha, she is a funny one. Much better than the boring old guy they had before her. He was no fun."

Bugen turned and regarded the two old women seated on the bench, both chuckling immoderately. He had half a mind to berate them for their attitude, but he stilled his tongue; he had not met the priestess yet, and even the followers of Sol were not faultless.

Best to err on the side of caution, and gallantry, in Bugen's opinion. "Good day to you," Bugen replied. "Pray tell, what did you mean by 'another priest'? I was under the impression that the current priestess had been serving Sol in these lands for a number of years now."

"Aha, there you're right, but as a rule we don't distinguish between priests of the different houses. In Port Adeline a priest is a priest is a priest, see?"

"Oho, yes, you're very right, as always: except for when they're a priestess, of course," agreed the first crone. "But really, I was talking about that priest of knowledge: that Higgens. Oho, but he cracked, didn't he deary?"

"Like a leaky chamber pot he was, aha, after whatever it was that happened to 'im. Mind leaking rubbish everywhere!" At this both women began snickering again.

"We're here to see Higgens," put in Ed. "So tell us: what happened to him?"

"Oho, nobody really knows, do they?"

"Aha, nobody does deary, no. All we knows is that this Higgens was looking in his crystal, as he was wont to do, and whatever it was that he spied broke his mind. Never the same again, he was."

"I saw them taking him away from his church, I did. About two months back. Oho, but he looked a treat, all writhing around and wide-eyed. Whatever it was, it gave him a real fright, I'll wager."

The second woman turned to the first and said, quite seriously, "It was probably you in the nuddy... Aha!" Both women erupted into gales of laughter.

Bugen had no idea what to make of these two. Fortunately the guardsman chose that moment to re-enter the room, this time *via* the corridor. "You pair can come with me," he said to Bugen and Ed, though looking curiously at the women; the latter were now unable to make eye contact without giggling hysterically. He then turned and made off down the hall.

Ed and Bugen followed, amused but still glad to leave 'Aha' and 'Oho' back in the waiting room.

The three men continued along the hallway until reaching what seemed to be a dead end. The guard then stooped, drew a large key from his belt, and inserted it into one of the floor tiles. With a moment's exertion a heavy trapdoor was lifted and a narrow passageway revealed. "Higgens is down there," indicated the guard. "I wait here."

"Is he dangerous?" enquired Ed, wondering at the heavy security Higgens was under.

"Not so much: not more than anyone not in their right mind," came the reply, "but he's bloody good at escaping, so we need to keep him locked up tight."

With that comfort in mind, Ed and Bugen descended down a narrow ladder into the dingy cell. Buhbuh remained with the guard.

The space into which they emerged was cramped, to say the least: little wonder the guard had remained above. Higgens was shackled to the far wall, and if the man's wrists were not bound above his head by thick chains he would have been able to reach out and touch Ed and Bugen, even though the two stood with their backs to rock. Despite the shackles and the confinement, the city guard evidently looked out for Higgens' well-being; just as well, thought Bugen, for the man was imprisoned through no fault of his own.

"It's never just one," came tumbling from the deposed priest's lips. Bugen could not tell if there was a spark of recognition in the man's eyes, or if he, Bugen, just wished to find some signs of sanity in his counterpart. "She always needs more. Never just one."

"Friend, I am Bugen of the Sun house," said Bugen solemnly.

"Never just one!"

"I have come to Arcana to help," continued Bugen, speaking slowly and clearly.

"Always more. One in ten; She needs at least one in ten."

"What did you see?" asked Ed directly. Even he was moved by Higgens' condition.

"The Reaper! I saw Her..." The man strained against his chains, pupils suddenly dilating in fear. "She always needs more!" he fairly screamed. "Every hundred years... one in ten!" The grating of metal on rock filled the room as Higgens continued to writhe against his constraints, still jabbering rapidly and affirmatively.

Taking pity on the man, Bugen stretched out his left hand and placed it on the thin prisoner's chest. "Friend, may Sol give you her peace," he intoned. A brief glow came from his buckler and hand, then Higgens slumped against his restraints, spent.

"Every hundred years," the dazed man murmured. "Every hundred... She needs more. It is coming."

Bugen and Ed exchanged a significant look; the Festival was held every hundred years, and it was approaching quickly.

By unspoken agreement they left Higgens behind, still murmuring quietly to himself.

"And old fat-face still doesn't think there are Fae 'ere..." murmured Ed.

The pair were filled with an odd sort of nihilism; the light streaming through the waiting room door seemed falsely cheery, and the jokes that the old women wore were just a thin veil covering their own frail mortality. The travellers both paused on the threshold.

"Well, if they're 'ere I'm gonna need some cold iron," said Ed finally. "Best I make sure our supplies are in order too."

"Aye. In that case I shall make my way to the House of the Sun. I wish to worship our Lady, and to talk with the priestess here. She might be able to shed a little light on what is really happening in Arcana."

ℒ ⊷✕ᴄᴏ ⊷✕ᴄᴏ ℘ᴄᴏᴄᴏ ⚔ ⊷ᴄᴏᴄᴏℛ ⊷✕ᴄᴏ ⊷✕ᴄᴏ ᴄᴏ

"Woah!" burst out Artyom as soon as he was permitted to. "This place is sooo awesome! I mean, even your receptionist can use magick. She just put a spell of silence on me. On *me*!"

The lad's jaw continued to flap about, but no words were permitted to come forth; the Archmage had just reinstated said incantation, to, in his opinion, rather marvellous effect. "Listen, Master Tilin," he lectured. "I am Brett Silverstone, Archmage of Port Adeline and keeper of the great community of arcanists formed here. *You*, on the other hand, rank lower in my interests than my lowliest apprentices, no matter what skill you might possess. Make no mistake, you are here only because of that letter you bear. Do not try my patience."

'Here' was the topmost room in a rather lofty spire which sat above the library of Port Adeline, which itself occupied a goodly portion of the mages' sector. The room contained an expansive desk, upon which perched a small, white stoat seated on a red pillow.

Silverstone was attired as one might expect. His head was crowned by a red skullcap, no doubt concealing a bald pate, and he wore a matching set of sweeping robes. Besides a few gold rings his only other adornment was a drooping moustache which twitched with impatience.

Artyom nodded vigorously until Silverstone removed the binding with a flick of his hand (and his moustache). "Well Brent, I have some questions, you see. About the Fae, that is."

"Oh, not this again," groaned the older man. "Do they not teach deductive reasoning in Faust?"

Artyom stroked his chin thoughtfully, as though formulating an answer.

"Never mind!" Silverstone exclaimed, seeing the wheels turn in the lad's head.

Young, socially inept, no regard for seniority, and disgustingly talented: the worst kind of student, in Silverstone's experience.

"Look, it goes like this," he began in the tone that one adopts when explaining something irritatingly obvious to someone dense. "There are no Fae in Arcana. Fae are trouble, and trouble is easy to spot. And those who make up stories of trouble where trouble simply does not exist are just going to make trouble for themselves, see? That's why you are here: to put the trouble back away so we can get on with business as usual. Interrupting business, well, that causes a lot of trouble, does it not? People do not like that, not at all."

Artyom regarded the man for a moment, then lifted the map he was holding and pointed to it. "What do you know about the murders in Newtown?" he asked evenly.

The other man was unable to determine whether Artyom had paid even the slightest amount of attention to the lecture he had just received. "You can't possibly extrapolate the presence of Fae from that data," scoffed Silverstone. "Humans had been doing an admirable job of killing one another for aeons before the Fae even showed themselves, and we've not changed a great deal."

"Okay, so you don't know anything useful about Newtown then," Artyom said brightly. Silverstone wondered whether this stranger was deliberately winding him up, or if the lad was genuinely oblivious to social niceties. "How about Maerin?"

"Nothing exciting has happened in that village since they caught an unusually large clobster."

"I've heard that there have been reports of strange lights out to sea there," persisted Artyom.

"Look, it is *nothing*," retorted the old mage. "Nothing. We have sent people to look on three separate occasions and nothing is ever there, despite the protestations of the townsfolk. And I know what you're going to ask next," he continued, holding up a finger pedantically. "The four disappearances in Evergreen and two in Briss, yes? Well, forget it. Yes, it is unusual for so many children to go missing around the same time, at least in Arcana, but we have no reason to think Fae are involved.

"The fact of the matter is we have scoured every inch of the land hereabouts and found no sign of the Fae, not even the small ones. The very idea is simply preposterous!"

In response to this Artyom whipped out his notebook again. *Preposterous* he wrote across the page beneath the previous information. "Well, Mr Silverstoat, you've been quite unhelpful," said Artyom as he tucked the book away, as though complementing Silverstone on a fine achievement. "I like your magick and all—it's really cool—but is there anyone more knowledgeable that I might speak with?"

That was the final straw for Silverstone. His face now matched the colour of his skullcap, and against this backdrop jiggled the moustache, keeping time with the man's rising pulse. "Why don't you go and talk to the Nature priestess?" growled Silverstone through gritted teeth. "I happen to know a shortcut."

"Oh, *that's* useful," began Artyom, before being yanked into the air and thrown through the open window as though by an invisible troll. "Awesome!" he yelled as he fell, flailing upside-down through the air.

Artyom came to a sudden halt about a handsbreadth from the ground. No sooner had the lad breathed a sigh of relief than the mystical force supporting him vanished, planting his face into the turf. Tamtem floated gently down after him, alighted smartly, and stood waiting for his master to arise. After a moment Artyom stood, ran one hand across his face, and groaned. "Well, that's the first time we've ever been magicked out of a window," he said excitedly to Tamtem. "Thanks!" he yelled toward the tower. "That was cool!" With a last wave the arcanist—unconventional, as Alfazar would say—turned and made his way out of the mages' sector, his dirty face earning him many scandalised looks on the way.

ৎ ৵৯✖️৵৯ ৵৯✖️৵৯ ৵৯৵৯৵৯ ✖️ ৵৯৵৯৵৯ ৵৯✖️৵৯ ৵৯✖️৵৯ ৵৯

"Come one, come all," announced the bard. "Witness acts never before seen in Arcana." Alfazar was fairly certain that his particularly flamboyant performance style would not have travelled this far previously.

The man stood in one of Port Adeline's numerous public gardens. Many of those on the nearby thoroughfare caught his words and decided that a break was just what they needed at that moment.

"Oo are you, then?" queried someone from the gathering crowd.

"I am Alfazar d'Barouse, famous amongst the courts of Graea and Faust, entertainer of peasant and noble alike. My knives have even flashed before the King himself," came the smooth reply, as Alfazar pulled two knives from his belt and began juggling them. The straight weapons, with flaring, double-edged blades, twisted gracefully through the air.

By this stage a great number of onlookers were ensnared: about fifty, all told. Alfazar felt it time to ramp up the intensity a touch. "I have seen distant ports, and strange lands where lights hang in the skies, and the earth itself spews forth fire and smoke." He flicked an unlit torch into the air with his feet and seamlessly added it to the intricate pattern traced out by the knives. The crowd was rapt, intently following his movements to such a degree that when Alfazar ignited the torch with a hidden taper many were shocked. Their loud exclamations drew even more eyes towards the performance.

"Travellers must take care in those lands," warned the bard, "that the ground does not unleash its wrath upon them." So saying, Alfazar made to flick another torch into the procession. By some ill luck, or perhaps a hidden depression in the ground, or maybe the slight remnants of the rolling sailors' gait he had acquired over the past months, Alfazar stumbled at the last moment. He tripped over the torch and landed uncharacteristically heavily. Before long the feeling of his wounded pride was joined by a screaming pain in his left leg. Looking down, Alfazar noted the hilt of one knife protruding from his thigh, its twin and the torch having mercifully landed elsewhere. He clenched his jaw and flared his nostrils as he bit back a curse. Looking up, he saw that the majority of the audience was attempting to not look embarrassed for him.

Their efforts were quickly undone by a lone old man, standing far to the rear of the crowd, who roared with laughter. "Well, it's unleashed its wrath upon you!" wheezed the geezer, shaking with mirth the whole time. He continued to do so as the crowd began to disperse; it was like Alfazar had become something unspeakable.

"Hospital's just over there," mouthed one woman as she made to leave, pointing surreptitiously towards a purple building with a large red cross emblazoned on it. Nodding, Alfazar finished bandaging his leg with part of his ruined pants and began to make his painful way towards the indicated structure. As he hobbled, Alfazar gave fervent thanks, through gritted teeth, to whichever deity had arranged for his three companions to be elsewhere.

The houses of worship were crammed together in a space much smaller than the marketplace, which irritated Bugen. How could these people rank the gods and goddesses below the economy?

Looking through a narrow archway, Bugen espied the House of the Sun sitting next to the Nature House, itself nestled up against the House of the Moon. Whilst Lune was not inherently evil, those who worshipped the moon goddess often associated her with death, which the followers of Sol did not, as a rule, appreciate. Despite that, devotees of the deities of Order tended to get along with one another.

Bugen stepped through the archway and was confronted by a woman dressed in familiar red and yellow: evidently a worshipper of Sol. "Hey, you're new here, arncha?" she said. She was young, somewhere around Bugen's twenty-five years, of middling height, and had shoulder length brown hair framing an angular face. The woman's clothing was of a different cut to Bugen's, which was not unusual, and she bore a silver necklace on which was scribed the symbol of Sol. Bugen felt a faint stirring of unease, but could not place why; maybe he was just unaccustomed to female attention. "Oh, I bet you're here to see her: Dell, that is."

Bugen cocked an eyebrow in query.

"She's only the high priestess of Sol," teased the girl.

"Well then... yes, I am here to see Dell."

"She's pretty grumpy at the moment; I'd steer clear if I were you," the woman advised. "Hey, I can show you around town in the meantime."

Bugen had little choice but to fall in step with her as she strode off. His hesitation meant that he walked along behind the woman, who was certainly not out for a stroll.

As he stepped through the portal a second time Bugen's world tipped alarmingly, and he threw out an arm to break his fall. Fortunately the priest landed on his face, and not the sword sheathed at his waist. Bugen sprang to his feet, clutching his buckler, and was halfway through turning around when he felt the wire wrapped around his foot. Too late now: the sky and ground traded places again. This time Bugen was careful to stay on the ground.

"Ooooo, got you twice, I did!" burst out the woman raucously. "That was excellent! I didn't even have to ask for the encore." She seemed to be greatly enjoying her little malicious joke, chuckling to herself as she watched Bugen attempt to extricate himself from the snare. From his new—rather lower—vantage point Bugen quickly noticed that the woman was wearing a darker set of clothing under the tabard. He also realised that the necklace she wore was cheap tin, not silver.

He had been duped by the imposter priest. Or perhaps not; this sort of tomfoolery smacked of the antics of those who dedicated themselves to following the more unstructured deities. "I take it I have just been acquainted with a priestess of the House of Chaos?" Bugen asked mildly as he stood and brushed himself off.

The woman nodded, her giggling unabated.

A loud guffaw drowned out the mischievous chuckling. For all its apparent mirth it was a callous laugh; the sort made by someone small-minded and cruel when they tread on others to make their own existence seem more palatable. "Good one, Flavia," called the laugher, a stocky fellow whose pale skin was thrown into contrast by scraggly black hair and a sparse beard. Bugen did not need to look at the other man's robes twice to realise that he was a follower of darker deities. "New priests make for such... marvellous entertainment."

His eyes never left Flavia.

"Do they *ever*!" came the excited response. "I just wish they came in more often."

The reply was a monotone, "That could be... arranged." Flavia looked at the newcomer for a moment, quiet now, before bursting into laughter again.

"Always so serious, Vincent," she said in the same teasing manner she had earlier turned on Bugen.

The dark priest, Vincent, managed a facsimile of a smile which failed to reach his eyes; eyes which still had not left the woman's face.

Flavia did not seem to notice the man's gaze. She turned back to Bugen. "Yes: Flavia of the House of Chaos. A pleasure to make your acquaintance." She held out a hand, which Bugen thoroughly inspected before shaking.

"The pleasure is... mutual," replied the young man, almost questioningly. He inclined his head toward Vincent too, but refrained from speaking. It is not healthy to ignore dark priests, nor to antagonise or insult them. "Whether Dell be angry or no, I shall see her now," proclaimed Bugen.

Flavia giggled yet again, but this time with a wholesome laughter borne of appreciation for the one who is laughed at. The girl was so capricious: yes, capricious and malicious, but not evil, and, in her own way, naïve. The other priest, Vincent, made Bugen's skin crawl.

Best to be gone, he thought. With one last adjustment to his tabard and armour he was off, striding off across the square to the House of the Sun. It was high time for some answers, and perhaps a spot of peace and quiet.

༺ ✦ ✦ ✦ ⚔ ✦ ✦ ✦ ༻

"So, you got any cold iron?" enquired Ed.

He was standing inside a small, dark shop, the entry of which was filled with a jumble of assorted ironmongery—swords, axes, even a suit of plate armour arranged on a mannequin. The small forge situated at the back of the room provided a little illumination but also made the cramped space stiflingly hot. Ed inwardly snorted at the smith, a short man whose excessive arm musculature made him look too top-heavy to stand upright; as a result of the oppressive atmosphere the man was clad in little more than a loincloth, a pair of thick leather gloves, and a sooty apron.

The man laid down his hammer and turned towards Ed, not bothering to hide his stormy expression. "Now, why would I have cold iron?" he growled.

"Well, y'know," Ed replied. "Cold iron. The Fae hate it."

"The Fae, you say," the smith said with a look of disgust. "Well, there ain't no Fae in Arcana, so I ain't got no cold iron, savvy?"

Ed could see that the man was holding his temper in check, but not by much. Still, cold iron could be the difference between life and death when fighting the Fae. 'Cold' was a misnomer, if Ed understood correctly; cold iron was still forged, but at a lower temperature than usual for steel weapons. It took skill to make a decent cold iron weapon, and a masterful smith to fabricate one that would last more than a few fights. Despite this, cold iron was in huge demand because of its apparently mystical Fae-slaying qualities.

Ed believed that the metal somehow tampered with the Fae's connexion to their magicks, making them more susceptible to injury.

They certainly hated to touch the stuff even more than they hated regular iron.

Time to try a different tack. "I can pay," Ed pointed out in a low voice.

"What with?" asked the smith, still eyeing the hunter dubiously. "You don't look like you could afford cold iron, if I were t'have it, that is," he said, then spit to the side. The forge let off a brief but violent sizzle.

In response, Ed waved his letter of credit under the short fellow's nose.

"Ainsworth! Just get out," the smith hissed, pointing to the door. "I don't want no trouble."

"But—"

"Out, I said!" The man continued to gesticulate towards the door, now with his hammer in hand.

Ed decided it was time to cut his losses; he already had his lucky cold iron horseshoe, and there were likely to be other smithies around town or in the surrounding villages. No point stirring up trouble... yet. Without another word, Ed walked out, making sure to 'accidentally' knock over the armour on the way. That ought to keep the smith sweating for a while longer.

Bugen enjoyed the warm light of his goddess filtering through the enormous stained glass windows above the altar. There was a matching set at the rear of the temple, to allow the morning sunlight in also.

He sat with his legs folded beneath him and his hands clasped in his lap, unsheathed sword resting across his knees. Although he sat quite erect, Bugen could still feel a faint sensation of gently rolling from side to side: a phantom remnant of the extended sea travel.

Despite the great power of Sol that he could call upon at need, Bugen always felt closest to her when simply revelling in her presence. He was not one for spectacles or shows, although the young cleric feared the great power wielded by his deity. She was as much in the whispers as in the shouts.

"I remember feeling like that," a voice intruded. The owner was an older woman, Bugen surmised. Her voice had a rough edge, as if she had indulged in too many pipes. He opened his eyes and focussed them on her, and for a moment she was struck motionless by the awareness radiating from the green gaze. Man and woman stood connected by a moment of understanding, bathed in the yellow-gold radiance of a sunset streaming into Sol's temple.

"High Priestess Dell." Bugen rose and bowed to her respectfully, then turned and bowed to the altar before sheathing his sword. "I'm certain you still feel like this when you are at peace."

"Peace... is hard to come by, kid," came the gruff response. "Even here in Adeline." She beckoned for Bugen to follow her away from the few others sitting in the pews or kneeling on the warm stone floor.

The young cleric studied his senior counterpart. Her long dress was red with yellow trim, to match Bugen's tabard, and Bugen noted that it was split up to the hip on either side. Dell wore a pair of men's leggings underneath, perhaps to allow her to ride a horse. The woman's frame was lean and unarmoured, and although she carried only a small poniard it was clear to Bugen that she had once been a woman of arms. Such was common in the priesthood. Her greying hair carried no stain of pipeweed, which led Bugen to believe that her rough voice was the result of a life spent largely on the road, spreading Sol's light through the Kingdom.

She ascended a short staircase into her study, which was nestled in behind Sol's altar. As Bugen entered the room she gave him an appraising look. "Peace will be hard to find where you're going too, boy."

Bugen smiled at her forthrightness. "I am prepared," he stated simply.

"Is that so?"

"Aye." Bugen hoped that was the only piece of sailors' language that he'd picked up on the *Steadfast*.

"And when you must face Fae?"

"I will pass Sol's judgement upon them." *They took my sister. I will have answers.*

"Fair enough, kid. How about when your companions are wounded or killed?"

"They know the dangers," Bugen said gravely.

"They know only the worldly dangers, kid. Do you see them here, shriving their souls or praying for protection and mercy? At any of the temples? No. Their type—Ainsworth's type—see only the mortal dangers. How will you respond when they're dying? Plead with Sol for mercy on their souls?"

Yes. "May Sol guide them with me as Her tool." *Guide them into Her embrace and Her justice.*

Dell sighed and raised a hand to her forehead. "I don't know whether I feel pity for you or ashamed of myself. Once I was that faithful."

"You still are, priestess: you're just wearied by the hurts of the world. If you look you will see all of the good that drove you to Sol many years past."

"Hey, kid. I'm glad you came," came the slow response. Dell smiled briefly and coughed a few times to cover her emotions. "Well," she said, suddenly brusque. "We can't stand around yammering all day. Let's get to business."

"Aye," nodded Bugen again, shooting a quick prayer to Sol as he did so.

"You've already been told about the sightings in Maerin and the disappearances in Evergreen and Newtown, right?"

"Yes," Bugen began. "Ainsworth briefed us about the following facts..."

"Well, that must be the houses of worship over there then Tamtem," mused Artyom as he scrutinised his map. The boy and his familiar drew a significant amount of attention, even with all the wares of the marketplace competing for the notice of passers-by. The attention went unrequited, for Artyom was now fixated by the small archway he had identified as the ingress point.

Tamtem reached the gate ahead of his master and stopped suddenly, going on point and growling like a dog spotting a hare. "Hmmm..." came Artyom's response. He cautiously continued forward and identified the tripwire. "Pfft, what a bunch of amateurs. Anyone worth their salt could spot this thing from a mile off," the lad proclaimed in a carrying voice, playing to his no-doubt concealed audience. He stepped over the wire and continued into the courtyard.

"Aww, that's ruined all of my fun now," a voice whined behind him. "And I was having such a good day, first with that pious little munchkin that came through, and then with the stodgy priest of Sol." Flavia stepped out of the shadows and into Artyom's view.

"I take it that Bugen didn't spot the tripwire then?" asked the lad.

"Oh, you know him?" Flavia asked eagerly. "He's good value, I'd say. Got him twice." Her face broke into a wide grin.

Artyom paid her no attention, occupied as he was by making a mental note that 'Bugen is poor at detecting traps'.

"So, what's your squirrel's name?"

"Tamtem," replied Artyom absently, as he tried to discern the markings on each of the surrounding buildings. He squinted out from underneath his hand as he shaded his eyes from the westering Sun. "Where can I find the Nature priestess?"

"Nature is that one there," Flavia responded, indicating a building to the right. Artyom could just discern an engraving on its pearly marble lintel: an anvil. He turned his gaze slowly towards Flavia.

"Ermm... you're not very good at this, are you?"

"Huh?" came the overly-innocent reply.

"That's the House of Ferrous...," instructed the mage. "And that," he continued as he indicated the sightly ramshackle building behind Flavia, "would be the House of Chaos, no?"

Flavia stamped her foot and crossed her arms before pouting like a truculent teen. "You *are* no fun."

"But new priests are *ever* so much fun," drawled a voice which would have been mild if it were not so dead. Vincent emerged from the shadows beyond the gateway and began circling Artyom. "So...

much... fun," he said through narrowed eyes. Tamtem cringed under the priest's baleful gaze, and even Flavia took a step away.

"I don't think this one's a priest Vincent," said the latter in an uncertain quaver.

Vincent ceased pacing. His eyes raked Flavia up and down, as though scanning for signs of weakness. "Oh, so you've got a new devotee then?" he jested eventually.

Artyom was completely unfazed. "I'm no priest; I'm a mage, of course."

Vincent turned slowly on the spot to face the arcanist. His voice, when it finally reappeared, had apparently spent its absence carefully cultivating sarcasm. "A *mage*. Oh, how *silly* of me. *Of course* you're an arcanist. I should have bloody well guessed.

"Damn you arcanists and your damned uppity lip!" he practically howled. "How about I show you some new magick!"

"Oh, that would be c—" Artyom began, but he was interrupted by Vincent thrusting one hand forward, glowing palm outwards. Artyom felt his hair stand on end for a split second before the priest's malice burst forth with a sound like lashing whips. Unable to react in time, Artyom was seized by red tendrils of power which forced themselves into his eyes and filled his sinuses with unbearable pressure. His ears whined and popped, then the pressure vanished and his world went pitch black. "What the—" cried the mage, pawing at his face.

Then he fell silent.

Vincent hawked up a glob of phlegm which struck the ground with a wet *thwack*. "Bloody mages," he cursed.

"Woah, that's a neat piece of magick! I can't do that one," Artyom said, practically bouncing with excitement. "The eyes thing, not the snot," he clarified.

Vincent had no response to this except to turn incredulously to Flavia, who was watching proceedings with apprehension. Of course, this exchange was completely wasted on the arcanist. "Blasted right, mage boy," the dark priest replied. "Get you gone, or I'll teach you a few more things you can't do," he instructed gruffly, somewhat mollified by Artyom's praise. "It'll wear off by tomorrow."

"Ooh, now I'm all intrigued. See you around... well, not *now* I guess..." said Artyom as he stumbled off.

After a few moments Flavia burst out laughing and called teasingly across the square. "Oi! My newest devotee: you're going the wrong way, moron!"

"Huh? Oh, right. Come on Tamtem."

"Hi... I want... to speak... to... the Nature priestess."

The few people who were praying in the House of Nature threw Artyom filthy looks and moved closer to the stream in a vain attempt to blot out the intrusive noise.

A woman clad in dun robes flowed her way over to Artyom, her gait smooth and deceptively fast. The lady's dark skin and long brown hair blended with the browns and greens of the floor—which was carpeted with leaves, soil and fungi—and her green eyes matched the verdant vegetation bordering the watercourse wending its way from the altar down to the Nature worshippers. "May I help you?"

"Are... you... the priestess?" enquired the mage in a carrying whisper. Some of the frogs fell silent.

"Yes. What brings you to my House?"

"Fae," he replied tactfully.

Artyom stumbled out of the temple's doors, which shut firmly behind him. "What's *with* everyone today? So angry..." He tapped around with his feet, trying to navigate the stairs which led back down into the courtyard. *Where's the blasted temple of Sol?* he thought, laughing on the inside.

The two priests stood in the narthex below the great windows showing Sol's mortal guise. Now that the Sun had gone down fully the temple was lit from within by ingenious use of polished bronze plates and oil lamps; the effect was to generate a metallic glow which bathed the stained glass and the altar of Sol, leaving the rest of the space in twilight. Light glinted from Bugen's armour.

"And be sure to check in with the innkeeper at Newtown," Dell was saying. "The man was a regular worshipper here for years, but has stopped attending recently. I'd rather like to know why." Bugen nodded, adding a mental note to his list. "Any questions, kid?"

"No, High Priestess, I will attend to my companions and those whom I meet on this quest. Sol will reveal my tasks to me as we travel."

"If I had half of your faith left, kid..."

Bugen's reply was curtailed by a faint knocking sound. Dell gave him a quizzical look, before the thick oaken doors to the temple were thrust open. Bugen had his buckler in hand before he recognised Artyom standing on the threshold. "You sure know how to make an entrance, mage."

"Hey, it's Bugen," Artyom said, more to Tamtem than to anyone else.

"This is your mage?" Dell asked, trying to hide her incredulity. This young slip of a man was an arcanist? Why was he behaving so erratically, stumbling around the doorway?

"Artyom... did you fall?" queried Bugen once he noticed the dirt still smeared across the mage's face. Maybe he had a concussion.

"Oh yeah, it was really cool. I got magickally defenestrated and then the dark priest guy out the front here blinded me." Artyom sounded genuinely enthused as he jerked a thumb back over his shoulder, mistakenly indicating the House of Lune. "But he said it is temporary, so it's all good, right?" Artyom's face bore a wide grin.

"Best you take your companion to the inn, kid."

"Of course, High Priestess. I wish to rest before we leave tomorrow."

"May Sol's peace go with you," Dell replied ceremonially. She added, almost introspectively, "I might be seeing you around."

"Three ales and a water," Ed called to the barmaid. The woman was middle-aged and looked overworked, with brown hair brought up in pigtails. She shot Ed a look of acknowledgement as she bustled off to acquire the beverages, wending her way between the tables in the common room of Findlay's Inn. Ed eyed her ample bodice, wondering how she managed to squeeze between tables without smacking their occupants in the back of the head with her chest.

The companions were seated at one of the quieter tables near one of the internal pillars which supported the arched roof and the guest rooms above. There were plenty of people in the inn, but though the room was rowdy nobody was causing trouble. All in all, it was one of the more palatable establishments in Elandria, Bugen thought. The familiar scent of ale permeated the thick air, hearty stew could be smelled bubbling thickly in a cauldron over the hearth—guarded by an employee wielding a heavy ladle—and a haze of tobacco smoke clinging to the ceiling sent down blue-grey tendrils to touch each of the many lit pipes in the room. Whilst he waited for his drink to arrive, Bugen idly wondered how there was enough proper air left in the room to breathe. Ed and Artyom were nattering to one another again, and Alfazar was keeping a low profile, as far as possible. There was a purple bandage on his leg, Bugen noted absently.

Four tankards were set down on the table, covering up a few of the many rings adorning its surface. "Thanks!" Artyom said brightly to the barmaid, reaching for his cup with more vigour than caution. Still blinded by the dark priest's spell, Artyom knocked over two of the heavy pewter containers, sending them crashing to the floor in a mess of diluted ale.

The maid bent with a sigh and began mopping up the ale with a rag which she drew from somewhere about her person; evidently this was a common enough occurrence to be prepared for immediate action. Artyom, bearing a chagrined expression, ducked beneath the table to help. After a few moments of pawing around the mage found one of the steins and lifted it back onto the table. "Found another one, darl. Be a honey and put it on the table," muttered the barmaid, holding out the empty vessel for Artyom to take hold of. The young arcanist, ever helpful, reached for the container and missed, seizing a sizeable handful of the woman's top instead. After a moment of puzzlement Artyom realised his error, hurriedly let go, and apologised whilst blushing a furious red. The barmaid, to Bugen's surprise, chuckled and threw Artyom a mischievous wink. Her cleaning complete, the woman departed.

Ed looked away and fumed, wondering why he never got that response... Blasted mage boy.

Chapter 4

A Bit of a Pickle

One might almost be forgiven for thinking that man is the only intelligent race which inhabits our world (besides his predators, the Fae); however, the truth is far from this simplistic.

There have, of course, long been tales of dwarves living in caverns still deeper than any delved by human hands. These may or may not have foundations in reality. Certainly no conclusive evidence for their existence has been found. For this reason we will not concern ourselves with dwarves in this book (dwarves are discussed in 'Digging for Dwarves' by L. G. W.).

There is no doubt whatsoever that elves do exist, though they have withdrawn from affairs with humans. Historically they have played an instrumental role in shaping our society. Therefore the majority of this book is occupied by an account of the dealings of men and elves, up to and including their mysterious disappearance shortly after orchestrating the formation of our modern Kingdom.

Let us introduce the main characters in our story. There are essentially four races of elves, related in much the same way as the many races of humans. The longest-lived and wisest are known as the grey elves, their eyes filled with memory and even-temper; bright elves, on the other hand, are known for the vibrancy and immediacy of their revelry; intelligence and unpredictability are the hallmarks of the halfling elves, of smaller stature than others; and most dangerous to mankind are the wild elves, the least civilised, and the least trusting.

Elves have a close link with the divine, them being charged by the deities and demi-deities with maintaining the balance of the world. This is, of course, a weighty charge, and it speaks volumes that humans were not entrusted with the same responsibilities (for discussion see 'On the Balance of the World', volumes I-XXIV, by L. G. W.). This has led many *to believe that elves have abandoned humans out of disgust for our new-found blasé attitude towards divinity (the role of arcane magick in modern human society is detailed in 'Straying from the Supernal', volumes I-XVI, by L. G. W.). Though there is a gem of truth in this, the whole truth is, as usual, far more complex...*

Introduction to *A History of Elves and Men* by L. G. Wright

 HE companions met in the stables of Findlay's Inn an hour after dawn. Ed was first on the scene, having eschewed his bed in favour of a swag pitched in the rear of the supply cart. He preferred the organic smells and animal noises of the stable to their human counterparts. Bugen arrived next, after spending the first hour of sunlight making his daily devotion to Sol. The priest waited patiently until Alfazar and Artyom arrived, practically together. "Good morning," Alfazar greeted Bugen, not noticing that Ed was still asleep.

Buhbuh opened one eye and let out a perfunctory growl before settling back down to sleep.

Artyom moved over and prodded the hunter. "Oi, wake up... I mean, 'Good morning.' "

"Not for me it isn't, being 'wakened by an impertinent little mage," answered Ed, opening his eyes. Contrary to his words, he appeared wide awake and happy. Evidently Ed too was keen to get under way.

Alfazar, who seemed to have taken a liking to Artyom, wore a grin similar to that evoked by a particularly precocious niece or nephew. His leg, Bugen noted, was free of bandages, having been healed overnight by whatever unguents the healers had applied. Small wonder then that fewer people felt the need to rely on the divine.

As Ed had already secured all of their provisions in the cart, there was little left for the travellers to do, bar saddle their horses, mount them, and point them in the right direction. This turned out to be more difficult than expected, as Artyom had little experience with mundane beasts of burden. After a few minutes of watching Artyom struggle to saddle his horse Ed stepped in and corrected the lad, and a few moments later Alfazar had to point out that the rider traditionally does not face the tail. Meanwhile, Bugen was watching Tamtem tease Buhbuh, who was less than impressed at having to share the cart with the familiar.

Nevertheless, the group was soon off. They made their way along the boulevard—one of the four which quartered the city—in the direction of Newtown. Not having much to go on, their plan remained necessarily simple: reach Newtown by noon, reserve rooms in the local inn, which would serve as a temporary base of operations, and begin their appraisal of the settlement. All four agreed that Newtown would serve as a hub for travellers and their gossip.

People were already out and about, but in this direction the throng would not truly be joined for a few hours hence, when the farmers' markets swung into action. The same could not be said for the road leading towards the docks, which was already thick with traffic; after all, the tides wait for no man.

As the five horses—two drawing the cart, driven by Ed, and three bearing the remainder of the motley party—drew abreast of the great gate there came a quiet voice. "Wait!" said a figure, hooded and cloaked in umber, waiting out of sight of the guards who stood beyond the portal. Drawing near to Bugen, the person held aloft a golden chain from which swung a flat pendant. "Take it. You'll know when to use it. Keep it with you." The priest silently leant down and took the trinket, inclining his head towards its previous bearer. With that, the figure vanished back into town at a brisk pace. Bugen briefly inspected the object hanging from his hand; a rectangular gold medallion into which was set a rough-hewn ruby scribed with the symbol of Sol. Then, wondering why Dell had felt the need to hand over the item in such a manner, the young cleric fastened the chain around his neck and slipped the pendant under his gambeson.

The company continued through the archway and passed the guards as though nothing unusual had happened. Each kept their emotions to themselves; Ed, who was sure the rumours were true, was pleasurably anticipating hunting down Fae and destroying them; the mage was grateful that the trip, on which he might earn some small fame and knowledge, was not to be undertaken by boat; Alfazar was at ease, as usual; and Bugen, though appearing outwardly passive, was troubled by the weight of the token about his neck.

The morning passed without event, save for the passing of a swelling number of carts, laden with goods for Adeline's markets, and a few instances where Ed veered from their path to examine some unfamiliar local flora. Though greenery—both cultivated and natural—was in great abundance, there were few stands of any height, allowing the travellers to clearly see the road ahead; the red soil of its bed cut through the surrounds like a lazy red river. No true rivers were in sight, yet water was carried to and fro by numerous streams, many of which were clearly artificial.

At the eleventh hour of the morn, or so Bugen judged, the settlement of Newtown hove into view. A collection of mean dwellings were loosely clustered about the centre of town, which was identified by the presence of a large two-story stone construction set amidst a small sea of canvas tents. Alfazar speculated that the former was the inn, and the others were inclined to agree. The canvas probably indicated a market place.

Soon thereafter the four found their suppositions confirmed. A large gravelly square occupied the centre of town, into which roads debouched from three directions; travellers from Maerin would arrive from the right, whilst those from Evergreen and Briss entered Newtown from the left. Taking pride of place was the inn, which stood behind a sign bearing a painting of a scantily-clad maiden ploughing a field, underscored with the words *The Lucky Sod*. Bugen did not think much of the local humour.

The companions made their way past the markets, which were quite lively, but far smaller than their counterparts in Port Adeline, and onward into the square. Bugen noted a dingy stone building, single-storey and windowless, set off to the right, and a number of smaller and better-kept houses away to the left beyond the farmers' stalls. The first he judged to be a guardhouse. No churches or other places of worship were evident, which struck Bugen as unusual. In his experience the residents of smaller towns made the most faithful devotees, being less exposed to the apathy emerging in larger cities.

They came to a halt outside the inn. Alfazar dismounted and handed his reigns to Bugen, who was driving the cart; Ed tended to wander off, and Artyom was still having trouble handling a single horse. "I'll see if I can secure us some rooms," said Alfazar before entering the inn. A minute later he emerged and motioned for the others to follow him around to the stables. "It's not bad, as inns go. I might even sleep in the bed," opined Alfazar as they walked.

"So, what are we going to do after noon?" asked Bugen as he divested a horse of its tack.

"Well, I'd like to talk to the families of the murder victims," piped up Artyom. "It's likely that I'll be able to find some sort of evidence. I mean, if there's evidence that it wasn't Fae then our job will be a lot simpler."

And more honest, thought Bugen, who was still not comfortable with proclaiming a message that he did not believe wholeheartedly.

Ed pulled a grim face. "More likely you'll find evidence that shows it *was* Fae. I got this feeling..."

"C'mon Ed, you always have that feeling," said Artyom, waving away the hunter's comment. "Remember that time near Fewburg?"

"Yeah, remember the bloody great hobgoblin that jumped us?" shot back Ed.

Artyom raised a finger in protest, mouth open as if to speak, then slumped in defeat.

"Come, let us eat," suggested Alfazar once the horses were stabled. He led the way back to the inn's main entrance and opened the heavy door. The four emerged into the taproom, which was dominated by a large, well-used bar stretching the length of the facing wall. The room's walls were lined with booths—so heavily stained that their original colour could not be discerned—save for in the far right corner, where a staircase ascended to the upper level of the building. It was a curious space, neither clean nor filthy, dark nor well-lit, busy nor empty.

A smattering of locals were spread across the room like a rash: a few congregated in the booths, some around the tables occupying the centre of the room, and some on stools at the bar itself. A lone waitress wended her way across the floor whilst the innkeeper stood guard over his extensive stock of stupefying beverages.

Ed headed straight to the bar and called for an ale, though a weak one, it being still early in the day. Artyom requested a pitcher of water, which seemed to strike some of the regular patrons as odd. After serving both of these drinks the innkeeper turned to Bugen, who had seated himself next to the other two, and took the priest's order for a portion of pheasant stew. In the meantime Alfazar had ensnared the waitress' attention and procured a meal at a heavily discounted rate.

Well, he *was* the most effervescent man in the room, even when doing nothing of note.

"Oo, that's real sweet," Ed blurted, pulling a face after sipping one of the local brews. "But she'll go down right," he added awkwardly in case the innkeeper, who was polishing glasses a little way along the bench, had overheard. "So, we heard your town had some trouble in the last couple o' weeks," Ed addressed the barkeep after a few moments.

"Well, there were two murders," replied the innkeeper in a jumpy manner. He moved closer, bringing a glass with him. "They happened right here in my very inn. Kind of scary, it was, but nothing more has come of it."

Ed inspected the man as he spoke: nothing out of the ordinary or otherwise suspicious. The barkeep's only memorable feature was a most peculiar beard. A forest of wispy hairs clung to his neck and threatened to encroach upon the territory of his face, but it seemed that some force prevented it from surmounting the man's jawline. Bugen noted the neck beard too, and grinned as he imagined a community of miniature woodcutters holding the forest in abeyance by ceaselessly depilating along its borders.

A moment later Bugen realised that he should not appear to be grinning about two murders, and quickly wiped the expression from his face.

"It started about a month ago."

Artyom had already brought out his book and was poised to take notes.

"I had a stranger staying in the inn—got no idea who he was or where he was from—and he didn't come down for breakfast. Well, that wasn't too strange, so I let it lie until lunch. Lunch roles around and he still hasn't come down, so I says to meself 'I wonders if that fellow is doing alright?' and goes up to check his room. I knocked on his door," the innkeeper demonstrated by rapping his knuckles against the bar, "and nothing happened, so I opened it up and found him. Dead as a doorknob, with nary a mark on him.

"Well that was mighty strange, but then, about a week ago, one of my patrons went down to the stables, about to leave, and he finds a local fellow! Dead as a doorknob. Lying on the floor of the stables, he was." The man paused and leant in close to Ed, Bugen, and Artyom. "The strangest part though, is that there weren't no blood left in him! He'd been stabbed, right in the back if you please, but there weren't a drop of blood to find."

This last piece of news sunk in and Bugen felt the hair on the nape of his neck prickle. Humans, even the most vile, rarely drained the blood out of others, and neither did most animals. Ed and Artyom exchanged a significant glance, to which the barkeeper was oblivious.

"Of course, this got the town into a bit of an uproar. Some unknown traveller mysteriously dying didn't mean much to most, but when it was one of our own... well, people started getting paranoid about Fae. So I tells them 'Don't worry. Fae only eat children, remember?' and that calmed most of them down." The bartender went back to polishing the schooner he was holding, before adding, "Still, I'd bet you're here to do something about rumours, right?"

Bugen was forced to re-evaluate the man's intelligence; that was a particularly penetrating question. "What gives you that impression?" asked Bugen.

"We had another group come through yesterday," said the bartender with a grin. "From Ainsworth, they said, and they had a priest with them too. 'You must take a priest with ye on all matters of state,' says the king, and Ainsworth's got to listen to him."

Bugen felt that the man wanted to say more, but thought it too risky.

Artyom interjected. "Do you know where they are headed?"

"No: probably south to Maerin, north to Briss or east to Evergreen. Flip a coin, I say."

Ed said nothing, but glowered at his cup in response to the inanity of this comment.

Bugen spoke again, before Ed could summon up enough anger to respond. "I heard from High Priestess Dell that you have not been able to make the journey into Port Adeline of late. Is this because of the murders?"

The innkeeper looked completely blank for a moment, then grinned sheepishly. "Yeah, well, I didn't want it to look like I were the murderer, see?" He scratched his beard as he continued. "Thought it was best to stay in town."

"Very well. Forgive my curiosity," finished Bugen. The cleric was left casting around for a new topic, since Ed was still fuming and Artyom was staring at the far wall with a glazed expression. "That building to the right of the main square: what is it?"

"Well, young priest, that would be the militia house. Between you and me, they don't do much militia-ing... more like sleeping." He set the glass down with a thunk. "Don't get me wrong, they're not stirring up trouble, but when there's trouble being stirred up they just seem to sit around doing whatever they please."

Ed looked up. "Didn't they investigate the murders?"

"Not really," sighed the barkeep. "They came into my bar and says to me 'Show us the place,' so I take them out the back and they dig around the hay for a bit then make to leave. I says to them,

'Are you done then?' on the way out.

'Of course,' they says. 'If he's gone he's gone, and if he's not he'll still be here for a while,' and then they're gone." He made a shooing gesture to accompany the last line.

"Sound like a bunch o' layabouts," grumbled Ed.

Alfazar shook off the waitress' attention and made his way over to join the other four. "Sounds like it's been trying times for you folks," said the bard in a tone of sympathy, voice raised a little so that everyone could hear. This was answered by numerous small noises of agreement from about the room. "I'd bet that the townspeople would love a little performance tonight, don't you think?"

"Oh, that would be grand!" responded the innkeeper as conversation in the rest of the room rose to a buzz. "I actually used to do a little performing, you know. I sang."

"Well, you can be the grand attraction then," put in Alfazar smoothly. "My companions and I shall accompany you." He dipped his hand into his shirt and withdrew a small drawstring bag. "This ought to cover the cost of hospitality for the townsfolk."

The innkeeper picked up the bag, which clinked as he peeked inside. "It certainly will," he grinned. "Drinks all round!" The buzz rose to a roar as the patrons responded with great enthusiasm.

"Well," came Alfazar's voice smoothly over the din, "I shall go and ready the stage." He departed the taproom with a cheer from its occupants, save the waitress, who looked too smitten to make a sound.

"It sounds like we have work to do too," said Bugen to the others, and they tipped the innkeeper before following Alfazar outside.

Once out of earshot, the mage grinned broadly at Alfazar. "Well played!"

Alfazar made an exaggerated bow in response.

Bugen looked on with a mystified expression.

Artyom glanced around before turning to the priest. "A performance is a fantastic distraction for us," he said in a low tone. "We can explore town under the pretence of spreading news about it; it will get everyone in one place, which will make it much easier for me to check for magick; and if we decide we need Ed to snoop around some of the buildings he can do it without his absence being noticed." Bugen could see the truth of what Artyom said.

Ed rubbed his chin thoughtfully. "I hope you arranged for plenty of booze."

"Oh, certainly," Alfazar replied. "How much booze do you think you could buy for ten crowns?"

"Ten *crowns*?" Artyom nearly yelled, while Bugen thumped his chest to dislodge the bit of spittle which he had inadvertently attempted to inhale. Even Ed had to pick his jaw up off the floor.

"That man would not have made ten crowns in all the time since he built the inn," said Bugen, in a bit of a daze.

Alfazar just shrugged and smiled with a slight shading of apology.

After another moment Ed burst out laughing. "That ought to be enough booze then," roared the hunter, thumping his thigh. "Ohoo... okay. Well, we'd best start 'advertising' then."

"I'm off to the graveyard," piped up Artyom. "Then I'll try to find any family of the local victim. Oh, and I'll be looking for magick, of course."

"Hmm." Bugen stroked his chin thoughtfully. "I'm going to pay the militia a visit."

"Ed, you'll be more useful to us at night, I think. Perhaps you can go for a wander now, then return and assist with setting up a stage and so on," suggested Alfazar.

Ed agreed this was a good idea.

With a final nod to one another the four went their separate ways for the moment.

Bugen quickly gave up on trying to talk to the militia captain. The latter was clad in a crumpled black tabard and a week's growth of facial hair. Lounging in a canvas hammock in the guard room adjacent to the inn, the man responded to questions only with 'Yes,' 'No,' and great exasperated sighs that said 'Must I talk to you?'

Deciding it wasn't worth the effort of getting angry, the priest bade the disgruntled guardsman good day and left.

Before he exited, Bugen did briefly explore the rest of the building—feeling somewhat rebellious—and found nothing of note. Everything seemed to be in place.

Re-emerging into the main square of Newtown, Bugen spied Alfazar preparing a large cloth sign for the upcoming performance ('featuring the Grand Innkeeper of Newtown himself!') and quickly identified Ed's whereabouts; the bushman had assembled a work crew of a half dozen drunkards to erect the wooden stage, and was busily berating their lack of coordination.

"How goes it?" Bugen asked of Ed.

"Bloody slack lot, this one," replied the bald hunter, tugging at his beard and jerking a thumb towards his work crew. "Blasted drunkards. Oi, you! Don't go sticking things into that!" Ed ran off to prevent one of his lackeys from puncturing a barrel of ale with a rusty nail.

Feeling like a spare wheel, Bugen set off for a stroll through town. Perhaps the graveyard would be worth a check; Artyom may have found something there.

In short order the priest arrived at the town's cemetery. A few rows of neat headstones sprang up out of the thick turf which thatched the little patch of land, although the living carpet was marred in two places by human-sized patches of red earth. Bugen intoned a short prayer to Sol as he read each headstone ('*L. G. W., who didn't live as long as he wrote*'; '*In memory of Douglas Quaide*') before finally stopping near the two newest epitaphs. Bugen supposed these belonged to the unfortunate former guests of the inn.

"Ah, it was *you* I could feel."

Bugen started and then attempted to look calm as he turned towards his arcanist companion, who had walked up silently whilst the priest contemplated. "Feel?"

"Well, I was trying to detect if there was magick being used nearby, or magickal creatures," the mage silently mouthed 'like the Fae', "and I was finding nothing until a few minutes ago."

This was a surprise to Bugen, who had not realised that he could be detected like that. "You can tell if I'm nearby?" he asked, trying to mask his disquiet.

Artyom looked thoughtful before replying, "Well, yes and no. Normally magickal creatures, arcanists, and so on stand out like pinnacles on a flat landscape. Priests... well, most priests have no magick of their own, but I can usually feel something emanating from them. It's weaker and more diffuse than an arcanist, but definitely there." The young mage wrinkled his brow for a moment. "But you feel... different, somehow. I thought I'd gotten used to your feel on the *Steadfast*." He stood like that for a moment and then added brightly "Maybe I'm just not seasick any more!" before slapping Bugen genially on the shoulder and heading off. "See you back in town."

Bugen just stood, feeling the pendent resting against his chest.

The buzz of the crowd filled all of Newtown. The Sun was westering, the rickety stage was set, and the townsfolk well on their way to being suitably intoxicated. Vast quantities of fermented products were arrayed along the makeshift bar beside the militia house. Bugen could feel the carnival atmosphere in the air, hear it in the chatter of nearby adults, and see it in the faces of excited children playing near the stage. Beyond this, he spied Alfazar talking calmly with the innkeeper, and distantly he thought he could make out Ed, Buhbuh, and Tamtem in the shadows near the inn itself. Artyom was standing close at hand, but bore a slightly glazed look. Bugen supposed this meant that his young companion was observing the world through the senses of his familiar.

The cleric wondered if Sol sometimes used his body in a similar way.

Despite the din, Bugen remained introspective until Artyom prodded him. "Hey, Ed says it's nearly dark enough now. Let's get this show on the road." The two men nodded to each other and took their positions.

Bugen climbed onto a barrel (one of the many that had already been emptied by the villagers) and held aloft his buckler. Then, dimly at first, but growing brighter, his hand began to glow, until eventually the reflection cast from the priest's buckler threw a gleaming pool of radiance on the stage and its makeshift backdrop.

The entire crowd fell silent, save for some grunting and shuffling as people shifted to better viewing positions. Bugen, whose raised vantage point allowed him to see Alfazar waiting in the shadows behind the stage, watched the bard let the moment play out with consummate ease. Then, when the tension was just right, Alfazar sprang into the light with a flourish, and the crowd erupted in deafening cheers. Bowing low in Graean fashion, Alfazar ushered the innkeeper up, and then made a great deal of fussing over his ridiculous clothing.

"Hark, from what fantastical beast did you cull such a hide?" Alfazar loudly enquired of the innkeeper, gesturing towards the latter's flamboyant orange doublet.

"My former wife," replied the innkeeper impishly, earning hoots of laughter from his audience.

"And those hose, man! Were they your wife's too?"

"Actually I think they belonged to her lover... though I cannot tell how he was not impotent." The innkeeper adjusted the tight hose—complete with ludicrous codpiece—whilst bearing an overly-pained expression, earning some hysterical giggles from the onlookers.

In the background, unheard, Artyom sidled over to Bugen and spoke in a low voice. "Well, there's no magick here that I can detect,"—he glanced up at the priest's glowing hand—"except that... but something still feels off about this town. Ed's going in." Bugen took that in and nodded, not letting his light waver. Holding the buckler aloft was starting to take its toll on the priest, especially with the unfamiliar Arcanan climate, but, really, Bugen felt that he had the easy job.

The ale-sodden crowd let out another cheer and Ed caught the flash of one of Alfazar's many knives as the bard performed some silly trick. How people could find this sort of thing entertaining was beyond Ed, whose pragmatic view of the world was equally incomprehensible to many. Not that he thought less of the bard: Ed could recognise talent when he saw it. It was one of the reasons why he'd stuck by Artyom for so long after their chance meeting in a small Faustian inn.

As per their plan, Ed had mingled with the villagers until sunset and then surreptitiously extricated himself, taking up post between the stage and the inn. The latter was empty, what with most of the booze being out near the militia house anyway: exactly as Ed wanted it. The darkness and distractions would leave him free to get a good look around the inn without any untoward interruptions.

"Alright, that ought to do it," the hunter murmured to Tamtem, who gave off an air of listening attentively. Ed sure hoped that Artyom was listening in too. "I'm going in. C'mon Buhbuh." The pair moved off as a single unit, as though they were telepathically linked too, leaving Tamtem on sentry duty.

The front door was mercifully unlocked. Stealing into the room, Ed canvassed his surroundings with a glance. Buhbuh mooched around and sniffed at the booths, but did not find anything worth reporting to his master; he gladly ate the left over pie silently. After another cursory inspection Ed moved over to the stairwell, hardly making a noise. The passageway was barred by a thick iron grating and padlock, which elicited a soft snort from the hunter. He grinned to himself as the lock clicked open under the gentle caress of his dagger's tip, and mounted the stairs. It was a pretty safe bet, Ed thought, that there would be nobody inside the inn, given the performance outside and the fact that the innkeeper had barred the internal door.

Padding around the top floor of the building turned up nothing interesting except a small folding knife that had been lost down the back of one of the straw mattresses—Ed promptly pocketed it— and a chest which contained a surprising assortment of women's underwear. Nothing seemed to be out of place. Still, Ed had this feeling... had he forgotten to check anywhere? He carefully opened one of the upper windows and peeked out to see how much time he still had.

ౕ ౕౚ✖ఌ ౕౚ✖ఌ ౕఌఌౚఌఌ ✖ ౕఌఌౚఌఌ ౕౚ✖ఌ ౕౚ✖ఌ ఌ

"Thank you, thank you. You're too kind. What a marvellous audience!" boomed Alfazar as he strode around the stage, collecting his knives and replacing them in his bandoleers. Several small coins and trinkets were flung onto the stage in response. "And now, it is my pleasure to introduce to you the main act for our performance tonight. The Grand Innkeeper himself shall sing for us! Make him welcome!"

His proclamation was met by cheers and the clanking of schooners being raised in salute. Artyom caused some showers of sparks to fly into the air, and cries of delight were added to the furore.

Everyone eventually fell silent as the innkeeper prepared himself and Alfazar readied his flute to accompany him.

ౕ ౕౚ✖ఌ ౕౚ✖ఌ ౕఌఌౚఌఌ ✖ ౕఌఌౚఌఌ ౕౚ✖ఌ ౕౚ✖ఌ ఌ

After inspecting the upper floor again—tapping floorboards and the ceiling to check for any hidden alcoves—Ed had come up empty-handed. He grumped his way back downstairs, now not bothering to stay quiet. He plumped himself down on one of the moth-eaten seats and sighed. One hand scratched his head in thought, and the other scratched Buhbuh, who was oblivious to his master's confusion. Ed's irritation mounted when he realised that, of course, the innkeeper would have locked away the reserve booze too...

Ed was on his feet so quickly that it startled Buhbuh. The booze! In his excitement the hunter vaulted over the bar and grabbed the heavy padlock on the small wooden door leading into the cellar. After a few moments the lock had not yielded to the woodsman's attentions, but Ed didn't mind; the thrill of the chase was on him now, and he relished the challenge. His new folding knife was brought out and jiggled around inside the lock too, but to no avail.

After a few more minutes of tinkering Ed decided it was time for more drastic action. They'd be gone tomorrow anyway, and Alfazar had already paid the innkeeper a king's ransom in gold. Out came Ed's small axe, and with two strokes the lock lay broken. Ed paused for a moment and listened, but it seemed that no-one outside had picked up on the sudden noise. Putting the axe back into his waistband, Ed pushed the door open and whistled at Buhbuh. Both of them moved into the darkness beyond.

Once his eyes adjusted Ed found himself in a large dusty cellar which was redolent with wine, beer, ale, and the waxes used to seal their fragrant wooden casks. There was just a hint of corruption, like a suggestion of spoilage in the still air. Ed and Buhbuh began moving along, methodically checking the large stacks of barrels which blocked their view of the end of the room. These were arranged in two loose rows, with a central passage between them.

Each tap of Ed's axe against the casks sent off a small puff of dust.

The mage had drifted past a few times during the performance to let Bugen know that Tamtem had not heard anything untoward from the inn. Now, as the crowd of villagers roared with laughter—the innkeeper was reaching the end of a bawdy tune concerning the exploits of an amorous duck—Artyom sent up a jet of green sparks.

A surreptitious nod from Alfazar indicated that the latter had understood their prearranged signal; he needed to stall for more time. "Well, I'll never say 'quack' quite the same way again," Alfazar chortled, throwing an exaggerated wink to the audience. He paused for a moment, then continued with a sad air, "I think we're just about done for the night."

The effect was immediate; people rose up and started to loudly voice their displeasure with particularly imaginative phrases. Bugen was somewhat taken aback by their vitriol.

"Did you hear something?" Alfazar enquired of the innkeeper over the din.

"Hmm... well, now that you mention it, I did hear something," the other man replied, as the villagers began to settle down a touch.

"Did you hear something?" they both asked the audience.

After waiting for the roars to subside Alfazar turned to his orange counterpart and, with an air of amazement, said "I think they heard something! Was it... this?"

The crowd cheered as Alfazar whipped a tin whistle from within his voluminous pants and began to play.

A growing feeling of disquiet marred Ed's excitement. The only sound in the cellar, apart from the occasional hint of revelry from outside, was Buhbuh snuffling around in a few of the tighter spots that Ed could not get too.

As he reached the back of the cellar Ed's foot came down with an abrupt crunch, as of a meringue being squashed. He started, as did Buhbuh, whose sniffing ceased for a moment before resuming.

Ed reached down and felt the hard crust on the dirt. His questing fingers traced it to a stack of barrels at the very back of the room.

Tap... nothing. Try another barrel. *Tap...* nothing. *Tap—thunk.*

The barrel sounded partially empty, and had obviously leaked onto the floor, which explained the crusty patch. The smell of something wrong lay heavily here, and Ed surmised that the shipment of—he checked the stamp—rum had simply soured whilst left open to the air.

Ed turned to go, but decided that thoroughness was the best policy. He climbed onto a nearby crate, braced himself against the rear wall of the cellar, and kicked the offending barrel away. It fell with a crash and the lid rolled free, spilling torrents of liquid across the floor. Clambering over the barrel, the hunter peered inside.

There was a misshapen object inside the cask. Ed reached inside cautiously. At first he felt a fibrous material brushing against his calloused skin, then, further in, this gave way to a leathery surface. It was hair, a face! Filled with a sudden foreboding, Ed thrust his hand further in and found, as he suspected, a bushy beard below the pallid corpse's chin. With one great haul the hunter pulled the pickled body of the innkeeper of Newtown from its improvised resting place.

It wasn't a great loss in Ed's opinion—he had never liked people with neck beards anyway—but his excitement quickly shaded to anxiety. Who was outside in the village square? Ed decided that he ought to get out and alert Tamtem as quickly as possible.

"So, you've found me out. That's just vexatious, you know."

Alfazar decided that the knot of children close to the stage would enjoy an item targeted at their demographic, so began singing, trusting that his companion would play along.

> *"Baa baa, black sheep*
> *have you any wool?"*

The innkeeper replied in time-honoured fashion.

> *"Yes sir, yes sir,*
> *three bags full."*

They joined for the final segment.

> *"One for the master,*
> *and one for the dame,*
> *and one for the little boy*
> *who lives down the lane."*

Alfazar could see some children in the front row were disappointed by the song's end, so he started an impromptu second verse. The innkeeper would probably pick up what was happening.

> *"Baa baa, black sheep*
> *it's mighty beautiful."*

The innkeeper responded without appearing to pause for thought.

> *"Thank ye sir, kindest sir,*
> *It took a while to pull.*
> *First from the farmer,*
> *and then from his maid,*
> *and then from the little brat*
> *who wanted to be paid."*

Wondering where this was going, Alfazar played along, grossly exaggerating his acting.

"Baa baa, black sheep
you mean this stuff is hair?!"

In a sweet voice which grew more menacing, the other man continued.

"Yes sir, yes sir,
and yours will go in there."
Out came the sheepy's knife
and shanked the poor dear
and as he lay on the floor
the sheep got out shears.

The innkeeper finished by making scissoring gestures with the first two fingers on each hand whilst wearing a caricature of a dark, leering grin. After a moment of silence Alfazar sprang back up from where he had mimed being viciously stabbed, and bowed low. The villagers shouted and hollered in appreciation: even the children, who were intimidated not at all.

Ed's heart rate jumped four-fold and the hairs on his neck stood up like hackles. He stilled his breathing and backed against the far wall, keeping the stone behind him so as to not be taken unawares. Buhbuh, maybe smelling the change in his master's mood, followed quietly.

"Poor little woodsman, why could you not have left well enough alone?" The voice sounded almost conversational, but laden with inhuman threat. It seemed to issue directly from the air. Ed strained his senses but failed to hear any footsteps, breathing or other noises over the sound of his heart pounding in his ears. "I never take many. Always frugal. But now you have found me out; I shall have to leave and find new grounds, shan't I?"

The cellar shaded to deeper colours as the malevolent but strangely chirpy voice spoke. Shadows became inky purple, and the dust motes caught in stray light from the open cellar door shone with iridescence.

"Frugal. Did the innkeeper and the traveller sate you?" Ed tried to inject some sarcastic venom with the shaky words as he cast about for an escape route.

"Everybody wants to eat, hunter. Surely you of all people understand that," came the lazy reply. The entity let the implicit threat hang, congealing, in the air. Insouciant. "I only take as many as I need, never more."

When Ed reached the back corner of the cellar he inwardly sighed with relief; the barrels and casks were not stacked up hard against the wall. This was probably to keep them from rotting, a small part of him surmised absently, though the vast majority of the hunter's mind was focused on escape.

"And the innkeeper's body? A trophy?" he spat at the being (wherever it was) before working his way up the wall towards the door. Mould grew in some patches, musty smell resonating in the woodsman's nose.

Talking: he needed to keep the creature talking.

ↄ   ↄ✕ↄ   ↄ✕ↄ   ↄↄↄↄↄↄ ✕✕ ↄↄↄↄↄↄↄ   ↄ✕ↄ   ↄ✕ↄ   ↄ

Realising that it was about time for the finale, Artyom raised his hands and summoned a shower of red and gold sparks which seemed to pour from Alfazar's side, where he'd clutched the imaginary wound moments ago—a nice touch. The bright dots of light swirled from there to Artyom and then back towards the stage, twisting through the audience in strange, fluid patterns. Cavorting specks gathered around the two performers, shimmering in time with the mad applause from the townsfolk.

Alfazar bowed and waved at the peasants, soaking up their enjoyment. It had been months since the bard had given a successful performance; he had almost forgotten what it felt like.

After a minute or so of cheering the crowd suddenly quieted, then broke into applause again. Alfazar glanced sideways, wondering what the commotion was. He did a double take; the innkeeper was glowing. Unlike Alfazar, who was bathed in the lambency of Artyom's sparks, the innkeeper himself was throwing out light across the visible spectrum. The pattern of vivid illumination shifted like something living.

Near the back of the crowd, Bugen let Sol's light fade; the performers hardly needed any more illumination. Eyeing the curious sphere of brilliance surrounding the innkeeper, Bugen turned to congratulate Artyom. "That's some interesting magick..."

Artyom was pale and frowning intensely at the stage. Before Bugen could ask what was wrong, the mage turned to him and said in a strained voice "It's very interesting. And it's not me."

Almost as if this were a cue, the innkeeper blazed brighter and began, slowly but surely, to rise into the air.

The bard, assuming that Artyom was behind the whole act, did not miss a beat. "He can fly!" Alfazar exclaimed over the din of the crowd, egging them on. "A man of many surprises! Come, sir. How is the weather up there?"

Bugen's pulse quickened as he contemplated this rogue magick. He could not make out the levitated man's expression through the glare of colours being thrown from his visage. At one point the priest fancied that he saw a look of contempt, but it was gone the next moment.

Artyom quickly pulled his sparks away from the innkeeper, sending the luminous dots to Alfazar instead. The former was by this stage a good fifteen feet from the ground, and glowing a uniform white; the effect looked cold next to the warm tones bathing the bard.

With that, the innkeeper let out an enormous laugh, clapped his arms above his head, and vanished in a spray of colour, leaving Alfazar alone on the stage. A strange sucking rush echoed through the nearby cane fields.

The crowd shrieked with enjoyment.

With his characteristic decisiveness, Artyom formulated a plan. "Be ready to get him," he said to Bugen in an undertone, jutting his chin in the direction of Alfazar. The priest set off, keeping to the fringes of the crowd.

Once the audience had quietened down somewhat Alfazar took centre stage again. "And now, enjoy the remaining booze!" he boomed cheerily. Artyom's sparks bowed low with Alfazar, then gathered in a lambent pillar which shot into the sky and burst into fading blues and greens. Rowdy applause went on.

The illumination faded, leaving Alfazar unable to see. He started when a hand emerged from the darkness and clasped his forearm, but he quickly recognised Bugen's outline. "That was something," Alfazar said quietly to the priest.

Bugen could hear the smile in his companion's voice. His reply quickly wiped the smile away. "Aye, it was. But we don't know what. Come, Artyom needs us."

"Trophy? Hardly, little human." The apparition gave a smug laugh, echoing from every direction. It continued in a patronising tone. "You see, it is vastly simpler to impersonate somebody if you have... well, their *person*. I should think that even someone of your mental stature could appreciate that fact."

"So much for being frugal," Ed retorted, cupping his hands and speaking towards the corner that he had just vacated. Hopefully the echo would convince the Fae bastard that Ed was still over there.

"Oh, I drained him well, worry not," came the response, complete with chuckle. "I will need lots of blood when the time comes."

As he edged along, Ed noticed the shadows changing again. They shone with radiant blackness. Peeking through a gap, it became apparent that this phenomenon was fairly well localised. Wherever the voice was coming from, it had to be somewhere in that patch of strangeness. Even as the realisation hit him the temperature plummeted and the shadows changed, abruptly becoming deep voids of colour burning with cold malice.

"You are resourceful, I'll admit," the voice spake from somewhere near the ceiling. "But know that I know exactly where you are." The creature laid a delicate stress on the 'exactly' to drive home the message. Visual phenomena swirled dizzyingly. "You are out of your league."

At that Buhbuh let out a great whimper and bolted between Ed's legs—no mean feat in the cramped space—and scrambled out of the cellar. It happened so rapidly that Ed did not have time to respond, except to break out in a cold sweat. He lifted his axe and followed as quickly as he could, heedless of the noise he was making. "Bloody Fae!" he yelled maniacally, ripping his knife from its sheath and casting about with wide eyes as he moved. "Bloody Fae!"

Ed veered to his left, through a gap in the stack of casks, towards the central passage. He emerged from the gap with chest heaving as though he had run fifty miles, not fifty feet, and he chanced a glance towards the far wall of the cellar.

Dark.

Darkness blanketed the wall, spreading like flat tendrils out across the full width of the cellar. At their centre may have been a figure enveloped in shadow, taller than a regular human, thin without being whispy. Ed was not really sure. He stared for a moment, frozen on the spot, with sweat dripping from his nose. "Bloody Fae," he whispered.

The maybe-figure took a step forward and Ed's will broke. Pale like a corpse, he fled out of the cellar, tripped up the steps, and slammed the door behind him.

The thick wood did nothing to blot out the laughter of the creature in the cellar.

Chapter 5

Darkwood

Been one year since Mother passed. My life has been duller since then, and this winter feels even colder than normal.

Father did try to look after me, in his own way; he urged me to become a cartographer. Business is booming since the discovery of Arcana, and cartography is prized at the moment. That is certainly true, but just as certain is that transcribing maps is dull compared to studying the forces of magick. I longed to recapture my Mother's dreams of harnessing nature!

Father did not take it well when I expressed this to him, about a month ago. We had an enormous row. Feeling ashamed and trapped, I stole away that very night.

I wandered aimlessly until reaching Nuln. There, having spent all of my coin, I became embroiled in a hare-brained scheme to save a young girl who had been kidnapped by the Fae. The Fae hunter who hired me was good to his word, and together we recovered the child. Her parents repaid us handsomely, considering their circumstances.

Since then, I have found some comfort in a renewed purpose: not only to master the arcane, but to codify our knowledge of the Fae, and to fight them with my new companion.

I hope Father is well.

Diary found at Fewburg Inn

" HY are we fleeing? Surely we should stay and make sure the beast does not attack the townsfolk?" Bugen panted, voicing his concern as the party rode into the night. Ed had paused only long enough to relate his story before saddling the horses.

"No need." replied Artyom tersely. "Whatever it was, it isn't after the townsfolk." There was a pause whilst the mage righted himself in the saddle. "It's after *us*. Clearing out is the best thing we can do for them now."

Bugen could not help but admire his ally's clarity of thought, and was relieved that his flight was in fact aiding the villagers of Newtown.

"Besides," continued the mage, "tomorrow they'll realise that the innkeeper really is gone, and then they'll decide that we were the ones that did it." Another fair point, in Bugen's opinion.

"So now they'll think we were Fae," groused Ed, who had regained some colour. He was leading the supply-laden mare that had drawn their cart to Newtown; in their haste the travellers had left the latter behind. "Ainsworth ain't going to be happy about this."

Alfazar merely looked grim about the mouth as his smooth face reflected the weak moonlight.

After cantering along for an hour or so the companions left the road and wended their way through the countryside. Ed guided them on a path designed to confuse any potential pursuers.

"It'll keep 'em busy for a few hours, which ought to be enough for some rest... That looks like a likely spot to camp," opined the hunter, pointing out a relatively tall thicket of cane growing not far from the road.

After the horses were picketed near a small irrigation channel,

Ed distributed the few blankets which the group had retained, and the four men bedded down around the small fire which Alfazar had kindled.

Bugen stirred restlessly. "Artyom?"

"Yeah?"

"Why could you not detect the creature's magick?"

There was a brief pause during which only the crackle of the fire intruded. "I'm not sure," sighed Artyom, weary beyond his years, and with extremely sore legs from their ride. "With the correct training arcanists can conceal their spells, but I know not how one would conceal their magickal presence... their 'aura', if you will. And it's dubious that the same rules apply to Fae and other eldritch creatures. Oft-times I can feel them—their magick almost spills out of them—but some types of Fae are nearly undetectable."

Bugen found this disquieting. The priest wished for the stormy, hard, and familiar landscape of Faust; he felt naked and exposed on the soft Arcanan earth under the open sky.

Alfazar piped up. "It is likely that the creature is Fae. Many are the tales of these sorts of killings, across all of Graea and Faust: blood drained from bodies and doppelgängers created. Nobody is truly sure of the perpetrators, but the tales are ubiquitous." After a pause he continued, "I suppose that our first course of action should be to decide what to do tomorrow, regardless of the nature of the beast."

"Should we return to Adeline and try to convince Ainsworth that the Fae really are a threat?" Bugen queried.

Artyom jumped on the question. "He won't listen," he said flatly. "We have no proof. If we go back he will force us all to depart Arcana; he'll hush it all up as swiftly as possible."

This seemed like a reasonable assessment to Bugen, although it ran counter to his sense of duty.

"We're halfway to Darkwood already," put in the hunter. "I brought you this way for a reason."

"Oh?"

"Well," supplied Alfazar, "I remember the innkeeper mentioning that Ainsworth's first group had passed through Newtown on their way to Evergreen."

"Only a bunch of inbred idiots would build their town that close to Darkwood. Bloody Fae central, I'll bet," Ed spat.

Bugen pondered this for a moment. "So we're going to Evergreen on the advice of a man that turned out to be an illusion, potentially of the Fae?" he asked mildly.

"Not quite," said Artyom with a wry smile. "I heard the same news from a few of the villagers too. At any rate, we'll do better if we can catch up with the other party. We just might find out what's going on too."

Well, that was comforting. The priest sat and listened to the crackle of the fire, which was joined before long by Ed's snores. Bugen placed his sheathed sword close at hand before falling into a fitful sleep. What would tomorrow bring?

Bugen rose with the Sun and made his daily devotion to Sol. The rest of the party soon awoke, arranged a meagre breakfast, packed their few belongings, and doused their small fire before leaving.

They had scarcely set foot on the road when they heard the sound of an approaching cart, hailing from the direction of Evergreen. Shortly it came into view: an unusually large cart, thought Bugen, to match the unusually large man who drove it. Next to him was propped a blunderbuss of matching proportions. The fellow would push seven feet standing, was nearly as wide as Ed was tall, and sported a fantastically large brown beard, which wound about his face like a briar. He glared at the passing travellers with beady eyes. No words were exchanged between them, though Bugen politely inclined his head toward the man.

It was soon clear why the cart needed to be so unusually large; half of its hold was filled with hefty logs, evidently on their way to market in Adeline. A dirty green tarpaulin covered the other half of the vehicle.

Ed, ever the suspicious type, slowed as he passed. He quickly marked the odd lay of the cart's covering, and, after a further moment of consideration, noted that whatever it concealed was not moving in time with the cart's jostling passage. He calmly drew his horse alongside Artyom, who was riding behind the others. "I think there are people in that cart," he said to the arcanist in an undertone.

Artyom turned in his saddle and caught a glimpse of a young face peering out from beneath the tarpaulin. It vanished back into the cart, letting out a faint exclamation as it did so.

Without waiting to consult with the others, Artyom raised both hands and made an upwards yanking motion. In response, the cart's dirty covering flew into the air, exposing a huddle of some dozen children who screamed in distress at their unexpected revelation. They ranged in age from around three to twelve, in Ed's estimation, and had the sickly white look of those kept indoors for too long. Artyom promptly dropped his hands, and the cloth settled over them once more.

Bugen and Alfazar were flabbergasted.

The cart ground to a hold in a small cloud of dust, the shifting logs let out a massive *thump*, and presently the large man confronted the travellers, blunderbuss in hand: if indeed he was a man, and not a child-smuggling Fae. A film of fine grit clung to his sweaty visage, and he bore the look of one on a hair-trigger.

"Hi," Artyom chirped, characteristically diplomatic. "Are you a Fae?"

Bugen suppressed a wince and began edging his hands closer to his sword and buckler.

"You wouldn't believe me, even if I said 'no,' " said the man's gravelly voice. "Just as I won't believe the four of you." The last statement was punctuated by the click of the blunderbuss' firing hammer being cocked.

"Sir, I th—" began Alfazar.

"Shut it!"

Ed slowly reached into his jacket.

His movement was not lost on their large friend, who swung the trumpet-like muzzle of his weapon to bear on the hunter. "Get your hand back where I can see it!" His nostrils were flared.

Bugen was fixated by the beads of fresh perspiration which rolled from the man's forehead into his beard, where they followed twisted and intricate trajectories before dripping to the floor. Tension charged the air through which they fell.

Ed slowly brought his hand back into view, but it was now clutching a horseshoe.

Bugen blanched: what harebrained scheme did the hunter have in mind?

"This shoe is pretty cold, catch my drift?" the hunter asked. The question was rewarded with narrowed eyes and a brief nod. Slowly, Ed turned and touched the iron against Artyom's face, then equally slowly dismounted, handed the reigns to the mage, and went to place the horseshoe against Bugen and Alfazar. After this was finished Ed turned back to the man. "Convinced?"

Their counterpart lowered the 'buss slightly and gave another nod.

With a swift motion Ed threw the horseshoe at him, softly enough that it would not harm him overly, but fast enough that he would be forced to either dodge or catch the hunter's missile. For a terrible moment Bugen expected to hear the thunderous crash of the 'buss, but it never came. He unscrewed his eyes and found the tall fellow holding the horseshoe, seeming almost as surprised as Bugen that he had not fired his great weapon.

"And now we are too," Ed said, almost a little smugly.

Everyone visibly relaxed, although Bugen kept his hand on his sword's pommel, and the stranger did not uncock his firearm.

"We are named Alfazar, Artyom, Ed and Bugen," said Alfazar, indicating each in turn. "We are here on behalf of Sir Hupert Ainsworth, and work for the good of Arcana. How may we call you?"

Briar-beard scratched his face for a moment, still gazing at the travellers with infinite suspicion. "Willem, if it pleases you," came the grudging response. "Be warned that Ainsworth's name will bring you little respect in these parts; it certainly didn't for his other band of adventurers when they reached Evergreen. Ainsworth has forsaken us."

"Too damn right!" burst out Ed.

Bugen still dared not speak. The priest's thoughts lay with the children in the cart: they must be frightened, not knowing what was going on outside.

"Your cargo is precious," began Alfazar. "Where are you headed?"

Willem threw a quick look off to either side of the trail before answering. "We hail from Evergreen, on the border of the Darkwood. Things have been none too good of late, and we decided that the children were too vulnerable, so we're getting them out to Port Adeline. It's the safest place in Arcana."

"Vulnerable?" queried Bugen.

"Yes, rather," came the abrupt response.

"Vulnerable to kidnap, I would say," put in Artyom, earning him a sideways glance from Bugen.

"You're mighty well informed," Willem said with suspicion, hugging his blunderbuss more closely.

Alfazar rode forward in an effort to defuse the tension. "We are charged with investigating these incidents," he said with conviction. Bugen thought that was rather stretching the truth, but decided that now was not the time to be pedantic. "Tell us what you can, pray, and we will be finished—and the Fae gone—sooner."

"Four children have been kidnapped from their homes recently. Two lived in the woodcutter's camp, not too far into the forest, and the others were snatched from the fishing hamlet on the edge of the lake."

"The lake that drains into the sea off Maerin?"

Willem turned back to Artyom and nodded the affirmative.

"Has anything of suspicion been occurring there recently?" Bugen asked.

"Nothing much, except that foreign lady who started coming by there."

"Foreign lady?"

"About so tall,"—Willem indicated at chest height, being about five feet—"and all dressed up like a Graean." He inclined his head towards Alfazar. "She began visiting the town from the lake about six weeks ago. She's got one of them little Graean boats, all chock full of anti-Fae wares. Crystals, powders, amulets: she's got them all. Says she's a trader of some kind."

Ed mused and scratched his beard, mirroring Willem, and spoke again after a lengthy pause. "We should check it out, methinks."

Artyom brought the conversation back to more practical issues. "If it were me," he piped up, "I'd lie low in Adeline and see if things settle down after the Festival of the White Lady. Right?"

"Right." Willem was still scratching.

"Stay out o' Newtown if y'can. They've had a touch o' bother recently," Ed advised sagely. "And don't go to Ainsworth; he'll turf you out of Adeline if he thinks you're rumour-mongering." The hunter handed over a pouch of coins, which Willem secreted inside his dirty vest. "This ought to put you 'n' the kids up in an inn for a week or two. Should be enough time..."

Willem said nothing, but gave a single short nod, as if in appreciation. He finally uncocked his firearm, then turned and adjusted the tarpaulin, murmuring a few words of comfort to his charges. Soon he had the cart trundling along again.

The four watched him for a moment before heading for Evergreen. Bugen released a pent-up sigh as soon as the cart was out of earshot, and gladly took the reins in both hands.

The great glacier cracked and groaned as it ground its way down the mountainside until it reached the edge of the sea, pulverising all in its path under the inexorable momentum of millennia of snow and ice. Its shear face, riven by deep crevasses, would occasionally fragment and plunge a new berg into the ocean.

Bugen blinked. No, that was not the glacier that he had encountered on his first pilgrimage as a servant of Sol; it was a great pine forest. That was not ice; the tall, dark trees formed a wall of wood which seemed to flow from the high hills in the distance down to the tiny hamlet of Evergreen, where the forest ended abruptly, as though pressed against an invisible barrier. That was not an iceberg; that was a stack of coniferous corpses waiting to be sawn and carted to Port Adeline. Nevertheless, the forest carried all of the weight and majesty of the glacier that Bugen had beheld as a child.

The collection of buildings known as Evergreen sat immediately below the cliff of trees, as though in supplication to the immensity of the forest. All were of wooden construction, fittingly, and seemed to be closer to well-insulated Faustian designs than the airy dwellings which the travellers had encountered in Arcana thus far. Bugen surmised that this was because of their altitude—the land had sloped upward all morning—until he noted that mist clung to the gaps between trees in the Darkwood. Apparently the forest played a role too. Whatever it was, Bugen fancied that he could feel the temperature dropping as he and his companions continued towards their destination.

As they drew athwart the village the four travellers heard none of the usual noises of rural life, and they saw that the mean town square was empty. The only sign of occupation was a thin haze of smoke that hung in the still air, scarcely distinguishable from the mist.

"Let's see if we can't find an inn," said Ed in a hushed voice.

The four men spread out and began searching, staying within sight of one another. Bugen was inspecting the well in the centre of the square when he heard a soft exclamation from Alfazar.

"A man, over there!" All four of the companions turned and stared in the direction indicated by the bard. They saw a little man dressed in filthy clothes scuttle out from beneath the eaves of the forest, shuffle over to a small wooden hall, and knock rapidly at the door. After a brief delay, during which the short fellow cast an anxious glance about town, the door was opened and he slipped inside.

"Do you think he spotted us?" Bugen thought out loud.

"Aye, you bet he did," Ed snorted. The priest could not decide if Ed was being sincere or cynical.

"Yeah, I'd bet that we'd best take a look at that building," Artyom said to his bald counterpart. "Tamtem and Buhbuh haven't found anything else, so to the hall we go."

Ainsworth's 'ambassadors' dismounted and picketed their horses alongside a small fence running behind one of the houses before striding across to the door which the anxious villager had entered. Artyom managed a fair reproduction of the man's knock, and—to Bugen's amazement—the door cracked open. A hand emerged from the darkness and beckoned them across the threshold.

Bugen stepped through and was rewarded with a brief glimpse of a dimly-lit huddle of people before feeling sharp lashes fall across his back, arms and legs. His training taking over, Bugen used his buckler and armoured arm to shield his head whilst reaching for his sword. The weapon was halfway out of its sheath when a commanding voice cried out.

"Hold!"

The lashes fell no more, but silence did.

After a moment Bugen peered out from under his buckler. Alfazar had one of his knives to hand, and Ed was wielding his small axe. Artyom held no weapon bar a small dagger, which he clutched uncertainly. Straightening up, Bugen noted that the shadowy entranceway was lined by half a dozen ill-shaven men, each brandishing a thin metal switch and a wooden cudgel.

"All must be tested," said the voice, which seemed to belong to a man to Bugen's right. "You could have been Fae."

"Tested?" said Bugen without thinking, struggling to mentally keep abreast of this turn of events.

"Those will be cold iron, yes?" Artyom said to the voice's owner, indicating the rods held by the other villagers.

"Yes, and by their touch we are assured that you are not Fae," came the response.

As if this was some signal, the other villagers placed their switches and clubs in a pile near the door, and melted back into the hall.

Alfazar took charge of diplomacy. This was just as well, thought Bugen; Ed's rough manner did not sit well with most 'civilised' people, Artyom's grasp of social niceties was unreliably erratic, and Bugen was still shocked by how near he had come to slaying the door wardens. "We four have come to help," Alfazar said to the commanding man, whom he presumed was the *de facto* governor of Evergreen. When several of the nearby villagers shot Alfazar hostile and distrusting looks the bard decided that transparency would be the best policy to take with these people. "Aye, as you have guessed, we were sent forth by Ainsworth," the bard said in soft tones, being sure to address his whole audience. Then, in a voice projecting confidence and empathy, he continued, saying, "But we have spurned his indifference to you, and taken it upon ourselves to ease you in your suffering." Faces softened. "We are Artyom, the mage; Ed, the tracker; the priest of Sol, Bugen; and the bard, Alfazar. It is our pleasure to be of assistance to you."

Bugen was so grateful for Alfazar's skill with crowds that he offered up a short prayer of thanks to Sol. The priest did not forget his other companions, and uttered a petition for Sol's protection upon them all, and the surrounding villagers.

The mood in the room swiftly became more relaxed.

"Have you any wounded?" asked Bugen shakily.

"Nothing life-threatening," answered the governor. "A few minor scrapes and burns." After a pause he swayed in closer to Bugen and said in an undertone. "Perhaps your efforts would best be spent refreshing yourself and tending to the spiritual well-being of Evergreen. We are scared more than scarred."

Bugen nodded in understanding.

With slightly trembling hands, he unstopped his costrel and took a draught of water. In an effort to regain his calm he took stock of the single large room. Probably fifty people were huddled together here and there, in what the priest presumed were family groups. They all bore the same look as the children with Willem: pallid, kept indoors for too long, and tense. There seemed to be several vast barrels of supplies stacked towards the rear of the room, and from Bugen's earlier inspection of the well just outside he conjectured that lack of food or drink was not an issue, at least not yet. The people had fortunately had the good sense to ensure that the privy was not in the same room.

His eyes picked out a few symbols of the Nature goddess around the room, which made sense, given their proximity to such a demonstration of her power. No other adornment was on the walls or the floor, so far as Bugen could tell. All of the windows around the hall had been boarded up from the inside, and in a few places the packed earthen floor had been fashioned into fire pits. Looking up, Bugen could see that some small holes had been punched into the roof to permit smoke to escape.

As the room's occupants relaxed somewhat the general background mutter of conversation picked up. Random titbits of news, gossip, and opinion wormed their way into Bugen's head as he strolled between groups, on the lookout for the wounded, or anyone bearing a symbol of Sol.

"The last group didn't stay long, they'll be gone soon..." So, Ainsworth's other group had come through here too.

"Did you see Johm sneaking off with Gert last night?" Bugen supposed privacy would be hard to come by in a single room.

"...hope she visits again soon." The foreign lady, with the anti-Fae wares?

"But I'm hungry!" A universal experience, Bugen supposed.

With a start, Bugen realised that he had returned to his starting point, having circumnavigated the room. He grinned sheepishly to the governor, still near the door. "It seems I have calmed down somewhat." The priest's apologetic inflection made the statement sound like a question.

"We've been menaced for too long to take chances," came the gruff reply.

Bugen offered his hand and the men shook.

"Clive's the name."

"Pleased to meet you."

Judging from his manner, Clive was perhaps into his fortieth year, though Bugen would have expected his face to bear fewer lines. It was otherwise narrow and angular, but not sharp, with hair greying at the temples and black elsewhere. Bugen fancied that Clive would have made a fair bard, if given the opportunity and the training. He wore simple woodsman's clothes: robust and utilitarian.

"Well, priest, you and your companions have made a better impression on us than your predecessors."

The cleric cocked an eyebrow in response.

"One of their number objected vociferously"—Bugen nearly lost the next part of the statement as he marvelled at Clive's impressive vocabulary—"to being tested, and one of them had so much armour on that we could scarcely find a bare spot to touch his flesh."

"I can see how that would upset your friends here," Bugen responded, making a sweeping gesture to the rest of the room. In the background, Ed and Artyom sat together, drinking water from lathed cups and animatedly discussing something; Alfazar was entertaining a group of adolescents with a tale that earned their chuckles but also drew scowls from the old women seated at the next fire.

"Indeed."

"Tell me: how have you been menaced?" Bugen asked, moving closer to Clive so that others would not overhear their conversation.

"You know that they took four of our children?"

"Aye," Bugen responded, nodding gravely. "We were told they were taken from within the Darkwood."

"Correct," Clive said, with a distant look in his eyes. He scratched at his chin. "One, a young girl, was taken from her family's hut on the shores of Mirror Lake."

Sister.

"The other three were children of two logging families who have built houses within the forest. Two brothers lived near the mountains, but the third boy was much closer. Still, we always told the families they were foolhardy, long before we had any evidence of Fae presence... no lights or sightings."

"Neither you nor they could be blamed," Bugen said, resting a hand on the man's shoulder. "Are the rest of the encampment living here now?"

"Indeed."

Bugen surveyed the room, noting that Artyom and Ed were now merrily eating dried fish with one of the larger family groups. Ed was rubbing at an elongated welt on his cheek. Meanwhile, Alfazar had moved to the circle of little old ladies and was making up for his previous behaviour by performing sleight-of-hand tricks for them. "We can stay for a few hours, but then we will need to be off. Time grows short for us all..." He exchanged a significant look with Clive. "Is there somebody who could be convinced to show us where the children were taken from?"

Never before had Bugen desired a guide with *less* experience.

"Everyone's on holidays, eh?" Their guide spoke with the uniquely gummy tone of those who have lost all of their teeth, and wheezed a little as he led the party along the logging path through Darkwood. "Kids gone on holidays too, eh?"

Bugen felt a species of pity for the geriatric man—poor dental health, poor memory, poor fitness and poor situational awareness—but it was tempered by a crawling uncertainty about this place. Unlike his aged companion, who was pottering along the trail with his arms crossed against his back as though he were simply out for a stroll, Bugen was on edge. One hand held his buckler, and the other was rested on his sword's fish-tail pommel.

Artyom and Alfazar followed on foot, strung out behind Bugen, whilst the hunter led a mare and a gelding laden with supplies at the rear of the train. Tamtem and Buhbuh skittered back and forth along the wagon trail, smelling here and listening there as they went.

The darkness under the trees was oppressive, even though enough light remained to make out the path ahead. Everything to the front and rear faded into a nondescript grey at a distance of about a hundred paces, so it seemed to Bugen that the forest opened ahead of them and closed behind. Of course, he did not believe that the trees actually *moved*; the amount of energy required to shift one of these gargantuan trunks was more than Bugen could readily conceive of. Maybe Sol could displace one of the conifers... Bugen's eyes widened in amazement as he realised that, for all of their apparent might, these trees were at the mercy of the mere mortal loggers living in Evergreen.

Any hope that this produced—any thought that perhaps steel and spirit, science and sinew could win out against whatever malevolent beings lurked under the gloomy eaves of the forest—was rapidly dispelled by the gathering shadow.

The travellers travelled on, subdued. Not even Ed left the trail to investigate the unfamiliar flora sprouting from the forest floor. There was no trace of any animals.

After a short eternity the companions came across a fallen tree which blocked their path. The rational part of Bugen reckoned they had been travelling for just over half an hour.

"Good thing we don't have the cart," Ed grumbled as he led their horses around the obstruction.

Another quarter of an hour passed before a clearing came into view, and beyond it a wide lake sitting under a grey sky. Several large nets in varying states of disrepair were strung up around the clearing, and after a moment the priest spotted a handful of clinker row boats which could be launched directly from the water's pebbly edge. To the right lay a dishevelled house, weathered wood showing through a coat of flaking red paint. The only other buildings were a few mean huts, little more than boat sheds, which could be seen around the curve of the lake to the left.

Bugen tried to get his bearings. A light layer of mist lay over the lake, obscuring the far shore and lending the clear water an eerie quality, but the young cleric could nevertheless make out a bay extending out to his right, southward; he suspected this was the river which drained into the sea near Maerin.

The clearing's most notable feature was the short jetty which protruded from the shore into the placid water. Moored to this stout wooden pier was a boat which Bugen recognised as being of Graean design. All three spans of the vessel were painted brilliant turquoise, though subdued by the dull lighting, and the white furled square sail adorning its single mast was decorated with patterns of umber. A whitewashed cabin was built over the bow, continuing back to amidships. Brass fittings gleamed like gold in the twilight and the soft light of a lantern shining through shuttered windows.

The old fellow did not seem at all perturbed by the boat's presence, but none of his companions really felt that amounted to much; he had not been perturbed by the forest either.

"There is someone aboard." Artyom's whisper broke through the still air.

"You can *feel* them?" Bugen asked sharply, feeling his heart rate ratchet up.

His only response was a nod and a grim look.

Ed drew his kukri.

Their elderly companion was oblivious to the tension. He continued merrily towards the boat, hailing whoever was inside with
his gummy, wavering voice. Bugen hurried to keep up, ready to
protect him if need be. Meanwhile, Ed hung back; *let the old geezer
go forward first—better for gramps to die than us, and we might learn
something beforehand.*

Faint noises drifted across from the boat; it sounded like someone was hastily grabbing anything of worth out of the cabin,
caring not at all for whatever was being knocked over or thrown
to the floor in the process. After a moment a figure emerged on
deck. She was dressed in traditional Graean garb—the colours of
which matched her sailing vessel, to quite pleasing effect—and had
a large bag slung over her back.

She disembarked quickly and trotted down the pier toward
them, looking apprehensive. Bugen noted that her pale, young face
was flushed pink, and she kept glancing back over her shoulder
as she came on. The sight of four armed (and one geriatric) men
also obviously unnerved her. She continued straight past gramps,
who, being completely ignored, mumbled something to himself
and trundled off towards the boat sheds.

"Hold!" commanded Alfazar, whose blue clothing mirrored
hers. He held his hand outstretched, palm outwards, in the classic
'stop right there' posture, but his tone was less aggressive than
Bugen might have expected.

The slight woman came to a stop. She gnawed at her lip, shooting glances at each of the five men; then Buhbuh and Tamtem; and
finally back towards the lake. Bugen noticed a thick curl of deep
walnut brown hair, an escapee from beneath her embroidered white
shawl, twisting across her forehead. He also noted that she had not
put the bag down.

"We are investigating several abductions which occurred here
recently, believed to be due to Fae activity. Do you have any information?" Alfazar asked.

She gave no reply.

"You trade in anti-Fae devices, no?" he continued firmly.

"I do not have time to answer, sir," she said, her face screwed
up as if in pain as she grasped the bag tightly.

"Why? Pray tell." It was clear that it was not a request, although Alfazar somehow managed to say it without menace.

"I'll tell you why," growled Ed darkly. Bugen had not noticed the hunter sidle up behind Alfazar. "Because *she's* a filthy Fae, that's why." He jabbed a finger towards her and spat on the ground at her feet to punctuate his remark. Bugen was astounded by the hunter's sudden wrath.

"Let's not be hasty now," Alfazar said calmly to Ed, trying to defuse things.

The woman cringed away from them.

"Here, it's easy to check." Ed brandished his knife, suddenly calm. "Just take this and I'll be all polite-like to you, missy." Unlike the the bard, Ed *was* menacing.

A moment of pained indecision passed, during which Bugen saw a myriad of expressions flit across the girl's face, before she sighed deeply— emotionally and physically spent—and slumped in weariness. "You know I cannot. Kill me if you must; otherwise I need to go." The last was almost a plea; a plea which struck Bugen with its piteousness.

He would have been deeply moved, save that in the back of his mind rested the sure knowledge that many Fae could appear as this beautiful girl, only to later erupt monstrously from that form into terrible flesh-rending beasts for whom pity had no meaning. Legitimate terror, or cunning ruse?

"See!" Ed exclaimed fiercely, with a matching mirthless grin. "A Fae. Off to capture some more children, are we? Desperate to find your next meal?" he jeered. Dark blotches coloured the hunter's face, but all colour had been driven from the Fae's.

"My kind do not capture human children," she whispered. "Nor do we eat them. We have done no wrong against you."

"Your kind?" Artyom put in, before Ed could continue his baiting.

"Yes: the phearsanú. We are Fae, you would say, of the desert south-east of here, and there are precious few of us left. We do not serve Him like the others. We do not capture children for Him." Each utterance of 'Him' was accompanied by a slight shudder, of fear or loathing. She wrapped her arms about herself protectively.

"Let me go: I am fleeing from Him, and He is more dangerous than you—even all of you combined. Do not think I am unprepared to force my way past you if I must." A small amount of colour returned to her face and she stood up straighter, no longer shying away from Ed, though her limbs still trembled.

"Empty words."

"There may be some truth to her, Ed," Artyom opined. After all, the arcanist could *feel* her. "I should like to hear more of her story, at any rate."

"Who is 'He'?" Bugen asked, trying to keep the conversation going so that Ed would not decide to let his knife speak for him.

"The Red One." Her nerve seemed to crumble, and—apparently to accentuate her proclamation—a splash of red appeared on her lips as she gnawed at them again. For a moment Bugen thought that her eyes flashed black, but it was gone so quickly that he decided it must have been a trick of the light.

"Where do we find him?" Ed asked voraciously, his eyes twinkling with an almost lustful desire for a confrontation.

She looked at him, terrified, blanched, then hissed in a trembling voice, "If you seek Him in Esra'Nell it will mean your death, foolish man. He is far more terrible than you!" And then she swept away into the twilit woods, running as though her life depended on it.

Artyom threw his hands in the air. "Why in the blazes didn't you try to calm her?" he asked his priestly companion with some ferocity. "Ed told me what you can do. She could have been a mine of information."

"I was too busy being worried about calming myself," Bugen responded defensively. "Besides, you could have worked some arcane magick too. Both of us did not do so out of fear of retaliation. But that is moot now: do you think we're in immediate danger here?"

"Doubt it." Ed looked at each of them in turn. "If this Red Guy has other cronies to do his work then he's not going to come charging down here himself. Just be wary for lesser Fae sneaking around."

Gramps reappeared holding a pair of cane rods and a bright expression. "Anyone wanna go fishing?" he enquired brilliantly.

"Anything?"

"Nope," Ed replied with a sigh, looking past Bugen into the centre of the lake.

Bugen sat next to the old man on the end of the pier. Both held rods attached to crude hooks by delicate cat-gut lines; their floats, fashioned from pig bladders, bobbed gently on the water. Bugen was unsure where the old fellow had procured their bait from, but the wriggling worms were the length of his fingers.

"There are signs of water Fae," Artyom said. Bugen briefly asked Sol to ensure that no water Fae ate his bait, then continued listening to the mage. "The child's bed is still dripping wet. Apparently she was taken into the lake..."

"We won't find 'em. Slippery buggers'll be gone if they've not already killed the kids."

"Kids on holidays, eh?" gramps wheezed.

Bugen silently prayed for Sol's peace upon the missing children. He did not hold out much hope that they would ever be found.

Alfazar's head popped out from inside the cabin of the Fae girl's boat. "This thing is crammed full of phony anti-Fae wares. There are horseshoes, iron rods, perfumes, prayer beads: all sorts of junk. I wonder why a Fae would decide to sell these to humans..."

"Anything useful?" Ed was always practical.

"Not really: no weapons, nor any maps or navigation gear. There's some exotic foods."

"Strange," Artyom mused. "A boat of this size would usually carry at least a compass. Did she take it with her, or did she not need one?"

"Who knows the mind of a Fae?" Bugen asked generally, concentrating on his float. There had been a distinct tug on the line. Ripples radiated out across the water as the float bobbed.

"I daresay Alfonz Higgens does," the mage retorted. Bugen looked around and shared a significant look with Artyom.

Plunk. Bugen's float was pulled under and, distracted, he struck too late. He brought in his line with a sigh, then stowed it when he saw that there were no worms left.

Abruptly, his old companion, who was dangling his feet in the water from the end of the pier, laughed broadly and pulled hard against whatever had snagged itself on his hook. A moment later he hauled a large mottled fish onto the pier and tried to unhook it without it flapping its way back to freedom. Ed waltzed over and struck the fish squarely between the eyes with the haft of his axe; its paddle-like tail abruptly stilled. "Still got the touch, eh?" gramps exulted, slapping Bugen on the back with a fishy hand. "I got me dinner... shame I lost me teeth last week. Oh well! See you wusses later." He trundled off towards Evergreen with his catch, leaving Ed, Artyom, Bugen, and Alfazar staring after him.

"Who woulda thunk it..." Ed mused.

"So, where lies our path?" Alfazar recovered.

"That's easy," their arcane expert piped up. "Esra'Nell." Bugen shivered. "Our phearsanú friend—didn't catch her name—was running away from 'Him', so if we want to find out who 'He' is we should be heading *that* way," Artyom said, indicating the far shore of the lake.

"Do we take the boat?" Bugen wondered.

"Too risky: there could be water Fae. Slimy critters'd be all over that little boat, and there wouldn't be nothing we could do to stop 'em." Ed sounded as if he knew this from personal experience. "Better to go on foot. We'll leave the horses: the forest is no place for them anyway."

After the companions had divided their supplies amongst themselves, stashing excess equipment in one of the boat sheds, they sent the horses back toward Evergreen with a slap on their rump. "Maybe they'll catch gramps on the way." They then prepared to enter the forest again.

Artyom retrieved a rope from the sheds nearby and threw it over Ed's shoulder. "For you."

"We'll stick close to the edge of the lake for the first bit," Ed advised, seeming to ignore the mage.

With no clear path to follow Bugen felt more oppressed than ever, so he hefted his buckler and summoned the light of Sol. The buckler glowed brightly, illuminating him and his companions, but the surrounding trunks and undergrowth remained as dark as ever. *This cannot end well*, thought the young priest, following Ed into the gloom.

ᔕ   ᔕ✖ᕈ   ᔕ✖ᕈ   ᔕᕉᔕᕈ ✖ ᔕᕉᔕᕈ   ᔕ✖ᕈ   ᔕ✖ᕈ   ᕉ

Ed whistled and stuck his thumbs into his belt. "Wouldya look at that!" he exclaimed, grinning.

"I'm looking at it," Alfazar agreed. "Phenomenal. Like there was some cataclysmic magickal schism millennia ago."

Artyom was too busy rummaging through his backpack to comment.

Bugen hurried to catch up with his companions, who had evidently emerged from the darkness. Unfortunately, the eaves of the forest here were just as abrupt as at Evergreen, and in his enthusiasm Bugen emerged from beneath them too quickly. As he attempted to blink away the bright image of the Sun imprinted on the back of his eyes—the irony was not lost on the young cleric—Bugen began to make sense of his surroundings.

He could make out a strip of green land about fifty yards wide, and bordered on one side by the huge forest trees. Bugen rubbed his face in frustration; why did the the trees appear so *small* now?

When the penny dropped it could have bounced into Bugen's mouth, which was hanging open in amazement. Rising from the green avenue were the sheerest cliffs that the young priest could conceive of. The walls were formed of smooth grey rock. They erupted suddenly from the ground, as though driven vertically through from below, and stretched so high that their summits (Did they have summits? Bugen could not see them) were clad in ice. At their base was a jumble of loose shale, stretching perhaps ten cubits in width. In both directions the enormous mountains curved gently away from Bugen, and he felt a faint stirring of memory. It was almost like...

"These are the peaks Uncle spoke of," Artyom said, seemingly reading the priest's mind. Artyom was pointing to the map that Ainsworth had gifted to them, finger resting on the uncharted circle. "The Staufen Mountains."

"Who cares what they're called?" Ed asked, and for once Bugen agreed. "What's on the other side, that's what I wanna know."

Esra'Nell?

"And how do we get there?" mused Alfazar, stroking his face with one hand whilst alternating between eyeing off the mountains and the map. None of them even suggested climbing, for it was obviously futile.

All four turned and looked at the great walls barring their path, gaping upwards. After a few moments Artyom's glasses started to fog up. "Well, if the other party reached here then I doubt they headed back into the forest, so our best chance of finding them is to stick within this grassy strip," he opined as he polished his spectacles with the tail of his shirt.

"Aye, but which way did they go?" Ed pondered.

Buhbuh chose that moment to urinate at the foot of the cliff, breaking the thoughtful silence that had fallen on the group. Tamtem was not to be outdone, leaving Artyom chuckling in a paternal manner.

Once things settled down Alfazar spoke up. "The Fae girl came from the direction of Maerin. I'd wager that means the entrance to this place—if it even exists—is towards the south."

"That sounds reasonable," Artyom said.

"Alright, let's go." Ed whistled to Buhbuh and the company set off to the south.

Bugen reserved his comments; the priest thought one path would be much like the other, and trouble would lay down both.

The mountains' scale was misleading. What Artyom and Bugen had taken to be thick turf stretching around their base soon turned into a bed of rushes waving in the gentle breeze. Their motion struck Bugen as somewhat off: too stiff and lopsided, like an arthritic joint. The group picked their way through the crooked marshes, ever on the lookout for any evidence of Fae or Fae hunters.

Fortune was with them, it seemed, for after scarcely fifteen minutes Bugen noticed wagon ruts in the soft earth. They emerged from the forest and turned to the south. Ed reckoned the tracks were made by a small cart drawn by a single horse.

After a few minutes of following the trail Bugen was starting to feel uncomfortably hot, so he was glad when Ed halted the party: for a moment.

"There's something over there," the hunter said quietly, pointing to a lush stand of rushes a dozen or so yards away.

Everyone froze into silence while Buhbuh went to investigate, Tamtem trailing close behind. Buhbuh rustled around for a few seconds before Artyom hurriedly turned to Ed. "Get him out of there!"

Ed, unquestioning, whistled for his companion to return, and the mage visibly relaxed as Buhbuh came back into sight. Alfazar and Bugen remained tense, ready to draw weapons.

"It's alright," Artyom offered after a moment, registering his allies' unease. "There is some sort of booby trap in there; Tamtem spotted one of the tripwires. No Fae or other creatures nearby though, it seems."

"Let me check it out," said Ed, stumping off towards the reeds. Bugen took the opportunity to refresh himself from his costrel, and Alfazar began regarding the mountains again. No doubt the bard was formulating an epic song about them.

A few moments passed before Ed returned, looking grouchy but intrigued. "There are tripwires all around that patch of overgrown grass. Some of 'em are really well hidden, but they all seem to connect to the same trap, whatever it is. Someone's cut down a bunch o' reeds to cover whatever is in there too." He sounded grudgingly impressed.

Artyom was first to respond. "Why not send Tamtem in there, bypass the traps?"

"Too many wires. Too well hidden."

The young mage accepted this judgement with good grace. "How do we find out what it is then?" he asked, looking thoughtful.

The bard spoke up tentatively. "Could it be the cart? Do the tracks continue past the stand, Ed?"

The hunter replied in a doubtful tone. "Aye, it might be the cart, but it looks pretty confused past here; there are ruts everywhere, all crossed over one another. The cart could be anywhere."

"It could be a really cunning trap," Artyom said, almost to himself. "We're supposed to think there's something important in there, but there's not... and then we spring the trap for nothing."

A thought sprang to Bugen's mind, and he turned excitedly to the mage. "So why don't we spring the trap?"

"Wha?"

"You can cause cloth to become animated, no?" Bugen asked in an isn't–it–obvious tone.

"Yeah. Even more animated than Ed is sometimes."

The hunter threw him a filthy look whilst Alfazar chuckled.

"How about rope?"

Comprehension slowly dawned on Artyom's face. "Ahh, great idea! Why didn't I think of that earlier."

"Too busy being smart to be smart," Ed grunted. The hunter pulled a pained face and scratched behind his ear sheepishly. "Think o' what, exactly?"

The party was ready in short order. They took cover behind one of the larger trees—thick enough to hide a small house behind—and Tamtem scaled its gargantuan trunk until he was perched in its lowest branches like an over-large squirrel (Ed was not shy about making the comparison loudly and frequently). Once Artyom was sure that his familiar was secure he trotted out from behind cover and fixed his gaze on the nearest tripwire.

Bugen was rapt; this was his first opportunity to really observe the mage using his arcane powers in detail. Firstly, he noted that the mage's face was set in concentration, and his eyes were glazed; he was looking through Tamtem. Then, Artyom reached out in front of himself, and it seemed to Bugen that hints of an enormous spectral limb extended out from the arcanist's body to the rushes. Bugen turned to Alfazar in amazement, but the bard could not make out the ghostly appendage. The almost–limb reached down, mirroring the motion of its owner's flesh-and-blood arm, and grasped one of the trip wires. Artyom yanked, and fifty yards away the tripwire was pulled loose.

"Oh, it was a du..." the mage managed before there came a thunderous crash. The party cringed behind their cover—Artyom lost his glasses diving behind the trunk—as dozens of objects collided with the tree, and the sound of metal on rock mixing with the echoes of the initial explosion blended into a cacophony that had Buhbuh whimpering.

Once the noise died away they all stood and brushed themselves down.

"Everyone okay?" Ed asked, making his way around the trunk. "How's Tamtem?"

"Could be worse," opined Artyom.

Looking up, Bugen could see that Tamtem was pressed flat against the trunk of the tree, slowly and carefully extricating himself from between enormous steel fléchettes embedded in the bark; one was next to the familiar's head, and another was pinned between his legs.

"I'm glad we had that tree on hand." Alfazar was inspecting the damage.

From above, or so Bugen supposed, the scene would have had the appearance of a steel flower. In the centre was a small cart—now clear of reeds, and smouldering slightly—and the petals were composed of waves of deadly harpoons spread around for hundreds of yards in all directions. Many of the fléchettes were embedded in the trees nearby, and several dozens were strewn randomly around; Bugen guessed they had ricocheted off the cliffs.

The group picked their way towards the cart, being sure not to stand on any stray projectiles. Ed quickly declared that the booby trap was, "Completely disarmed," and that it was safe to investigate the little wagon's contents. He then stomped off to set up a camp, sending Bugen to find water—the hunter had pointed out the silvery sheen of meltwater coursing down from the peaks in a few places nearby.

Bugen quickly found icy water at the foot of the mountains. It came down in a rivulet which pooled briefly on a rocky shore before draining into the marshes. From there, or so he reckoned, it probably fed into Mirror Lake, back near Evergreen. Regardless, it surely served as a prime breeding ground for midges and other unnamed biting insects. Bugen scratched his face and thanked Sol for his long garb, despite the heat and humidity.

As he worked his way back to camp Bugen suddenly realised why the rushes seemed off-kilter to him; they were all bent away from the feet of the mountains. The priest mused on this for a moment and came up with a likely explanation, based on his limited understanding of meteorology. He was rather pleased with his hypothesis, for it could also explain the rocky pools at the mountains' feet, and the curious fact that the forest did not continue all the way to their base.

The priest knew that during the hot tropical summer the ocean air became laden with moisture because of the power of Sol's light. When blown into the Arcanan countryside by the usual winds this moisture would give rise to the regular rains which kept Arcana fertile. However, if the warm mass of wet air were to be blown into the Staufen Mountains... Bugen could practically see, in his mind's eye, the enormously heavy rains that would pummel the mountains' slopes, and the furiously large hailstones pulverising their very rock. The resulting slurry of ice, stone, and untameable water would careen down and crash into these marshes with terrific force, flattening everything in its path before finally spending its fury in the fringes of the forest.

The priest gave thanks that this temperature and humidity passed for an Arcanan autumn; he suspected that no creature could survive such a deluge.

"... not much of use beyond food," Alfazar was saying as Bugen neared the cart again. Ed was squatting beside an iron-rimmed wheel, listening intently to the bard's report. "There was also a strange scroll, but Arty believes it is both harmless and useless." The bard waved a piece of parchment absently as he spoke.

"That settles it then," Ed murmured.

"Settles what?" queried Bugen, placing his load of full waterskins carefully onto the diminutive wagon.

"What to do with the cart, o' course," Ed supplied, standing and rapping his knuckles against the wood. "Either Ainsworth's other group set up that booby trap, or it was some of their enemies," said Ed generally.

"Aye?"

"Just wait a moment. I don't wanna have to explain this twice." Ed summoned the mage with a loud call, and shortly all four travellers had gathered around—or in Alfazar's case, on—the cart. Bugen felt like a mourner at some bizarre sort of funeral. "Well, here's what we do..." the hunter began.

The young priest had not received much training in espionage or counter-espionage, understandably, so he listened intently as Artyom and Ed fleshed out a plan. It seemed that there were two possibilities. Firstly, Ainsworth's second team may have stashed their supplies here for a return journey through the area, and left a trap to prevent them being pillaged by Fae or vagabonds. Alternatively, Sir Hupert's other group may have simply left their excess supplies here, and said evil creatures had laid the trap to injure or delay the group when they returned to reclaim them. Either way, Ed and Artyom were certain that the best way to proceed was to set up a 'double booby trap'. As Bugen understood it, the plan was to pilfer anything useful from the cart and then set it up to look like a second booby trap had been laid. Then, the companions would have a few moments to assess the threat if an adventurer or Fae greeblie turned up to check on its original snare.

In the meantime, the travellers could get some rest and take stock.

Half a sweaty hour later they were ready; several bundles of reeds had been cut and draped artfully over the top of the cart, leaving a clear area around it. This was important, emphasised Ed, because it would mean that nobody could get close enough to inspect the wagon without revealing themselves. Artyom and Alfazar had jammed clusters of stray fléchettes into the ground around the area, but left many undisturbed. Finally, they strung ropes around the fléchettes, leaving somewhat of an obstacle course which could be mistaken for legitimate tripwires.

Having done that, the group availed themselves of the water which Bugen had collected, and retired to finish making their camp. The wary hunter had selected a location in the fringe of the forest around fifty yards from the defunct booby trap.

Bugen hesitated to refer to it as a camp; four bed rolls, four packs and a smattering of equipment hardly constituted an encampment.

Wait... there were *five* bed rolls, although the fifth was no longer than Bugen's sword.

Tamtem was obviously spoilt by his master.

Alfazar took first watch as Sol's light began to disappear beyond the horizon, and the shadows of the storm-battered reeds grew long and grim. The young priest offered an exhausted prayer to Sol, volunteered for the second watch, ate his oats in silence, cleaned the rush's grime from his sword, and then dropped off to sleep fully clothed. He did not climb into the bed roll: hardly needed it.

Bugen dozed fitfully. At the end of Alfazar's uneventful watch he woke Bugen and immediately fell into a deep and easy slumber. His priestly counterpart had hoped to emulate this sudden, miraculous sleep at the end of his allocated time, but to no avail. Despite his weariness, Bugen was finding it difficult to rest.

An hour or two passed and Bugen reached that half-way place between sleep and wakefulness where the sleeper is aware of their wakefulness but not of the external world. The small part of his consciousness that remained was, paradoxically, excited by the prospect of proper sleep.

But it was not to be.

Ed stooped over Bugen and roused him with a gentle shake, one hand held up to his lips to indicate that the priest should remain silent. "There are things out there," the hunter whispered urgently into Bugen's ear. "Wake the others and make ready."

Bugen quietly crawled over to Artyom, who was lying nearby, which was no mean feat given the priest was encumbered by his bronze scale maille. It seemed imprudent to remove it before sleeping, and Bugen was grimly pleased to see his choice vindicated. "Wake up!" he said breathlessly. After a moment the priest shook Artyom again. "Artyom, awaken!"

"Huh?" The sleepy noise rang in Bugen's ears.

"Shh!" hissed the young priest, glancing anxiously over his shoulder towards the cliffs. "They'll hear you."

Artyom looked instantly alert, flicking the tail of his striped nightcap over his shoulder so as to better observe the scene. Next to him, Tamtem roused himself from sleep, and shook himself so that his own stripy headgear was out of the way. "I'll wake Alfazar. Get your gear ready," whispered the arcanist.

Drawing his sword, Bugen scrambled back towards his blanket and snatched up his buckler: foolish to leave it lying so, when he could better defend himself with the small holy shield than with the sword.

Soon all four adventurers could hear the sounds that had alarmed Buhbuh, and thereby alerted Ed. There was some thing, or things, over near the faux-booby-trapped cart.

Bugen crept over, his companions nearby, and strained all of his senses. Squinting into the darkness, he could just make out a peculiar tableau.

Three bipedal creatures were cavorting around the clearing. Their massive hunched shoulders supported long arms draped in matted black hair, from which protruded three-fingered hands tipped by scythe-like talons that glinted white in the weak moonlight. These enormous claws were also visible on the creatures' feet. Perched on top of oddly small legs were tapering bodies clad in sheaves of dark fur sticking out at wild angles, so that each animal bore a passing resemblance to a woolly haystack with pitchfork arms. Despite all of this, Bugen thought that their most peculiar, and disturbing, feature was their faces. From the front of each haystack emerged a long snout filled with gnarled teeth and a lashing tongue, tipped by a sensitive nose, and supporting a single enormous eye which seemed to flash in the darkness.

Two of the creatures were capering around the small wagon, apparently inspecting it, and jabbering to one another in a guttural language that consisted of deep gruntings and the occasional high-pitched hoot. Meanwhile, the third was vigorously sharpening its talons by rubbing them against its alarming dentistry, pausing every now and again to behead a rush and hoot angrily at its companions.

Bugen shifted his weight to obtain a clearer view. *Snap.*

The small noise of the stick breaking was enough to bring all three creatures to silence, and three eyes flashed Bugen's way. All he could see was a baleful blue glow emanating from each orb, and he broke out in a cold sweat at the sight. He held his breath. A moment passed—or several, Bugen could not tell—before the cold sweat turned very much to a *hot* sweat. The blue light intensified, and now the priest felt like he was being slowly roasted, too bewildered to even cry out, to alert his comrades to the danger of the eerie light.

Several things happened in rapid succession. Mastering himself, Bugen brought his hand up to unbuckle his armour, which was beginning to glow red hot under the power of the creatures' magick. The metal seared his flesh, forcing his hand back down. Ed, who had sneaked forward with considerably more stealth, chose that precise moment to leap into battle with the shaggy beasts, axe in one hand and kukri in the other. Buhbuh followed close behind with hackles raised. Simultaneously, Alfazar charged into the fray from the right, trapping two of the creatures between himself and the hunter. The lithe bard wielded a knife in one hand and a small flute in the other, which struck Bugen as completely ridiculous until Alfazar demonstrated the creatures' dislike of the short, shrill bursts of sound that the diminutive instrument could produce.

The haystacks recovered rapidly from the unexpected assault. Two of the hulking beasts faced off against Ed and Alfazar, and the third, with a bizarre rollicking gait, skittered towards Bugen. Fortunately for the toasty cleric, his comrades' distraction bought him enough time to dull the worst of the pain by emptying his costrel into his gambeson, so that he was not taken entirely unawares by the approaching enemy. Facing into the blue cyclopean visage, Bugen hefted his sword and prepared to swing. Then Artyom's ghostly hand reached past the priest, seized one of the tripwires still strewn across the clearing, and violently introduced that visage to the ground.

"Okay, priest?" asked Artyom, flashing a quick grin past his nightcap.

"They're doing something to my armour. I can't touch it, it's too hot," Bugen explained, a little panicky.

"Onto it," affirmed the mage, and the edges of Bugen's scale maille soon ceased to glow incandescently.

Bugen took the opportunity to glance towards Alfazar and Ed, gauging their status. The duo were acquitting themselves well. As Bugen watched, Alfazar—who was now wielding a flaming torch in one hand—unleashed a powerful burst of noise towards his opponent. The creature threw its arms up towards its gnarled ears to block the hated noise, and in doing so clipped the bard, sending him sprawling away from the fight. The other creature, hooting viciously, grasped Ed around the middle and punctured the hunter's leather jerkin with its impressive talons. Ed ignored the small injury, even using the added lubrication of his own blood to evade the creature's grasp and deliver a counterblow with his axe. Two of the offending claws fell to the ground.

Alfazar's opponent covered the ground between them in a single bound, pouncing on the prostrate bard, who barely managed to fend off the scything nails by jabbing frantically at the beast's eye with his torch. Bugen could see that Ed was still occupied with the first Fae, which was gnashing its teeth at Buhbuh, and the mage was concentrating his resources on redirecting the flow of energy which would crisp Bugen if left unchecked.

The bard was too far away—some thirty feet—for Bugen to physically assist him. It was time to employ his, Bugen's, own brand of magick.

A sharp intake of breath helped the priest focus his mind on the Light of his Goddess, and he used the weak moonlight as a physical anchor to assist his efforts. Then, drawing on the power of Sol, Bugen swung his sword in a powerful arc, as though to cleave an exposed head in twain. Mid-way through the swing, with a sound of rushing wind and curling fire, there burst forth from his sword an incorporeal counterpart. The gleaming summoned blade, wreathed in tongues of flickering flame that let off no heat, sped across the intervening distance—hurtling over the third beast, still struggling to right itself—and buried itself to the hilt in Alfazar's assailant like a comet of divine retribution. The monster, taken by surprise, stiffened and let out a strangled groan before falling dead at the bard's feet.

Bugen was pleased, but he quickly clamped down on the emotion. He had saved Alfazar from injury and defeated one of the creatures by employing his favourite piece of priestly magick, yet two foes still remained.

No sooner had he finished the thought than the nearest creature sprang back to its feet, rubbing debris out of its eye. Its gaze fixed on the source of its embarrassing clumsiness, then it loped towards Artyom with fell intent.

Bugen moved forward, sword and buckler held ready to intercept the beast before it could close with its unarmoured target. Fortunately, the demise of the creature's erstwhile companion had lessened the magickal assault on his maille. Artyom too must have sensed the changing flow of aetheric energies, for Bugen heard him mutter something, and the shaggy monster came to a halt. It teetered on the spot, eye half-lidded as though dazed.

Taking advantage of the unexpected lull, Bugen—still on his guard and still picking his way forwards—looked across to check on his other companions again.

Alfazar was heading to Ed's aid, the latter having earned a scratch across the forehead which sent blood dripping into his eyes. Their assailant was not faring any better though, as Ed had managed to put his axe into its knee. The limb, matted with blood, was now a hindrance to its hulking owner, although the wound would clearly not be fatal. Together now, Ed and Alfazar began herding the creature towards the cart, where its mobility would be impaired even further.

The nearest abomination started to growl like an angry bear waking from hibernation, wrenching Bugen's attention back to the fight at hand. With obvious effort it forced its glowing eye fully open and turned its magickal fury on the priest once more. Faster than seemed possible, a whiff of smoke rose from the top of Bugen's gambeson, singing his sinuses. Artyom yelped and terminated whatever spell of lethargy he had been attempting to maintain, opting instead to protect Bugen.

The priest, not realising this in his panic, lunged forward and thrust at the aberration's horrible orb in an attempt to disrupt its magick. This hasty move cost Bugen; his foot snagged on one of the many faux-tripwires and he fell to one knee, his thrust going awry. The Fae hooted maliciously and charged towards Artyom, crashing through Bugen's poor defence and knocking him aside as it passed.

Fortunately, the mage was not completely defenceless. He clutched a long-bladed dagger, double-edged and adorned by decorative brass quillons. With a surprising display of agility, Artyom side-stepped the oncoming claws and struck out at the offending beast, only to have his blow go wildly astray.

Bugen arrived shortly behind and scored home on the creature's other arm, but the thick fur was sufficient to prevent the gleaming sword from finding purchase. The priest retreated temporarily and summoned his spiritual blade from the body of its previous victim—the weapon was not marred by the creature's welling blue blood—before sending it arcing towards his assailant.

Evidently these creatures had some measure of intelligence, for the beast stooped low to the ground and allowed the flaming weapon to pass harmlessly overhead. It stood with a powerful thrust of its legs, which sent its massive, hunched shoulders surging into the arcanist, throwing Artyom's second blow off. Then, with one arm poised ready to swipe down Artyom's face, the monster let out an ear-splitting shriek and slumped to the ground. Alfazar's thrown knife had taken the creature in the throat, causing massive damage.

After briefly inspecting Artyom for wounds Bugen swung his attention towards Ed and the sole remaining monster. The wounded creature was still awkwardly backing towards the cart. As a result it did not see the mage's familiar scurry onto the top of the small wagon. In the dim moonlight and flickering illumination provided by Alfazar's torch, which was sputtering on the ground, Bugen could see Tamtem raise a bulging leather waterskin above his head. The unlikely projectile sailed towards the final beast and split against its wounded leg. A dark fluid burst out, and from the fluid expanded a murky vapour which seemed to solidify as it rose, encompassing the creature's lower limbs in shadow wadded with inky strands. The hunter, who did not seem surprised in the slightest, quickly moved in on his immobilised quarry, and removed the beast's remaining few claws. It was now alone, trapped, and essentially impotent.

After a moment or two the creature stopped trying to free itself, and began to growl and hoot in a miserable and frustrated kind of way, occasionally gesticulating with its long arms, or blinking and rubbing at its eye. Bugen noticed that the fierce blue glow had vanished from the latter, and quickly verified that his scale maille was back to its regular temperature. Just to be sure, the priest unbuckled the armour, so that he could remove it rapidly if needed.

Alfazar stepped forward cautiously, retrieving his torch from the ground and stoking the flame to a greater intensity. "A craicte, as I thought," proclaimed the bard, exhausted. The beast chittered in the back of its throat and gnashed its teeth at Alfazar in a desultory fashion. "Filthy creatures. Not as filthy as their mouths though."

It took Bugen a moment to register this last comment. "They speak?" he asked in amazement. His unearthly blade, lodged in a tree behind him, vanished with a slight sucking sound.

"Aye, they speak. Craicte are Fae creatures with a penchant for violence and foul language"—a few people who fitted that description sprang to Bugen's mind before he quickly banished the uncharitable thought—"although not language as most humans understand it. Craicte speech is closely related to an elvish language, but debased."

"Other Fae use craicte to do their grunt work," Ed added, face twisted in distaste. "They like booby traps: one of their few intellectual gifts. And they like... cooking. Makes people easier to eat, apparently. Looks like they tried it on you, Bugen?"

"Yes," the priest replied simply, indicating his unbuckled maille and burnt hand. Fortunately the remainder of the damage was only cosmetic.

"Good."

Bugen was a little taken aback.

"Last time I saw a craicte they heated my knife up: burnt me hand too, and ruined the knife's damned expensive cold forging. Didn't want them getting my horseshoe."

That explained Ed's attitude, but begged a plethora of further questions. "Why cook my armour, though? Or a knife?" Bugen settled on.

"Weaker Fae: metal seems to interfere with their magick," Ed responded, looking somewhat intimidating in the firelight. Blood dribbled down his face, chest and leg. "Jus' be glad you had some on you."

The priest nodded and decided he ought to do something about those injuries. "Are either of you hurt?" he asked Artyom and Alfazar. When he received two replies in the negative Bugen gestured to Ed. "Come away over here so that I may heal you," the priest said, pointing away from the craicte.

"Why do I gotta go over there?" came the grouchy reply.

"My healing power is indiscriminate," explained the priest. "If I call on Sol's power too near to the craicte it too will be mended. I do not want it to break loose."

"Oh, it won't break loose, I can promise you." Artyom had joined the conversation. "See that?" he asked Bugen, pointing to the broken waterskin. "I prepared that snare myself. Not even a kraeling could escape from that web. Last one I have, though..."

Bugen guessed that a kraeling was a variety of Fae, but chose not to demonstrate his ignorance to the mage.

"So go ahead and heal Ed here," Artyom continued. "I'm tired, and I'd rather question this craicte in the morning; we might as well make sure it will live through the night."

The craicte must have understood the gist of this exchange. It settled back onto its rump, as best it could with one leg trapped and mangled, and started to sharpen the stubs of its claws against its teeth. Maybe it hoped to have them ready to employ against its interrogators in the morning.

Bugen healed Ed and himself with a sunburst of power, in the process mending the craicte's leg wound, then the five settled in for some sleep before morning arrived.

Shortly the only movement was Tamtem's eyes as, standing at attention like a meerkat, he kept watch over his master: except no meerkat ever had such fantastic pyjamas.

The plan, as Bugen understood it, was quite simple: question the craicte about its activities and then dispatch the vile creature. Things had gotten rather more complicated, however, and now Bugen found himself walking briskly through a strangely coiling cave which smelt of mushrooms and stale cat urine.

The first hint that all was not going as Bugen had foreseen should have been when he returned from his morning meditation to find Ed and Artyom hunched over their small camp fire, conversing rapidly in hushed voices. This did not strike Bugen as unusual though, since the two obviously had a shared history and would be wont to discuss things without consulting their other companions.

Alfazar had been admiring the mountains, so Bugen strolled over—in the opposite direction to the craicte, which had its head tucked under its arm like a gigantic bird—and took up post next to the bard. Bugen had then split the loaf of bread he was holding and handed half to Alfazar, who nodded his appreciation.

"What's a kraeling?" Bugen had asked.

"Kraelings are a type of water Fae which have the appearance of chubby human children and the consistency of chewed tobacco." The well-travelled bard had chuckled a little as he answered, making the connexion between the early morning's events and Bugen's question. "Their entire bodies are lubricated by some manner of foul secretion, and they have no hard skeleton to speak of, barring their skulls, so they are exceptionally good at writhing into small spaces and out of traps."

"Thanks."

Ed and Artyom had then gathered their whole party around the craicte, which was quite agitated, as evidenced by the steady stream of invectives flowing from its monstrous snout whilst it attempted to free itself from its imprisonment. After listening to the ramblings for a minute or two Alfazar had made some comment to the effect of, "It is essentially saying 'get your own children,' or 'find your own,' if you cut out all of the cursing, swearing and questioning of your ancestry."

"Who's your master?" Ed had asked the craicte belligerently, brandishing his horseshoe towards the creature. The only response he got was a high-pitched chittering as the craicte followed the shoe's movement with its single great eye. "I know you know what this is," Ed had assured it. "Don't even think about it," he warned, indicating that Artyom was on the lookout for any magick that the Fae beast might employ.

A few more shouts from the hunter had coerced the craicte into answering, and after a moment Alfazar had translated its response for the group. "It's very vague. There are a lot of mentions of a 'Him', and it seems that this creature and its companions"—Alfazar had then gestured towards the two dead craicte stacked beside the cart (the remaining creature hawked a gob of phlegm at the bard in retaliation)—"were sent here by 'Him' to check that 'nobody else gets inside.' "

Ed and Artyom had shared a significant look at this point, which should have been Bugen's second warning.

Some further loud noises and threats of pain from Ed had not gotten anything more out of the Fae, so Artyom and Ed had decided to 'cut their losses'. The hunter tramped over to the craicte, raised his axe, and began an exaggerated swing targeted on its head.

Bugen recalled the scene vividly; out the craicte's arm flashed, smashing the axe off course, and Ed had responded with a seemingly-desperate blow that bit into the creature's calf, inadvertently shearing through many of the tangled webs of darkness that bound it in place. Even as it let out a great howl and smote the hunter with its stumpy claws the craicte had pulled itself free of the snare and run off, leaving spatters of blue-black blood in its wake.

Bugen and Alfazar had rushed to Ed's side; fortunately, the hunter had only received a shallow cut for his botched execution attempt.

"After it!" Artyom had cried, prompting the other three to scramble for their supplies before setting off along the path laid down by the craicte's lifeblood.

About ten minutes had passed before the bloody trail, which was begin to wander from side to side, reached a dense stand of rushes. Thick smears of congealing gore on the plants had made it abundantly clear that the craicte had passed through the stand; Bugen did not need Ed's skills to tell him that. With their weapons readied, the group had plunged into the reeds, Buhbuh going first so that he could spot any obvious booby traps.

They had followed the trail to a small overhang concealed at the base of the mountains, hidden behind a mound of scree. A narrow fissure was cloven into the rock's face—the only real imperfection Bugen had seen in the mountains so far—and from it emanated a sort of murky stillness that made Bugen's skin crawl.

"Excellent," Ed had sighed, satisfied.

Bugen had turned to him in surprise.

"Yep, well done. Here it is," the mage had said, spreading his hands widely to indicate the cleft.

Bugen, mystified, had turned to Alfazar, who was looking confused too. Then the bard's face had changed into one of sudden comprehension.

"You sly dogs: you deliberately botched killing the craicte, knowing that it would lead you back 'inside'. Lead you with its own blood, no less: that's cold." The accusation was delivered with an even tone that had left Bugen wondering whether Alfazar secretly approved of his companions' methods. There was certainly a timbre of respect for the results of their cruelty.

"Craicte ain't that intelligent," Ed had explained. "We"—he jerked a thumb in Artyom's direction—"pulled this trick on some back near Russeldorf: found their nest and destroyed it."

"They'd taken a dozen children over the span of a year," Artyom had lamented with a sour face, prompting Bugen to wonder whether their cruelty was warranted. Something to consider later, he decided.

"We didn't tell you 'coz we thought you might put a stop to it," Ed had told Bugen unabashedly; the hunter was right about that much.

With a sigh and a murmured prayer Bugen had invoked the light of his holy symbol, and between his glow and Alfazar's torches there was enough illumination to ensure they did not all plummet to their doom down some unseen pit in the floor of the tunnel. And so the adventurers had entered the dank, urine-scented cave.

"Oi, what are those symbols?" Ed enquired as he hurried to keep pace with the craicte. Bugen, Artyom, and Alfazar were following the hunter along the damp and rocky cave floor, with Tamtem going behind and Buhbuh ahead. It was fortunate that the ceiling was relatively clear of stalactites, for it was so low that only Ed could stand upright; the others had to hunch. Alfazar was holding one of his knives, and had given another to Bugen, partially for security, but predominately because the weapons scraped on the ceiling when in their shoulder-mounted scabbards. Bugen was thankful for the knife, with its short blade. The stone walls of the tunnel—close enough on each side that Bugen could run his hands along both of them—did not leave enough room to swing a cat, let alone a sword. They shone with a faint green phosphorescence, despite the yellow tint of Bugen's divine light and the fiery glow of the torches. Still, the walls' sickly fluorescence provided no real illumination.

Bugen snapped out of his reverie and looked at the wall which Ed was indicating. At about navel height there was a plethora of symbols carved along the wall. Some were deeply intagliated, others small and shallow; some were carefully carved and finished, and others appeared to have been scratched into the rock with little thought for aesthetics. The mass of symbols lay one on top of the other, forming a patchwork of glyphs.

One repeated symbol stood out: a circle bisected by a line which sat slightly rotated from the vertical. The priest found it oddly familiar. He cast his mind back through his memories, trying to recall the lesson in which he had come across these markings. Something to do with a deity...

The priesthood of Sol was educated about more than Sol Herself, though they revered Her above others, and pledged themselves to supporting their Goddess in preference to other deities. It was so with nearly all of the deities; each gathered about themselves, deliberately or inadvertently, a quorum of dedicated followers through whom they could act in the mortal world. It was thus necessary that most priests were educated about the devotees of other powers.

Now Bugen recalled the relevant lesson clearly.

His thirteen-year-old self sat cross-legged on the cold stone floor whilst alternately gazing at his tutor and out of the immense stained glass windows—three inches thick, so as to resist the stormy Faustian weather—at the darkening sky. The tutor was an old fellow with a stereotypical priestly tonsure, white around the edges, and a pair of half-moon glasses that somehow matched his dusty voice. Bugen rubbed his hand across his cropped hair and tugged on the one thin braid hanging at his neck, then pulled his brown robes closer about himself.

"There is a single god of the Moon, known to us mortals as Lune. She is a being to be reckoned with, as most of the gods are..." He paused briefly before continuing, "Although our observations indicate that much of her influence is dependent on the power of Our Lady.

"Lune is worshipped by many. Evidence suggests, however, that she favours the elves. She is associated with the qualities of mischief, evil, madness, and even death: a far cry from the benevolent light of Sol. We have reason to believe that Lune is in fact foremost amongst the death gods."

"These glyphs are the sign of Lune, the Moon goddess, although of an archaic variety. Humans have not used that sign since before the Unification," Bugen informed his companions.

"Moon goddess?" Alfazar said sharply. "Ill are the tales I have heard of Lune."

"Aye," concurred Bugen, remembering the remainder of his lessons (the brother who taught him would have been proud of the priest's recall).

Ed was silent, not having had much experience with deities of any flavour.

The four of them were following a bleeding Fae creature along a narrow, spiralling tunnel, bored through the most gargantuan mountain range in the known world, leading to an uncharted region of Arcana potentially infested with Fae, elves or other questionable Moon worshippers... Bugen had a bad feeling about the situation. Still, he strode along as briskly as the cramped ceiling allowed, clutching his buckler and the knife with white knuckles.

Chapter 6

Esra'Nell

I... this record to preserve the knowledge that... are not all the enemies of mankind. Many would be surprised ...re are those amongst us who are able to do so.

Our horror began with the birth of the Red One... true name is forgotten. He... Erdis [n.b. this was the closest match our translators could find] *... enslaved... bloody rite...*

Partial translation of hieroglyphs from Fae-infested cave, based on drawings by Corporal John Waite made during the Purge of 250–251 AU

 HERE was definitely light ahead; Bugen could see it on the wall of the tunnel where it curved away to the left in front of him. After so long in the darkness it was as plain as... well, day. Artyom, Alfazar, Bugen, Ed, Buhbuh, and Tamtem emerged onto a rocky ledge perched on the mountainside and gazed out across a startling vista. They had *definitely* gotten 'inside'; no place not steeped in Fae magick could possibly be so gloriously and unnaturally beautiful. It struck wonder and fear into Bugen's heart.

Nestled inside the indomitable mountain fortress—the rock was purple, like at Port Adeline—was a forest. Enormous trees, some far taller than their mundane counterparts near Evergreen, grew in great stands, their grey branches twisted in intricate and gravity-defying shapes, white foliage twinkling with unearthly shades of green, blue, and orange. They looked almost crystalline, inorganic, like living structures of mineral shooting up from the bedrock. But no, Bugen could not deny the flocks of small, multi-coloured birds swarming between the trees. The priest imagined that they were searching for fruit which sparkled like translucent gemstones.

At the centre of all this was a perfectly circular lake, filled with the clearest water Bugen had ever seen. On second thought, maybe it was not water at all. That seemed too mundane, too expected, for this place. Something was poised over the middle of the water's surface, but the priest could not make it out; many Faustians had poor distance vision, on account of the fact that the weather rarely permitted them to view the distance anyway. Whatever the object was, it seemed to be the centrepiece of this strange land—the focus. A dwelling? Magickal device? Maybe 'He' was there...

Bugen was glad that the Sun, at least, was the same one he was used to. Sol had not abandoned him in this beautiful, terrible place.

Nobody broke the silence.

Ed drank in the beauty too, but his shrewd mind quickly returned to the task at hand. Where was the craicte? A moment of scanning the surroundings made it abundantly clear that there were only two ways to the valley floor: walk down a winding trail, little more than a goat track, or fly. Ed elected for the former.

He permitted a quick break, during which they wolfed down some trail ration and water, then the four were off once more.

The trail was cut into the side of the cliff, fairly smooth but exceptionally steep. Every now and then a smear of craicte ichor assured Ed that the beast had come this way. The companions laboured down the hill, trying not to slip and crash to their deaths. As usual, Buhbuh and Tamtem went ahead to seek out any traps or ambushes.

After scarcely ten minutes the comforting Sun slipped from the sky. No stars slid in to take its place, but the moon did; it seemed to Bugen that it loomed large over the valley like a celestial eye casting all beneath its gaze in a cold, silvery light.

"The day passed so rapidly. Could we have walked into another plane?" wondered Alfazar, enthralled.

"No, we're in the same plane," Artyom stated categorically. He offered no explanation.

"So there won't be madness awaiting us?" Alfazar asked generally, gesturing towards the eldritch valley.

"Oh, I never said there would not be madness," Artyom half-grinned, half-cringed.

Thus comforted, the four began down the trail again. Bugen handed Alfazar back his knife, favouring his own sword now that the environment was more clear. Besides, the longer weapon made a good counterbalance. Its familiar weight sat reassuringly in the priest's hand.

The sight that greeted them at the valley floor about an hour later was both pleasant and unsettling.

The arrangement was essentially a series of concentric circles. Firstly, a clear space, perhaps twenty feet of barren soil, stretched around the base of the cliffs like a moat. Inside this ran a stony creek bed some ten feet wide in which crystal-clear water bubbled. The stream curved away to the left and right, and Bugen noted that the chattering flow of water seemed to be unnatural, as the ground was quite level. Beyond the stream was a formidable fence of amethyst crystals as large as a man, jutting up at odd angles like glittering craicte teeth. Finally, there was the forest itself, breathtaking trees towering over the travellers. Their strangely angular branches were twisted and turned chaotically about one another, casting disquieting yet beautiful moonlit shadows over the scene. A few birds perched above, cracking open angular fruit with their fearsome beaks. The whole tableau dripped with pulsing, unnatural vivacity, and a cold light: full of soft glows and sharp edges.

The beautiful symmetry of the circles was marred by a path about four feet wide and covered, seemingly, with the contents of an enormous lapidary drum. A graceful stone bridge—complete with carved bannisters—carried the path over the moat–river, from whence it speared through a gap in the crystalline fence before being lost in the twinkling undergrowth.

And in the middle of the bridge lay the craicte.

Ed cursed violently, surprising Bugen. "Damnation..." the hunter added as he ran over to the corpse, drawing his axe.

Alfazar unsheathed a knife and Bugen tightened his grip on his weapon, wondering what had prompted the outburst.

"It almost made it back. The wound you gave it must have been more dire than you thought," Bugen suggested as he drew nearer to the hunter and his quarry.

Alfazar scanned their surroundings with keen eyes.

"Nah, that was just a piddling little scratch to this beast, barely enough to slow it," Ed groused. "I wasn't what did it in."

"So...?"

"Imps."

"Huh?" Bugen asked eloquently.

To answer, Artyom simply lent over and indicated a number of small holes punctured in the craicte's body.

On closer inspection, Bugen could see that they were arranged in groups of three, and that the craicte's flesh seemed to hang strangely from its frame. "What magick is this? Has decay set in so rapidly?"

"Not decay." Ed shook his head darkly.

"Imps... drink the fluids of those they kill." Artyom's voice was clinical, dispassionate.

That explained it: the craicte was deflated like a punctured wineskin. The anaemic tongue protruding from its muzzle was the last pitiful splash of colour on its body.

Ed swore ferociously again. Under normal circumstances Bugen would have rebuked him, but he had to make allowances. "They know we're here. They knew my strategy, so they arranged for the sodding creature to die. Whatever we're dealing with, it's intelligent, and it's ruthless." This assessment coming from Ed—whom Bugen thought of as ruthless (and adequately intelligent)—was enough to send a shiver of fear up the priest's spine.

Their adversary, whoever 'He' was, was smart, qualmless, cunning, and likely backed to the hilt by Fae magick.

"No point staying out here." Alfazar said it as if it were a simple observation. "Do we press on, or go back?"

"We go on," Ed responded quietly. "He's here somewhere."

"As are the children," Bugen added pointedly. "Probably."

The four companions stepped over the craicte's corpse and continued up the path, multi-hued gravel crunching under foot. Behind them, Tamtem stopped to investigate a peculiar, squat plant by the wayside, but was quickly dissuaded when it shot thousands of glittering needles into the air. Buhbuh, more easily amused, merely sniffed at the craicte and wished that they could stop for a bite of real meat for a change.

The landscape was mesmerising and terrifying in equal measure. Bugen and his companions had walked along a sinuous path which meandered along the forest floor and sometimes ascended briefly into the trees before returning to a sensible height.

"Keep an eye out. There are marks on the trail: could be footprints. Looks like another group of about our size," Ed opined after a few hundred yards. With a practised eye aiding him, Bugen began to make out the putative footprints. This was particularly difficult because the trail was spattered with variegated patches of gravel and criss-crossed with runnels of glistening water, even when raised well above the ground. Bugen fancied that the water even ran uphill on occasion.

Alfazar constantly scanned the surroundings, letting the others focus on the trail.

Despite stretching his senses to a maximum, Bugen could not detect any life beyond the occasional flock of tiny glittering birds which swooped through the tangled trees in the distance. Perhaps he could not isolate any animals because there was just *so* much life pulsating all around. The hard-edged vegetation glittered with phosphorescence and acute angles, but was undeniably alive.

"Artyom, can you *feel* anything?" Bugen asked, turning to the mage. Perhaps arcane magick would succeed here, where priestly insight would not.

"Dunno. Let's see..."

Artyom dropped to the ground and cried out in pain, grinding his fists into his temples. For a moment he rolled and the whites of his eyes showed, and Bugen began to panic in earnest. Tamtem whimpered in unison with his master.

The fit passed as suddenly as it came, leaving Artyom shaken and grimy. "So *much*. I can't feel anything at all because I can feel *everything* in this place." He took a shaking breath. "It's unnatural, eldritch... Fae."

Bugen unstopped a costrel with hands that shook slightly, and passed it to the mage, who was still on the floor.

"We'll just have to do things the old-fashioned way," Ed said grimly, helping Arty to his feet. The mage took a mouthful of water and passed the costrel to Bugen, who followed suit.

Further down the unnatural trail, at the apex of a sweeping bend, Ed halted the party. "What's this?" He stared at a patch of soft ground which undeniably showed footprints.

After a moment it registered. "They've split up!" Bugen exclaimed, aghast. Why would Ainsworth's second party split up in this inhospitable place?

"Don't you know, you never split the party..." Artyom said in a sing-song voice which seemed totally out of place. Bugen shot him a quizzical look, but got no response.

"There are four of them," Ed decided after a moment's inspection.

Bugen could plainly see the prints here. One set, fairly small compared to the others, continued on down the trail. A second, the faintest of the four, left the path and headed off into the forest at right angles. The third went off in the opposite direction, accompanied by a set of tracks of some four-legged creature; Bugen suspected that this person was a mage or a hunter of some description. Finally, deep, broad prints led backwards at a tangent to the path.

"Let's leave the one on the trail 'til last," suggested Ed. "See what happened to the others. If they're still alive."

Artyom nodded in agreement and the pair made to leave the trail.

"Wait," Bugen said hurriedly. "This place is full of Fae magick: what of Fae shape-shifters? We've run afoul of one already, and there may be others."

Ed cocked an eyebrow at the priest, but Alfazar nodded in understanding. "We need some sort of signal to prove to one another that we're our real selves. Then if we get separated we can be sure that we are reunited with one another, not with some Fae creatures."

"Aye," said Bugen, glad that the bard was so sharp.

"Well, no Fae would know the name of the ship we came here on," Artyom said. "We'll use its name as a signal. Agreed?"

Bugen rolled the name around in his mind: *Steadfast*.

"That'll do," said Ed, clearly wanting to be off. "Let's not tarry here any longer." He threw a glance into the trees as he led the party off the path, following the second set of tracks.

Scarcely twenty metres from the path Ed drew to a halt. "Stop." He took a few further steps forward and peered down in a most peculiar way. "That's... odd." The hunter gestured for the rest of the party to join him.

They suddenly perceived that Ed was standing on the edge of a sheer precipice, gazing down at a twisted figure caught in the crystalline branches of one of the strange trees below. Bugen felt a species of sorrow for the black-clad figure. They had obviously not noticed the sharp cliff and simply stepped off into thin air, and their doom.

"Why did they not notice the cliff?" Alfazar wondered. "Were they running, Ed?"

The latter inspected the prints leading up to the sheer drop and shook his head. "Nah. Weird."

It took Ed five minutes to find a safe route down the cliff. The party clambered down a rock slide of dark stone with smooth faces and sharp edges; Bugen worried that he might be cut by the edges of the glassy flakes. Fortunately, they made it to the bottom without any incidents, barring some choice curses from the hunter.

Eventually they stood below the tree they had spotted earlier. The corpse hung in its branches like some sort of macabre decoration, painting the limbs below it with now-dried blood.

"Blood: no imps then," Artyom observed dispassionately.

"Looks like a rogue," opined Alfazar. When that drew a blank look from Bugen he continued, "Usually fringe-dwellers, members of society with sociopathic tendencies who are employed as assassins or thieves by those who wish to keep their own hands clean. Some are no more than pick-pockets, but others are exceptionally well-trained, athletic, fleet-of-foot, and skilled in observing their environment. I doubt Ainsworth would have wasted gold on the former, but..."

"But why did he not see the cliff if he was not running?" Bugen finished for him, stroking his bearded chin.

"Exactly."

"Best get him down, see if we can find out any more. Might be carrying something useful, too." Ed was always practical.

The image of Alfazar scurrying up the tree forcefully reminded Bugen of the bard's antics in the rigging of the *Steadfast* on the way into Port Adeline, what seemed like several years previously. Had it really only been four days ago? The priest tried to count the time as he stood vigil at the base of the tree, buckler and sword drawn, whilst the unnatural Esra'Nell light grew once more. At any rate, Bugen was glad to be free of the baleful glow of the moon. He briefly wondered whether he would need to perform his early morning devotions again—he normally needed to in order to maintain his mindfulness of Sol—but quickly decided that Sol would gift him with mercy, given the circumstances.

Eventually, Alfazar and Ed managed to extricate the body from its arboreal resting place; they had needed to use the rope from Mirror Lake to set up a makeshift pulley system to lift it off the branches and manoeuvre it down.

In the light of morning the party gathered around the corpse and scrutinised it. Numerous puncture wounds, some still with crystalline shards of tree embedded in them, decorated the rogue's torso and legs, though its head was curiously unscathed. Alfazar le-ant over and tenderly removed the faded black bandanna covering the rogue's face and scalp.

It looked like a young lad. He was clean-shaven—hardly looked like he needed to shave at all—and could have passed for one of the mild-mannered gentry of some older Faustian towns. Not at all what Bugen had expected.

Nobody made comment: it seemed too disrespectful. That did not stop Ed from rummaging through the corpse's pockets and scabbards, though the usually stoic hunter did have to look away from the cadaver's glassy, accusing gaze. He came up empty, barring a short knife with a blade that folded up into its handle. Ed pocketed this, claiming that it could be used as proof that the youthful rogue had fallen afoul of Esra'Nell.

There was a convenient cavity at the base of the tree, between two of the major trunks, which the companions appropriated for use as an improvised mausoleum. Bugen gravely offered a prayer for protection of the lad's soul—the others joined in half-heartedly—and silently petitioned his goddess to watch over them all.

The four companions found their counterparts' parting-of-ways again, though the Sun was overhead by the time they did. It relie-ved Bugen that they had reached the trail again safely.

He had a prickly feeling all over, like they were being watched by something malevolent. Judging by the way that Alfazar kept glancing over his shoulder, Bugen was not the only one. Still, he could not detect anything, by means mystical or mundane.

Artyom, on the other hand, was already hypothesising. "Perhaps he was blinded. Or maybe they made an illusion which disguised the cliff. He could have been distracted by something nearby. Drugged so that he couldn't perceive his surroundings..."

"Shut up, will you?" Ed cut in. "Maybe he was busy hypothesising instead of paying attention."

There were three more sets of tracks to explore; one wide, deep, and well-spaced track leading backwards, towards the head of the path; another which Bugen could only make out with Ed's help; and a set of small, slight, and shallow prints which headed further into Esra'Nell.

"Remember what Clive said about an armoured one," intoned Bugen.

"Huh?" Ed asked from where he was crouching to examine the prints.

"Oh. Right. The leader back in Evergreen told me that, 'One of them,' from Ainsworth's other groups, 'had so much armour on that we could scarcely find a bare spot to touch his flesh.' "

"Aye, this'll have been their warrior," agreed Ed. The use of past tense was not lost on the priest. "Usually a huge, muscular guy with an ego bigger than his biceps. Some are pretty noble, though. Hard to faze, these types."

"Not much can harm you when you're wearing a king's ransom in plate armour," Alfazar said, nodding. "Did you know that actually was how King Duplieren II was ransomed from the..." He trailed off, realising now was not the time or place. "I'll tell you when we get back to Adeline."

If we get back to Adeline, Bugen mentally amended, then chastised himself for his pessimistic outlook.

With Ed in the lead, the four travellers followed the footprints back at a tangent to the trail. The impressions rapidly got wider apart—Bugen estimated them to be separated by about two of his stride lengths—and deeper. With a start the priest realised that this meant the man must have been sprinting. Shortly he saw further evidence: several low-hanging tree limbs seemed to have been shattered by the man as he fled, leaving gem-like shards scattered haphazardly around.

Bugen and Alfazar took up post on either side of Ed and Artyom with weapons drawn, allowing the latter pair to concentrate on tracking their quarry. The priest briefly noted that there were no other tracks evident in the vicinity. Did this mean the armoured juggernaut had not been pursued?

Ahead was a clearing formed where one of the strange trees had collapsed, pulverising a section of nearby forest. Did such trees rot, as did their mundane versions? The cleric could see bright sunlight twinkling from a thousand glassy leaves waving gently in a soft breeze. Their brilliance cast a shifting amber glow over the scene, such that it took the companions a moment longer to discern what should have been immensely obvious to them.

At the head of the clearing, leant against the base of an angular rock, was a mass of polished armour. Ed hurried over and checked for anything behind the rock, whilst Alfazar moved to cover Artyom and Bugen, who were inspecting the mass.

Neither man could see signs of life. Artyom removed the warrior's helmet—a rounded affair which mated with the gorget rising from the armour's breastplate—and immediately registered the bloodshot eyes staring lifelessly up at him. Dark eyes set into a dark face made the white and red of the warrior's sclera stand out dramatically. The man's visage was twisted in terror. There were no obvious signs of a fatal wound, so Artyom gave Bugen a dark look and set about trying to determine what had killed the heavily-armoured warrior.

Bugen's nose picked up a faint scent of something foul as Artyom struggled to move the warrior around. Decay, so soon?

"He died of terror!" gasped Bugen as the answer flashed into his mind. "And he's emptied his bowels, before or after."

"A brave warrior, frightened to death," Artyom muttered.

"Ironic," Ed chipped in. "He even threw his weapon away," he said, indicating a shape out in the clearing which Bugen eventually identified as a massive metal hammer. The weapon looked as though it would require several men just to lift it.

"There were no obvious signs of pursuit," Alfazar added, corroborating Bugen's earlier observation.

"Just more confirmation of Fae involvement," Artyom replied gravely.

Artyom removed the warrior's belt, which was stamped with scenes of Graean peasants going about their business, and buckled it about his own waist.

Moving the unfortunate man's body was out of the question, but the four companions did their best to restore to him a measure of dignity in death. They lugged his massive weapon across the clearing—the man must have had great strength to have flung it so far—and wrapped his stiff fingers around its haft; Bugen shut the dark eyes and closed the man's mouth; and Alfazar tucked the helm under one arm.

Bugen led the group in yet another mortuary benediction, and felt despair. Yet, as the final words faded into silence, the golden sunlight streaming into the clearing revived the dying embers of Bugen's hope, and he found peace within himself. No matter what evil filled this day, Bugen knew the day itself was a good gift from Sol: a gift which evil, for all of its power, could not hope to match or to undo.

Another body. It lay face-down near the base of a tree, as though its owner had simply fallen there and expired.

The most peculiar element of this tableau, Bugen felt, was not the dead woman. Nor was it the dead lynx nestled against her still body, nor the twisted skein of tracks leading from the path to this location. It was the fact that this woman had evidently died of thirst, clutching an empty canteen, despite the stream chuckling just twenty yards from her drying mortal shell.

Alfazar, Artyom and Bugen again took up watch whilst Ed searched for any items which would be useful in identifying his deceased counterpart. He eventually cut a lock of her long brown hair—which was sparsely adorned with blue feathers—then bound it with a short thong and tucked it into his tinder kit. It would be impractical to remove any of her leather armour or her weapons.

Now that she was rolled over Bugen could see that she would have been tall and rangy in life, and in his mind's eye he had no trouble picturing her striding purposefully through a Faustian forest with her lynx as a guide. Unfortunately, he also had no problem picturing the pair wandering fruitlessly through this unnatural domain as some dastardly Fae intelligence repeatedly and maliciously interfered with their ability to find water.

There was no need to imagine the look of exhausted despair that she bore as she finally lay down to die; the expression was still frozen on her face. Bugen sighed and shuddered inwardly.

The priest administered the final rites. Afterwards, Alfazar and Ed gently carried the pair of bodies the short distance to the stream. Grotesquely, the bodies remained frozen in their positions by the rigour of death. The hunter, in an uncharacteristic display of tenderness, washed the deceased woman's forehead with the water, then nudged her into the main flow. After a few moments her parched body, lynx perched atop, vanished around a bend, finally uniting both with the water they had so craved.

"A rogue with his agility removed, and a ranger with her tracking foiled. Whatever happened to their priest?" Alfazar mused, drawing a knife and looking back towards the path.

Bugen wondered. A priest with no deity? The possibility disturbed the young cleric profoundly; what terrible power could cut him off from Sol?

The Sun was setting, casting red across Esra'Nell for a few short minutes. Bugen knew that the moon would soon take predominance once more. It bothered the priest; only a few hours had passed, subjectively, yet already the day drew to a close. Truly, this place was both terrible and wondrous.

The party had barely travelled twenty feet further along the pathway when they found bloody footprints. About ten yards beyond that they found her: a slim form, lying face down in the gravel. The last member of the other party. Artyom, Alfazar, and

Ed looked briefly from her to Bugen and back, then stepped away from the body.

He had been preparing for this; every group on state business was obliged to include a cleric.

Bugen moved closer, solemnly inspecting the slight figure clad in the quartered yellow and red of Sol. Blood pooling around two knives driven into her back disfigured the clean lines of her clerics' garb, leaving uneven red blotches across the yellow. The woman had long hair splayed around her head, white and fine, but seemingly ruddy in this light. Bugen did not recognise her features.

Her male counterpart removed the knives as tenderly as possible—one was lodged in gristle and took some effort to extricate—and rolled her onto her back. Bugen knelt and checked her neck and hands for any trinkets bearing Sol's symbol; every priest of the Lady of Light carried her token with them somewhere. He shortly found a petite dagger, slim and about a hand's span long, with the sacred crossed circle engraved on its pommel. Bugen unbuckled the leather sheath and hooked it to his sword's scabbard using a simple bronze clasp that the woman had carried. He noted a sign of the Nature goddess thereon, but did not think ill of it. It was not uncommon for clerics to pay obeisance to multiple deities, within reason.

There were no questions from the others; they knew that it was proper that Bugen be the one to take the dagger.

He stood, hands clasped and head bowed over the body. After a respectful pause Ed moved up beside the priest. He lifted a bloody knife up for Bugen's inspection. "These blades," said the hunter pensively, running his hand over the grip. "The rogue was wearing two empty sheaths..."

The implication hung in the air between the travellers. "Be on your guard," Alfazar intoned softly, eyes staring blankly off into the distance. "Some terrible power has deceived our erstwhile comrades. Let us be careful..."

"Check your targets," Ed huffed, though Bugen could see that the hunter was unsettled and trying to cover it with bluster.

"Let us hope we have some advantage that they did not," contributed Artyom. "Or at least some good fortune."

"We need more than luck," muttered Bugen, silently petitioning Sol yet again. Part of the priest—the more scholarly part—wondered whether he was showing a lack of faith in Sol by reiterating his prayers to her so frequently, as if he did not trust her to remember or to act on them; the majority thought that a bit more prayer could not possibly go astray.

Bugen took a crunching step further along the path before he felt Ed's hand upon his shoulder. "Ain't you gonna bury her? Pay your respects, like with the others?"

The priest calmly drew the stiletto, grasping it by the blade, and showed Ed the engraving. "Sol willing, I will return this to this woman's home monastery, where it will be displayed in a place of honour reserved for those who have died in service to Our Lady." He looked directly into Ed's eyes as he said this. "This is the greatest respect I can give her." He paused briefly and made eye contact with each of the three other men in turn. "If I should fall, I ask that you do the same for me." He indicated his buckler. Without pause, the others nodded gravely. "Dell will know the details."

They turned and proceeded as one, leaving the woman's body staring sightlessly at the setting Sun.

ᔊ ᥤᗱᕐᓀ ᥤᗱᕐᓀ ᒧᕆᕐᓀ ✕ ᒧᕆᕐᓀ ᥤᗱᕐᓀ ᥤᗱᕐᓀ ᕆ

"It's cold, wouldn't you say?" Artyom muttered as the party trudged along the path. The twisted trees threw disquieting shadows under the light of the obscenely large moon.

"It's more comfortable than the rest of this island's bizarre weather," Bugen opined. " 'Tis definitely cooler though."

The group fell silent again, almost instinctively. After a few more minutes Alfazar quietly said "And now it's cooler again."

"Something isn't right," Ed grumbled. "It feels almost like Faust in here."

"Aye," concurred Bugen.

They rounded a corner and found a figure standing in their way. It was a short humanoid, hooded and cloaked in blue so deep it appeared black. "You again!" hissed Ed, reaching for his kukri. The figure drew back its hood, revealing long, walnut-coloured hair.

"The Fae girl from the wood," Artyom murmured. "Is this your doing?" he asked her. "The cold?"

"No," replied the phearsanú woman, shaking her head. "You are being hunted by one of His creatures."

"Bollocks," Ed scoffed.

"It is a Naked One, and it will be upon you shortly if you do not hide."

Ed snorted.

"This creature: can we fight it?" Bugen asked, wondering if it was more dangerous to listen to this Fae or to ignore her.

"You are not equipped for this battle. Please, you must hide," the woman pleaded, wringing her hands.

"Fine," Ed relented, shooting her a filthy look: the temperature was still dropping, and his exposed flesh now bore goosebumps. "But first: what's your name." It was a demand, not a question.

"Vera. Now let's get off this road, quick!"

Vera turned and trotted about twenty yards further up the path, then ducked off to the left. Bugen drew level and saw that a cluster of shrubs grew to about shoulder-height there. Their glittering leaves were sufficient to hide the phearsanú from view. He was wondering precisely where she had gone when her head popped out from between two bushes. "Quickly," she mouthed, beckoning frantically and shooting glances back up the path.

The band got in behind cover as stealthily as they could, then crouched there, trying to still their breathing. Bugen could hear his pulse thudding in his ears, drowning out any other sounds, until it gradually lessened in frequency and volume. Meanwhile, Ed unsheathed his knife, ready to react if Vera should prove false or if they were otherwise detected.

After a minute or so of crouching Bugen began to hear a distinct external noise. Had he not been informed otherwise, he would have guessed that the sounds were those of a simple horse walking the path at a leisurely pace; instead, Vera's warning made the commonplace *clop* of hooves on gravel evoke fear.

Bugen's heart rate rose again, but the steps remained audible; the rider was getting nearer.

Buhbuh stirred and sniffed the air, which was growing more and more chilly, but a hasty hand gesture from Ed ensured that the dog did not make any noise. It did not take long before the humans could smell it too: raw meat. The air seemed to thicken and congeal as the odour grew and the temperature plummeted. Bugen was forcefully reminded of the atmosphere inside the Faustian caves used to store and preserve meat.

He was trying to find a gap in the bushes to peer through when something settled on his nose. The cleric was astounded to see a snowflake perching there. It persisted for a moment, then his body heat melted it, and it vanished into the cold sweat coating his face. Uncrossing his eyes, Bugen returned his focus to the imminent danger.

The steps halted immediately opposite their shrubby conceal-ment. A snort sounded—as of a horse, but subtly altered—and one hoof scraped across the ground impatiently. Bugen waited for the sounds of a rider dismounting, but they never came.

Puzzled, the cleric peered through a small gap in the foliage. It was just possible to see through, if he turned his head at an unnatural angle.

The creature that he spied through the narrow hole was repug-nant. Its lower half could have feasibly been a horse's body, but one totally stripped of skin. Powerful cords of flayed muscle stretched and coiled as the beast stamped restlessly. Small beads of straw-coloured fluid squeezed out of the flesh with each motion, then froze and flaked away on the next. The horse's body was topped with a nearly-skeletal head, from which snorts of vapour gusted rhythmically.

Looking further upwards—his gorget now digging into his neck uncomfortably—Bugen saw the creature's crowning travesty. Where a rider would normally sit there was instead a legless hu-manoid torso, also totally flayed. The priest could not tell if this hideous addition was grown there or grafted on, but he did know that the result was odious in the extreme. Whatever had made or bred this *thing* was evil.

The rider's helmeted head—adorned with the antlers of a stag—turned here and there as it strove to catch sight of its quarry. After a moment the whole creature wheeled to its right and inspected the crystalline bushes growing there by pushing leaves aside with the haft of the icy halberd it clutched in its clawed hands. A few jabs of the wicked spike assured the rider that nobody was hiding in there. Bugen was beginning to feel like discovery was inevitable.

There was movement next to him. Turning his head carefully—he did not want to have his armour inadvertently clink and give away their position—he saw that Ed was tensed up and crouched as if ready to pounce on the creature whilst its backs were turned. Vera was tugging on the hunter's sleeve, trying wordlessly to convince him that this was a very flawed idea. Meanwhile, Alfazar was looking undecided, as if he had reservations but was still ready to back Ed up if need be.

Artyom, on the other hand, was gazing blankly into the middle-distance, looking totally detached from their predicament. Bugen puzzled over this for a moment before he recognised what was going on; Tamtem was missing.

Bugen carefully reached out and tapped Ed on the shoulder. Having gained his attention, the priest shook his head slightly and flicked his gaze towards Artyom. Ed threw a look towards the Fae monstrosity, which had finished inspecting the other side of the path, then glanced back at Artyom. Bugen could practically hear Ed's thoughts. *Hurry up, you blasted mage!* they shouted.

The rider was nearly upon them—Bugen grasped his sword tightly, ready to spring up into the creature's belly—when a tinkling sound floated down from further along the path. Antlers twisted as the rider turned towards the noise, and its halberd came up into a defensive position. Its breaths caught, then resumed.

After a few tense moments another bush rustled, a little further away this time. The naked one stood as though undecided, its humanoid head turning briefly back towards the travellers' hiding spot. Sweat ran down Bugen's back and his leg ached from the awkward crouching position. Finally, the horse's head huffed, spraying an enormous gout of fog into the chill air, and the entire Fae beast moved off in the direction of the offending noise. Bugen was so surprised by the snort that he nearly yelped involuntarily, but—Sol be praised—he managed to suppress that reaction.

Nobody dared speak or move for another few minutes, though it felt like much longer. The temperature rose palpably, and the little snow that had fallen vanished as if it had never been.

Eventually, Tamtem returned, slinking carefully from tree to tree and avoiding brushes with the undergrowth. Artyom woke from his apparent daze and scratched behind Tamtem's ears, then fished out a small edible treat for the familiar. "Well done," the mage smiled. Everyone visibly relaxed, and Bugen took the opportunity to finally seat himself properly. Ed did not put away his kukri, but he seemed fairly satisfied that Vera was not about to betray them just now.

When he was done taking a swig from his costrel, Bugen— motivated by habit more than real concern—wordlessly offered Vera a drink, which she demurred with a shake of her head. "I drank yesterday," she explained briefly, leaving Bugen puzzled.

Yesterday? And why was her hair so odd? In the moonlight it was difficult to tell, but Bugen could have sworn that it was clumped together in thick bunches which hung heavily from her skull.

"I must leave," Vera continued abruptly, rising to her feet and replacing her shawl.

"Not so fast," Ed grumbled. "You've got some explaining to do."

"And it seems we are in your debt, Vera. Thank you," Alfazar put in smoothly.

"Aye," Bugen echoed, still wondering about the hair.

"Yes," nodded Artyom.

"Fine. Thanks," the hunter sulked. "But still: answers."

"Be quick," Vera sighed, glancing around nervously.

Artyom's curiosity was piqued by the beast. "How does he make them?"

"The riders? He does not," Vera answered, face wrinkled in disgust. "He may... modify them, but Naked Ones existed long before Him. They are a type of Fae *so* corrupt and evil that they willingly work for the Red One."

"What is it doing here? Is their master near?" Bugen asked, skin crawling. If these abhorrent creatures worked for this Red One, how terrible must he be?

Vera's paranoia did nothing to help the priest's nerves. "It is searching for you. He has many agents," she said, glancing up at the trees. "But though he watches, I do not think He is near."

That was at least a little comfort.

"Many agents," Ed repeated, stroking his beard. "So nowhere is safe in this place?"

"There are few places of safety anymore," Vera responded solemnly. "In fact, this place is not on that list. I must leave." She turned to go.

"Blast! Will you not help us?" Ed hissed angrily.

"The dryads can answer your questions. They live beyond the Lake. Fare thee well!"

It did not seem to take long for them to reach the lake which Vera mentioned: the one they had seen from the cliff. The moon loomed monstrously, reflected in the lake's surface. No waves lapped at its unearthly shore. Not even a ripple could be seen. However, the curious water paled into insignificance next to the strangeness of the thing located at the precise centre of Esra'Nell.

Bugen could not decide what the object was, or even if it was an object at all. It floated half a foot or so above the water's surface, and stretched up perhaps six feet. At first it seemed to be a hanging silvery orb, but the longer one looked the more confused one became. It was evidently not solid, for it seemed to flow like smoke caught in a bubble, yet its ethereal outline was quite well defined. Bugen eventually gave up on trying to comprehend the device and simply accepted its absurdity.

Even as he looked the orb shone, and it seemed to Bugen that some doorway opened at its centre. Unfolding from this point came a shape which grew rapidly in size. Bugen caught a flash of pink and then, with a strange twist, out stepped a humanoid figure.

The party stared at the creature from across the water, and it stared back. Bugen could not fathom how it did not sink into the lake below. Its body was almost uniformly flesh-coloured, a tad too pink for a human, and it stood perhaps five feet tall at most. The legs, arms and torso were those of a normal man, but the large head and wide, panicked eyes were of a horse. This whole disparate ensemble glistened as though wet.

The creature glanced down at the bundle in its arms, then turned and ran full-tilt towards the forest. Artyom, not waiting to consult with his companions, took off around the gravelly shoreline. Ed immediately followed, whistling to Buhbuh and pointing at the creature. Meanwhile, Alfazar and Bugen exchanged a confused look before following with weapons drawn.

"What is it carrying?" Bugen asked as loudly as he dared, in case the rider was still nearby.

"A child," called back Artyom, pounding along the water's edge.

The pursued creature had managed to reach the treeline and Bugen briefly lost sight of it. Fortunately, Buhbuh demonstrated his Fae-hunting prowess. The large dog rapidly outpaced the group, and once close enough he pounced upon the creature's back and began worrying its leg. Bugen watched through a gap in the trees as he ran to catch up; the child had been dropped but had not stirred or cried out, whereas the Fae shrieked and spit at Buhbuh. Ichor ran from a bloody wound on its leg, and Bugen was surprised to see that the fluid was red.

Ed and Artyom reached the area first. The hunter immediately stood between the child and its erstwhile captor, whilst the mage ran to check on what Bugen could now see was a little girl. He guessed she might be five years old or so; about the same age he was when the Fae tried to take Elanor.

The mage made a cursory inspection and turned to the concerned priest. "She appears to be fine," he said in a matter-of-fact tone. "I have heard of a type of Fae beguiling magick which matches her symptoms. She is unconscious, but it should be reversible."

The priest was glad of this fact, although the effect was slightly creepy; the girl's brown eyes were wide open, and she blinked occasionally. "No wounds?" Bugen enquired, to which Artyom just shook his head before answering.

"Doesn't appear to be."

Artyom arranged the girl a little more comfortably on the ground—not that she would be aware of it—and stood. He and Bugen turned their attention back to the others.

Ed was kicking the Fae creature with bloodlust in his eyes, although Bugen now knew the man well enough to see that Ed was restraining himself. Still, he seemed to be glad to have an object on which to focus his wrath.

Bugen resolved to step in if the hunter went overboard.

The creature was hissing and spluttering in some strange, sibilant language. From the gesturing, and Ed's replies, the priest surmised that the pink Fae was swearing at its captors.

"Say what about me mum!"

Hissing...

"Say what about me *dog*? Then ye shouldn't have run, eh?"

"What is it saying?" Artyom asked.

"Just cursing at Buhbuh an' me... an' Mum," Ed replied, giving another kick for good measure. He then whistled to Buhbuh and made a circling gesture with his hand, instructing the dog to check their perimeter. With one last longing look at the Fae, Buhbuh obeyed.

Tamtem popped onto Artyom's shoulder and perched there like a furry parrot.

"You can speak with it Ed?" queried the bard. "I can catch some of its meaning, but the dialect is unfamiliar."

"Yeah, I can speak with this thing."

"What is it?"

"A kelpie." Ed's pronouncement was met with silence, although Artyom nodded knowingly. "Some kinda water Fae; one cut me up a few weeks ago. You'd know all about that, eh Bugen?"

"Aye," replied the priest, remembering back to the *Steadfast*.

After a pause the hunter continued, reluctantly. "Well, that's all I know about 'em."

"Ask it what it was doing with the child," Alfazar suggested, and Ed began interrogating. Bugen listened carefully, though he could only understand half of the conversation.

"What're you doin' with the kid, eh? Answer or I'll kick you! You've got to? Or The Reaper will take yours, eh? I don't care about ye blasted leg."

"Would you care to translate for the rest of us Ed?" Artyom put in sarcastically. The short hunter shot him a foul look but complied.

"It said it has to take the kid to The Reaper." Ed pulled a grotesque face and sketched quotation marks in the air with his hands. " 'Have to, have to, The Reaper, or me,' " he mimicked in a whiny voice. "It says that it's always been like that. If it doesn't take the kid then The Reaper will take it instead: or its kids."

Bugen felt like this statement was the icing on an already strange cake. If this short, wet creature was to be believed—which it might not be, Bugen reminded himself—the Fae were driven to abducting humans out of a desire to protect themselves and their own progeny from this Reaper. Somehow it made the odd horse-beast before him seem more human than alien.

"The Reaper is the being that the insane priest back in Adeline saw," mused Alfazar, who had sheathed his knife.

"Higgens. Alfonz Higgens," Bugen clarified, feeling compelled to remember the man's name.

"So this Reaper is here somewhere," Artyom mused.

"Where is the child from?" Bugen asked Ed; the priest had moved to watch over the girl during the conversation because it occurred to him that four people intent on one Fae creature might miss another which wanted to snatch the bewitched child.

Ed relayed his question to the kelpie. "It says it came through 'the shiny' and that the kid was on the other side..."

Bugen felt a species of disappointment, but guessed he should not be surprised by the vague answer.

Ed continued to listen to the Fae, then translated for his companions. "The 'shiny' links through to water it seems. It says it goes to every ocean, stream, river, lake, puddle of p... you get the picture."

Another fit of hissing and spluttering came from the kelpie, though it made no threatening move. If anything it seemed more tired and afraid than threatening. Its webbed hands gesticulated into the forest, and a few red fins strewn around its body wobbled futilely. "It says it can take us to Her," Ed said cautiously. "The Reaper." Evidently the creature understood, for it began nodding vigorously, and appeared less stressed than before. Artyom responded first.

"So let's go. There won't be anything untoward waiting for us. In fact, taking the directions of this Fae to this Reaper lady is the best idea we have had in a long time." The mage's comments dripped sarcasm, but he threw Ed an exaggerated wink. Bugen realised that Artyom was banking on the kelpie having a poor grasp of the nuances of human conversation.

"You *can* take us to The Reaper, right?" Ed asked the creature again. Once more it nodded, and its face split into what might be described as a grin. "Do get real!" Ed told the kelpie forcefully, though he did not strike it. "Take us to the 'shiny'."

The only response from the Fae was more hissing. This time even Bugen could see that it was protesting about its mangled leg. Ed stepped aside with a sigh and asked the priest if he could heal the creature enough to let it walk. Bugen complied; he called upon Sol and trickled Her energy through to the creature, stopping short of healing it fully so that it could not run without causing itself pain. The Fae's story lodged in the cleric's mind, causing him to feel some pity for it as it rose to its feet and tested its stance. Still, caution was warranted.

"Put this 'ere rope on for now," Ed commanded the creature; it slipped the lasso over its shoulder and under an arm without complaint, seemingly resigned to its fate.

Artyom walked into the Fae's line of sight and addressed it as one might address an idiot. "Now you"—pointing at the kelpie—"take us"—casting a hand around the group—"to the portal."

The party moved out and trundled back towards the lake. Ed and Artyom were in the lead, just behind the kelpie; Alfazar came up behind with Bugen, who was carrying the child in his arms. She breathed deeply and regularly, oblivious to her predicament. Probably a good thing, Bugen thought.

"Quit dragging yer feet," grumbled the hunter, occasionally tugging on the rope to make the Fae go faster.

They were back within view of the 'shiny' when Artyom stopped suddenly. Everyone else followed suit, though the Fae only did so because the rope pulled taut. It was visibly disappointed, and kept throwing glances towards the otherworldly orb. "Doesn't it seem a bit daft to lead a water Fae back to the water?" the mage queried generally. His companions all exchanged looks and began nodding, glad that the mage was so attentive.

"Perhaps we can put it to better use," Alfazar mused. "Know you the way to the dryads' grove?" he asked it, not unkindly. The kelpie looked truculent for a moment—though it was hard for Bugen to read the expression on the horse face—then indicated yes, though not with the vigour it displayed before. The young cleric wondered if this meant that the kelpie thought the dryads were less likely to kill him and his friends than The Reaper was.

With somewhat of a start Bugen realised that he had not heretofore thought of the three men as his friends. How quickly things can change. He gave thanks for their bond, despite their differences.

"Sounds good to me," Ed opined. "Let's do it."

Artyom again stepped up, and in an obnoxiously loud voice he commanded (complete with gestures) "Take us... to... the dryads." The mage finished with his hands above his head, fingers spread to mimic tree branches. Bugen did not know whether to laugh or cry at the lad's behaviour, so he remained impassive instead.

The kelpie shuffled off with a roll of its eyes and a huff which sounded like a wet neigh. It walked roughly around the circumference of the lake, though far enough away that only occasional glimpses were seen through the trees. These glimpses seemed to alternately excite and upset the Fae, which edged steadily closer to the water until Ed instructed Buhbuh to walk between it and the shoreline.

Bugen's arms were beginning to feel the weight of the girl, but he persisted. To distract himself he asked Ed to explain what he knew of dryads. The reply was encouraging. "Dryads are forest Fae which look like trees and suchlike. They act as guardians of forest life, 'specially plants, and trees most of all. From what I've heard they're usually pretty benign. Some keep humans or humanoids around as guards for the dryads' dwellings. Said humans are basically their vassals. They're sometimes magickally drugged into doing their job, but they get a great life in exchange."

From the tone Bugen realised that Ed was genuinely jealous of these putative magickally-compelled forest people. It warmed his heart to see Ed's genuine appreciation of nature, even if the hunter seemed unable to articulate it in as many words.

As they walked the companions and their hostage all noticed that the forest grew more dense, and that the many trees were taller than elsewhere. Though their trunks were definitely unnaturally enormous, Bugen could not help but feel that the forest was growing more *normal* as they walked on. The biggest difference, he decided, was that the trees had regular, rough bark in warm brown hues; it seemed more vivacious than the anaemic grey he had seen everywhere else in Esra'Nell. The Sun also seemed to be rising again, which added a further layer of colour.

Artyom stopped again, pulling the party to a halt. "These dryads... will they be understanding if we bring a bound prisoner into their midst? Do they get along with kelpies?" he asked of the others. A short discussion ensued; Ed was for killing the kelpie, but he was talked out of it by the others, who argued that they were so close to the dryads now (maybe) that killing the kelpie would be unwise.

They only stopped when Ed noticed that Buhbuh had stopped pacing and was instead staring fixedly at the kelpie. "Oi!" he cried as he jerked the end of the rope, causing the kelpie to lose eye contact with the dog. "Trying to bewitch him. Ugh!"

Buhbuh snapped out of it pretty quickly, but the large dog seemed unusually buoyant for a few hours afterwards.

"Let's cut our losses," Alfazar suggested. "Just let the beast go; it seems incapable of doing much harm, and I doubt it is in cahoots with that cold, naked horse creature."

The group soon reached consensus, and Ed commanded the kelpie to remove its bonds. Once free it did not even spare a backward glance, but ran directly for the lake as quickly as its tender leg allowed.

"There," Artyom said, hands spread in the direction of their former prisoner. "Now the dryads will know we mean no harm. The worst that can happen is that they take us for sex slaves."

This pronouncement, delivered with matter-of-fact certainty, was too much for the priest, who broke into immoderate laughter. He laughed at the absurdity of the situation, laughed at the fact that nobody had ever said such a thing in his presence before, laughed for the joy of being capable of laughter despite the terror inside. The young girl lolled nervelessly in his arms.

When he regained his composure Bugen gave a pained grin. "Shall we press on?"

"Yes, we shall," Artyom replied, one finger raised pedantically. "And remember, we are entering the dryads' domain! Every tree, every branch, every bush—why, even every *mushroom*—must be treated as though holy in their sight." He ticked off each item as he spoke.

Soon the undergrowth grew thicker, and the air more redolent with the smells of a normal wood. Ed was in his element, moving through the forest with scarcely a noise as he revelled in the sights and sounds of small animals. Good, wholesome, mundane creatures were here: birds chirped, insects sung, and frogs called to one another. To Ed—and even to the others, who had less experience in woodlands—this part of the forest felt less 'otherworldly' and more 'super-worldly', as if this was the standard which all other forests failed to quite live up to.

The going became tough and Bugen stopped briefly to hang the girl over one shoulder instead of carrying her in his arms. He trudged off after the others without any finesse, constantly becoming entangled, and having to skirt the bigger bushes in his path. As a result he did not see the large mushroom in his path until his foot had already come down on it and squashed half of its cap into the ground.

By fortune Artyom had been glancing back to check on the priest at that very moment. The mage's eyes went wide, theatrically, and he dropped to his knees. "Bugen, no! I told you there would be mushrooms... You better hope the dryads forgive you for squashing their holy mushroom!"

The young priest just looked at Artyom incredulously whilst mirth and anger waged a brief internal war. "Well you'll have to forgive me," he said tightly. "Did it occur to you that I'm a little more encumbered than you?" Bugen tried to not be sarcastic.

"He's got a fair point," Ed chimed in as he joined the pair. "Hand her over for a bit Bugen; I know what I'm doing in the forest.

"Don't worry about the mushroom, it'll be fine," he added under his breath as he took her from the priest. He slung the child over his shoulder and resumed walking. Artyom turned and continued too.

Tamtem, riding on Artyom's shoulder, looked back at Bugen. He pointed at the priest, then smashed one tiny fist into his other paw, mimicking Bugen standing on the mushroom. The familiar finished by shaking his head emphatically. Bugen wondered if this was Tamtem's own little performance, or if Artyom was somehow instructing him. He shook his head and fell in with the group.

Unseen by anyone, Buhbuh skulked around for a moment more and gobbled up the mushroom before trotting back to the front of the party.

Alfazar's introspection was only broken when an awful noise began. What was... was that Ed *singing*?

Hi ho, hi ho,
It's off to the dryads we go!

The bard winced and screwed up his face; Ed's pathetic singing was an insult to Alfazar's very profession! "What *are* you doing?" he asked pointedly.

Ed stopped his song, giving his companions a reprieve. "Just lettin' 'em know we're 'ere," he said without a trace of embarrassment. "And that we're comin' with peaceful intentions and what-not."

"What do they do to those without peaceful intentions?" Alfazar queried.

Ed pondered for a moment, then answered. "From what I've heard they will try to enchant people to sleep, then remove them from their lands. Otherwise, if they've really made a mess of things, the dryads turn them into good fertiliser."

Charming.

Ed resumed his soft warbling—Bugen hesitated to call it singing—as they continued. Instead of falling silent, the small creatures of the forest seemed to respond positively to the unusual noise, as though they understood Ed's words and were glad to hear them.

The atmosphere continued to grow thicker as the trees became larger, but the air remained fresh, and it was not dark on the forest floor despite the enormous boughs overhead. Grateful to be unencumbered, Bugen did much better than before, though he still made so much noise that the mage started referring to him as 'old leadfoot'.

Abruptly the troupe came upon a small clearing planted with thick, green turf. In its centre was a sunken bowl-like area with a fence of mossy rocks arranged around it. Without prompting from Ed, Buhbuh stopped and sat before the mysterious ring. Alfazar and Artyom filed into the clearing next, followed by Bugen.

"This feels like the spot," Ed whispered, looking around with wide eyes. "The mixture of tree types 'ere: it's not natural. More like a garden."

Even as he spoke there came soft noises from all around, including overhead: here a cracking, there a susurration, and over yonder a scratching. Bugen watched, enthralled, as a branch quivered and rippled along its length, revealing what were recognisably arms and legs of some tree-being. The thing—Bugen supposed it was a dryad—dropped to the ground and alighted elegantly, as if the twenty-foot fall were nothing to it. The priest's attention was immediately caught by another dryad; this one extricated itself from the earth at the base of a mighty tree, where it had been masquerading as a root. Others seemed to extrude from trunks, and some poked inquisitive heads from within hollows at the bases of huge branches.

Within moments Ainsworth's band of adventurers were surrounded by dozens of the graceful dryads. A handful of larger ones, tall and thin, advanced towards Ed and stopped near enough to touch the hunter, who looked stumpy by comparison. With no regard for his personal space, they leant in close and inspected him and the child he carried. The ranger held his ground and resisted the urge to reach for a weapon. "We come in harmony," he said.

Bugen maintained a passive face, but mentally cocked an eyebrow; he'd always thought the line was, 'We come in peace.'

"Sorry about your mushroom," Artyom cut in before the dryads could reply.

"Whose mushroom?" replied a dryad who wore the appearance of a woman in perhaps her thirtieth year. She looked vivacious but stately, and had small flowers arranged throughout her long hair. "I don't have a... do any of you have a mushroom?" she asked the other dryads lightly. A few distinguishable 'no's were given in response, along with much muttering and shaking of leafy heads; it sounded like a light wind passing through the clearing. The tree-woman bent down closer to Artyom. "We tend this grove," she said solemnly, "and maintain its balance. One mushroom is a loss we can recoup." She smiled gently and Bugen was surprised to see that her face was supple enough to allow her cheeks and eyes to crinkle; he had expected a wooden creature to be more deadpan. She straightened and addressed all of the strangers, saying, "Welcome. What may we do for you, travellers?"

"We wish to know of The Reaper," Ed simply stated, trusting that the dryads meant no harm. As a gesture of trust, he moved over to one of the enormous trees and gently propped the girl up against it. When he stood again he saw that tree-woman seemed at a loss, but then she gave a single nod.

"We cannot tell you of The Reaper," she began, making Bugen's heart sink. "But we will fetch an elder who can."

Then the dozens of dryads in the clearing spread back into the forest, sinking into trees and roots, and were gone. It was so fast that Bugen was still mentally catching up when Ed caught his attention. The hunter was looking up into the trees overhead, where he spied great fruit and the occasional massive bough, larger than seemed physically possible.

"Some of those branches don't seem ta come from any tree in particular." With the dryads apparently gone, Ed had reverted to reverent whispering.

One of said branches quivered and cracked, then a large shard of it fell to the ground and landed in the circle. It stuck upright in the turf. Then, with a groaning which sounded like an old man waking from sleep, the top half drooped towards the ground. Suddenly Bugen could see the outline of a humanoid figure bent and stooped by age. Leaving some fragments of bark on the grassy floor, the outline resolved into a fully-limbed body. The dryad turned and regarded the companions with wise eyes. Bugen was shocked and somewhat amused to see that the walking stick which the creature carried was in fact grown directly from its hand. The elder coughed a few times, shaking loose some orange leaves from his bushy beard, and then went to speak.

"Sorry about the mushroom," Artyom cut in again, and Bugen suppressed a groan.

"The loss is lamentable, though I will not mourn over-long," the tree-man responded, speaking slowly and giving the words an odd lilt.

"See Bugen? You trod on the *elder*'s mushroom!" Artyom and Tamtem both pointed accusingly at the priest. "Leadfoot," the mage confided to the dryad, shaking his head. "City boy."

"Apologies," Bugen said to the elder, bowing slightly from the waist as he tried to suppress his irritation. The priest realised that the Fae would tower over him if it stood up straight, and that it had probably been alive for many, many human lifetimes.

"As I said," the dryad responded, waving the hand which was not sprouting a walking stick, "think it of no consequence."

Bugen bowed again.

"I can answer your questions," wheezed the ancient Fae as he hobbled to the centre of the clearing, "but you will soon have to leave this place."

"We want to know about The Reaper," Alfazar stated succinctly and respectfully.

"Ah, yes. The Reaper," mused the hunched fellow. "The Reaper is our friend."

Chapter 7

The Reaper

Gnome: little childlike buggers with big noses and funny hats. No strength or magick. Not dangerous alone. <u>Never alone</u>. Like living with other Fae. Good at repairing stuff. ~~Sometimes~~ armed with little hammers.

Faun: funny goat-human critters. Human top, goat bottom, and silly little beards. Agile. Can trick people with their <u>music and dancing</u>, but easy in a <u>fight</u>. Like forests and green grass. Pinches kids by dancing them to sleep.

<u>Spriggan: small</u> but <u>very heavy</u>. Bouncers for bigger Fae or special Fae spots. ~~Bards say~~ able to <u>grow huge when angered!</u> Some carry <u>little bottles of sorcerers fire!</u>

*Bauchan: dangerous little bastards, like Brounies, only more pissed-off. **<u>Did Dad in with poison daggers</u>**. Squishy, once you get hold of them...*

Kelpie: Water Fae. Like a Centaur, But upside down—Manish body with an asses head.

Ragged sheet of parchment found in Findlay's Inn stables

ॴ   ৶✕৶   ৶✕৶   ৶৶৶৶৶ ✕ ৶৶৶৶৶   ৶✕৶   ৶✕৶   ৶

149

UGEN'S mind reeled and he tensed instinctively; The Reaper was a *friend*? He could not process the statement, nor reconcile it with the apparently gentle old being before him. How could the dryads countenance the wholesale slaughter of humans—especially human *children*—and other Fae? The priest experienced an uncharacteristic flush of anger, followed by a deep confusion. Uncertainty sank its roots into him, paralysing his decisiveness and sapping his will to act on the strange wrath.

"The Reaper does what is necessary," continued the old Fae, as though the atmosphere were not charged with tension. He was gazing vaguely into the forest, recalling the past. "She has done so for many, many moons, even by the reckoning of Fae," he murmured. Then his awareness seemed to hurtle back into the present, and he made very deliberate eye contact with each of the companions in turn. Gravely, he elaborated. "Her job is to maintain the balance, now that we Fae are immortal." The old creature turned away at the last, as though upset or embarrassed by the fact.

"Now that the Fae are immortal?" Artyom repeated rhetorically. Bugen found it curious that the mage was showing a recognisable measure of respect to the ancient dryad. "I thought the Fae were always immortal. At least compared to humans."

The hunched dryad turned back to the group and straightened somewhat, looming over Artyom. "And so most creatures are, compared to humans. But you misunderstand me, child; when I say 'immortal' I mean precisely that. Truly, no Fae now dies save those caught by misfortune or the ill-intent of others. We do not wither, nor rot. Our bodies do not fail, and no pestilence takes us." By this stage the elder sat on one of the larger boundary stones, hunched nearly into a semicircle. "At first many were overjoyed and thought of immortality as a gift. Some of us rejoiced. But many of us came to recognise it as a curse." He laughed grimly, then stopped to cough for a moment. "I do not expect you young ones to understand," he continued when he recovered. "Especially you, humans. But consider this: what would become of human realms if your race was to become immortal? You breed faster than us—even faster than the lesser Fae. Your cities would overflow, your lands become barren, your people threaten war with one another once more.

"So it was with we Fae. Our immortality angered Death, and we must now pay the price for the Red One's meddlings. Because of this The Reaper is our friend: she maintains our account."

Bugen stood, still tense but no longer frightened. So much of the dryad's careful explanation made sense, yet there were so many gaps in the priest's knowledge that he did not have the faintest inkling of how to go about filling them. Ed and Alfazar, it seemed, were equally paralysed by the creature's revelations.

The mage, on the other hand, waited only a moment before asking "Who is this 'Red One'?"

"A Fae born bearing the mark of Death. His coming was prophesied many centuries ago by, of all things, a sick gnome on its death-bed. Would you believe? At any rate, it was foretold that the Red One would invite death and destruction into the world. And when the child was born, that is what he did. He meddled in the affairs of Death, and as payment for our inability to control him we have the Tithe. We—all Fae—must pay for the deeds of the Red One."

Artyom was sitting and scribbling this down madly, so Alfazar continued the conversation instead. "The Reaper: is she Fae?"

A faint rustling and creaking accompanied the dryad's response in the negative. "She is mortal."

"What is this place?" Ed questioned, trying to bring things back to a level that he could comprehend without straining a mental muscle. "How long have Fae been in Arcana anyway? There weren't supposed to be any Fae here."

"Fae have been here far longer than your people, little fellow," came the reply. "You might describe us as native to this isle."

"Then this is where all Fae are from in the first place?" exclaimed Artyom, looking up from his notes like a startled hare.

"More or less."

The mage jumped to his feet in one swift motion, upsetting his notebook and backpack in the process. With uncharacteristic vehemence he cried "Well done Uncle, you total *idiot!*" and threw his pencil to the ground. Bugen sympathised with him; the priest too was liking Ainsworth less and less with each passing moment.

The dryad regained its feet carefully and wheezed "Are you alright, lad?"

"Yes, I'm fine." After a moment Artyom relented, and added, "My adopted uncle is the human who discovered your island and began its... resettlement. He is responsible for a rather great mess, I'm afraid."

In response, the dryad simply laid a gentle hand on the mage's shoulder. It was an extremely human gesture, and it dispelled a great deal of Bugen's unease.

"Children, we cannot talk much longer, for we dryads must prepare for the Tithe." This brought Bugen's unease surging back, with interest.

"With respect," Bugen began, wondering at his own nerve, "how do you prepare for the Tithe?"

"You care for the child," observed the elderly dryad, who was peering intently at Bugen. "Be at ease. She is safe with us."

"How then do you meet the Tithe?" asked Alfazar, who had heretofore been content with listening attentively.

"The dryads are few in number. We select from our own: elders who have lived long and full lives. They go willingly to The Reaper."

Bugen found himself deeply moved, and his fears evaporated like frost before a flame. He realised that the creature before him was likely going to meet its doom within the week. It was a humbling thought, and revealed much of the creature's character. As

Ed had supposed, these dryads were not bloodthirsty monsters; in fact, they were a great deal more temperate than most men.

Ed missed the implications of the dryad's explanation. His mind was working over something else the tree-geezer had said. "Whaddya mean, 'angered Death'?" the short hunter queried, voice respectful but sceptical. "You speak of Death like it's a person."

"Death could be several people... or rather, several gods," Bugen clarified. "This Red One seems to have interfered with one of them."

"Isn't it obvious?" Artyom piped up. "The Red One is the spanner in the death works."

"Spanner in the..." repeated Bugen as he cocked an eyebrow at the mage.

"In the works of the different death gods. Listen, what do you know of the death gods?" Artyom was becoming quite animated as he mentally worked through whatever line of thought he was following.

"Not much," the priest admitted grudgingly. "Sol is the one source of life; the death gods are lesser than She. We were taught the names and symbols of the more powerful of them, and learnt of the dangers of necromancy."

"Sure got your blinkers on there, priesty-buddy. Allow me to explain." The mage stood again, stretched, and cracked his hands in preparation, evidently enjoying being more knowledgeable than his clerical companion.

"Right. There are multiple death gods—as you said, there is only one way into this life, but many ways out. As a result, each death god has their own... fetish, if you will. War, pestilence, famine, *et cetera*. It's how they collect souls and gain power.

"So, let's imagine one of the death gods likes eating pickles, and another prefers olives." The mage indicated to his left and right respectively. "Everything is okay so long as they don't try to eat off each other's plates.

"Problems start when the Earl of Extra Virgin tries to move in on his fermented friend's territory." Artyom mimed plucking a pickle from his left and transferring it to an imaginary plate on his opposite side. "The Pickle Master spots a missing snack and goes,

'I say, did you take my pickle old chap?' " Artyom turned towards the right and affected an accent which seemed somewhat aristocratic: it vividly reminded Bugen of some Elandrian gentry he had met on a previous assignment. "And then the Olive Oily One says, 'Heavens no. You know pickles aren't my thing. Olives are. Why, I'm even the *God* of Olives!' " This new unctuous voice evoked images of a scrawny weasel of a sycophant in an overly-fashionable outfit. Still in character, Artyom gave an unconvincing chuckle, and the young cleric amusedly wondered if Artyom was thinking of Ignatius too.

"But this is not enough to satisfy the Prince of Pickles," lectured the arcanist. "He's still suspicious, so *he*'s like, 'Very well, but one of my pickles is missing,' and the Olive Overlord goes, 'Wasn't me.' Then, 'Are you sure?' 'Quite sure.' 'I think you're lying,' 'No-no-no. What could possibly give you that impression?' " Artyom paused to let the tension build a little—not as adeptly as Alfazar, it would have to be said—before continuing. "Then His Great Gherkinship leans in and takes a big whiff. 'I can smell it on your breath!' "

Bugen hoped that maybe the mage would get to the point soon. " 'Lies! Have at you!' " Artyom put up his fists and, in his clipped Pickle God voice, he bawled, " 'Scurvy knave! I will press you to pulp! Hya!' "

Bugen and the others looked on as Artyom enacted a small brawl between what were apparently the Minor Deities of Delicious Death. After a few moments the punches, vulgar gesticulation and incoherent insults trailed off into a series of small whimpering and choking noises. Artyom terminated the performance with the Picker of Pickles suffocating the King of Kalamata by stuffing fistfuls of preserved cucumbers down his throat. "And that's what I meant by 'spanner in the death works'," Artyom proudly concluded.

Buhbuh scratched at his ear, but all else was silent for some moments.

The dryad in particular had no idea what to make of this display. The elderly tree-spirit shook its head in confusion. "I do not understand. Is he alright?" the ancient creature asked Ed with evident concern. "I have heard tell of a 'stroke' before, but never have I seen the symptoms..."

"He's fine," Ed assured the old Fae. One hand run over the stocky hunter's head spoke of his frustration. "What's your point Arty?"

"I begin to see," Alfazar said. "You think this Red One–"

"Yes, that's exactly right Alfazar. I think this Red One is the Mover of Pickles."

The group spent another hour or so arguing amongst themselves and discussing with the elderly dryad. A few of the younger Fae joined them also, but they knew little lore and could not answer the travellers' questions. These ones were content to watch and listen, or to amuse themselves by petting Tamtem and Buhbuh.

After the mage's little 'Gods of Antipasto' episode the conversation had turned to whether there was a specific god whom had previously managed the mortality of Fae; the consensus answer was 'no', though this conclusion was highly speculative. The dryad then made a passing remark about undead, which steered the discussion into the realms of forbidden lore. Bugen explained that necromancy—that dark art which twisted dead flesh into a shallow but terrifying facsimile of life—was prohibited by Elandrian law, yet many darker worshippers of Death still practised it. He was astounded to learn that the banshees which appeared during the Festival of the White Lady were in fact undead Fae. Moreover, they were undead Fae which were not under the control of The Reaper, or so the tree-spirit seemed to think; it insisted that the banshees only appeared because The Reaper's power was otherwise occupied during the Festival. This confirmed that the Festival of the White Lady must coincide with the offering of the Tithe.

By the time the discussion concluded Bugen could feel that it was nearing sunset again, although he doubted the others would register the subtle change here in the peaceful glade with its strange lighting. After a moment of contemplation he amended the thought; Ed would probably notice.

Bugen's armour weighed unusually heavily on him. Perhaps it was just the sheer weight of outlandish information which he had absorbed over the past day. It seemed to settle on his shoulders like a physical presence, and the young priest resolved to spend some time working through its implications.

"Friends, you must rest," the elderly dryad finished. "You have our leave to remain here for some days hence, so long as you do not interrupt our preparations. Leave the girl in her enchanted sleep until you are ready to leave; she will require no nourishment in this state. When you ask, we will take you to The Reaper."

Ed surprised his companions by bowing to the tree-spirit. "Thank yee kindly."

Everybody else added their thanks. Then Artyom sat and sleepily scribed some further notes; the bard lay with his hands behind his head, contemplating the leaves above; Ed whistled softly and scratched behind Buhbuh's ears; and Bugen unbuckled his armour and lay down to sleep. His last sight before drifting off was the elderly dryad being gently hoisted back into the canopy by a team of younger Fae.

He dreamed of wooden people being scythed down at the hands of a laughing giant swathed in darkness. The giant's bloody hands turned into a crimson moon, then that moon was obscured by the passage of a thousand pale wings as banshees flooded across the sky. They merged into a single field of white, which resolved into a bedspread dripping water. The bed was in a windswept shack. Bugen emerged from the shack and beheld Vera, who fled away across a lake without sinking. "He is far more terrible than you..."

Bugen rose, began his morning rituals, and remembered the dream not at all.

She awoke without transition. Where was she? Vague memories brushed at her conscience. She had been asleep and then had had a dream about a weird horse. She was quite sure it was talking to her, but she could not remember what it said. The strange horse then turned into a funny pink man, and she had wanted to wake up quite badly. The dream had continued for a few moments longer, and she recalled an impression of slimy wetness, then nothing more.

She scrunched her hands underneath her; this was not her bed! Focusing, she saw branches overhead—monstrous branches—and then she spotted a man crouched beside her. It was the pink man! She scrambled to her feet, wanting to escape, when another figure came into view. This one was intimidating too, and nearly as wide as it was tall. By this stage she was panicking in earnest, and beginning to cry. Where were Ma and Pa?

The second figure raised an arm and said some words that did not penetrate her brain. She shied away from the sudden glow which leapt from the figure's upraised hand, shielding her eyes from the painful light. Finding her feet, she ran towards the nearest cover she could see: a tree trunk. She ducked behind it and sobbed, worrying that the pink man and his giant friend would hear.

When she stopped wiping her eyes and looked up she saw a most unusual face. It seemed to be a woman—it reminded her of Ma, but made out of wood. "Be still, child," the face implored her gently. Some leaves and petals fell from above, leaving a faint perfume, and the woman straightened up.

The child beheld the dryad and was not afraid; in fact, when it reached out a hand she gladly took it and stood. The woman and the girl joined hands with a group of dryads, and together they danced gaily on the lawn.

"Tree roofies," Ed muttered, whilst Artyom rolled on the floor and laughed at Bugen.

"Is he alright?" a nearby dryad asked, looking at the mage with concern.

"Having performance issues, Bugen?" the mage managed to get out between fits of mirth. At this, Alfazar joined in the laughter, and even Ed gave a few guffaws. Bugen studiously pretended to not understand the double entendre. The dryad, nonplussed by this human behaviour, shrugged and moved off.

Bugen looked at his left hand, which was no longer glowing, and then across the clearing at the little girl who was now laughing and spinning in circles with the dryads. He was glad to see her smiling, but it still puzzled him that he had been unable to calm her fears with Sol's help.

"Not your usual audience, Bugen. Think nothing of it." Alfazar gave Bugen's shoulder a brief squeeze to drive home the encouraging comment.

"She will be well cared for here," Bugen said peacefully, turning to Alfazar and smiling. He was glad that the child was safe. "But we must move on."

The party had spent three strangely short days in that peaceful clearing after their audience with the elder. All of them felt an urgency to leave, despite the glade's beauty. Each had the impression that they were somehow standing on a pinnacle with doom all around, and only one clear path laid before them; they needed to confront The Reaper, and then maybe even this Red One. To do otherwise would lead to failure and death.

It was a shame, Bugen thought, that failure and death seemed to lay down all paths into their future.

A tall dryad, male in appearance, strode into the clearing. His skin was smooth and predominately grey, but light brown showed in places. His short beard had the look of lichen or moss. The young priest wondered if the dryad grew this 'facial hair' from its own body or if it cultivated actual lichen and moss in its place. Bugen stroked his own beard as he contemplated this, and was mildly put out by how unkempt he was. Still, a few days of untamed growth were the least of his concerns.

The creature bore wise, green eyes set into a solemn face which looked ready to break into boisterous song at any moment; it was a look common amongst the dryads. The eyes looked over the travellers and then in a reedy tenor the creature told them, "I have been sent to show you the path to The Reaper. You may call me Trimblewind." It gave a graceful bow.

"Greetings Trimblewind," Alfazar replied, matching the dryad's gesture.

"I already know your names, so let us not tarry. You must be on your way," Trimblewind explained in a firm but gentle voice.

The party reluctantly hoisted their packs and made some final checks on their gear. Bugen tested the buckles on his armour, and then confirmed that his sword and buckler, and the unnamed priestess' dagger, were at his belt. Finally, he extracted the rectangular amulet from underneath his gambeson, inspected its golden chain and clasp, then tucked it back out of sight. Ready.

As Trimblewind led them out of the dryads' grove the entire party could feel the forest grow less vibrant and welcoming. The feeling was especially strong for Ed, who was more attuned to nature than his companions. For Ed, the gradual increase in the number of unearthly, inorganic trees was like a growing chill. Bugen felt it too, though he could not point to the source of his unease in the same way that the hunter could. Not even Artyom spoke much.

After a quarter hour their guide stopped abruptly. "Here you will find the path, friends. The Reaper is not far, but we dryads dare not approach before our preparations for the Tithe are complete. Remember though: she is a friend."

In this bleak setting Bugen could not help but doubt Trimblewind's words, despite the good faith shown by all of the tree-spirits thus far. He chided himself for his lack of trust. "Go in peace."

"Thank you," Alfazar added.

"And your people too," Ed continued.

Trimblewind bowed once more and strode back towards the grove, vanishing rapidly.

Bugen sighed deeply and contemplated the path ahead.

"I know what you mean," Alfazar sympathised.

Strangely, the path reminded Bugen of the way up to the monastery which Priestess Sabine had delivered him to as a child. That particular monastery was perched atop a rocky pinnacle, creating a fortress-like structure protected on all sides by precipitous drops. Pilgrims and priests—often one and the same—ascended from the plains below by braving a set of stairs carved directly into the rock of the cliffs. Over the ages, since well before the Unification, these traipsing travellers had worn away at the rock of the stairs, until now the centre of each step was sunken and rounded by the passage of thousands of feet. So too was this pathway obviously well-trafficked and ancient; it sank nearly half the height of a man below the surrounding ground level, and its floor was hard-packed by the tramp of feet, hooves, fins, and whatever other exotic means of locomotion the Fae used.

He set off along the trail after the rest of his company. They travelled at a brisk pace for some twenty minutes without incident before Artyom halted at a spotless gate of wrought iron set across the path. He surveyed whatever it was that lay beyond for a moment, then turned to the rest of the party and said in a tight voice "Brace yourselves."

Heart sinking, pushed down by a growing foreboding, Bugen joined his friends at the gate and gazed out upon the scene before them.

He beheld a perfectly circular clearing, the antithesis of the dryads' grove. Where the grove had been verdant and teeming with life, this place was grey and desolate. No tree or plant grew within the circle; in fact, Bugen could see now that the trees arrayed about its perimeter bent up and away from it, as though they would depart the place if their roots would but permit them. Not even a branch protruded over the low wall bounding the clearing. The very air was filled with a clinging mist which drifted aimlessly, like a spectre of sterility hovering over the barren earth.

Yet there were strange shapes on the ground; bundles of various sizes, bound in white shrouds and lying haphazardly around the place. Bugen quickly realised that they were bodies, though from this distance he could not tell if they were quick or dead. The majority seemed to be children, judging by their stature.

In the midst of this madness was a most unexpected object. Where Bugen had expected to see a monstrous beast there was instead a dwelling. The small house of white-washed stone sat at the precise centre of the clearing. It too was circular, with a conical roof tiled in grey slate and punctured through by a chimney which released a faint stream of smoke that nobody, not even Ed, could smell in the air.

Each member of the company was stunned into silence by what they beheld. Each, in their own way, felt that here was a nexus of Death. The tableau drove any puerile conception of The Reaper from their minds. No longer did they picture her as some malevolent entity bearing an enormous scythe, revelling in the harvest of souls; instead, they came to understand that she might instead be dispassionate—that her brand of Death might no more celebrate the passing of a sentient life than a banker would celebrate striking a line from their ledger. Truly, Bugen began to understand what the old dryad meant by 'keeping an account'.

And yet, there was still threat. Here was a place where life was not snuffed out by the violent destruction of all the organs and pulsating operations of the body, but simply by the removal of the *prima vitae* itself.

Here was Death: cold, clean and efficient.

Artyom tried to place a hand on the gate, but it was repelled sharply.

"You have arrived, travellers," stated a voice. It might have issued from the air around them. "Though I am surprised at the routes you have taken."

Bugen cast around, looking for the speaker, and gripped his buckler for reassurance. He did not want to make any overtly threatening moves, but he was resolved to act if the need arose. He subvocalised a hasty prayer to Sol, yet again.

In the silence which followed Bugen considered the voice. It was feminine, dispassionate, and precise, as though every word was weighed and evaluated before being spoken. The utterance was utterly devoid of warmth or colour. Neither was it threatening, nor welcoming. It was grey, like the clearing before them, and it gave Bugen the chills.

"What do you want?" it probed, betraying a faint hint of curiosity. Bugen was now convinced that his ears were not involved at all with this eldritch mode of communication.

His companions exchanged glances quickly, trying to communicate silently. Meanwhile, Buhbuh edged closer to Ed and Tamtem wrapped himself around the mage's shoulders.

"We come to learn," Artyom answered resolutely after a few more moments.

"What a pleasant surprise. The last group were not so wise as you."

Suddenly, it became achingly clear to Bugen that there were four adult-sized, cloth-bound figures lying stacked inside the circle: apparently another one of Ainsworth's teams.

"They attempted violence upon me. Learn from their mistake, travellers." Again, this was just a statement of fact, not a threat. Then there came a faint *click*, and the pristine gate swung open. "You may enter. Do not leave the path or attempt to interfere with the bodies."

The party steeled themselves and crossed into the circle without a word to one another. They walked briskly along the path, gazes directed immediately ahead in an effort to shut out the cadaveric cocoons strewn across the clearing. The house's door swung open silently ahead of them. Bugen felt it would have been more appropriate for it to shriek in protest, like every nerve in his body. Trembling but not unmanned, the cleric stepped over the threshold.

Inside the house was a single large room. Bugen's first impression was of a library, for the entire space was littered with furled scrolls, thick grimoires, dignified tomes, loose folios, and even engraved tablets and plaques. The warmth of the leather bindings complemented the rich brown of the enormous wooden bookcase encompassing the room, lending the scene some much-appreciated warmth and colour. The floor was decorated only by these repositories of knowledge. Otherwise, it stepped up in tiers from the entrance and came to a peak on the far side of the room. At its apex was set a stone desk of about chest height, and resting upon it was a large book. Behind this was a statue of matching stone in the form of a grey figure dressed in black robes. It was seemingly bowed over the volume before it.

Bugen cast around, seeking any movement, but saw nothing alive. Judging from their frustrated expressions, Ed and Alfazar's visual inspection had also been in vain. Meanwhile, Artyom was standing slack-jawed, ogling the copious volume of knowledge surrounding him; he could read titles including *On the Balance of the World vol. X*, *History of Natural Arcane magick vol. I–XV* and *A Conjurer's Compendium: Revision VII*. Despite their circumstances, the mage was practically drooling.

The companions gingerly made their way towards the reading statue, sensing that this was the focal point of the room.

When Bugen was within three paces of the pedestal the voice spoke again. "What is your purpose?" Simultaneously, the reader raised its head and stood more erect. Everyone stared in amazement at the ersatz statue come to life.

Under the raised black hood could be seen a foreboding face. Its skin was pale and ashen, a match for the irises set into pure white orbs. The eyes fixated each traveller in turn, swivelling between them without any motion of the head, and then two grey hands rose and pulled the dark cowl back. This revealed a head of long grey hair held back by two small plaits. With a start, Bugen realised that this was precisely the way he wore his hair. Furthermore, the figure's exposed ears were slightly up-swept and gently pointed.

"You are a grey elf," Alfazar stated.

Bugen had never interpreted *grey elf* in such a literal way before.

"Indeed. And I ask again: what is your purpose?"

"Ms Reaper, we want to learn," Artyom stated once more, apparently fearless.

"Indeed." She eyed Artyom for a moment. "Tell me then: what do you wish to learn?"

"Who our enemy is," Ed answered with trepidation and anticipation.

"The Red One," Alfazar clarified.

The Reaper gathered her thoughts for a moment, shutting her disquieting eyes. "He has watched you this past week, as have I. Fear not: he cannot eavesdrop on our counsel here. You may ask what you wish."

"Pray tell us of the Red One," Alfazar instructed politely.

"The Red One is a Fae—a phearsanú, to be precise. He is the one predicted, as the dryads have told you already. His true name is Sanguinar.

"One thousand, three hundred and fifty nine years ago, a child of the desert was born bearing Lune's mark upon his forehead. At that time the phearsanú were a gentle people who enjoyed music, dance and theatre; their colourful tent village was known as a place of hospitality and entertainment in the otherwise harsh desert.

"The phearsanú knew of the prophecy regarding the Red One, so when Sanguinar was born his parents were instructed to kill their child, lest he become a very great threat. They refused, and Sanguinar's family were forced to flee from their village into the desolation which we now know as the Bone Desert. Sanguinar's siblings hated him for driving their family out. At first they merely taunted him and belittled him, but as the child grew older and began to stand up for himself his brothers started physically intimidating him. Eventually they graduated to outright beatings.

"Sanguinar's parents decided that they must reintegrate with their former society to stem the extremes of their children's emotions. To some extent they managed this, and their children returned to village life.

"This exposed Sanguinar to the combined fear-driven hatred and contempt of the rest of the phearsanú. He was systematically denied access to public locations, barred from the theatre, treated with wilful contempt, and often assaulted. He responded with theft, vandalism, and the occasional mugging. Eventually even his parents came to believe that their child was evil. They cast him from their home, and he was so enraged and distraught that he murdered them both ere he fled.

"And so the phearsanú, out of fear and anxiety, created the very evil which they had sought to prevent: the Red One of prophecy."

The Reaper delivered this entire sad history with a clinical detachment, as though merely reciting a collection of facts instead of recounting the downfall of a young Fae and his family.

"But why is He so dangerous? It sounds like this Sanguinar might be mad, but surely one Fae can be overcome?" Ed asked from where he was leaning against a pile of books.

"Because He is the Mover of Pickles, remember?" Artyom answered briskly. "So, Ms Reaper, which pickles did this Sanguinar move?"

"What do you know of Death gods?" she riposted, fixing Artyom with an unblinking stare. Even the mage quailed a little under her gaze.

"Not much more than we discussed with the dryads," Bugen supplied, feeling somewhat more confident now; The Reaper would not bother explaining all of this if she planned to kill them. "Essentially, there are many death gods; some are neutral, and others are evil, though the latter seem to be a minority."

"Essentially, yes. But there is much more that you are missing, human.

"Your people tend to pick and choose whom to worship; some worship Life, some Nature; others worship Death or Chaos. We elves, on the other hand, are wont to pick and *balance*." Bugen was somewhat startled to hear the strong emphasis placed on 'balance', given The Reaper's monotone delivery thus far. "I too am a cleric of sorts," she said as she raised her hands before her, indicating her robe. "But I, and my people, do not serve a single deity."

"You balance the death gods," Artyom blurted out.

The Reaper lowered her arms and turned to the mage. "Indeed. We grey elves aim to find balance between Life—the one you know as Sol—and Death."

"Why is there a need to strike a balance?" mused Ed. With a wry smile, he added, "Don't the gods take care of themselves?"

"Your ignorance betrays you, human. The relationship between the gods and the Mortal Plane of existence is more complex than you suppose."

"Mortal Plane?" asked Alfazar.

"Attend carefully." The Reaper adopted a didactic manner. "The gods are beings of immense power, though the immensity varies greatly from god to god. They dwell in realms separate from ours; we reside in the Mortal Plane, and they in the Realms Beyond. You humans might divide these other planes into the Heavenly Realm, the Dread Realm, and the Unaligned Realms.

"What then is the source of the gods' power?" This was clearly a rhetorical question, so none of the companions interrupted. "It is derived from their connexion to the Mortal Plane. You, priest, worship the deity of life, whom you name Sol. As you have rightly observed, there is but one source of life. This means that Sol is strongly tied to the Mortal Plane, and so her presence in the Heavenly Realm is powerful beyond the measure of other deities.

"Others, such as Nature, are also ubiquitously manifest in the Mortal Plane; they enjoy much power in the planes beyond. In general, the more worshippers a deity has, the more powerful they become. What then can be said of the minor Death gods, of whom there are many? Each has only a few followers, and so their power in the Mortal Plane is tenuous."

"But death is everywhere!" Ed protested. "We see it all the time."

"Yes," The Reaper lectured patiently, "It must seem that way for you, human. Yours is a short-lived species; death is often near to you. However, it is not so with all. Elves, for example, can live for many centuries, even without... assistance."

"So where does balance come into this?" Artyom queried before Ed could respond.

The Reaper nodded sagely. "It was decided by my people that steps needed to be taken to ensure that the minor Death gods could never pass away."

"Pass away!" Bugen exclaimed. He was practically beside himself with wonder and fear. "How does a *deity* pass away?"

"By losing their connexion to the Mortal Plane," The Reaper explained calmly. "If a god or goddess finds themselves without worshippers or other anchors to the Mortal Plane they quickly attenuate. In essence, they die." She paused, then added, "This synergistic relationship between the Mortal Plane and supernatural power is a great irony of our world."

Bugen's mind boggled at the implications. None of what The Reaper had said contradicted the teachings of Sol's priests, but neither was her lecture a simple extrapolation of his beloved truths. It felt as if he had been gifted a great insight, and with a curious glow he thought that human theology had progressed more in the past few minutes than in the century preceding that. And how small that progression was, compared to what this singular elf had already encompassed!

"So the grey elves took steps of what nature?" Alfazar asked respectfully, seeing that Bugen was too enraptured to ask questions just yet.

"We ensured that the minor Death deities have permanent physical ties to the Mortal Plane," The Reaper replied.

"By spreading the worship of your people amongst them?" enquired Artyom sharply.

"Indeed, but we are so few that this alone was insufficient. We grey elves sought a more permanent solution."

"Other anchors..."

"Yes." She paused for a moment, then continued, "My people crafted a set of orbs, which came to be named Moons in honour of Lune, whom we revere as the mother of most Death spirits. Into each orb we instilled a fraction of a single minor Death god's power, binding that portion of their being onto the Mortal Plane. Thus, we ensured that the god can persist with few or even no worshippers.

"In this way we attempted to safeguard the balance of Life and Death." The Reaper looked from Alfazar to Ed, then to Bugen, and finally Artyom. "You may find it humorous to know, human, that the orb of Erdis is in fact a deep green: Mover of Pickles indeed."

"Erdis?" Bugen asked after a moment.

"A child of Lune, and a minor God of Pestilence."

"Pestilence!" Artyom cried. "But then... the Great Plagues began in 377 Pre-Unification; was that because of Sanguinar?" he asked excitedly.

The Reaper nodded gravely.

"My grandfather died in one of the most recent plagues..." Artyom trailed off quietly, as if speaking to himself.

"That was the year that Sanguinar captured the orb from us," The Reaper explained after a short pause. "The year he became immortal."

"In the same way that the Fae are?" queried Alfazar.

"Yes, but because he is the possessor of a significant fraction of Erdis' power he is also immune to poisons, all sickness, and even extensive wounding will not damage him irreparably. Sanguinar can wield magick beyond his remaining phearsanú kin: even necromancy." It was clear that The Reaper disapproved of the latter immensely.

"So let me get this straight," Ed said. "You're saying that this Erdis, some minor God of Pestilence or something, is cut off from our world because a phearsanú stole his magick green ball? And now that phearsanú—this Sanguinar guy—can use that ball to become a demigod himself?"

"In short, yes," The Reaper responded. Bugen was somewhat impressed by Ed's ability to synthesise their lengthy discussion in such simple terms.

"And the Fae are all immortal because the entire group of Death gods are out of whack with Erdis missing?"

"In a manner of speaking."

"And you have been left here as a way of dealing with the fallout?" Ed continued.

"Yes."

"So what's the Tithe got to do with this?"

If The Reaper felt any frustration she did not show it. "Its primary purpose is to prevent Erdis from attenuating entirely; its secondary purpose is population control of the Fae, now that they are immortal."

"What does 'prevent him from attenuating' mean exactly?" Artyom asked.

"I feed the souls of the reaped to Erdis, thereby sustaining him."

In Bugen's mind there formed an unbidden image; he saw thousands of souls crying out in terror and then suddenly silenced as The Reaper fed them into the slavering mouth of Erdis, who appeared as a nude, famine-thin figure covered in green-tinged skin and suppurating pustules. The mental image was so repulsive that Bugen's gorge rose, and he had trouble forming a coherent sentence. "Does he... Erdis... *eat* souls?" Bugen choked out. If Erdis ate them, every soul which had been sent to him, every human and Fae ever in the Tithe... maybe Bugen's sister...

"You are distressed," The Reaper stated.

Alfazar, Artyom and Ed were all staring at Bugen, wondering at the priest's reaction, but he was too worried to notice their quizzical expressions.

"I meant 'feed' in a figurative sense," she continued after a moment. "It would be accurate to say I direct souls to Erdis. He does not consume them."

"But you said that the souls sustain him," Bugen managed.

"Yes, but not in the way you suppose. Unaligned deities are unable to consume or gather souls to themselves permanently. Instead, they are sustained by the flow of souls through their realms into either the Heavenly or Dread Realms. Most souls become self-absorbed and fall into the Dread Realm; some come to understand their purpose in life and death, and rise to the Heavenly Realms; but it is a rare soul that is able to persist in the Unaligned Realms indefinitely."

Understanding flooded through Bugen and he relaxed, suddenly buoyant. There was hope yet. He gave thanks to Sol; She had not abandoned those caught in the Tithe. Truly She was great! "Thank you," Bugen said to The Reaper earnestly.

Ed looked from The Reaper to Bugen and then back, wondering what all that had been about. He had other worries on his mind. "How did Sanguinar capture this ball thing anyway? Didn't your kind keep an eye on it or somethin'?"

The Reaper turned her gaze to the floor, hiding her face. It was the greatest display of emotion that the four companions had seen from her thus far. "Yes, but we failed. Sanguinar is a phearsanú—even when mortal he was a wielder of illusion magick—and we grey elves are oft-times gullible."

Something clicked in Bugen's mind, and a few moments of consideration yielded a growing certainty that his insight was correct. "Sanguinar can use illusion magick... you said he has been watching us... Sanguinar was the false innkeeper, wasn't he?"

The Reaper raised her eyes again, a shadow of a smile across her face. "Yes."

"That little bastard!" Ed burst out, his face blotchy. Bugen could not tell if this was due to anger or embarrassment. "Music and theatre, eh? Creepy little ponce." He paused for a moment. "No offence, Alfazar."

The bard simply inclined his head graciously and waved the unintended insult away.

"So he can do magick. What else?" Ed asked The Reaper forcefully, wanting to learn as much as possible about his foe. "He got any face-melting biological tricks: poison teeth, acid spit, or anything like that?"

"The phearsanú have odd hair," Bugen added, thinking back to Vera. Ed grunted and shot Bugen an approving look, as though impressed that he had noticed.

"Their head covering is not hair, but rather dozens of tail-like appendages which assist them in keeping cool. Do not worry; they are harmless," replied The Reaper. "Apart from that, phearsanú possess a set of nictitating membranes–"

"Wha?"

"–eyelids, which help to keep out sand and glare, and they can happily survive for days with little water. You have already been appraised of their other abilities."

Ed stroked his beard, already calming down as he mulled over the possibilities.

"So how did Sanguinar take the orb?" Artyom brought the topic back, evidently intrigued by the possibility of learning some arcane knowledge.

"Well..."

Bugen listened as The Reaper spoke, and his imagination ran into overdrive. He could practically see Sanguinar's diminutive figure stumbling into an elven dwelling on the edge of the Great Arcan Forest, half parched to death, and still covered in the stains of his parents' deaths. From there, everything swept along as The Reaper recounted the tale.

Sanguinar laying in bed being nursed back to health by the grey elves...
The elves—cognizant of the prophecy and of his history—deciding on an attempt to avert catastrophe...
Sanguinar, surprisingly calm when informed of their design for him...
The young Fae delivered to human realms, glorying in the freedom from his desert home which he so despised...

The elves attempts to integrate him into human society, itself in a state of perpetual war before the Unification...
The war between rival city-states which Sanguinar became embroiled in...
The young phearsanū's revelry in the carnage of battle, and his indefatigable commitment to mastering slaughter...
A conclave of elves worrying about this development, and talk of the prophecy amongst the Fae...
Sanguinar's confrontation with the elves, ending with Sanguinar being taken to one of their cities, now unknown to mortal man...
Sanguinar going without struggle, but scheming and plotting their downfall all the while...
Him learning of the orbs after years of compliance with the elves...
Sanguinar carefully concocting an illusion of sickness within himself, then seeking admittance to Erdis' temple...
The underhanded slaying of the temple's guardians...
Erdis' cries of anguish which reverberated throughout the Realms Beyond when his Moon was severed from him...
Sanguinar's terrible purge of the phearsanū hometown...
His revenge upon his siblings through torture and defilement over several terrible weeks...
The pogrom by which he single-handedly reduced his people to a drifting, fragmented shadow...
Sanguinar's thirst to fulfil the prophecy and visit destruction upon the world...

"We have come to a stalemate of sorts," The Reaper continued. "Sanguinar has not yet had enough time to bend Erdis' power entirely to his will–"

"Not enough time?" Ed burst out.

"It's been nigh on fourteen hundred years!" Alfazar added, aghast.

"The gods do not give up their secrets easily," The Reaper chastised them. "The power of Erdis has resisted Sanguinar for centuries, but it will ultimately fail; it is only a fraction of a god, and each victory that Sanguinar wins hands him new tools with which to attack. By my estimation, Sanguinar's usurpation is nearly ripe." She paused, then continued. "Yet, as I was saying, Sanguinar has not yet obtained the full measure of power contained by the orb. Thus he cannot outright attack us here in Esra'Nell. Neither can we mount such an attack on him."

"Why not?" Bugen asked, feeling that he might already know the answer.

"Don't you have a bunch of other orbs to fight 'im with?" Ed added.

"Silence!" commanded The Reaper, fixing Ed with a glare. She flashed with fury for a moment, hard as stone. "Foolish thoughts such as these are why humans were never told of the Moons before. We dare not endanger the balance further." She softened. "If Sanguinar were to capture another it would be disastrous..."

"And the Fae are terrified of him," Artyom concluded. "Which is why you need us."

"Yes. That is why you have been brought here."

Chapter 8

To Die Without Pantihose

Last night's performance was no exception. d'Barouse demonstrated once more the fecundity of his pulchritudinous imagination.

d'Barouse' distinctive performance style is free of the moribund palaver employed by many of his au courant *competitors. Instead, the peripatetic bard appeals directly to our prehistoric roots, crafting a mélange of the primal and irrational with which to ensnare our collective* id.

The flicker of his knives and the flare of fiery torches constitute a most cromulent verisimilitude of the alluring discourses of pre-Unification civilisation, resurrecting the thrill of the antediluvian lifestyle without invoking the concomitant terror of perpetual bellicosity.

Having witnessed many of d'Barouse' performances first-hand, I cannot help but hypothesise that the wandering bard is in fact discontent with his métier in its current guise. It is my contention that he is restlessly searching for a prelapsarian ne plus ultra *of storytelling: some fabled 'ultimate tale' with which to bring true entertainment to the masses.*

Ariadne Spinoza, eminent theatre critic

 HANK you for your help, Ms Reaper. Put the kettle on!" Artyom quipped as they left some hours later. Bugen, who was already on the threshold and could see into the foreboding graveyard beyond, felt this was highly inappropriate, but he was too preoccupied to chastise the mage.

As directed, they headed off towards the lake.

"What'd The Reaper say about this portal thing again?" Ed asked, about half an hour later.

Bugen suppressed a sigh; his companions' banter grated on his ears, though he tried to shut out their words.

"It opens a path to anywhere that you've been before, or that you can picture clearly in your mind's eye," the mage responded, footsteps crunching along the path.

"I'm not an idiot..." Ed huffed. The hunter kept a close eye on the surrounding crystalline forest. "I meant about the other bit."

"The bit where the path will close when we step back through it?" Arty answered innocently.

"Yeah. There was something else too."

"The bit where nobody else can use the path that we made unless they're with us?"

"Oh." Ed crunched along the path. "Right. That bit."

"You forgot one more thing," Alfazar added as he pushed a branch out of his face. The other two gave him a quizzical look. "The bit where we have to somehow kill a god at the other end of the path."

"Oh, we don't need to kill him," Artyom said cheerily. "Just separate him from the Moon."

"Then take it back to The Reaper," Ed added. "Try not to die and be raised as an undead minion. Don't get infected by some horrible plague that'll wipe out half the known world. Y'know: just the basics."

"Not to mention this business with the time differences," Alfazar sighed. "Such a strange place this is."

Bugen could not agree more. He trudged towards the lake and its strange central portal, which The Reaper had assured them would be able to take them straight to Sanguinar's dwelling on the outskirts of the old phearsanú village. Dark thoughts clouded his mind.

The young cleric was feeling overwhelmed by the amount of information that had been unloaded onto him and the stakes of the game before them. Slaying a god—even a fraction of a god—was no mean task. Bugen was worried about what might be necessary to defeat Sanguinar, and this worry manifested as frustration and anger. It was a shield behind which to hide from despair.

He prayed internally, churning the same line of thought over and over, treading mental water. *Sol, what are we going to do? Sol, how do we fix this? Sol, why did you choose us for this? What am I meant to do Sol?*

No answers were forthcoming.

Bugen clung to three comforts. Firstly, he was confident that his goddess was still with him, despite his inability to feel Her peace at the moment. He had company. They might be frustrating, but they were his friends. Thirdly, he had the necklace which Dell had handed him.

Bugen thought back to that day in Adeline not long ago. *Take it. You'll know when to use it. Keep it with you.* He still had no idea what it did or where it came from, but it seemed that Dell had inexplicably known at least *something* about Sanguinar. How? And what? Bugen wondered fruitlessly.

This went on for some minutes, until Buhbuh darted across the trail and nearly tripped Bugen. The priest shook his head and caught up with his fellows.

"Well, what do we know about Sanguinar? What sort of weaknesses or flaws can we exploit?" Artyom was asking the others in a business-like tone.

"Know more 'bout his strengths, really," Ed offered.

"He likes illusions. He can use magick, and necromancy, apparently," Artyom ticked off.

"A filthy art," Bugen opined vehemently. The Reaper had explained how it was Sanguinar who raised the banshees during every Tithe, whilst her power was otherwise occupied. How disappointed the majority of humans would be if they learnt that the Festival of the White Lady was merely another way for Sanguinar to slap the Fae in the proverbial... face. After chewing over this line of thought for a moment more, Bugen added "His weakness will be tied to his hatred."

"Huh?"

"Sanguinar's weakness may be something to do with his obsession with his prophecy," Bugen elaborated. "He feels that he must live up to it. Maybe there is a way of using that against him."

"Tied to his hatred..." Alfazar mused. "And he likes illusions, as apparently all phearsanú do. Drama, even."

Bugen wondered whether Vera shared a love of illusions, of subterfuge or drama...

"The Reaper specifically mentioned that Sanguinar was barred from the phearsanú theatre," Alfazar continued, thinking aloud. "And from our experience in Newtown we know first-hand that Sanguinar is a consummate showman; he put on a show for us, for the entire town, and even a private performance for Ed. I reckon that in his head it's all part of his hatred for his people; he uses their favourite past-time—the one he wasn't allowed to join in with—to show them that *he* is in charge now."

Ed glowered. "So we could fight him with singing and dancing?" he said a little combatively.

Alfazar shook his head. "We could delay him with drama and illusion. Make him think that all is going according to his plans. We only need to separate him from the orb, then high-tail it out of there; that could be much easier if we never have to fight him."

Everyone fell silent as they contemplated Alfazar's idea. "Well, I like it," Artyom agreed brightly.

"Aye, makes sense... still want to smash his poncy face in, but this plan is wise," concurred Ed.

"Bugen, what think you?" queried Alfazar. "Do you have any other ideas?"

"None that I like," responded the weary priest. And none that he was willing to share right now.

How entertaining Sanguinar would find a fallen priest...

Ed leant out over the water and tentatively extended a foot. Just as The Reaper had promised, the hunter's boot did not break the water's surface. Bugen, still lost in dark thoughts, felt his mood lift a little as he observed Ed's pensive expression. He then turned back to surveying the forest surrounding Esra'Nell's central lake.

Again, Ed tested the magickal water. His brow furrowed in consternation, but the water held once more. No ripples emanated from where his foot touched.

Artyom sauntered right past Ed and onto the enchanted lake. "C'mon slowpoke," he called cheekily. "Isn't this just the coolest? And I thought Adeline had amazing magick!"

"Blasted mage..." Ed grumbled, just loudly enough for Bugen to hear.

Alfazar chuckled.

Shortly Tamtem and Buhbuh joined Artyom; the three jumped and gambolled in their joy over the curiously solid liquid below their paws. Alfazar was much more calm; he walked around and peered down in wonder, observing the strange weeds and fish which lived in the paradoxical lake.

Bugen walked out to join Ed, who had taken a handful of nervous steps onto the water. The hunter was standing with legs apart and arms out to the sides, as though steadying himself. He was also uncharacteristically pale and angrily muttering to himself. Bugen caught a few words: 'blasted', 'unnatural', 'drown', and 'Fae'.

The priest had decided to simply trust to the magicks which kept him supported; they seemed to have worked just fine for the mage, and the kelpie earlier. Still, he refrained from looking down for too long. Instead, he looked to his companion.

After a few more moments of cursing Ed knelt, then lay down flat on his stomach with his arms and legs splayed. This elicited a chuckle from his priestly companion. Ed then began sliding himself towards the portal, looking like nothing so much as a curious brown and red penguin.

When Artyom turned and spied this strange beast approaching he burst into immoderate laughter. "The first—and most difficult— test," he said in a ridiculously exaggerated voice, "is conquering the Lake of Ultimate Terror!" In his normal voice he added, "You look more like a fool than I do half the time!"

"Ah, shut yer gob," Ed called back whilst waving Buhbuh away from his face; the dog retreated, sad that his master did not want to be licked. "You look like a fool more than half the time."

Alfazar chortled as Ed continued to drag himself along.

The woodsman refused any help until he was within a few paces of the portal, where he finally accepted Alfazar's extended hand to help him stand.

"Finished being a crustacean?" Artyom jested. "I thought they lived *in* the water."

"Let's just get this done."

The four companions composed themselves and formed a semicircle around the mysterious device suspended before them.

This close, Bugen could see that his earlier estimate was off; the portal was closer to eight feet tall than six, and it was slightly elongated in the vertical direction. The shape reminded him of a sugarloaf—one of the extremely expensive Arcanan sugarloaves, no less.

There was definitely an interface at the portals's surface, though the priest had not the faintest idea what it might be composed of. Inside he could see swirling mist rising and falling in peculiar convection patterns, and occasionally he caught a glimpse of colour. It came to him that he might be seeing the termini of paths opened from this point into the rest of Lorem. Was that flash of white a glacier or a snowfield? Maybe a saltpan, he thought. Who knew how far the portal could take somebody?

"Well, what are we waiting for?" Ed growled. He hefted his axe and walked through the mystic interface.

Nothing happened.

Artyom wasted no time. Indicating the portal, he put on a nasal voice and said to Ed, "Sir, I regret to inform you that our sophisticated magickal device has determined that... you have no brain. I am afraid the prognosis is poor."

"I'll give you a prognosis," responded Ed, raising his axe.

Bugen recognised the friendly antagonism for what it was, and his thoughts quickly turned back to the portal. "Why did it not work?"

"Because Ed wasn't thinking... of where we need to go," replied the mage, shooting a sideways glance at Ed.

"Perhaps..." Alfazar started, drawing his companions' attention before the hunter could get an insult in. "Perhaps we ought to use the portal to open a path back to Port Adeline. Maybe we can find something there to help us."

"Something like?" Ed asked.

"Maybe priests," said Alfazar, looking to Bugen. He added a rising inflection which almost turned the statement into a question. "Mages," he added, now eyeing Artyom. "Hunters."

The others paused.

"I do not think that will work," Bugen replied slowly and carefully. "At least, I think my order has given all of the help which it can." He raised his hand to his chest to remind the others of the mysterious pendant. "And Ainsworth will be on the lookout for our return; we are now a liability to him."

"I agree," Artyom added heavily. "I do not know if Uncle knew of the Fae presence when he began colonising this land, but he will not stand for us warning the townsfolk. We gain only risk by returning to Adeline."

"What think you, Ed?"

"Nothing, remember?" Artyom supplied.

Ed glowered at the mage for a moment, then turned back to Alfazar. "It seems someone or something has chosen us for this job." He said this very seriously. "I guess we'll just have to see how things pan out from here."

Bugen felt a little deflated—his faith outdone by the hunter!—but that rapidly changed into a strange buoyancy. He found Ed's attitude encouraging.

"So we're winging it," Artyom finished gleefully, rubbing his hands together. "My favourite kind of plan."

"Well, I'm going to try it," Artyom proclaimed. "Wait here, and send the cavalry if I don't come back."

"The cavalry?" Bugen asked.

"Yeah: you guys."

The arcanist composed himself for a moment, then Tamtem jumped up onto his shoulders. Together they strode into the portal and vanished. There was no noise or any other indication that the device had worked. Silence stretched for what Bugen thought was around thirty seconds. Then, with no warning, Artyom and Tamtem reappeared.

Seized by a sudden suspicion, Bugen drew his weapon and levelled it at the arrivals. Ed looked at the priest sceptically but made no other move.

"What was the name of the ship we arrived here on?" Bugen demanded.

"Relax, it's just me," Artyom said, brushing himself off. "And it was the *Steadfast*. Put your sword away. Besides, most people like spontaneousness."

"Phearsanú like deception," Bugen explained calmly, slipping his arming sword back into the sheath at his hip. "And it's 'spontaneity'."

"Whatever."

"Whaddya find?" Ed asked eagerly. "Did you get there?"

"Yep. Desolate tent city in the middle of the Bone Desert, just like The Reaper described. Very bright, very dry, very sandy. But we didn't see much else. Let's go. No point taking extra provisions or anything: we can just come back through the portal if we need to."

Steeling themselves, the party stepped through the mystical device with Artyom.

Just as described, their destination was bright, dry and sandy. Except Artyom had understated it, in Bugen's opinion.

The first thing he noticed was the dry heat. The nervous sweat which had accumulated on the priest's skin evaporated in a flash, sucked into the hot and thirsty air. He could feel the skin around his eyes tightening in protest, and each breath seemed to parch his nostrils and lungs. Though a gentle wind stirred, it did nought to relieve the sensation; if anything, it exacerbated it.

Next came the glare, which forced Bugen's hands up to protect his eyes until they adjusted. The light of Sol blazed down on this place like a fiery, disapproving eye. Rays of brilliance reflected from every single particle of grit stirred up by the wind, turning them into miniature stars, and the sides of the dunes were initially painful to behold.

Finally, the wind-blown sand began to accumulate around his gorget and neck, immediately beginning to grate on him. It was all rather unpleasant, Bugen thought.

After a few moments of extreme discomfort he felt able to observe his surroundings properly. Squinting, he made out a city of sticks and torn cloth sitting in a valley formed by two dunes. These enormous mounds of sand towered over the ragged, Sun-bleached town like a pair of unbroken waves waiting to wash its existence away.

Bugen saw that Artyom and Ed had already fashioned themselves makeshift veils to cut out some of the grit and glare; Alfazar, of course, was already well-equipped in this regard. Bugen mimicked them, using a square of torn cloth which had been fluttering forlornly from a broken tent-pole. He then grasped his buckler tightly and turned to his companions.

"Mighty fine place this is," Ed said, kicking at a fragment of desiccated wood and wishing for some proper trees.

"I wonder where His Worship lives," Alfazar mused in response. "I had expected a... warmer welcome than this."

"Not too much warmer please," Bugen added.

"He'll be somewhere nearby, no doubt," Artyom stated. "And it seems that he's content for us to go to him."

"Let's get out of this hole," Ed continued, working a tent pole free from where it was being slowly subsumed by the sand. A shred of canvas at its end flapped like a grim flag in the breeze.

"Well, shall we go to him then?" Artyom asked, pointing towards the top of a dune. Bugen guessed it lay to their west. Squinting, he could just make out a curious red conical shape protruding over the top of the ridge. "Whatever that thing is, it's enormous," the arcanist added. "Got to be him."

The town's wreckage was so forlorn that the band did not even pause to pick it over. It was clear that were no provisions or anything else of use amongst the desolation.

As the group began to trek up the steep slope, it occurred to Bugen that there were also no bones there either. He tried not to dwell on that thought, but it kept intruding. *Trudge*. No corpses. *Trudge*. No bones. *Trudge*. God of Death. *Trudge*. Necromancy. *Damnation*.

The priest stepped onto an unstable patch, lost his footing, and tumbled ten feet or so down the dune's face before stopping. Bugen coughed and spluttered in protest, then carefully wiped his face free of abrasive particles. Lastly, he patted down his armour, sending rivulets of silica skittering away.

Artyom called down, "Careful there, old leadfoot."

Bugen ignored him. He therefore failed to notice when Artyom and Tamtem slipped a little way down the dune face too.

After a few minutes more Bugen and the others neared the summit. The climb was exhausting, despite the relatively short distance. Ed halted and explained that silhouetting themselves against the sky would give any attackers a clear target, so the four travellers reluctantly lay prone against the baking sand and crawled the last part of the way up. Bugen could tell that the hunter did not expect any attacks to be forthcoming—yet—but wariness was certainly called for.

As they reached the crest of the dune Artyom began shaking and wriggling in a strange fashion, which alarmed Bugen until he discerned that the mage was merely displacing the hot surface sand so that he could rest against the relatively cool layer beneath.

With that, the group passed around a waterskin and considered what lay before them.

In between this massive dune and the next was a relatively level area, perhaps one hundred and twenty yards square. At its centre was a gentle hillock of sand crowned by an enormous tent. Its walls rose vertically from the desert floor some fifteen feet before tapering to a conical top; it was this spire, coloured deep red, which the group had spotted from the ruined township. Overall, the monstrous tent reminded Bugen of some nomad dwellings he had seen sketched in a book or on the edge of a map somewhere.

Arrayed around the base of the yurt was a collection of humanoid figures of varying sizes. At this distance Bugen could make out little detail; however, he was confident that the figures were unmoving. Statues maybe, or something more sinister? "What can you see?" Bugen asked, turning to the others.

"They appear to be bones," Artyom observed drily.

"Why so many sizes though?" Alfazar pondered as Ed grunted his agreement.

Bugen paused for a moment, then queried his better-sighted friends. "Are there any phearsanú-sized ones?"

"Phearsanú sized?"

"If you were a necromancer who hated his family, what would you do with them?" Bugen pointed out.

"That's dark, Bugen," Artyom said.

"Our opponent is dark..." Bugen groused, wiping sand from his eyes. The priest was still worried about how to best Sanguinar, and still hiding it behind frustration. He made note of this and tried to reign his emotions back in.

"The trick," said Artyom, "will be to get close enough—and be interesting enough—that we will have time to find the Moon. Got to be adorable like a mouse, not a rat."

"There goes our chances then," Ed responded, as dry as the desert.

Artyom abruptly stood, showering everyone in sand.

"We've just got this ugly mage," Ed continued. He shook sand from his beard and stood too. "C'mon, little rat."

Alfazar and Bugen stood and began following the others down the dune. It was steeper on this side, and Bugen frequently had to steady himself with his hands as patches of sand slid out from underneath his boots. Fortunately for his ego, it was Artyom who finally lost his footing completely. The slight arcanist tumbled down the slope, spraying grit everywhere with his ungainly cartwheels. The others heard a slight 'oof' when Artyom finally came to rest at the foot of the dune.

"What were you saying about 'old leadfoot'?" Bugen called down. He regretted this almost immediately; not only was it foolhardy to make so much noise, but he now also had to make it down the rest of the way without duplicating Artyom's feat.

As the rest of the band worked carefully towards the valley floor, Artyom pulled himself free of the mound of sand he had loosened. After a moment he pawed around for his spectacles, and miraculously found them not far off. Sighing with relief, the arcanist donned the glasses. As he did so, he noticed that his face was in shadow.

One of the unmoving figures stood perilously close.

Wind-swept, Sun-bleached, desiccated bones. Twisted wire. Frayed ribbon, still pink, but probably red in a former life. The odd rusted nail or iron band.

Mismatched arms: one big, one small. Legs too. A human skull with an over-large mandible jutting out, tusks curving skywards. Too many ribs on one side, weaved through with frangible cloth. A pose which seemed to suggest fluid motion—only one leg touching the ground, the other pointed daintily backwards, one arm raised skyward.

Artyom carefully inspected the construct as the rest of the party caught up with him (rather more elegantly, it has to be said).

"It's a blasted dancing skeleton," Ed said in amazement. "Look, it's even got poncy little ribbons."

Bugen looked up and saw that the skeleton did indeed have two long ribbons fluttering from its up-raised arm. "What sort of a madman are we dealing with?" Bugen said, squinting as he was surveilled by the other skeletal figures. He held one hand raised to shade his eyes.

"The artistic kind," Alfazar replied. "Putting the 'art' back into the Necromantic arts, as it were."

"Hilarious..." Ed opined. "What a flaming loony."

Bugen noticed a pattern after a few moments of inspection. He could see perhaps fifty of the bony statues arrayed in more-or-less concentric circles around Sanguinar's lair. The outermost circles consisted of 'happy' figures: dancers, athletes, even one which seemed to be prancing over the sandy ridges with a bouquet of femurs. The next circle contained stern and noble characters. Bugen could see a solemn knight with an enormous, rusted sword driven point-down into the sand. Next to that was a skeleton sitting on the back of another, hand clenched under its chin as though deep in thought. The figures closest to the tent were imposing and quite obviously angry. One had its mouth hinged open in rage as it swung a scimitar overhead; another had been assembled with arms and legs swapped, and given enormous claws with which to silently menace the desert.

He returned to inspecting the closest figure. It seemed that the twisted creations had been designed rather carefully, if maniacally. Each joint was intricately tied with copper wire, and some bones had been strategically reinforced with metal armature. Fear and wonder knotted Bugen's stomach. "Can they be raised?" he asked of Artyom.

"Good question: can they be raised?" the mage responded, slinging the question back to the priest with a self-satisfied grin.

"Don't faff around Artyom," Ed retorted before Bugen could get an angry word in. The priest bit back his frustrated comment, satisfied that Ed had said everything necessary. Artyom was not at all fazed.

"The tales I have heard of necromancy would suggest the answer is 'yes'," Alfazar cut in before things got out of hand. Sol bless that man.

"Yeah, they can be raised," Artyom relented. "With enough evil intent it's possible to animate skeletons."

"But... but," Ed spluttered. "They don't even have a brain, let alone muscles!"

"Neither do you—a brain, I mean—yet here you stand."

"Cut it out; we need to concentrate." Bugen paused, then continued more calmly, "If they are raised, how do we defeat them?"

"Magick, or smash them so badly that they are unable to maintain structural integrity."

"At any rate," Alfazar said, "We ought not do anything to provoke Sanguinar yet."

"Aye."

"Agreed," Ed complied. "Only one thing for it then."

Eyeing the dancing bones one last time, the group set off. They passed through the first and second rings of sculptures with no incidents, then all came to a halt before crossing the final circle.

Buhbuh caught up from where he had been relieving himself against the leg of a skeleton.

"Cute, like mice. Not rats," Artyom said under his breath.

Bugen was sweating profusely beneath his armour and improvised veil, and not just because of the heat. He hastily commended his soul to Sol.

The four nodded to one another solemnly, then stepped across the final ring.

Nothing happened.

They reached the enormous entrance to the tent, covered by maroon curtains which towered above them. Artyom took a single step forward and a voice rang out from inside.

"Who approaches?" it asked in a sing-song manner.

"It is I, Artyom."

"Come in."

The companions stepped through the curtains as one.

Light flared in the darkness of the tent's interior immediately Bugen entered. The sound of a blasting powder detonation assailed his ears, leaving a characteristic acrid smell. Simultaneously, he felt tendrils of dry, papery flesh run down his face and around his head and shoulders. His mind filled with images of undead tentacle-beasts reaching down from the ceiling, waiting to latch onto the living like unnatural octopodes.

Buhbuh let out a piercing whine, like the Damned themselves. Even Tamtem whimpered.

Then something unexpected happened. "Welcome, welcome!" the voice proclaimed jovially.

Bugen batted at the tentacles and was astounded to hear one rip asunder with a familiar sound. Paper? Blinking away after-images, he saw green, blue, and red streamers draping across him and his companions. Glancing upwards, Bugen saw that confetti still drifted from the ceiling above. All of this, just so the party could make a grand entrance?

"After all this time, we were beginning to think you weren't coming. And it has been a $#&@ing *long* time coming," the speaker continued. He—for it was definitely a 'he'—had a strange way of accenting almost every other word, lending his speech a peculiar lilt. The emphasis betrayed the speaker's excitement and, behind that, hinted at his anger.

Quickly regaining his senses, Bugen located the speaker near the centre of the tent. It *had* to be Sanguinar.

The phearsanú sat in a polished wooden armchair, bathed in sunlight and perched upon the peak of an enormous mound of treasure; chests of clothing and of weaponry; gold and silver coins; mannequins with wigs and gilded jewellery; shining heaps of silver tableware; candlesticks and other accoutrements pilfered from churches; even enormous banners embroidered with pre-Unification heraldry. Sanguinar stood, sending coins skittering, and daintily picked his way down the pile.

Bugen took in his appearance in an instant, memorising it as though his life depended on it. The necromancer stood a mere five feet tall. His frame was topped with a head of long, red phearsanú tails, pulled back into a neat plait but leaving a 'fringe' parted in the middle by a distinctive widows peak. Beneath this was the blotchy, brownish birth mark which was responsible for setting this whole long chain of events into motion. It was indeed in the shape of Lune's sigil. Sanguinar grinned mischievously, exposing pointed teeth beneath green eyes with over-large pupils. His ears were swept upwards, like Vera's, but were also studded by numerous piercings which bore glittering gems and precious metals. His hands and wrists were likewise adorned. Finally, Bugen noted the loose-fitting white shirt (which showed off the wiry musculature beneath), red leather britches, long boots, and well-worn gilt rapier hanging at the phearsanú's side.

"Oh, we're going to have so much fun in the next half hour!" the demigod proclaimed.

Bugen blanched a little further at the implication.

"I've been so bored. Of all the gods I could have chosen, it had to be $#&@ing *pestilence*. Yawn!" Sanguinar fixed his eyes on each of the companions in turn; they all stood a little taller in defiance of his overwhelming personality. Bugen returned Sanguinar's stare resolutely until—like a reptile—darkened membranes slid sideways across the Fae's eyes. He shuddered involuntarily, eliciting a smug grin from the phearsanú.

"There's no pizazz! One moment you're kicking along fine, the next you're kicking the bucket. Where's the drama? The finesse? The $#&@ing suspense?" Sanguinar continued as he reached the base of his self-styled throne. "But you're finally here. There's so much I want from you."

"What do you want?" Artyom asked. Bugen was impressed by the note of authority with which the mage spoke.

"What do I want?" Sanguinar mockingly feigned thinking deeply. "Oh yes, that's right.

"I want to see the world *burn*. The whole $#&@ing thing. Every human, every elf, every Fae—especially my dear $#&@ing people—writhing and crying in terror at the sound of my name!" Sanguinar's voice rose to a horrible screech as he spoke, and he ended with arms raised high and face upturned. Bugen could see the cords in his neck straining.

Without transition, Sanguinar returned to normal posture and voice. "But from you I want something else." He paused and inspected them. "Blood. Every $#&@ing drop of it."

"Didn't get enough in Newtown? Water hard to come by in the desert?" Ed drawled, though he was visibly shaking. The hunter looked unnaturally white when he removed his veil.

"Not for a phearsanú, but I prefer the colour that blood leaves on my $#&@ing lips!" snapped Sanguinar. "You $#&@ing moron. I'm a *God* of *Death.*"

"You need a reagent," surmised Artyom. Bugen supposed this meant that the blood would be used to power some unholy magick.

"Yes," Sanguinar responded evenly. His unpredictable responses were unnerving. "I want your blood to help me make a Bone Dragon."

Fantastic.

Artyom tried to stall for time. Bugen could practically hear him thinking. *Cute like a mouse...* "What will you do with a bone dragon that you could not do yourself already?"

"Let's see." Sanguinar struck a somewhat effeminate pose and began listing responses on his fingers. "Fly, maybe. Terrorise small creatures—no, wait. I can already do that. Ummm... oh, yeah! Leave this gods-forsaken desert, start the next human civil war, then breed an army of undead with which to $#&@ing crush the bloody elves back into the Stone Age. That about covers it," he finished brightly.

With Sanguinar's attention fixed on Artyom for a moment, the others took the chance to visually inspect the tent. They too removed their veils, the better to see.

Bugen could see thick red and black curtains ringing the room. Sunlight streamed into an open panel in the tent's roof. Squinting up towards the glare, Bugen could make out a wooden platform near the top of the tent's cone, supported by a column which penetrated the centre of Sanguinar's piled riches. Maybe the Moon was up there?

Ed caught the priest's eye, flicking his gaze sharply skyward to indicate the platform. Bugen subtly nodded his agreement.

"An... an army," Artyom stuttered. "Well, that's certainly an ambitious goal..."

Sanguinar made to interrupt, but Artyom ploughed on.

"Oh yes, leading armies is difficult even for gods," Artyom blurted. Bugen suspected the mage was madly formulating a plan. "I mean, you've never seen Ferrous out leading troops, have you? Neither have I. It's difficult business."

"Is there a point to this, little man?" sighed Sanguinar. "I don't like being $#&@ed around by puny, squishy mages. I grow bored."

"Sorry. I haven't had much experience at *that* either."

Sanguinar laughed hysterically, throwing his head back in faux-mirth. "Did you hear that?" he asked of Alfazar, taking a few steps closer to the bard. "He's a good guy," he continued, pointing at Artyom with sharp, painted nails. "A real $#&@ing comedian. I might let him live the longest." Bugen could not tell if Sanguinar was genuinely enjoying this exchange, or if he in fact loathed the mage and was readying a wicked death for him.

He amended the thought; Sanguinar was definitely readying a wicked death for all of them.

"I might let you live longest instead, though," he continued with another step towards Alfazar. "The famed d'Barouse. Bard *extraordinaire*. Oh, we had such fun back in Newtown, did we not? Care to reprise the act?

"Or you, you filthy, little, bearded, humourless glob of a man," Sanguinar rounded on Ed, moving in to nearly striking distance. "Will you entertain me more than these three?"

"I'd sooner die," Ed vented, spitting at Sanguinar's feet.

"Hah!" Sanguinar crowed, ignoring the insulting expectoration. "That's the spirit. And so I shall grant your wish, shortly."

"He is rather short," Artyom jibed, trying to distract Sanguinar.

"Enough!" The word burst from the phearsanú like a physical force. Face blotchy beneath the birthmark, he cried out, "Your *time* grows short, all of you."

Even Artyom stepped back under the withering fury of Sanguinar's words.

"Fortunately, I've thought of a way you can help me with your last moments," the demigod continued mildly, as though the rage-filled outburst had never occurred. "As you kindly pointed out," he leered at the mage, "leading armies is potentially difficult. So I shall let you help me practice. My army against yours."

The companions exchanged confused glances. "Although I can guess at the composition of your army," Alfazar replied warily, "we unfortunately neglected to bring ours."

"Not to worry," Sanguinar grinned. From this distance Bugen could see every sharp tooth point. Were they natural or did he file them like that? "I suspected you might not bring one, so I went to the trouble of gathering one for you." The rictus widened. "Behold!"

Sanguinar threw his arms out to the sides, placed one foot delicately in front of the other and bowed low from the waist. Then, without stirring in any other way, he snapped his fingers.

The thick curtains which Bugen had noted earlier flew upwards with a flourish, revealing four enormous cages around the rim of the tent. Bugen could see dryads, tiny gnomes, beautiful nymphs, and an assortment of other Fae creatures through the thick mesh. The majority cowered in the corners furthest from Sanguinar. Some seemed oddly pallid, which puzzled Bugen momentarily. Livid bruises showed on many.

Damnation.

"Your foul deeds will not go unreckoned," Bugen finally spoke out, incensed at Sanguinar's mistreatment of these sapient Fae.

"Oh, the hypocrisy burns," Sanguinar mocked. "My foul deeds. *My* foul deeds. What about my $#&@ing family's? My people's? They tried to stop me becoming this."

A sly expression stole over Sanguinar's features. He turned to face the forty-odd captive Fae, arms again spread wide, and asked in a loud, clear voice, "What of the abductions carried out by these pitiful creatures?" Bugen could not see the phearsanú's face, but he could hear the malicious smile in his voice. The priest knew what was coming next. Ironically, the knowledge calmed him immensely.

Sanguinar turned back to Bugen and continued in a soft, seductive voice. "What of the Fae responsible for the death of your sister, hmmm? Or your little companion's family?" He indicated Ed, who was glowering.

"Your choices are yours; do not pretend otherwise," the priest rejoined evenly, having already made peace with that over long years.

He thought back to their recent conversation with The Reaper and realised that knowing the full story made forgiving the Fae that much easier. Maybe even Sanguinar could be redeemed yet. "Still, the Lady of Light is merciful. You have time left to choose."

Their nemesis pulled a face which would not look out of place on a toddler deprived of their favourite toy. "$#&@. You're boring."

As he began ascending his treasure hoard once more, Sanguinar called, "I gifted you an army—do you know how $#&@ing difficult it is to capture live satyrs?—and soon it will be time for you to use it." When he reached the top he plonked unceremoniously into his throne, slouching over nonchalantly.

"But it needs something more, doesn't it?" asked Artyom, raising a finger in objection. The mage walked closer to the pile, trying to draw attention away from the others.

"What?"

"Drama," Alfazar piped up, sensing that Sanguinar might now be vulnerable to suggestion.

"Drama?" the demigod asked condescendingly. "What more drama do you want?"

"A story," Artyom suggested.

"A grand tale."

"A $#&@ing *epic* battle, between kingdoms!"

Sanguinar jumped to his feet, clearly excited. "What a glorious $#&@ing idea! I knew I didn't kill you already for a reason! So, what's the story?" The demigod practically bounced with anticipation.

"Errr... an important battle between nations because their kings are fighting over..."

"A princess," Alfazar supplied. "A beautiful woman whom the two kings both want for their own."

"Yes, yes. $#&@ing excellent. Clearly I am one of the kings. Bardy-boy here can be the other," Sanguinar conceded. "So let us begin. Gather your army."

"Wait!" Artyom cried.

"Oh, what now?" Sanguinar sighed.

"You still need a princess."

Sanguinar's eyes lit up and he clapped his hands together gleefully. "You'll do nicely. Come," he beckoned. "I have the perfect dress for you; you'll be $#&@ing *ravishing*. We can pick out your hair too."

Artyom shot a strained look at the others, trying to communicate 'hurry up and look!' to them without using words. He then walked over to Sanguinar, who was inspecting the clothing on one of his mannequins. "I hope you have underwear on those dolls too; I refuse to die without pantihose!"

Chapter 9

Winging It

"Damn, this could spell the end of our little venture. Potential evidence of Fae presence."
[sounds of a chair being moved, somebody sitting heavily]
"Is the evidence overwhelming?"
"Not yet, but it does corroborate previous claims."
[silence before speaker continues]
"Never mind; we need only suppress information for a little while longer."
"But if there are Fae there then it's just a matter of time until–"
"It matters not to us, so long as the colonists meet demand in the meantime. We were never interested in Arcana's survival, only her exploitation. Ainsworth is the one with the long-term vision."
"And if his vision survives? If the rumours are unfounded?"
"Then, when the time is ripe, we will expose his corruption and seize the lands back."
"Dangerous: a truth and a lie in one."
"Not half as dangerous as failing now. Send Ainsworth a message: aid is on its way. Tell him to look to the seas..."
"Very good, sir."

Transcript taken by false security guard, Faust

"PIN for me. Actually, wait." The Red One held up a finger, then turned and yelled at Bugen and the others. "Oi! $#&@ing pay attention. We're going to be fighting over this glorious bastard shortly."

Bugen, Alfazar, and Ed came in from where they had been fruitlessly searching for the orb under the pretext of examining the treasure hoard or the caged Fae. They all looked exhausted, pale, and drawn.

"Now, spin," Sanguinar commanded.

Artyom obliged, carefully. The mage was wearing a conservative, full-length maroon dress with delicate geometrical patterns embroidered down both sides and across the front. The material gathered just under his bust—or rather, where his bust *would* be—and fell in form-obscuring folds which covered down to his ankles. Artyom's sparse chest hair peeked shyly from the top of the bodice, framed on either side by ridiculously puffy, pleated sleeves. Above this hovered his pale face. Sanguinar had seen fit to apply a whitening powder, lip rouge, and, absurdly, a beauty spot, which hovered over the mage's visage like a bloated fly. The *pièce de résistance* sat perched atop Artyom's head: a red beehive wig some two feet tall, done up with jewelled clasps. The entire outfit would have been laughably comical in any other situation, Bugen thought.

"Show us some skin," Sanguinar jeered, wolf-whistling as Artyom revealed a leg clad in sheer, pink hosiery. "Glorious," continued the phearsanú, wiping false tears from his eyes. "Oh, I'll miss that dress.

"And now for your army. In the interests of time, I will select your warriors for you."

The phearsanú waved an arm airily and two of the four cages

opened. A handful of Fae stepped out, rising above their terror, but the majority tried to melt back into the shadows of their gaol. Bugen noted that Sanguinar had sickeningly selected the smallest and weakest of the Fae to be the first victims.

"I was worried they'd do this," the necromancer joked to Artyom. "Lazy creatures."

Without warning, Sanguinar's rapier flashed out and the nearest gnome fell back. The diminutive creature mewled wretchedly, clutching one of its overly-large ears. Red blood welled between its fingers as it vainly sought to hold the appendage in place.

"Now get the $#&@ out of there, or I'll cut off the other one!" Sanguinar screamed at the remaining Fae. His back arched violently and spittle flew through the air.

In each of the adventurers there hardened a grim core of determination to see this task through.

"It's showtime," Sanguinar continued angrily. "Get outside and try to last more than thirty seconds," he snorted contemptuously as he herded the Fae out through the tent flap, prodding Alfazar and Artyom too. The weeping gnome went with them, sticking close to Artyom's skirt.

Despite the confusion—or perhaps because of it—Ed managed to use an unlikely combination of hand signals and eye rolling to indicate the upper wooden platform to the mage. Artyom, blessedly fast, enchanted one of Ed's ropes so that it stretched up to the platform and tied itself off. It then hung there limply and innocuously. Bugen prayed that Sanguinar had not noticed.

The tide of movement out of the tent finished abruptly. Bugen realised that he and Ed had both managed to stay indoors, apparently unnoticed. He had no idea what to make of this, nor why Sanguinar would leave such a potential opening, but he knew what he had to do now.

He and Ed clasped wrists briefly and nodded once. When they broke, Ed instructed Buhbuh to keep watch—Tamtem went with Buhbuh, sticking close—then he immediately began to climb.

Meanwhile, Bugen rushed to the other two cages and set about trying to extricate the remaining Fae.

"I'm here to help. What can you give me?" the priest asked breathlessly as he inspected one of the cells.

"Naught," replied a female dryad. She stood and walked closer. Her voice trembled. "The Red One has bound our power within these walls. Once we are free, maybe we then can help, but..."

"But these are cold iron cages," Bugen finished, suddenly understanding. The Fae could not touch them, nor use their magick to free themselves.

He quickly disabused himself of any notion of cutting through the bars; that would ruin his sword, take far too long, and be far too loud.

"What of the floors?" he asked suddenly.

A shadow—a shadow of a shadow, maybe—swept across the sky. It left in its wake a horde of skeletons slowly coming to life.

Alfazar watched carefully as one construct turned its eyeless visage to gaze across at the small group of Fae arrayed against it. He tentatively identified its skull as that of a horse, but the recent encounter with the kelpie left him unsure. The skeleton rolled its over-large shoulders, causing a cascade of sand to rain through its exposed ribs. It then made off to join its companions, which were assembling some forty yards away.

The air bore a sharp, vinegary stench which Alfazar eventually attributed to the fear-drenched sweat of his Fae companions. A stream of a million other small details imprinted themselves on the bard's trained memory.

No time for that now, he reminded himself. For now, all he needed to do was survive.

"Here, take these," Alfazar said as he began pulling knives from his bandoleers.

Some of the Fae availed themselves of the offered weaponry, but many demurred. "Iron," they said simply, shaking their heads. The bard noted that those that were clutching weapons did so carefully, holding the knives at arm's length like something infected. He shrugged: nothing he could do about that.

"We have a plan," Alfazar told them all in an undertone. *Or a hope of a plan*, he amended internally. "Just try to keep him occupied." He tried to put on a brave but believable expression as he encouraged the huddle of Fae.

"You scurvy knave, she shall be mine!" Sanguinar called melodramatically from amongst his army of skeletons.

Alfazar turned and spied the phearsanú leaning casually against the hilt of his rapier, which was thrust into the sand. Undead clustered all round him. "Mongrel dog, you shall be put down this day!" Alfazar yelled back vehemently. "And she will belong to me," he added as an afterthought.

"A real woman will fight for herself!" a third, unfamiliar voice cut in. "Neither of you shall have me."

Artyom stood, hands on hips, staring Sanguinar down. The plucky lad pulled his elbow-length gloves on more tightly, rustled his skirts, and punched into the air, yelling "Shi–shi–shaboom!" in a ridiculous falsetto voice. In response, an invisible piledriver descended upon the nearest skeleton, clipping its side and sending bone shards spinning through the dry air. It fell, obliterated.

"Yes, let's go!" Sanguinar cackled, pulling his sword free and swiping it through the air.

Without warning, a dozen tiny warcries filled the air. The relatively small group of Fae behind Alfazar screamed and broke towards Sanguinar, brandishing whatever weaponry they had. Soon all of them joined the charge.

They were terrifying. Even as Alfazar watched, they all—down to the smallest—ran headlong towards combat with their captor's creations. In that moment Sanguinar's horrible treatment became their strength and their shield, spurring them on to feats of immense bravery and recklessness. Their faces came alive with viciousness; defiance and fury swirled in their eyes; hope was kindled within the breast of every faun, satyr, nymph, brounie, gnome, and human. Alfazar found himself deeply moved as he joined their glorious flight across the sands, in defiance of all odds and common sense.

Skeletons moved to intercept. The two forces met, and Alfazar only had time to react.

He threw a knife, then broke the nearest skeleton's knee with a well-placed kick. Its skull was smashed by the cloven hoof of a passing faun as it struggled to rise again. On Alfazar's right he saw a gnome—the one from before—scream and cast its severed ear at its unnatural assailant. Now totally unarmed, the gnome valiantly threw itself into melee. It clung to a bony shin for a moment, scratching and biting, until the skeleton kicked it free and smeared the impudent creature across the ground. Three more gnomes moved in to avenge their fellow, wielding long bones as clubs.

A shadow loomed across Alfazar's face and the scimitar-wielding skeleton swung its enormous weapon. The lithe bard jumped aside, letting the blow careen into the sand. He closed and grabbed at the skeleton's wrist, hoping to smother its reach advantage by getting into close quarters before it could recover. In this, Alfazar was partially successful. Reacting obscenely quickly, the skeleton dropped its weapon and punched Alfazar square in the chest, knocking the bard away. The blow crunched bones in the construct's wrist, but it came on implacably.

Alfazar snapped back into a fighting stance and readied himself to fend off the next attack, but the next punch never came; a sudden magickal assault twisted the skeleton's head half off, leaving it batting its hands aimlessly.

"Turning heads wherever I go!" Artyom proudly proclaimed as he skipped past. Alfazar spared a brief glance and was rewarded with the sight of Artyom wrenching the dancing skeleton's poncy streamers from its grasp, then entangling it with the now-animated ribbons. A brounie—a child-like creature with over-large eyes—dashed in and drove its dagger into a bony ankle as the skeleton struggled.

Returning himself to the task at hand, Alfazar grabbed up the scimitar and used it to smash his erstwhile assailant into a pile of bony splinters. That done, he cast a critical eye around the battlefield.

His heart sank.

Despite their best efforts, the Fae were outmatched. Alfazar could see numerous fresh bodies amongst the fallen bones. The skeletons were herding the survivors into two loose groups and slowly closing the noose about them. Meanwhile, Sanguinar was laughing uproariously as he skewered a satyr, sending blood spraying through the air. Only Artyom seemed to pose any real threat to the demigod's forces, and he was hopelessly outnumbered.

Alfazar sucked in a deep breath, hoping—maybe praying—that his friends were making headway inside the tent. Then, ducking below a flying brounie, he rejoined combat.

Ed frowned in concentration, heeding nothing but the task before him. Artyom's magickal rope trickery had gotten the hunter this far, but now he needed to get onto the wooden platform itself. The problem was that there was no gap between the cloth and the wood for him to get between. He could see no trapdoor either.

Nothing to it, he decided.

He drew his dagger and used it to slit the roof of the tent open. It was just like gutting a creature: a *really* big creature. Sounds of fighting filtered in through the man-sized hole. The hunter then clamped his knife between his teeth, pirate-style, and drew his axe. The plan was to twist through the hole onto the roof, slam his axe into the top of the wooden platform for support, then climb up and cut his way in from above.

The initial step went smoothly, but then his axe-stroke went awry. Ed found himself sliding feet-first towards the edge of the yurt-like tent. By the sounds of it, he'd likely have a polite pile of skeletons ready to break his fall: and then his body. Deciding that wasn't an option, Ed slammed his axe down into the fabric, punching a hole in the material and slowing his descent. It was not totally halted until he plunged his knife into the roof too, blade turned ninety degrees to catch instead of cut. He jerked to a halt with one leg hanging over the rim until he quickly snatched it back out of sight.

Not even sparing time for a peek into the chaos below, the hunter carefully began punching his way back up towards the peak. This was going to take a while.

As he worked Bugen contemplated the theological significance of his predicament. Was it significant that his most precious worldly possession was being rendered up to the service of others? Was it profound that the only digging tool available to him happened to be his holy buckler? Would it have been more convenient to have a holy spade? Yes, he thought, on all three counts.

Still, the buckler made a surprisingly effective tunnelling implement. Sand flew everywhere across the phearsanú's expensive, pilfered carpet. Bugen knelt by a hole which he had slashed into the floor covering, through which the priest was excavating a tunnel. Once there was enough space below the cages he could smash his way through their relatively flimsy floors, freeing the remaining Fae. Bauchans, dryads and the other species offered him whispered words of encouragement as he laboured.

He kept up a constant stream of prayer as muffled noises of destruction drifted through the tent door.

Poke.
Poke. Poke.
$#&@, I'm getting bored.
It was nearly time. He could feel the tension building within: that primal fury which had been his companion for as long as he could remember. The craving to prove the world wrong. This little farce with the skeletons was just the beginning.

Soon, very soon, he would have their blood. And then he would have his Dragon.

Sanguinar sighed and turned his attention back to what could laughably be called the 'fight' at hand. His deliciously malevolent creations had corralled the surviving Fae into a small group and were methodically picking them off. That $#&@ing mage was the only thing really preventing the skeletons from crushing the other little meat-sacks. He watched as the princess smashed the ribcage of a necrotic statue into smithereens, preventing it from beheading the one remaining satyr.

Still, Sanguinar had to admit that the lad made a *fine* woman. One half of the comic duo... speaking of which, where was the humourless one? Was that bumbling oaf still cowering in the tent? Or maybe they thought to steal his power from him. *Good luck*, Sanguinar thought. Smugness settled over his thoughts like a blanket. Even if Ed found the Moon, it would take more than mere physical separation to free it from Sanguinar's control. He had spent centuries bending it to his will.

Any man will fall if you grab his ball, he chuckled to himself.

The phearsanú got to his feet and admired the artwork he had carved into an expiring faun's face, gleefully noting that ichor still weakly pulsed from the stab wound through it's stomach. It made no noise: was too weak. *Excellent*, he thought viciously. *You will be the first.*

Leaving his rapier rammed through another corpse, the Red One stepped forwards and picked up a shattered skull. Turning, he knelt by the faun. "I know you can hear me," he told it gently, almost intimately. "Do not worry," he continued, caressing the creature's ruined face. "It will all be over soon."

His dagger plunged into the faun's stomach and dragged sideways. It let out one final, strangled bleat.

Sanguinar carefully inspected the ruined insides, then tracked upwards and grasped a weakly pulsating, fleshy rope. Holding tightly, he tore out the faun's aorta and jammed his improvised bowl below the mess. Blood drained slowly into the cranium.

His face split into a malicious leer. Time to make things more interesting... much more interesting.

"Slam shot!" Artyom yelled. Two skeletal automata, both wrapped in ribbons, were thrown off their feet. They met head-on in mid-air and collapsed into bony rubble.

"Nice," Alfazar commended the mage as he threw his last knife; the scimitar had been long lost in the melee. Alfazar's blade whickered past the mage's head and cracked into the undead behind him, spoiling the blow it had aimed at Artyom.

Quick as a cat, Artyom whipped around and entangled the new threat. He lifted the skeleton skyward, then sent it rocketing towards the ground. Alfazar expertly shoved another necromantic creation into the flying skeleton's path; neither got back up.

"Oh yeah, you just got Artyomed!" the mage yelled at the splintered bones. Alfazar shot the mage a look. "And Alfazared. Yeah... Artyom-and-Alfazared. That's the one I was going for."

"Just give me the knife back."

Artyom's ribbons seized the blade and tossed it back to the bard, who deftly caught it. They raced back to aid the remaining Fae.

ᗫ   ᗏᚷᗌ   ᗏᚷᗌ   ᗏᗌᗏᗌ ✕ ᗏᗌᗏᗌ   ᗏᚷᗌ   ᗏᚷᗌ   ᗌ

There was enough sand removed now for a dryad to wriggle through the gap beneath the cages, but Bugen was having trouble cracking through the floor. The iron mesh below the wood was not very thick, but the awkward angle prevented the priest from getting any power behind his blows. So far he had only succeeded in rolling over the weapon's edge in a few places.

The Fae dared not handle his sword, weakened as they already were by the cages.

Maybe a supernatural tool would be required where the mundane version had failed. So thinking, Bugen stepped back and summoned his ethereal blade. It flashed into being alongside its usual heatless fire. With a mental command Bugen sent it carefully between the bars of the cage containing the dryad. "Take it," he told her.

She tentatively passed one woody hand through the fiery tongues, then reached forth more confidently when it did not cause pain or injury. Her nervous expression settled into one of determination as her hand closed around the hilt.

Bugen breathed a sigh of relief. His hunch had been correct; Fae creatures, blood thick with magick, could wield the incorporeal blade. Never before had he attempted anything like this. It simply was not done. Still, he was glad, for it was much less likely that he would accidentally injure the cell's other occupants now.

"Cut the floor," he commanded. "Quickly!" The dryad braced one hand above the pommel and drove the weapon through the mesh. Bugen squirmed a little; he could feel the movement of the sword, and it was supremely odd to have someone else controlling it. Nevertheless, the blade punched through the timber and down into the space Bugen had excavated earlier. "Good. Again!"

Nearly ready, Sanguinar thought. He dragged another corpse into place, forming a small mound of the recently deceased. He fancied that it resembled a bonfire, and reflected that here was the spark which would set the world alight.

So thinking, Sanguinar turned and scanned the desert for fresh cadavers. There was no shortage, for nearly thirty or so of the pitiful Fae had fallen. He continued to collect and heap them up as an offering to himself. It was sweaty work, but the anticipation of what was to come more than compensated for the effort.

At first it displeased him that there was an unfortunate lack of human corpses in his gift, but he soon realised that it was better this way; they would experience the full horror of his success before being consumed. It was no less than what the $#&@ers deserved. And then... then he could move on the others.

Sanguinar turned back to his construction. Anger expanded in his mind, leaving no room for other thoughts. Yes, this was long past overdue. Now there would be a reckoning.

He was right, and wrong.

The pair's brief escapade had downed four of the damned skeletons, but the Fae had also lost numbers. Alfazar reckoned there were only a dozen left—it was difficult to tell amongst the chaos—versus in excess of twenty skeletons. Good thing the hideous statues did not get back up after they were struck down. This observation niggled at the bard's memory; something here seemed out of place.

The thought was put on hold as Alfazar spear-tackled a foe aiming to stove a nymph's face in. Its neck snapped and vertebrae tumbled free. The frail but decidedly daemonic-looking woman had just opened her mouth to offer thanks when a sharpened femur speared through her chest, spraying the bard with gore. She shrieked and fell amongst the remains of her vanquished opponent, lifeblood leaking into the sand.

Alfazar cast around wildly, trying to locate the new attacker. His eyes fell on the prancing bone-bouquet skeleton, which was readying another projectile.

The bard was in motion before the throw even began. He sprinted towards the revenant and launched himself into a roll as it completed its swing. The improvised javelin flew overhead and tumbled away into the desert. Alfazar rose to his feet and ran on, careening into the skeleton. The momentum of the fully-fleshed man collapsed it onto the ground, where it tried to rise even though both legs were broken. Alfazar scrambled away on all fours whilst the frustrated undead flailed at him with its shattered limbs. It stopped when one of the remaining gnomes clubbed it into submission.

"Thanks," Alfazar sighed. The gnome just nodded and let out a feral hiss, then began looking for a new target.

Sand squeaked underneath Artyom's feet as he trotted over, lifting his dress to avoid it getting tangled around his legs. "Alfazar! Something unusual is happening."

"More unusual than you in a dress?" the bard queried as Artyom helped him to his feet.

"The skeletons..."

It did not take long for the dryad to punch out a circle of mesh big enough to climb through. She relinquished control of Bugen's blade and jumped onto the weakened section of flooring. It took several thumps before the timber gave way completely.

Bugen looked around anxiously to check that nothing outside had noticed, but the noises of battle continued without interruption. Satisfied, he reached into the tunnel, reefed out the disc of wood and its dangerous cold iron covering, and cast it away.

"Go, go," the dryad urged its smaller companions. Several made faint noises of celebration as they slipped through the narrow tunnel. Meanwhile, Bugen moved over to the second cage and directed the flaming blade to slice another hole into the carpet. The Fae in this prison looked on with anticipation, hoping against hope to join their fellows in freedom.

Shortly about a dozen Fae were free of their gaol, and Bugen was on the way to digging another tunnel.

A hand fell on his shoulder as he laboured. "Allow me," the dryad said with a gentle smile. "I was made for this." The priest stood and moved away, nodding solemnly; perhaps she was, in more ways than she suspected.

She knelt beside the small furrow which Bugen had already opened, then buried her hands in the grit. Under her ministrations the little ditch rapidly grew into a sizeable hole, until after about a minute she almost vanished underground. Bugen could not tell exactly how she managed this feat, but he did fancy that he saw her fingers sprouting down into the sand like vivacious, grasping roots.

Bugen availed himself of the opportunity to retrieve his worldly sword and tend to it. He drew the deceased priestess' dagger and used it to turn over the rolled edges of his weapon before sheathing them both. Steel sharpens steel, he observed, before feeling that peculiar mental tug once more.

The dryad was driving his otherworldly sword up through the floor of the last cage. She cut a sizeable opening in short order, then retreated from the tunnel—sword in hand—to allow the captive Fae to escape.

They did so with celerity, helped clear by their already-emancipated brethren. As the group gathered in the middle of the tent Bugen noted that many looked stronger and more lively already, which he attributed to a combination of renewed hope and being free of the iron enclosures.

The priest opened his mouth to deliver some words of encouragement, but then felt a malevolent presence. The tension, which had abated somewhat with the freeing of the Fae, returned tenfold. "Wait here," he mouthed. Drawing his sword, Bugen walked briskly to the door, through which he could now hear the Red One's muffled voice and a sound like rolling thunder.

Everywhere they looked, skeletons were collapsing, unravelling. The clatter of disintegrating automata filled the air, yet there was no cause for celebration. Artyom could see the comprehension dawn on Alfazar; it manifested as a tightening around the eyes and a slight flaring of the nostrils.

The sky was growing dark overhead, well ahead of dusk, as unnatural clouds drew over the desert. The mage instinctively knew that this was a spectacle not seen in millennia.

One of the handful of remaining Fae yelped and jumped forwards a little. Artyom tore his gaze away from the weather and watched as the Fae peered down at a stray metacarpal by its foot with suspicion.

The minute bone twitched from side to side, then resumed its creep through the sand, prompting the Fae to dance out of the way again. The mage could see the short track which the bone left now, like an obscene version of the lines left along beaches by children trailing sticks. Seized by a sudden suspicion, Artyom gazed back across the battlefield.

Everywhere, bones were on the move. Femurs slid like rigid snakes, hips ploughed up sand as they dragged, and skulls rolled with obscene irregularity. Even the bones of the fallen Fae, still encased in flesh, were in inexorable motion. The multitude of trails they painted across the desert were converging on a single point.

Following the lines with his gaze, Artyom spied a small mound of Fae corpses: perhaps a dozen.

And behind it stood Sanguinar, cradling a skull in one hand as if it were a goblet of wine. "I was wondering how long it would take you to notice me," the Red One drawled.

The sky was now quite dark, but the clouds still offered no relief from the arid air. Sanguinar waited for the survivors to congregate in a loose group before continuing his monologue.

"You $#&@ing idiots were never a threat," he explained. Corpses continued to magickally pile onto the mound, making it broader and deeper even as Sanguinar began climbing it. "You danced your way here like puppets." His ascension was slow and seemingly relaxed, but Artyom could see the tension in his posture even from this distance. "I let you come. We had already enjoyed the opening act together. 'Why not more?' I asked myself."

Sanguinar's face split into a mocking grin. "My favourite part..." he began, then he halted and made a show of laughing smugly. Arrogance dripped from his every pore. "My favourite part is that you think you came here to defeat me. Me!" A look of disdain stole over his features as he continued towards the ever-growing summit. Artyom estimated around eighty bodies—fleshed and unfleshed—were contained in the pile now. "As if!"

The mage watched as a cascade of vertebrae and skulls flowed up towards Sanguinar. He thought he knew where this was heading, but he knew no way of stopping it.

"You did not come here to defeat me!" the Red One yelled. Vertebrae knotted together beneath him, lifting him higher on a skein of twisted spines. Darkness and baleful power spewed from the phearsanú like an aura of evil as he rose. Artyom could feel it; he could practically smell it. "You came to be the jewel in my crown," Sanguinar screamed, eyes pitch black. "The final ingredient."

ℒ ⚜ ⚜ ⚜ ⚔ ⚜ ⚜ ⚜ ℛ

Bugen peered through the door, horrified by what he was seeing. A seething mound of flesh and skeletons flowed and crunched beneath a tiny figure held aloft on a teetering pylon of bone. Then Sanguinar thrust his hands skyward.

Power coruscated up the Red One's arms and into the object he held; Bugen guessed it was an upturned skull. "And now, in your closing act," Sanguinar cackled, "I will give you the privilege of witnessing my apotheosis!"

Ethereal energies took hold of the phearsanú. He glowed with a negative light, and a nimbus of dark power lifted him further into the air. This phenomenon soon enveloped the entire churning mass of bodies below, lifting them free of the desert too. It made Bugen's skin crawl.

Then Sanguinar dashed the skull into the hovering grave.

Waves of sickly green light burst across the desert, accompanied by a horrible ripping sound. Bugen was forced to turn away from the flare, but not before seeing every Fae corpse torn asunder simultaneously, liberating skeletons from fleshy prisons. Blood, innards, and gobbets of meat exploded outwards and were consumed by—or maybe they powered—the fell magicks being worked, leaving only naked bones behind. In the midst of this hung Sanguinar, revelling in the carnage.

Bugen turned away and retched at the revolting smell. He took shallow breaths, trying to keep his gorge down. His eyes remained squeezed shut until the powerful waves of light began to abate, but he did not have an opportunity to open them before he heard it.

A swelling, trumpeting roar. A noise culled from a thousand tortured throats simultaneously. It was the stuff of nightmares: the sounds of damnation dredged up from the bowels of the Dread Realms and sent echoing through the bone dragon's unnatural maw. The cry cycled up in pitch until it was lost to human hearing, leaving behind only a subsonic growl which shook Bugen's organs inside him.

All at once the fell light stopped. The swirling atmospheric phenomenon collapsed down to a pinpoint and winked out of existence. Dead silence fell.

Bugen's eyes flew open and darted around wildly, desperate to reacquaint themselves with their surrounds, until they fixed on the new, overpowering addition to the desert landscape.

There was something intrinsically abhorrent about the fleshless monster, something which went far beyond the fact that it was constructed from the bodies of the dead. In a moment of hysterical logic Bugen reflected that *all* creatures—him included—had bodies formed from those of the dead, and he therefore concluded that the revulsion he felt now stemmed from more than fear or instinct. As he watched the dragon he realised that it was the parody of life which was most disgusting. Though it roared, growled, and crouched like a living animal, the necromantic creation was in reality a travesty, an empty, hollow creature, like a shell of hatred and malice draped over a decaying scaffold. Sol was not in it.

So realising, Bugen turned his attention outwards once more.

Sanguinar sat nestled at the crook between the dragon's shoulders and its neck. The phearsanú's hands were stretched skyward, and his upturned face bore a beautific expression. A combination of closed eyes and an off-kilter smile suggested a satisfaction which was almost sexual in its intensity; Bugen blushed at the thought, then pondered how ridiculous that reaction was under the current circumstances.

Before anybody could recover enough to move, Sanguinar exhaled and lowered his hands. The sound came clearly across the desert. Without opening his eyes, Sanguinar held up a finger and said, "Hold on." Bugen was taken aback by how mellow the corrupt Fae sounded. "Before we continue, I'd like to point out that things have become a bit unfair." Green eyes snapped open before Sanguinar continued. "There's only two of us now, against... eightish of you. Still, I feel like we should press on," he chuckled from his perch.

"We defy you!" Artyom yelled as he stepped forward. "Me and..."

At that moment Artyom spotted Bugen in the doorway of the tent. "...the cleric!" the mage finished triumphantly.

Ed stood, panting and pale, on the small wooden platform. The strenuous climb and stress had left him exhausted.

A ray of sunlight angling its ways past the hunter revealed a simple piece of metalwork in the centre of the space. This held a marbled globe roughly the size of a severed head. The sphere was smooth but its surface roiled with chaotic patterns in ever-changing shades of green. Deep green.

The Reaper's voice rang in Ed's head: *Mover of Pickles indeed.* He had found it, and he permitted himself a short moment to enjoy the glow of success. Perhaps now they stood a chance.

Ed moved forward and was about to pick up the Moon when he had a sudden foreboding. This orb was the power of a God of Death...

He turned to the wall he had cut his way in through—the one opposite Sanguinar and whatever awful critter he had summoned out there—and quickly sliced away a large square of fabric. This was thrown over the orb, then the whole lot was bundled unceremoniously into Ed's pack. He felt mildly nauseated, even with the cloth between the Moon and his flesh, but it passed quickly.

Clutching his kukri, Ed jumped out onto the roof. He bounced past an open panel, giving it a wide berth, and slid until near the lip of the tent. At a precisely chosen time, he twisted and plunged the knife through the wall. The sound of tearing fabric accompanied his descent, until he touched down gently on the desert floor. He butchered his way through the back of Sanguinar's tent and proceeded inside, where he joined the huddle of Fae which had apparently been freed by Bugen. "What'd I miss?" Ed asked them quietly, trying to spy the priest or any of the others.

A shout from the doorway interrupted any answer.

Bugen did not miss a beat. "Drop it!" he commanded over his shoulder, then, when he felt the dryad's grip vanish, he hurled his spiritual sword at Sanguinar. The fiery blade flew straight and true, streaking over the sand. Alfazar, Artyom, and their companions watched the weapon complete a full revolution, heads moving in eerie unison as they tracked its path; then it crashed into Sanguinar.

Chapter 10

Aggressive Theodicy

I remember when I first clapped eyes on it. We had been at sea for eight months straight; the alcohol was gone and our water was salty and stagnant. Our food was fair crawling with weevils, and some of us—not naming any names—were mighty happy whenever we managed to catch one of the 'orrible little mice. Tasted better than their droppings, y'see?

We were beginning to think we'd go the way of the other voyages of 'discovery': just motes on the seafloor or in the gullet of some leviathan.

Anyhow, there I was in the crow's nest. There was a speck on the horizon, and it was the first speck we'd seen in moons. I called out the heading and we hauled rudder to get there. Most of us didn't care if it was a new land or nothing; it was land! And when we made it to shore—fresh water!

The boys dashed off to drink their fill, but y'know what Ainsworth did? He staggered off the longboat—we were all pretty thin and shaky by then—walked to the tideline, and sat on the sand. He just sat there and wept like a child.

After ten minutes I asked him 'What's wrong?' and he just looked up, eyes all red-rimmed, and said "I'm naming her 'Arcana'." And I knew that he had plans for it already.

Crewman from Sir Hupert Ainsworth's expedition

 UGEN'S blade ricocheted off the phearsanú with a plangent *ting*, leaving nary a bruise. Sanguinar smiled evilly and opened his mouth as if preparing to gloat.

Then pandemonium broke loose as everyone moved at once.

The group of twenty-odd Fae burst from the tent, practically shoving Bugen out of their way. They spilled across the sand and threw all manner of spells at the bone dragon, which was painted with flickering lights and bursts of colour. The magickal assault did no discernible damage to its target, but the dragon was definitely aggravated; it hissed and snapped at the frustrating, popping specks of energy assailing it. Under cover of this barrage, the Fae converged upon their brethren near Alfazar and Artyom.

"Keep him distracted!" Ed yelled to Bugen as he sprinted past and headed for the others. Buhbuh ran after, panting in the heat.

"Aye." Bugen pointed and his ghostly weapon sped back at the dragon, picking up speed as it arced across the sand. This time it struck home with somewhat more success, biting away a section of rib from the beast's torso. The chip of bone fell to the ground without the dragon even noticing; it was too busy pulping the brave dryad, who had strayed too close in her defiance of the beast.

The whole situation, Bugen reflected sorrowfully, was like trying to sink a ship using only a limp feather, except that the ship was forty-foot long with gnashing teeth, rending claws, powerful limbs, and a wingspan to match. He fervently prayed that the skeletal wings were insufficient to permit true flight, but he could not rule out magickal assistance.

At that moment Ed bawled Artyom's name and threw a bundle of rope skyward. It uncoiled even as Ed ran beneath it, then the rope shot towards the bone dragon like a striking snake. In a flash

Artyom had it wrapped around the construct's skeletal legs, hoping to stymie its movement.

It was not to be; after one or two frustrated attempts to eat the nearest living Fae the enormous wyrm gathered itself and pulled its limbs free of the makeshift bonds. Sanguinar cackled as he spurred the dragon onwards.

Bugen felt it would be prudent to move to support Artyom, who was likely to be the object of Sanguinar's wrath shortly. He trotted towards the mage, readying his weapons but keeping his distance from the dragon for now. He could see Ed and Alfazar were engaged in a hurried conversation—which the priest could not hear over the rattle of animated bones—and it was also apparent that most of the surviving Fae were fleeing into the desert. Bugen could hardly blame them.

Artyom bravely—or foolishly—held his ground as the wyrm came on. The plucky mage waited until he could see the fell light in Sanguinar's eyes, then threw one of his arcane punches. It slammed into the dragon's torso and knocked its advance off course, but failed to do any meaningful damage. Horribly sinuous, the enormous construct recovered and whipped its tail through the air. The whistling appendage was too far away to strike Bugen, but Artyom was forced to duck.

He let out a cry of pain as the tail made contact.

"The nexus portal: can anyone here access it?" Alfazar asked desperately as Fae dispersed around him.

"Oi, listen up!" Ed chimed in to no avail.

Small groups of Fae fled in seemingly random directions away from the dragon, and a small part of the bard wondered why he did not follow their wise example. But no, he had a job to do.

"I feel really bad," Alfazar told Ed in a hushed but hurried voice. "We shouldn't leave them," he gesticulated towards Bugen and Artyom, "behind, but this is probably the best distraction we're going to get. We'd better hurry and get it out of here before all the Fae are gone."

"Yeah. Don't worry, they can handle themselves," Ed said tightly, trying to convince himself of the fact. Their best hope now was to get the Moon to The Reaper before the others died. He began to move off.

At that moment a distinctly human yell of pain and alarm rang out. Ed looked over his shoulder and saw something tumbling away over the sand as the dragon completed its tail swipe.

"No!" Alfazar cried.

"New plan!" Ed said. He threw his pack off and Buhbuh grasped it in his mouth. "You keep those two alive. Me and Buhbuh will take care of the rest."

The hunter and his companion sprinted off towards the ruined Phearsanú town, spraying sand as they ran.

Alfazar turned back to the fight, fearing the worst but ready to face it.

The bone dragon was weaving on its feet and shaking itself, like a wet dog with a hangover. A small part of Bugen speculated that Sanguinar was having trouble exerting his will over the construct, but the only real evidence for this was the look of intense, passionate concentration on the phearsanú's face.

At any rate, now was Bugen's chance. He made ready to dash in towards where Artyom had fallen, but the mage was already rising and moving out towards Bugen.

"Ow. I regret choosing the tallest wig he had now," Artyom observed as he reached the priest. His fingers reached up and probed the bloody patches on his crown where chunks of hair had been torn free along with the beehive hairdo. Relief coursed through the priest, but he reminded himself that there was still a ton of necromantic dragon—literally—and a demigod to deal with.

The wyrm still stood around as though confused, growling and whipping its tail but not advancing. Seeing this, Artyom hoiked up his skirt like an angry governess and stamped one hosiery-clad leg down. He magically regathered the rope and twisted it around the dragon's limbs once more. This time he managed a much more convincing snare, complete with knots.

"Hah! Puny, squishy mage," cried Sanguinar. "Let us see how squishy you really are!" His face contorted into a snarl.

Once more the bone dragon attacked. Ropes parted like warm toffee as it lunged forward and twisted, trying to duplicate the feat which had so nearly removed Artyom's head before. It seemed to be able to learn, or at least to respond to Sanguinar's commands, because it now swept its lethal tail much closer to the ground.

Artyom attempted to throw himself out of the way of the attack, but the tail made contact with him in mid-air. Bugen heard ribs crack under the onslaught, and saw the mage deposited onto the sand some ten metres away like a rag-doll.

No time to concentrate on that though: Bugen had himself to worry about. The wyrm's ram-like tail came on inexorably, barely slowed by its encounter with Artyom. Bugen's perception of space and time shrank down to that single object, that moment of impending impact. He knew beyond a shadow of a doubt that he could not dodge the attack; after all, he was encumbered by heavier armour. The scale maille would prove of little use against such a percussive blow. It seemed, then, that this was to be the end—or at least very painful.

Bugen was surprised to find a sort of tired acceptance inside himself. If this was to be his fate, then so be it; he had faith that Sol could turn his demise into something beneficial, even if he could not divine such a plan himself.

He did not even have time to complete a prayer before the tail slammed into him and... stopped.

Bugen was totally bewildered and confused, but his training quickly took over. He slammed his sword down into the now-stationary vertebrae, and punched into them with his buckler for good measure.

Alfazar saw the dragon's skeletal tail hammering towards his companions and wondered whether there would be any parts of them left to salvage. Artyom was knocked airborne, then the tail struck Bugen.

It was as if Bugen had been replaced by a pillar of stone; nay, an immovable pillar of the legendary adamantium, set on foundations which plumbed the depths of the earth. The tail simply folded around him. Alfazar heard a dull *thud* overlayed by the sound of bones splintering near the point of impact. Puffs of dust shot from over-stressed vertebrae as they crumpled and twisted. The end of the tail continued to whip around under its own momentum, bending nearly completely around Bugen, before the priest provided the last iota of force required to shatter the over-stressed structure.

Six feet of tail fell and writhed snake-like in the sand for a moment, then separated into component bones. The wyrm trumpeted its chorus of the Damned again and retreated.

"$#&@ you, you son and heir of a mongrel bitch!" Sanguinar raged at the priest. "How?"

Bugen's silence earned another round of vituperation from the apoplectic phearsanú.

Meanwhile, Alfazar dragged Artyom a little further from danger. The mage lived still, though it was clear he had taken a severe battering. Blood and sand crusted his hair, and his breath wheezed. Alfazar knew he was risking damaging Artyom by moving him without checking for internal injuries, but he thought that the alternatives were much worse.

"Bugen?" the mage moaned weakly as Alfazar dragged him.

"Alfazar, actually."

"Oh, good. Alfazar?"

"Yes?"

"I refuse to die in a dress."

How does one respond to a statement like that? Alfazar wondered. "And I refuse to see you naked," he replied after a moment. "Chin up, boy: you'll be okay. It looks like Bugen has some tricks up his sleeve."

"Huh?"

Look at that pathetic blood-bag Sanguinar told himself as he eyed Bugen. *How'd the bastard damage my Bone Dragon? What a smug $#&@er, thinking he even has a hope of defeating me. Well, little does he know...*
The Red One screwed up his face in concentration and mentally groped out towards his Dragon's severed tail.
...that I can...

It required a peculiar sort of psychical twist—something like coordinating a new limb, or interpreting input from a heretofore dormant sense—but Sanguinar managed to set in motion a particular piece of necromancy.

...do this!

He maintained fierce concentration and was delighted to see his efforts paying off. The scattered bones began to draw together once more, reforming into a section of tail ready to be grafted onto the Dragon once more. The priest's shocked expression gratified Sanguinar.

It soon became apparent that much of the bone was so structurally compromised as to be essentially useless. After a moment's consideration Sanguinar decided to loot materials from his Dragon's wings—which were basically decoration at the moment—to reinforce and weaponise its tail. After the pitiful party was defeated, he reasoned, he could render up their blood and bone to complete the Dragon, wings and all.

So thinking, Sanguinar began making alterations. The construct's wings folded in onto its body, then the individual bones began migrating down to the stump of its tail, forming a socket of sorts for the reconstructed component to slot into. His Dragon squirmed as though uncomfortable, and he found that if he did not consciously maintain the process of change it would halt by itself, as if the Dragon resisted the meddling.

I didn't realise I'd have to fight my own $#&@ing Dragon *in addition to these four bumbling idiots.*

Wait: four. Where was the hunter?

Sanguinar cast his gaze outwards, searching for the leathery git. He spotted a few small groups of Fae fleeing away across the desert haphazardly, but quickly dismissed those. Within moments he had identified Ed and his useless quadruped companion legging it towards the old town. *$#&@ing coward. Running already?* Sanguinar thought condescendingly. *We can't have that; I've got a Dragon here with your name on it. Just as soon as I finish... Would you hurry up?* he mentally shouted at the Dragon. *Get a move on!*

Oh, for $#&@'s sake.

The demigod raised his arm and fashioned an eldritch projectile from the little will that he could spare, then threw it in Ed's direction. The ball of magick—for that was how Sanguinar conceived of the warped patch of reality—arced unnaturally across the intervening space and collided with the sand at the hunter's feet. Streamers of power, all but invisible in the bright conditions, sprayed across the man like an alcohol fire in sunlight. The hunter ran on, slowing noticeably, then beginning to weave. This elicited a chuckle from Sanguinar.

The phearsanú's expression turned to one of seething fury when the idiot man shook off the lethargy and continued running; maybe he had no $#&@ing brain to put to sleep. *Fine: flee. I will find you shortly, little puppet...*

Bugen was as amazed as anybody else at the sudden turn of events. Why had the dragon's attack failed so spectacularly? The priest had no answers, but he also had no time to contemplate now. Sanguinar was clearly distracted—perhaps even on the back foot—and Alfazar needed a diversion in order to get Artyom clear; for now, Bugen needed to press the attack.

He once more took mental control of his eldritch blade, and poured his hope, fear, and righteous anger into the orders he gave it, attempting to spur the ethereal weapon on to glory. Flames hissed around the sword as it soared directly towards Sanguinar, who was still gazing off into the desert with a sour expression. It struck him square in the face.

The blade's momentum knocked Sanguinar sideways a few degrees, but once again it failed to penetrate the phearsanú's arcane defences. He must have readied some manner of additional wards since Bugen's last attack, for the blade was banished from the Mortal Plane immediately it hit Sanguinar. There was a slight sucking sound as it vanished.

The Red One's expression changed from rage to surprise, then mirth as he threw his head back and laughed uproariously, revelling in the priest's successive failures. However, his gloating did not last long. His laughter and the tiny impulse from the failed attack conspired to unseat the demigod. Sanguinar's expression now turned to one of shock, and he groped blindly for a handhold as he tumbled sideways off the dragon's back. Bugen could hear the air burst from Sanguinar as he collided with the sand some fifteen feet below.

"Well done, Bugen," Alfazar called from where he was desperately trying to patch up the mage's injuries.

To their mutual astonishment, Sanguinar began laughing once more. "No, no no no. I'd much prefer rare Bugen." He pulled himself to his feet and rearranged his bangles, blinking sand away with those uncanny eyelids. "So rare that it still bleeds!" Sanguinar cackled hysterically as he dusted himself off. He began pawing at his belt for the rapier sheathed there, but the sudden intensification of his maniacal laughter prevented him from summoning the coordination required to draw it.

The laughter doubled and redoubled until Sanguinar was *bent* double, occasionally choking and coughing, then laughing on. Soon he went red in the face and began to gasp for breath. Sanguinar, unable to indulge his tendency to lalochezia, levelled a furious gaze past Bugen's shoulder between paroxysms.

Bugen was puzzled immensely until he turned and saw that Artyom had just barely managed to prop himself up on one elbow and cast some manner of arcane magick with a one-handed gesture. These small physical actions had taken their toll on the mage, who now collapsed back into the sand and clutched his side with trembling hands. "It... hurts," Artyom gasped weakly. He coughed violently, leaving red-tinged fluid on his lips.

Nevertheless, the mage was still conscious, and potentially dangerous.

Sanguinar must have had the same thought, for at that moment the wyrm exploded across the sand, dashing forward decisively. It skirted around Bugen before he could move to intercept its advance, then its terrible head stooped over Artyom and Alfazar. Dozens of skulls had been fused together to form its unnerving visage, replete with multiple sets of unseeing eyes; baleful green light leaked from the empty sockets. Mighty jaws, scaled with mandibles, yawned wide.

Alfazar bravely tried to interpose himself between the terrible maw and Artyom, but the wyrm was not to be denied its target. Butting the bard aside almost negligently, it clamped its many hundreds of teeth around Artyom's upper arm. Skin broke and blood welled. It ran onto the bone, where it soaked in and vanished as if into a sponge. Bugen could see Artyom staring at this effect with an expression of mingled horror, pain, and curiosity, then this view was lost as the mage was hoisted into the air. The wyrm threw its head back like an enormous egret—Artyom's shoulder dislocated with a tortured *pop*—then it caught his torso firmly in its mouth. Non-existent muscles flexed, and Artyom screamed.

Sanguinar merely continued to gasp.

Faint but frantic sounds of pain spurred Bugen into desperate action. What he needed now was time, time to get to the dragon and then extricate Artyom in one piece.

So he had better *keep* Artyom in one piece.

The priest focussed his will on Sol and Her divine Light. He could have sworn that the Sun itself flared brighter for a moment, then healing energies speared down from the sky, coursed through him, and spilled over the surrounding landscape. The channelled energy felt like a warm but refreshing wind, and smelt like an airy, open woodland. Bugen loved that smell. Rich, golden light—not thin and yellow like the desert glare—burst from his buckler, and the dreadful wyrm, born of dark necromancy and hatred, shied away from it.

Bugen ran towards Artyom in an attempt to concentrate the swirling supernatural wind near the mage. As he closed the distance he noticed from the corner of his eye that the dragon's vestigial wings were disintegrating. It seemed that the wyrm was actually being *damaged* by Sol's gift, which was anathema to vile creatures of un-life. Blessing his Lady, Bugen veered towards his foe. It yelped, released Artyom from its maw, then swatted at Alfazar with a claw before retreating toward its master.

Both men crashed to the ground.

Bugen sprinted to Artyom and crouched beside him. The mage was horribly mauled—so much so that Bugen doubted his ability to deal with the injuries—and one leg was shattered such that the bone protruded from the flesh. Nevertheless, he marshalled his concentration and discipline, and soon Sol's power began to wash Artyom's life-threatening injuries away. Bone disappeared from view as the compound fracture straightened, then healed over. Blood ceased to bead from minor lacerations, and Artyom's shoulder re-seated with an audible *click*. The cleric continued concentrating for long enough for Artyom to regain consciousness, then checked on Alfazar. The bard was sitting upright and prodding at his chest through a sizeable rent in his shirt. A six-inch-square patch of shiny red flesh attested to the massive damage inflicted by the dragon's attack.

"Thank you," Alfazar said, voice betraying gratitude and uncharacteristic amazement.

"Not at all," Bugen replied wearily as he ended the flow of energy. He felt mentally drained but knew the sensation would pass shortly.

"I think I lost my beauty spot," Artyom lamented weakly. "But I'm not dead," he added, still looking deathly pale beneath his make-up. "Not yet," he continued more quietly.

They all turned to gaze at the uncanny dragon crouching next to its master. Sanguinar too was beginning to rise from the sand where his undignified convulsions had deposited him.

"Your spell seems to be wearing off," Bugen opined quietly to the mage.

"Spell..." Artyom mused, eyes glazed. "Bugen, what tricks was Alfazar talking about?"

"The dragon's tail stopped when it ran into me," the priest replied hurriedly, keeping an eye on Sanguinar. "But I had nothing to do with it, I don't know what happened."

"Something to do with your amulet, perhaps," Alfazar said as he regained his feet and took stock of his weaponry.

The mage nodded sagely, then winced. "Yes, very likely."

Something like hope swelled in Bugen's breast; perhaps they were less alone than he had imagined. "We need to keep him busy," he said, stabbing a finger towards Sanguinar. The phearsanú was busy working some sort of dark magicks to restore his favoured creation to full functionality.

"Onto it," agreed Artyom, who was regaining his characteristic optimism. "Alfazar!"

"Yes?"

"I think it's time to heat things up."

The bard immediately began digging through his pack.

"Bugen!"

"Aye."

"It's your time to shine."

"Right," the priest nodded resolutely. He snatched his weapons up off the sand, then paused and looked to Artyom. "What about you?"

"I'm a utility mage, baby," Artyom grinned, displaying bloodied teeth. "Got spells for everything."

Bugen shot yet another prayer to his Lady before springing to his feet and intoning Her light. Now prepared in body and soul, Bugen charged, sword afire with Sol's radiance. Sand squeaked and crunched under his boots; his armour grated faintly as grit rubbed against metal; sweat dripped from his brow, and his breath was loud in his ears; but the priest made no other noise.

Even as he ran he saw Artyom use his arts to take hold of a length of rope. It slithered over the ground and tied itself around Sanguinar's feet, then began coiling upwards. The phearsanú was so lost in concentration that the rope reached his thighs before he noticed, and by then it was too late. The remaining length swirled and blurred, binding Sanguinar like a fibrous python. "$#&@ you!" the demigod managed to get out before Artyom gagged him with the tail end.

Sanguinar's violent attempts to free himself simply landed him back on the ground, where he wiggled and rolled like a furious caterpillar.

At that moment Bugen reached the dragon's side. Twenty years after that fateful night with the axe, Bugen braced and delivered a blow. His glowing sword descended in an arc powered by the momentum of his charge, slicing through two of the beast's many ribs. He followed this up with a buckler strike to the same location, smashing another few bones to smithereens.

The dragon roared and pulled away, trying to bring its head around to face the unexpected assault. In its hurry it very nearly stepped on Sanguinar, but—to Bugen's disappointment—its enormous foot missed. The wyrm swiped out with its claws to keep Bugen at arm's length as it clattered out of distance.

Its attack was not entirely futile; Bugen had to pause to blink some stray sand out of his eyes. This brief lull was all that the dragon needed to regroup. It drew itself up and hissed at Bugen, then prowled back towards him like a panther, interposing itself between Bugen and its master. Its massive shoulders rolled sinuously, as though preparing to pounce.

Aware that it was likely a futile gesture, Bugen nevertheless kept his sword and buckler up in a defensive posture. He began circling warily.

ఞ   ఞ✖ஐ   ఞ✖ஐ   ఞஐఞ   ⚔   ఞஐఞ   ఞ✖ஐ   ఞ✖ஐ   ஐ

She did not know where—or even who—she was, but she did know this was not a nice place to be.

An incandescent speck flew past her, trailing a cloying smoke and emitting an eerie groan. The foul emission thickened and hung in the air like a solid entity—some horrible, gelatinous mass of pollution—as the particle wandered off. Faint groaning continued to emanate from the floating mass, then it slowly liquefied and drained away, as though siphoned off into some other dimension.

She became aware of a high-pitched keening. Looking around for its source, she found only a featureless landscape of deep red in all directions. The effect was extremely disorientating, and she felt a stab of panic. It quickly dissipated.

It returned. There were more specks: dozens of them, flying around haphazardly and singing a mournful dirge. Overlapping groans, moans, wails, and sobs filled the air just as palpably as the multi-coloured smoggy trails which snaked haphazardly around the place. And that keening...

I have to get out of here. I have to...

What did she have to do? She could not remember, until an overwhelming external Will thrust itself into her mind and supplied the answer for her.

...KILL, MAIM, BURN, REND, HATE, SLAY...

Yes: that was it, she thought vaguely, momentarily totally subject to the Will. *Or was it to protect–?*

THE PRIEST: KILL THE PRIEST!

...DECAPITATE, AMPUTATE, EXSANGUINATE, EXTERMINATE...

How was she supposed to do that? Images—strangely fractured images, with ever-shifting perspectives—fed into her mind. She tracked a quartered yellow and red shape through dozens of eyes which were not her own, trying to pin down its location. Then, acting on the Will's instructions, she lashed out at the frustratingly elusive colours.

Bugen sidestepped a clumsy attack, letting it pass by harmlessly.

For a moment everything was drowned under a red mist, then she came to and felt another surge of panic. Those colours... that shape... some significance...

She tried to remember, but the keening came back and drowned out anything resembling coherent thought.

...RAGE, CONSUME, SUBJUGATE, CONTROL...

The cleric launched a cut with his glowing sword, shearing off one of the wyrm's claws as it began to withdraw. The tiny wound generated a much greater reaction than Bugen had expected. Wondering what was going on, he retreated a step or two and made sure to keep his guard up.

Light! Blazing, incandescent light tore through the non-space that she and the specks occupied. It seared through her mind and expunged all trace of the Will for the briefest of moments. The pain was intense—even worse than her death. *What?*

She screamed a terrible scream, and dozens of other voices joined with her. Then it was gone.

The sky faded to black, and roiling clouds of darkness spun into being. Specks began churning violently, pumping out their smog, and no matter how far she fled she could not rid herself of the choking fumes, nor the infernal keening. It was terrible; by far worse than the Light.

END HIM! DO NOT LET HIM TOUCH YOU.

...SMASH, CRUSH, BITE, TEAR...

The Will again invaded her mind, taking hold of it and moulding her thoughts as it pleased. Suddenly furious, she reached out and bit at the coloured shape dancing across her mind's eye.

"Yes, yes, good." cried a few stray voices which did not seem to originate from her or the Will. Again, she could locate naught but the noxious specks. "Smash, crush, bite!" the voices chorused.

HE CANNOT DEFY ME FOR LONG. AIM FOR THE SHIELD!

...DISEMBOWEL, LOATH, SUNDER, DENY...

There was a sense of movement. Her view altered through no actions of her own, then she again felt a wash of rage, but now attenuated; it was as if she was only experiencing part of the emotion. She was still puzzling over this when another burst of light assailed her.

That second attack had been more coordinated, but Bugen still managed to back out of biting range without too much trouble. He ducked under the third, feeling a claw bounce harmlessly off his buckler. As the dragon's arm passed overhead, Bugen launched strongly off his rear foot and sprang forward to attack the creature with Sol's light once more; it did not seem fond of Her glory. His blade made contact but bounced away, leaving the wyrm angry but unscathed.

This time the dreadful Will did not depart wholly. It shrieked its commands through her mind, leaving raw mental welts.

SMASH HIS $#&@ING HEAD OFF!

Keening...

I can't. Can't, can't, can't... I need to–

BLOOD; TAKE HIS BLOOD.

Some shred of instinct which survived from her former life warned her not to, that she would become something abhorrent by doing so. She was repulsed by the idea, yet drawn to it by a powerful undertow of invasive Will. Somehow she summoned the urge to resist. *I will not! I have to... to...*

The wyrm's other forelimb lashed out and smashed into Bugen's guard, but the enchantment of his amulet held firm. He gave thanks and attempted to press a counter-attack, but the sand slid treacherously beneath his feet and prevented any retaliation.

She never managed to complete the thought, for at that moment a swarm of specks descended upon her. Their howls and gibbers filled her mind, and their secretions fouled the air, blotting out the surrounds.

Now in a total panic, she picked a direction at random and fled through the vapour. Time passed, but the noisome fog did not. *Please, please, let the specks be gone,* she pleaded internally.

Monstrous laughter swelled through the entire non-space, filling the infinity.

BUT MY DEAR, NOT EVEN I CAN GET YOU AWAY FROM YOURSELF.

The speck wept bitterly, crying a pool of cloying smoke, feeling mingled despair and disgust at her fate, all while the Will gloated over her. But it did not last long. There was just not enough of her left to hold on to anything for long.

⚜ ⚜✖⚜ ⚜✖⚜ ⚜⚜⚜⚜ ✖ ⚜⚜⚜⚜ ⚜✖⚜ ⚜✖⚜ ⚜

Alfazar darted in with a lit torch and threw it towards the dragon, hoping that the flame would catch on some of the cloth which had been incorporated into its structure along with the original skeleton army. The torch completed two, three revolutions, then bounced away from the dragon's leg and fell to the floor. A few strips of fabric smoked fitfully, then went out.

Bugen was given a momentary respite as the dragon turned its attention to the bard. He gulped down a lungful of dry air and wiped the sweat from his brow; even with the extreme aridity he was sweating faster than it could evaporate.

The fight was exhausting. Neither side seemed to have the upper hand yet, but Bugen reflected that the dragon—though apparently unable to harm him—could simply outlast him. Still, it shied away from Sol's light, which was a potential advantage.

"Bugen. Bugen!" Artyom called, weakly at first, then with more force when the priest failed to hear. The mage stumbled over the sand, panting. "The amulet: it contains a spell. I can feel it now. You need to cast it."

"Cast a spell?" Bugen replied evenly, though he was internally screaming, *I have no idea how to cast a spell; I'm a priest. Do I look like an arcanist?*

"Yes. Just—Alfazar!"

Returning his attention to the fight, Bugen saw the bard side-step an attempt to squash him into jelly. The manoeuvre was successful, but a treacherous divot in the sand left Alfazar off-balance, and the dragon pounced on the opportunity. As it raised a clawed hand and prepared to swipe at its fallen prey, Bugen did the only thing he could think of. Forsaking his weapon, he ran in under the wyrm's twisted neck and grabbed hold of its torso with his glowing hand.

The necromantic beast pulled away and unleashed a foul scream, but even this was not enough to send its stroke totally awry. The tip of one claw raked across Alfazar's torso, cutting through the skin and exposing red muscle beneath. It was a fell wound.

Bugen could not help. Hoisted into the air as the dragon reared up on its hind legs, he was left hanging twenty feet above the ground, clinging onto the ribcage of the enraged dragon with one hand. The other clasped his buckler, and there was no way in the Dread Realms that he was relinquishing his holy symbol.

After several fruitless attempts to bat him away the dragon changed tactics. Bugen white-knuckled the rib he was holding as the entire world seemed to sway perilously. He glanced downward—foolishly—and was distressed to see that a spreading cloud of smoke had obscured Alfazar, Artyom, and the dragon's hindquarters. Then, on the edge of the miasma, he spied a loose pile of rope. Damnation!

What do I do, Sol? Whatwhatwhat... Bugen thought desperately as he tried to locate Sanguinar. *Cast a spell? I don't know how!*

The dragon reared again and tried to shake Bugen free, making reconnaissance or introspection impossible. The bone he grasped remained firm for one or two vicious shakes before disintegrating, and for one heart-stopping moment Bugen fell backwards into empty air. Though the dragon might not be able to hit him, the ground surely could, Bugen thought as he cried out. Then his free hand closed around another rib, and he slammed into the constructs's flank again. His scream mingled with the dragon's as it made ready to body-slam him into the desert sand.

Bugen leapt away at the last moment and cannoned into the ground. His legs took the brunt of impact, but the momentum of his maille-clad torso quickly threw him off his feet, sending him tumbling from beneath the wyrm. To his dismay, he was forced to drop his buckler, lest he land on it and break bones. It fell away, the light from its holy symbol winking out.

The sight tore at Bugen's heart.

The portal disgorged Ed onto the enchanted lake. His body revelled in the sudden change of climate, but Ed's mind was not to be distracted. "Buhbuh, come back here," he yelled before his dog could get too far away. "We can go through here," he explained through gasps. "Just need to rest up a tick."

That magickal bastard.

"Here, gimme that," the hunter said as he took the pack back from Buhbuh, who panted all the louder now that his mouth was free. "Good job."

With that, Ed concentrated really hard and stepped into the portal, making a new passage directly to The Reaper's gate. He didn't want to get any closer than that through magickal means; teleporting directly into her lounge room would probably not be a clever way of extending his lifespan.

He ran through the lifeless field of semi-corpses, then hammered on The Reaper's door. It swung open, and he burst into the room. "We got it!" he shouted triumphantly, holding the bag aloft.

The Reaper seemed almost surprised... almost. "Excellent. Come, quickly, lay it here," she instructed Ed briskly, indicating the centre of a large and complicated glyph which had been drawn onto the floor. "Do not disturb the lines." Meticulously prepared stacks of reagents, jars of unguents and lots of other arcane guff were arrayed around the convoluted pattern, along with an enormous book.

Ed opened the pack with trembling hands and fished out the cloth-swathed Moon. Carefully, very carefully, he lowered it into the prepared position, then swept its covering off.

Both paused to inspect the orb and its churning green marbling. It seemed more agitated than before, and Ed wondered how his companions were doing back in the desert. "Do you need help? How long will this take, anyway?" he asked The Reaper.

Bugen curled into a foetal position until he came to a halt, lying on his back in the baking sand with his gorget digging into his neck. Neither, blessedly, were broken. His buckler, however, was gone, and with it so was part of his bulwark against terror.

He sat up with a groan, sending rivers of sand flowing off him, then coughed violently as the thick, unnatural smoke assailed his lungs. Pawing at his eyes, Bugen frantically tried to locate his buckler. The dappled, muted sunlight which penetrated to his level did nothing to assist him.

As he searched desperately on his hands and knees he heard another screech from the dragon, and a strange, wavering light kindled somewhere nearby. He guessed that either Alfazar or Artyom had managed to set the dragon partially ablaze, and that it was not impressed. The fire cast perilous, jagged shadows through the magickally-enhanced smoke as its host searched for new quarry.

It did not take the wyrm long to locate the pair; Bugen could hear indistinct shouting coming from them as they no-doubt attempted to evade it. He had a sudden horrible intuition that his companions would meet their doom at the beast's hands in a matter of moments. Both of them were already wounded, whereas he, Bugen, was not.

So thinking, Bugen attempted to summon the Light of his Lady to draw the dragon's attention. He screwed up his face and tried to focus on Sol, but worries churned through his mind and derailed his thoughts. Bugen felt his panic beginning to take over, so out of sheer desperation he slapped himself across the face. "Focus," he berated himself out loud, then he once more hunched over, squeezed his eyes shut, and clenched his fists tightly. He drew in a sharp breath and held it until his lungs burned. Blood thudded in his ears along with Artyom and Alfazars' cries.

Eventually the air burst from Bugen and he was left to stare at his hands in disbelief; he had failed to find Sol's presence for the first time in over a decade. It was a horrible and alien feeling which sent shame and inadequacy crawling up his spine.

Everything seemed to be going sideways at a rapid rate, and he now felt truly helpless. His companions were once more fighting for their lives; he did not know where Ed was; he had no idea how to cast the spell contained in the amulet, nor what it did; and his buckler was lost. The priest also harboured a dreadful certainty that Sanguinar was not far away.

The last emotion grew stronger and stronger as the seconds ticked by. Some survival instinct pulled Bugen to his feet and sent his gaze darting around through the twisting smoke in an attempt to locate Sanguinar. Every ripple and swirl seemed to coalesce into a man-shaped silhouette as Bugen beheld it, and he briefly wondered whether the effect was mundane or magickal.

Even as he searched, the firelight faded and died. Perhaps the dragon had managed to extinguish itself, or maybe Sanguinar's power was blotting all illumination out. Terrified by what the darkness hid, the priest instinctively grabbed for the only armament left to him: the priestess' dagger.

The dagger! The tiny weapon was a poor substitute for the familiar weight and presence of his buckler, but it still bore Sol's symbol. Bugen beheld the familiar quartered circle and his feeling of ragged panic subsided somewhat.

Frenzied thoughts hardened and coalesced, reaching a resolution of sorts. *May Sol guide them with me as Her tool,* he thought, remembering back to his short time in Adeline. He needed to distract that dragon, lest it kill the others. And though he had no idea *how* to use it, he began to feel that *when* to use the amulet was fast approaching—if not already passed.

You'll know when to use it, he reminded himself: yes, that was what Dell said.

A few quick slices of the short blade opened up the front of his tabard and severed the clasps on his armour, exposing his sweat-soaked gambeson beneath. Bugen took hold of the flat medallion which lay innocuously against this, then yanked it away from his chest, snapping its golden chain. Panting, he held the rectangular amulet up to inspect it, hoping against hope for some manner of instructions to make themselves evident.

There were no instructions, nor were there moving parts, buttons or clasps anywhere. No matter: his actions from here on out would differ only a little.

Concentrating with every fibre of his being, Bugen summoned Sol's light. Unusually, this time he could not tell if the pillar of golden rays speared down from the sky or up from his shaking hands. Regardless, glorious radiance penetrated the murk and suffused the amulet which Bugen held before him. His skin tingled.

The ruby clutched in his hand sprayed ruddy brilliance all around, revealing Sanguinar scarcely ten yards away. "Found you. And now you die," the Red One—now literally red—gloated as he drew his rapier. He took a step forward and levelled his weapon at Bugen, surveying his prey through black eyes. "And don't think you'll go to your $#&@ing goddess when I'm done with you," he hissed.

Bugen blanched, wondering how he was supposed to fight a demigod with only a mysterious medallion and a dagger one tenth of the rapier's length. He held the dagger out at arm's length anyway, hoping to deflect any thrusts. So defended, Bugen began edging backwards, brandishing the amulet towards the phearsanú. Nothing happened. He desperately shook it at Sanguinar. Again, nothing. Despair sank its claws into Bugen once more.

Sanguinar laughed malevolently. "Sent here to die with a tool beyond your use. Pitiful creature. Now–"

The bone dragon chose that moment to vent its extreme displeasure at the return of the hated light. Spewing the sounds of a thousand tortured voices from its monstrous jaws, it wheeled around and bit at Bugen from behind. Even Sanguinar seemed surprised, but the cleric had no time to think on this as he threw himself out of the way.

The wyrm crawled over Bugen and pressed its blasphemous body down on him, pinning him against the ground. It was evident that the beast intended to crush the life out of him, to simply outlast his weak biological form, though it screamed and writhed in pain as it did so. "No, you idiot creature!" Bugen heard the necromancer rage over the din.

He felt five years old again: helplessly trapped by the overwhelming power of an eldritch foe. The cacophony was deafening, the darkness oppressive, and the situation dire. Panic faded, to be replaced with despair. There would be no priestess to rescue him this time; now *he* was the priest.

Bugen imagined that his skull would burst under the pressure at any moment. Breathing was nigh on impossible, and hope had all but faded. *At least my friends still have a chance.*

His right arm was trapped beneath the dragon's foul rib cage, but the left, still clasping the amulet, was free. Summoning the last of his strength and will, Bugen thrust the glowing medallion up into the wyrm's torso, right where a living creature's heart would be. *Oh Sol, ohSol, ohSolohSolohSol,* he prayed incoherently, gasping for air.

Sol's symbol flared into being on the amulet. He watched in amazement as it turned into a powerful, radiant beacon. There was a sound as of smashing glass, or a ringing bell, or a great, rushing wind, then intense violet fire burst from Bugen's hand. Spheres of it streamed outward in powerful, coruscating waves. Everything shook; the world groaned. The dragon came apart, and Bugen was buried under a pummelling rain of clattering bones. His vision tunnelled.

Awareness retracted down to a point.

Winked out.

Chapter 11

Ad Solis Ortum

Fae attacks were particularly audacious in the lead-up to the Festival of the White Lady of 249 AU (After Unification). This prompted the young and impetuous King Bartholomew II to gather a military force the likes of which had not been seen since the Unification.

The King's army began a campaign of extermination, sweeping through many Fae-held forests, caves, and other environs. Alas, this Purge was not to last. Bartholomew II was slain when his encampment was raided by Fae, leaving no direct heir to the throne.

Thus began the Great Schism (251 AU–310 AU), the closest that the Kingdom of Elandria has come to civil war in its illustrious history.

After a brief period of political turmoil, Faust united under the rule of Madam Fischer, a cousin of the royal blood. Shortly thereafter, Graea came under the leadership of Dante Cotillard, one of the late King's more charismatic and level-headed vassals. Faustians believed that Fischer had the strongest blood ties to the throne, whilst Graeans argued that their leader was proven by more than mere relation.

Tensions were high. Trade between Faust and Graea became fraught with disagreement. Neither ruler could effectively police the sea borders, so bands of Faustian thugs took up the age-old practice of pillaging from their neighbours. Retaliatory expeditions of Graean vigilantes became commonplace, and war threatened.

This situation lasted until 292 AU. The Fae returned from licking their wounds, and their increasing activity lead to a renewal of diplomacy. This resulted in a strategic marriage to heal the rift between the continents. Fischer's son, Klemens, and Cotillard's granddaughter, Corilla, became the parents of Queen Amaryllis I, widely recognised as the first monarch of the Second Dynasty. Her ascension marked the official end of the Great Schism.

Excerpt from *An Abbreviated History of Elandria* by C. L. Mitchell

"

HE ritual will take some time," The Reaper told Ed as she gathered a handful of reagent and prepared to cast it onto the glyph. "In this case it is necessary to undo a mental bond, which is always more difficult than undoing a physical one. You may wish to return and aid your compa–"

Suddenly, her grey mouth tightened and her eyebrows drew together, in what Ed recognised as a display of extreme emotion.

"What? What is it?" Ed nearly shouted, fearing the worst.

The Reaper turned to him with an expression of open bewilderment. "The ritual—it is complete."

"Bollocks!" Ed cursed as he turned. "Look after Buhbuh!" he added, then ran outside, through the yard, and into the portal. If even The Reaper had no idea what was happening... He had to get to his friends.

Ed bolted through the door of the tent, fully expecting to come face-to-face with a pissed-off bone dragon and its jumped-up creator. Instead, a desolate wasteland met his eyes. He pulled up sharply, panting.

The corpse of the bone dragon—if it could be described as such—dominated the vista. Its torso, neck, and most of its spine had been erased from existence, leaving behind a formless jumble of bones which littered the sand between its head and hind limbs like a confused forest. The wyrm's extremities had simply collapsed wherever they were when whatever had happened... had happened. Some parts smouldered faintly. Sanguinar was nowhere to be seen, and neither was Bugen.

All was eerily quiet.

He sprinted over to Alfazar, who was laying on the sand about sixty feet from the tent. Tamtem sat nearby. The bard's arm was held in a sling fashioned from a strip of Artyom's dress. "Ed," the bard greeted his companion solemnly. "We did it. Sanguinar is gone."

"Are you okay?" Ed asked, spying a blood-stained bandage wrapped around Alfazar's chest.

"I'll survive," Alfazar winced. "The claw glanced off my ribs."

Satisfied that the bard was not about to bleed out, Ed got down to business. "I got the ball to The Reaper, then something weird happened. Was it you guys?"

"It was Bugen," Artyom called from near the edge of the bone mound, about twenty yards away. The lad was pulling bones out of the pile and tossing them behind him, as though searching for something. His slow and careful movements attested to his lingering wounds.

"Bugen? Where is he?" Ed asked, casting around for a glimpse of red and yellow.

"He's gone," Alfazar explained.

"Gone? As in..?"

"Not dead, I think," Artyom interjected, still labouring. "Unless he is still in here somewhere, which I doubt."

"Alright, will someone tell me what happened here?" Ed asked in frustration, unable to make heads nor tails of the others' utterances.

Alfazar stood slowly and began hobbling over to join the mage, leaning on Ed for support. As they walked he told their tale to the hunter, who listened in amazement. Laughter-based magickal assaults, near brushes with death, arcane rope tricks, ethereal swords, untouchable amulets, broken limbs, flying priests, smoke screens...

"I didn't think I was gone long enough for all that," Ed interrupted.

"Time flows differently in Esra'Nell, remember? But even without that, many things happened very quickly out here."

"So how did it end?" Ed asked, still confused.

"After the dragon threw Bugen into Artyom's smoke screen we lost track of him. I managed to set its leg on fire, so it gave up on finding Bugen and attacked us instead. We kept it away for a few moments, but with both of us wounded... well, things did not look good. Then, all of a sudden, an enormous beam of light erupted from inside the smoke. It *had* to be Bugen. Anyway, the dragon spotted that, went absolutely bonkers, and attacked him.

"A huge noise started building, then everything seemed to *snap* a bit—like reality had turned into a huge drum hit by an enormous hand. After that—have you seen fireworks? It was like somebody set off a purple firework *inside* the dragon. Sparks of violet burst out of its chest and sprayed out in a sphere, until they all suddenly halted and joined together to form something like a glowing hemispherical cage, probably thirty feet across. It was not quite big enough to fit the whole dragon," Alfazar added, indicating the intact head, "but Sanguinar, Bugen, and I ended up inside it too."

They stopped behind Artyom and watched him methodically searching for a moment. Feeling a need to do something to help, maybe, Ed propped Alfazar up against a mound of bone, then joined the arcanist.

"All of the smoke was pushed out of the interior of the light–cage, so I got a reasonable view," Alfazar continued from where he was sitting, indicating the boundaries of the sphere with his good hand. "Bugen was pinned underneath the dragon, and Sanguinar was screaming at him. Bugen had that amulet in his hand—

remember the one from the priestess?—and it was obviously the source of the magick."

"There was a spell or something in there?" Ed asked in surprise.

"Yeah," Artyom answered, still searching. "And somehow Old Leadfoot figured out how to cast it."

Ed stopped his work and frowned, wondering how Artyom could be so irreverent when discussing a fallen comrade. "Shouldn't we be a little more respectful of the dead?" he asked pointedly.

Artyom turned and looked at Ed in confusion for a moment. "Oh, Bugen's not dead: probably," replied the arcanist, waving a hand dismissively. "You'll see. Finish the story, Alfazar," he commanded as he turned back to the bones.

"Well," the bard continued awkwardly, "Whatever the spell was, it worked. That light set the dragon unravelling, then the sphere collapsed and I felt a peculiar *twist* shoot through me." Alfazar paused and cast about for a decent simile to help him explain the sensation, but his fatigue defeated the search. "A twist that seemed to run through all of my organs, if you get what I mean. At the same time Bugen kind of wavered, then vanished, but it was hard to tell with all of the falling bone. When it was all over Sanguinar was gone too."

"So that creepy ponce might still be alive?" Ed asked, stricken. Maybe the phearsanú was buried under this mound somewhere.

"Not in any way which matters to us," Artyom opined calmly as he stopped and brushed his hands on his dress. "Let me guess; the severing ritual completed much faster than The Reaper expected?" the mage asked, apparently addressing his feet. He bore a peculiar expression.

"Yes," Ed supplied cautiously, wondering what the connection was, and what the mage was looking at.

Artyom nodded in a satisfied sort of way, then stooped and brushed away some sand. "I think that just about confirms it then," he grunted as he hefted something there. "I thought I recognised that spell." Standing now—slowly, so as to not black out—he revealed Bugen's buckler. The arcanist pointed at the etched quartered-circle symbol which adorned the small shield. "Bugen and Sanguinar were transported to the Heavenly Realms."

"The Heavenly Realms?"

"A grand irony," Alfazar added gravely.

Ed recovered his waterskin from inside the tent and brought it back out. The three companions sat and shared a drink in the shade of the enormous bone pile stacked by Artyom. Bugen's notched sword jutted from the sand beside them, holding up his buckler, which was hanging from its quillons. Each of the trio felt somewhat melancholy despite their unlikely success, and all of them were exhausted... bone tired.

"Well, do y'think Ainsworth will still pay us?" Ed asked sleepily.

"I don't think he will have anything left to pay us with after this gets out," Artyom replied, gazing off into nothingness.

"And I don't think we will need any payment," Alfazar pointed out, indicating Sanguinar's giant tent. The others were uncomprehending for a moment, then they all chuckled weakly.

"That wealth would go far towards resettling the colonists," the mage put in. Ed thought this was a wonderful idea, much to his own surprise. Maybe this adventure had changed him more than he suspected.

"Agreed," Alfazar nodded with a smile.

"We should head back," Ed said after a few more content minutes. "Water's all empty, and the other Fae will want to know what's going on."

"Yeah, let's get out of this sand," Artyom agreed, running his hands through it. "Oh look! My beauty spot." He picked up the dot and threw it into the desert. "Good riddance."

They all stood. Ed picked up Bugen's armament and cast a glance back towards the misshapen wyrm-skull, wondering how the priest was doing. Then the band limped back through the portal.

The hunter was the last through the nexus portal, by which time the uproar had already begun. Long practice and paranoia sent his hand darting downwards towards his kukri, but then the scene registered fully and Ed aborted the futile gesture.

The entire enchanted lake was crammed with Fae uncounted, and more were arrayed along the shore, and even in the forest beyond. Some perched in trees alongside the strange, glittering birds that Ed had seen earlier. Each and every one, from the smallest (no bigger than a finger) to the largest, was jubilantly celebrating.

The more rumbustious punched the air victoriously, whooping and hollering. Some hugged one another and wept for joy, whilst others— eyes twinkling and faces wrinkled in solemn smiles— simply applauded. Yet others were jumping about and laughing freely, or ebulliently performing aerial acrobatics. Never in his life had Ed seen such a crowd of Fae, much less a crowd of Fae which contained precisely zero individuals that he wished to shank. The cheeky thought made Ed chuckle, and he exchanged widening grins with some of the nearest Fae.

The mood was infectious, and soon all three men were smiling, embracing, and accepting the tearful thanks of the gathered Fae.

After some time—he could never quite recall how much—Ed once more felt his lethargy setting in. Alfazar and Artyom were likewise beginning to look drained by their exertions and wounds.

Fortunately, the Fae were aware of their honoured guests' needs. They brought forth water and some fruit for the companions, and after all had eaten a little Alfazar stood and addressed those assembled. The bard perched atop a chair which one of the Fae had fetched through the portal.

"Creatures of the forest. Through great sacrifice we have brought the Red One to an end." The Fae cheered again, then quietened when Alfazar raised his hands. "Our esteemed companion Bugen has gone to be with his goddess, taking the Red One with him. This action, and the brave and intelligent actions of Artyom the mage and Ed the... woodsman, have freed your peoples from the necessity of the Tithe." More cheering. "With this gone it may be that—in time—our races will come to friendship," the bard suggested hopefully. Some of the Fae looked dumbstruck, as if they had never considered the possibility, whilst others murmured and nodded to each other in agreement.

Alfazar decided to return to less controversial subject matter. "Today will be remembered in the histories of all peoples in Lorem! As you celebrate, take a moment to consider those lost, and to remember them. Eat and drink: be merry in their memory. For tomorrow will come sooner here than anywhere else, and the world will begin anew for all!"

Alfazar bowed to the crowd and graciously accepted their applause. "Thank you, my friends, for the greatest tale that will ever be told," he added, more to himself than anyone else.

Trimblewind moved forward to help the bard down from his makeshift podium, then bowed and retreated back into the crowd. Ed could see a group of the tree-people not far off, and he inclined his head respectfully towards that old codger they'd spoken to before.

"The pickles have returned, and the olives are where they should be," Artyom called to the delegation of dryads, giving them a thumbs-up.

"Is he okay?" a nearby centaur asked Ed in an undertone.

"He's fabulous," Ed chuckled.

Food was being distributed, and celebrations were getting into full swing. "Come," Alfazar said to his companions with a smile. "We ought to see The Reaper."

"Aye," Ed replied. "Wait up... Don't want to forget these," he added, picking up the sword and buckler again. "Bugen would have a fit if we didn't get these to his monastery."

"Why are you still talking about him like he's dead?" Artyom demanded again. Ed wondered about all that, but held his tongue.

Leaving the jubilant Fae to their celebrations, the trio slipped away through the portal.

They emerged on the edge of The Reaper's hollow. The sudden quietness was unnerving, even though all three men knew that The Reaper intended no harm to them.

Artyom opened the gate and they moved up along the grey path. All of the bound corpses were exactly as they were when the adventurers had set out. Alfazar reached out and politely knocked on the grey door, which swung open after a short pause. It was noiseless, as before, but this time there was a figure in the doorway. It stood on the threshold for a moment, then stepped out.

"Vera!" Ed exclaimed in surprise.

"Yes," the Fae woman answered. "Come, you are expected." She ushered them inside.

Ed cast around for something sensible to say. Why was she even here? "Thanks for putting us onto those dryads. Right lovely folk," he mumbled as he stepped into the house. Buhbuh dashed forward, and Ed paused by the doorway to scratch behind his faithful servant's ears.

"You're welcome," Vera responded. She seemed happy, but also fatigued and somewhat melancholy. The hunter supposed that was a reasonable response to having one of the last—but also most incredibly dangerous—members of your race destroyed.

The four climbed up and arrayed themselves around the high dais, on which sat Erdis' Moon. The Reaper stood behind it, staring intently at the green orb. Now that he did not have to busy himself about three companions in grave danger, even Ed felt some awe: here was the power of a god.

"Congratulations, all of you," intoned The Reaper. "Together, we have restored the balance of power amongst the Gods of Death, and returned the Fae to their intended state. Truly, these actions have echoed across this Plane and the Realms Beyond."

"All of us?" questioned the mage, who was also eyeing Vera curiously. "Then–"

"Yes; Vera has been in my employ."

"You had her guide us here," Alfazar declared. "Feed us the necessary information," the bard elaborated without heat.

"Yes, and at considerable personal risk," Vera piped up, smiling sheepishly.

Thanks for putting us onto those dryads, Ed repeated to himself. It made sense now; she had literally been guiding their steps, digging them out of trouble. "But why?" Ed pondered aloud.

"Because the phearsanú do not take children for the Tithe," Vera answered. "That at least was truthful. I was to be our next offering."

The hunter rubbed his red beard and pondered this development. "So we've been your tools all this time?" he asked the elf with words that held no rancour.

To his utter surprise, The Reaper laughed aloud. It was indeed strange to hear such a lively sound come from the heretofore clinical being. "My dear, we have *all* been tools all of this time. Yes, I manipulated you all, but I was merely following the course set before me. You might say that I have been... the biggest tool," she finished with a wry half-smile.

Ed chuckled at this, as did Artyom and Alfazar.

"Did you manipulate Sanguinar too?" Artyom asked after thinking back over the day's events.

"No," replied The Reaper. "Yet there is one who may have." She indicated the Moon sitting before them. "In the process of breaking Erdis' will, Sanguinar inadvertently exposed his own. Did you not wonder why he left you unsupervised in the tent, hunter? Even a little power, properly applied, can change history."

"Makes sense," the hunter agreed.

Artyom nodded, satisfied.

The Reaper sighed and closed her eyes. "It still feels unreal. Ever since the day that Sanguinar stole this Moon I have laboured to bring Death back into balance. And now my time of service draws to a close. Finally I can die in peace!"

This struck Ed as maybe a little sick, but after a moment's reflection he decided that it was not so bad; Bugen wanted to be with Sol, so why wouldn't The Reaper want to be with her deities? Actually, it was sort of endearing. Maybe the old elf had a human side after all.

"Come, child," The Reaper gesticulated to Vera. The phearsanú woman stepped up to The Reaper, who placed a withered hand on her shoulder and quietly said "You have done well. The Tithe is no more—go now and celebrate with the remainder of your kind. May your race prosper again."

Vera smiled and touched her forehead against the elf's in what Ed guessed was a show of respect. After that, she turned, smiled at the three remaining companions, gave a short bow, and left the building.

"What happens now?" Artyom asked, looking excited about something.

"That is up to you. Each of you. Those prepared for the Tithe will awaken at dawn tomorrow. You will care for these ones, and my people will see to the others. As for me: I will leave this place before then."

"What of the orb?" Alfazar pondered.

"To be returned to my people. It shall come with me," The Reaper explained.

"Good," opined Ed.

Artyom's hand shot into the air enthusiastically; he looked nearly ready to burst at the seams with excitement.

"Yes?" the elf queried.

A reply tumbled from Artyom's mouth."Can I have your house?"

The Reaper smiled and chuckled moderately. "I thought you might like it. Yes, it is yours."

Still smiling, The Reaper stepped back to the dais, and the Moon. She reverently enveloped the orb in her voluminous, black sleeves, then hugged it close to her body. "Farewell," she said simply, then she turned and stepped through an open portal, buoyed along by the travellers' goodbyes.

〜ঌ ঌ❊〜 ঌ❊〜 ঌ〜〜〜 ✕ 〜〜〜ঌ ঌ❊〜 ঌ❊〜 〜

At the rising of the Sun, The Reaper's—or rather, Artyom's—yard came alive with the sounds of drowsy children waking, just as promised. The eerie fog had vanished overnight, making the clearing a far more palatable place to be.

The three adventurers were on hand to help the kids out of their swaddling and to settle them down. This went well enough, considering that there were over a hundred of them, and they were all soon safely inside, enjoying a cup of tea with Artyom and some of the more enthusiastic Fae. As it turned out, the children were quite willing to get on with Fae so long as no adults were around to remind them of how terrified they were supposed to be. Tamtem was also a crowd favourite.

Outside, another group of Fae were helping Alfazar relocate said adults. There were only a few in the group, and all of them had been 'tree roofied' to prevent them creating panic amongst the younger ones. They sat in a circle together, linked arms, and sang songs until their turn to leave came, then wept melodramatically as they were shown to the portal.

Meanwhile, Ed procured a shovel from the stables of *The Lucky Sod* and used it to excavate a large hole behind the house. In this he buried the corpses of the other party—the ones that had assailed The Reaper. They had not re-awakened. He rolled them into their grave without ceremony, filled in the soil, then patted it down flat. When he finished, he added a simple rock in place of a tombstone, then leant against the shovel, patted Buhbuh, and pondered Bugen's fate.

ℐ   ⌘❀⌘   ⌘❀⌘   ⌘❀⌘   ✖   ⌘❀⌘   ⌘❀⌘   ⌘❀⌘   ℚ

The companions embraced and broke ways on the eve of the Festival of the White Lady.

Alfazar departed, taking the few children that had not been identified and returned to their homes already.

Now free of interruption, Artyom relaxed into his new home and began carefully sifting through the treasure-trove left to him by The Reaper. By around lunchtime the mage had found a book titled *The Transporting Guide to Portals*. He thumbed through the pages until finding *Chapter XLII—How to get to Heaven*, then glanced up at Bugen's sword and buckler perched on a stack of books nearby. Smiling broadly, Artyom and Tamtem wriggled further down into an overstuffed couch (procured from an unknown location by one of the Fae) and began reading.

Not at all interested by the book—and knowing that Artyom would now be all but unresponsive to the outside world—Ed quietly left and made for the enchanted lake.

He tried to reach Bugen through the portal nexus, to no avail. Not entirely surprised, but still a tad disappointed, Ed decided to join Alfazar as he travelled between Evergreen, Maerin, Briss, and Newtown, delivering children safely to their homes with great fanfare and rejoicing. The townsfolk, now having confirmation that Arcana was indeed *crawling* with Fae, began a mass exodus. Ainsworth was bankrupted and deported, and his magnificent city lay abandoned. Within only a few weeks Arcana was once again the home of the Fae.

With this done, Alfazar returned to Graea, whilst the hunter travelled to the dryads' grove. Much to his delight, the dryads granted Ed permission to build himself a small dwelling there. He learnt much from the tree-people, and together they enjoyed exploring the great, untamed forests of Graea and the alpine expanses of Faust. The woodsman became a dear friend to many Fae, but his hunting days were not left entirely behind; there were still plenty of unruly, corrupt, and plain evil Fae to purge. He and Artyom—who was becoming more and more learned in the arcane arts—had many more adventures together.

They frequently related their stories to Alfazar, whose fame had risen meteorically throughout Elandria. His grand Faery tale 'The Fall of the Red One' was enormously popular. Ed and Artyom often attended performances, and not once did they grow tired of remembering their adventures.

Epilogue

HE crushing weight is gone, as is the rain of bones. He becomes aware that he continues to exist. Bugen's eyes open. Sights and sounds, smells and tastes flood his senses so quickly that he cannot take them in, yet he feels no panic, just a joyous acceptance of the input. It is like waking from a half-remembered dream to the real thing, only to find that the real thing is far better than was ever imagined. The air is warm but comfortable, stirred by a gentle breeze which carries the chuckling sound of a nearby watercourse wending its way downhill. The scent of airy woodland strikes a chord deep within Bugen, as though it carries some profound meaning for him. Almost everything is fantastically bright.

The priest of Sol instinctively understands that he has been brought to the Heavenly Realms.

Before the realisation can fully sink in Bugen notices a cloud of darkness nearby. It is a blot on the otherwise brilliant landscape, blacker than any black he has seen previously. He conceives of the brilliant light as a fluid which streams across the Heavenly Realm, and the cloud as a void into which that fluid flows and is destroyed. Although he understands that this darkness should not be here, it does little to perturb his buoyant mood.

Sanguinar's face comes into view within the void. It is twisted with anger and disdain as it takes in its surroundings. His nictitating eyelids are shut, probably in a vain attempt to block out the light.

Bugen feels a shadow of disquiet, but remains peaceful. After a few moments he figures out why; the darkness already seems to be receding. Now Bugen can see Sanguinar's limbs distinctly too. The cleric quickly realises that his earlier supposition was incorrect; the darkness is not destroying the flowing light, but rather *being* destroyed itself—a vessel filled with the water of Heaven.

Bugen can see the same knowledge appear in Sanguinar's expression, which turns to all-out rage. The phearsanú draws his rapier back, braces his entire weight, and throws a deadly thrust at the priest.

Driven by instinct, Bugen stands his ground. The keen point of Sanguinar's weapon simply puffs into smoke as it contacts the cleric, and shortly the entire weapon has vanished, leaving only an astringent smell which rapidly clears.

"$#&@ you!" Sanguinar rages, his hand closing on Bugen's throat. The limb promptly vanishes too. "$#&@!" he shouts one final time, then Sanguinar is gone.

Bugen is stoically impassive throughout the entire assault. When it is over, he feels a deep peace and a pervasive happiness. His job is done.

He turns to begin exploring this beautiful Realm, and comes face to face with a woman. The cleric realises that in the Mortal Plane his eyes would be blinded by her sheer effulgence, yet here her aura is both welcoming and comfortable. He beholds her beauty—that of a vivacious young woman—and also the wisdom and grace of ages which can be seen in her bearing. Her face is tender, peaceful, noble, and unyielding all at once, and Bugen cannot shake the feeling that her expression is the epitome of the joyful radiance glimpsed on the faces of expectant women. He recognises the Lady of Light and the Mother of Life, for Sol herself stands before him.

Bugen sinks to one knee and averts his gaze downward in supplication before his Goddess, but She reaches down and extends Her hand. After a moment of hesitation Bugen grasps it, and Sol pulls him to his feet. She smiles broadly. Then, unexpectedly, She bows to him. "Well done, you good and faithful servant," She says warmly as she straightens up, making Bugen flush with joy.

"M'lady, it has been a pleasure," he replies.

"Think on that, Bugen. Was it all a pleasure at the time?"

The young cleric thinks back over the past week's events, considering the pain, anxiety, and hardship involved, yet somehow these feelings pale even as he recalls them. The memories remain, but are now shot through with divine purpose which lifts them up and exalts Sol in ways Bugen had never previously considered. "No," he replies. "Not at the time. Yet, it is all a pleasure now."

"Excellent. You begin to see," Sol responds gently. "With fear and trembling you have faithfully followed the path laid before you."

"How did Dell know?" Bugen asks, suddenly curious.

Sol laughs unguardedly, yet somehow remains dignified. Not understanding why, Bugen is caught up in Her mirth. "She listened, child."

"To you?" he manages, between bouts of laughter. He has never been tipsy, but Bugen imagines this is what it feels like, except that his mind remains clear.

"To the world," Sol answers. "Dell is a half-elf, Bugen; she is much older than she appears."

"She will be glad to hear that Your will has been done in this matter," the young priest decides, happy about this realisation.

"Aye," She responds.

Bugen is startled by that particular choice of word, and a quick glance at Her expression reveals suppressed laughter. Sol, Bugen realises, is *teasing* him like one teases an old and beloved friend. He laughs and weeps for delight, and Sol holds him: a mother and her child.

Time passes, or maybe it does not. At any rate, Bugen is unwearied when Sol once more addresses him. "My son, because of the unusual circumstances of your arrival—and your faithful service to me—I shall set a choice before you." He listens attentively, wondering what it might be. "If you wish, you may remain here, in my Realms. However, you may also choose to return to the Mortal

Plane and enact my will there. If you stay you will be exalted—as all are in my Realms—and if you return you will in all likelihood join me here again, in time."

Bugen considers, overwhelmed by the gracious offer. "Sol, do you not already know my answer?" he asks.

"Of course I do, child, yet that does not make the choice any less yours to make," Sol smiles.

The boy—for he now feels like a young boy once more—contemplates his options. His people are now free of the Fae, but his recollection of history is such that he knows of the paradoxical human tendency to devolve into ferocious internal wars when devoid of an external foe. Visions of a second Great Schism march across his imagination, showing only slaughter and pain for humanity. He feels deeply melancholy. Bugen realises he has made his choice.

"Send me," he says firmly. "I will go." Then he hesitates. "But first I wish to ask..."

"Yes," Sol answers before he can finish. "She is here. Come," She instructs, extending a hand.

Bugen walks with Sol and marvels at their surrounds. The land is of truly grand scale, yet also beautiful, intimate, and serene. Soon they come to a bright glade overlooking a deep canyon in which water like condensed light flows and tumbles. A young woman, seemingly in the prime of life, is waiting there, and Bugen immediately recognises her. Elanor—for it is definitely his sister—embraces him tightly, and Bugen is speechless. "Thank you," he says softly, knowing that Sol will hear and recognise that the words were meant for them both.

Two other people come forward and encircle the siblings with their arms. Despite having no memory of them whatsoever, Bugen knows that these are his parents. They laugh and cry as one, and soon Bugen can feel Sol's joy added to their own. He knows that their Goddess has looked forward to this reunion.

With a communal smile they all place their hands on Bugen's shoulders. "Go, my son," his father intones.

"Yes. Walk in Sol's light," his mother adds. Bugen sees that he has his father's nose, but his eyes are hers.

"You got out," Elanor says tenderly, cupping Bugen's face with one hand.

"Aye," he manages, before the landscape dissolves into shapes of solidified light hanging against a backdrop of glory. Bugen has no sensation of falling, yet the shapes rapidly stream upwards and away. His family goes next, until eventually only Sol herself remains.

"Go with my blessings, priest of Sol."

Then She too is gone.

He returns in a flash of light. Bugen looks around himself and is surprised to find that he is not in the desert from whence he left the Mortal Plane; instead, he stands on a flagged floor in a familiar but strangely dim room. Looking down at his arms and torso, Bugen soon determines that the room is in fact brightly-lit, and only seems dark because of the light streaming from his body like tongues of fire. He revels in the glory of Sol for another moment, eyes shut.

A cry of surprise brings his eyes open again, and he sees High Priestess Dell standing before him. "Kid, you're–" she manages, looking white as a sheet, before Bugen engulfs her in a hug.

"Thank you," he tells her earnestly. "Sol sends Her greetings, and Her blessings," he adds as he pulls away. Dell is still shocked, but soon accepts what her eyes and ears are telling her.

Promising that he will return shortly, Bugen leaves the stunned priestess and heads outside. The Sun shines warmly, and he is cheered by its presence, for he can already feel the unnatural vitality of the Heavenly Realms leaving him. Despite that, Sol sits somewhere just on the edge of his perception in a way which She never did before.

Striding purposefully across the square—and on the look-out for booby traps—Bugen heads for the marketplace. On the way he notes that his armour is now golden, and free of the hurts of its previous existence. A new sword hangs at his belt also.

Soon he reaches the wall beneath which is nestled the gaol. Somehow, he knows that this is right. He sweeps through the entrance—without the guard even noticing—and continues until he reaches a dead end. Bugen opens the heavy trapdoor and proceeds down the ladder thus revealed. At its bottom lies a cell, with a thin figure hanging from one wall by heavy manacles.

Bugen draws the sword, which glows red-hot, and cleaves through the manacles with two swift strokes. The prisoner falls forward, talking incoherently and looking bewildered whilst clutching at Bugen for support. Bugen gently lowers the fellow to the ground, then squats and places a hand on the man's chest.

Light flares in the darkness, and Bugen can see the intelligence come flooding back into his companion's expression. The cleric of Sol stands, and extends a hand towards the man. Smiling gently, he issues a simple command. "Rise, Alfonz Higgens. We have much work to do."

Pronunciation Guide

Emphasis is placed on capitalised syllables. The short 'u' sound (as in 'fun', 'run', *etc.*) is represented by 'uh'.

Alfazar d'Barouse	AL-fuh-zar d'Bar-OOSE ('oose' as in 'moose')
Artyom Tilin	AR-tee-om TILL-in
Bauchan	BUCK-orn
Brounie	BROWN-ee
Buhbuh	BUH-BUH
Bugen–Kynes	BOO-gen–Kines ('g' as in 'get')
Craicte	CRAYKT
Erdis	ER-diss
Esra'Nell	EZ-ra'Nell
Faust	FOWST ('ow' as in 'ouch')
Graea	GRY-uh ('Gry' rhymes with 'eye')
Phearsanú	Fuh-SHAH-noo ('shah' as in 'shark')
Sanguinar	SANG-gwin-ar
Vera	VEER-uh